*To*
GEORGE,
*and to*
THE TWO CORAS

# ENCHANTER'S NIGHTSHADE

*By*

## ANN BRIDGE

1968

**CHATTO AND WINDUS**

**LONDON**

Published by
Chatto and Windus Ltd
42 William IV Street
London W.C.2


*First Printed 1937*
*Second Impression 1937*
*Third Impression 1942*
*Fourth Impression 1968*

SBN 7011 1289 1


© Ann Bridge 1937

Printed in Great Britain by
William Lewis (Printers) Ltd
Cardiff

"As I drove through the streets I found that approval of what met my eyes was mixed with surprise, and I was forced to reflect with misgiving upon the attitude of mind which this surprise discovered. There was no doubt at all that from my conception of the universe, Hué had been left entirely out of account, for I confess that I had never even learned its name. And if Hué had been overlooked, was it not probable that a hundred other cities in other parts of the world had been passed over? And kingdoms too, perhaps, and princes and entire races, and whole worlds of thought and feeling, traditions and beliefs? Such reflections may seem to have little meaning in a state of existence where objective facts are infinite in number, and where the subject's knowledge of them, however great, must therefore remain forever infinitely small; but to this rigid logic I prefer the common view that travel does indeed enlarge the mind . . . inspiring the moderation and resourcefulness requisite to the conduct of affairs in which logic has never had the first nor the last word."

*A Journey from Peking*

## Chapter One

FRÄULEIN ROSA GELSICHER was sitting on a low stool, wrapped in a thick dressing-gown of purple flannel, cutting her corns after her bath, in the apartment of Count Carlo di Castellone in Gardone. In small provincial towns in Italy, thirty years ago, bathrooms were a comparative rarity—Fräulein Gelsicher's stool, accordingly, was placed at the outer edge of a broad pink mat, in the centre of which stood the flat enamel saucer-bath, painted pale green, with a wreath of flowers round the outside, in which she had just performed her morning ablutions, flanked by two large empty copper cans and a china dish, containing her bath-sponge, face-sponge, and Turkish glove. Beside the soapy and still steaming water, a pair of pince-nez perched rather precariously on her small sharp nose, under the grey hair thickly riddled with curling-pins, Fräulein Gelsicher, corn-knife in hand, worked with great apparent concentration. Her feet were a perpetual trouble to her, and with the warm weather coming it behoved her to treat them carefully. On each corn, as it was cut, she dabbed a spot of dark-green strong-smelling fluid out of a small bottle marked "Celandine"; on two of the worst she carefully arranged small circular pads of white felt, with a hole in the middle and one gummy surface to stick them on with, to protect these growths from the pressure of those sharp-toed shoes, a size or two too small, which fashion then decreed even for the most unfrivolous of women; but which were, in fact, the cause of the corns.

But in spite of her apparent absorption in her feet, Fräulein Gelsicher was really thinking very hard about several other things at the same time. She had come into the Castellone family twelve years before as governess to Elena, Count

1 ✓

Carlo's daughter, then a little girl of six. When Elena was twelve the Countess died, and since her death Fräulein Gelsicher had gradually assumed a position very different from that of the ordinary governess. The whole administration of the household had come, bit by bit, into her competent Swiss hands; her shrewd Swiss commonsense had made her the Count's valued consultant and adviser on matters extending far beyond the household and the health and morals of Elena and Giulio, Count Carlo's only son, three years older than Elena. She presided at the Count's table and saw to the comfort of his guests, but all with such a business-like modesty, such a strong sense of her position of stewardship, as made the relation a wholly satisfactory one. The Count both valued her and liked her—he had nicknamed her "La Gelosia" (jealousy) at the outset, partly because he never could either remember or pronounce foreign names, partly out of a whimsical pleasure in giving her a name which he recognised as being completely foreign to her character. At first it had been a secret joke in the family, but for years now Fräulein Gelsicher herself had shared it, and the Count's jocular greeting of *"La Signorina Gelosia come sta?"* when they met at lunch-time, while startling to guests, was a regular and pleasant feature of a very regular and pleasant family life.

La Signorina Gelosia's preoccupations, that morning, were mainly domestic in character. The family was about to make its usual spring migration from Gardone, where they spent the winter, to Odredo, the Count's property in the country some eighteen miles away. As a rule Anna the cook was sent out there in advance with a team of underlings, to prepare the house for their reception; but this year Anna had strained her ankle, and it was a problem whom to send in her place. Fräulein Gelsicher would really have liked to go herself for a couple of nights; but it was of course unthinkable in Italy, in those days, that a girl of Elena's age should be left for forty-eight hours without more adequate chaperonage than that of her father and her brother. Dabbing on another drop of Celandine, Fräulein Gelsicher sighed. She supposed they would have to send Umberto, though it was most inconvenient to do without him here. Umberto was Anna's husband, the butler and general factotum; he was Prime Minister, so to speak, under the undisputed sovereignty of Fräulein Gelsicher; he knew where everything was, and what everybody was doing. Anyhow he must come back to pack the glass and china, she decided, if he did go; if anyone else did it, things would be broken.

Then she must send round word quickly to Mme. Joséphine about Elena's dress for the Opera tonight. It had not arrived according to promise yesterday evening, and the child would be disappointed. Or had she better make time to go herself? Mme. Joséphine was temperamental and difficult, she was subject to *crises*, and when she had a *crise* she would fling a dress back at a patron half-done, and refuse to finish it ; it was really safer to see her than to write to her, for one could then observe on the spot to what point remonstrance could safely be pushed.

Mme. Joséphine was an important element in the life of the Province. Every Autumn and every Spring she arrived from Paris with her models from the "great houses," and with two assistants took up her quarters in a small apartment in Gardone, where she showed frocks, produced materials, advised, cut out, fitted and made, for a few hurried weeks. The ladies of the Province depended entirely on Mme. Joséphine for their more elegant clothes, and for their knowledge of the movements of fashion. Except for one or two families, who were either politically or socially important, the provincial nobility did not go to Rome for the winter—but neither did they remain in their large, rambling, unheated and unheatable country-houses. No, they moved in, ten, twelve, fifteen or twenty miles, in their broughams, victorias and waggonettes, followed by long narrow farm carts containing their plate and linen to Gardone, where each family had either its own town house or an apartment. How pleasant they were, those large-fronted houses, built with a certain nobility of plainness, with their narrow wrought-iron balconies, their long green shutters, their big and rather sparsely-furnished rooms, shadowily reflected in many mirrors —houses so large that two or three families could easily settle down in one of them, taking a floor or two apiece, in complete independence. This indeed was the usual practice. Various members of the same family would establish themselves, each with his household, under the roof which bore their common name. So the Castellone house in the Via Vittoria contained at this moment, besides Count Carlo and his establishment on the first and second floors, Countess Livia di Castellone, the widow of the eldest son, on the ground floor; the third floor would normally have been occupied by Ascanio Castellone, son of Count Carlo's younger brother—but Ascanio had married a smart rich Belgian wife who insisted on going to Rome or Paris for the winter, so it was empty; finally, on the fourth floor, in the smaller and lower rooms, lived two spinster cousins of Count Carlo, the Countesses Aspasia and Roma di Castellone.

So patriarchally housed, keeping their distance but able to keep also a close eye, if they so wished, on one another's comings and goings—a privilege of which the occupants of the fourth floor took full advantage—the various members of the Castellone clan passed their little winter season, wearing Mme. Joséphine's creations to concerts, to stiff evening receptions, and to the Opera, which took place in the small, richly rococo, and curiously elegant little opera-house; driving out to the library, to pay calls, or merely to take the air in her heavy fur-trimmed coats and enormous plumy hats, their hands in muffs hung on jewelled chains, and their cards in small silver or gold cases which dangled, also, on little chains. They gave luncheons and receptions, they ran in and out to one another and talked, they met at the Opera; but they seldom gave dinners, never went out to tea (because no one drank tea) and by no wildest stretch of the imagination could they ever have been conceived of as giving cocktail or sherry-parties, because cocktails were not invented and sherry, as an aperitif, was not yet in fashion even in England. Nor did they as a rule give balls. The young people danced informally and *en famille* among themselves in the livelier households, like that of the Marchesa di Vill' Alta (and in a place where everyone was related, more or less, to everyone else, to dance *en famille* was almost unavoidable) but balls they left for Rome and Venice; balls were not for Gardone.

Fräulein Gelsicher's self-communings on the subject of Mme. Joséphine and the green dress were interrupted by a knock on the door. Not on the door of the *cabinet de toilette* where she was attending to her feet, for this stood wide open, but on the door of the large bedroom beyond. Without moving, Fräulein Gelsicher called out "Who is there?"

"Annina," replied a voice.

"Avanti," responded Fräulein Gelsicher briskly, and began to put on her stockings; Annina was the maid, the daughter of Anna and Umberto, and the toilets of her two mistresses held no secrets from her. Annina came in, shutting the bedroom door behind her, and advanced to the *cabinet de toilette*, where she announced that if it pleased the Signorina, Umberto wished to see the Signorina.

"What is it?" Fräulein Gelsicher asked, pulling on her second stocking, of fine black lisle thread.

"Something from the Signor Ospedi," Annina answered

Fräulein Gelsicher sighed again. Ospedi was the bailiff at Odredo, and was in her opinion incompetent, if not worse. But so far she had not been able to persuade the Count to get rid of him. He made no difficulties about Count Carlo's innovations in wine-production, as most bailiffs would have done; and improving the qualities of the local wines being the Count's ruling passion, he looked no further, and was blind to what seemed to Fräulein Gelsicher the man's glaring defects in other directions. Telling Annina that she would see Umberto, she slipped her feet into a pair of grey felt slippers with long tongues, and closing the door after her, moved into the bedroom, where she took from a drawer a small fleecy shawl and wound it round her head, with a view to concealing the curling-pins. This was her only concession to appearances before interviewing Umberto; in the easy continental tradition, where the ladies of the household spent the morning in wrappers, and family life only began with *colazione* at twelve, it was perfectly normal to receive the menservants thus attired, and both Umberto and Paolo, the coachman, came regularly to her room of a morning for orders, or for what, in Umberto's case, might better have been described as consultations.

Umberto presently followed his knock on her door, a short stocky man just beginning to turn grey, clean-shaven, with the grey eyes that are by no means uncommon in North Italy, and a stubborn humorous mouth—dressed in a black and white striped pantry jacket and felt slippers. Bowing, he unfolded his business. The Signor Ospedi had sent a man in on a bicycle to ask about the waggons.

"What about the waggons?" the Signorina asked.

Two of the waggons, it appeared, had foundered in the mud fetching wood to the castle, and had each a wheel broken; Ospedi wished to know if he was to hire other waggons for the transport of the effects next week; they could not be mended in the time, as the wheel-wright had a congestion.

"Have you spoken to the Signor Conte?" Fräulein Gelsicher asked.

"Sissignorina," Umberto replied. "The Signor Conte said I should tell the Signorina."

Fräulein Gelsicher sighed, for the third time in half an hour. Count Carlo had been rejoicing yesterday over the arrival from Paris of an immense tome on a new system for pruning vines—until he had finished it, there would be no getting anything else into his head, she reflected resignedly. She thought rapidly, while Umberto watched her, with the eyes of a sporting dog watching a man whom he respects with a gun. Waggons they must have—but to hire was very expensive, and sheer waste; and with Elena growing up now, and needing more and better clothes, and guests coming to the house, money was not too abundant—at least, waste was more intolerable than ever. They must find some other way. And, her quickly-working practical mind having soon pounced on another way, she moved over to a small spindly unsteady walnut writing-table in one of the wide windows, and sitting down there, the streaming Spring sunshine falling incongruously across the purple flannel dressing-gown, the lacey shawl slipping back from her grey and curling-pinned head, Fräulein Gelsicher rapidly penned a note, in her pointed firm writing, to the Countess Livia downstairs, explaining the situation and asking if Count Carlo might borrow the wheel-wright from Castellone itself for a day, to repair the broken waggons. If so, she begged the Countess to have the great kindness to send also a small note to the Castellone bailiff, which might be shown him by the bailiff from Odredo. She gave the note to Umberto, explaining its import; Umberto nodded his head in a satisfied manner—the dog approved of the manœuvres of the man with the gun—and moved to the door.

"And Umber*to*," Fräulein Gelsicher called after him.

"Sissignorina?"

"If the Signora Contessa gives you the note to Taddei *separately*, do not come back, but send it, with a message. I am busy."

With a final nod and a "Va bene" Umberto removed himself. When he had gone, Fräulein Gelsicher continued the process of getting dressed. Her spring-weight combinations, mid-way between summer and winter ones, she had put on after her bath—now she added the rest. Her underclothes were not coquettish, but there were a great many of them—white knickers which fastened on a buttoned band, a white petticoat trimmed with fat embroidered scallops and flowers, a silk petticoat over that, tied round the waist with a tape; a woven bodice, buttoning up the front, with sleeves to the elbow and high in the neck, and, above all, stays.  Stays were stays, thirty years ago, and no nonsense about stretching in two or more ways; Fräulein Gelsicher's were made of fine slate-grey twill, with whalebone stitched into them at two-inch intervals all over, and fastening down the front with two solid steel contraptions called busks, one side of which hooked over a series of studs on the other side—they reached from her bosom well down over her hips.  Having clipped herself into this harness in front, she proceeded, very swiftly and expertly, to adjust the laces behind, drawing up the crossed loops with a hooked finger, from the top downwards, from the bottom upwards to the waist, where she drew out the slack and tied it in a long dangling bow.  When she was finally attired in her bodice and silk petticoat, she put on a loose-sleeved cambric jacket, embroidered with more of the fat scallops, and sitting down at the toilet table, which occupied the centre one of the three windows, she began to do her hair.

Hair-doing was also something of a business in those days. The essential thing was that the natural shape of the skull should be concealed as completely as possible.  To this end the hair was fluffed out, front, sides and back, into a sort of large cushion or cake, covering the head; on this structure was disposed, according to taste, either a coiled chignon, or puffs and rolls of various descriptions.  But whether chignon or puffs, it required a great deal of hair to create this erection and moreover to make it solid enough to support steadily the large hats then in fashion; and few women really had the requisite amount.  Fräulein Gelsicher had not the requisite amount.  Seated at her dressing-table, she took out of a drawer and laid on the embroidered cloth before her three stiffened pads of horse-hair and a long and glossy switch, made up of her own "combings"; also a neat lavender-coloured cardboard box, which contained her current comb-ings, the raw material of future switches.  Carefully she removed her curling-pins, brushed out her hair, combed it, and then proceeded to attach to her head the three pads, one across the front, one above each ear. She had just reached this stage, and was embarking on the process of fluffing out her rather thin grey locks before brushing them up over the pads, when there came a light tap at the door.

"Who is there?" Fräulein Gelsicher asked again.

"Me!" called a girl's voice, and without waiting for further permission Elena di Castellone ran into the room. She too was not yet dressed, but was wearing one of the cambric dressing-jackets over her petticoat; her black hair however was perfectly arranged in a large pompadour roll above her glowing complexion, with a thick twisted chignon, like a teapot-handle, on the top of her head. Her mouth was already open in laughter as she came into the room, showing irregular but deliciously white teeth; her brown eyes were sparkling with mischief; she carried two envelopes in her hand.

"Gela cara, such news!" she began, coming straight up to the dressing-table. "Zia Suzy is coming back! This very next week, to Vill' Alta! And listen! Marietta is to have a governess!"

Fräulein Gelsicher lifted one section of grey hair from in front of her face, turned it up neatly on the brush, and fastened it in position with a hair-pin. Through the gap thus formed she looked out at her pupil and said "Buon giorno, Elena cara," very pleasantly. Elena paid no attention whatever to this gently-implied rebuke; she caught her governess by her cambric shoulders, drew her up off the dressing-stool, and whirled her round in a sort of waltz, carolling "Marietta is coming back, Marietta is coming back! And she will have a governess, a governess, a governess! And our Gelosia will have company, someone to tell how bad I am!" With a final twirl she deposited Fräulein Gelsicher on the stool again, and stood laughing.

Fräulein Gelsicher took these demonstrations very quietly.

She raised another section of hair into position and asked: "What sort of a governess?"

"English! An English governess! She will have thick boots and flat hair and tweeds and spectacles, and will teach Marietta algebra! She will be much older and sterner than our Gelosia, and will make Marietta much cleverer than me!"

"The good God has already made Marietta that," observed Fräulein Gelsicher serenely, leaning forward to the mirror to effect a junction between two bits of hair, where the pad was showing a little—one or other of Fräulein Gelsicher's pads was usually showing a little. "Senta, who tells you all this?"

"Marietta! I have a letter just now. Princess Asquini has recommended the governess to Zia Suzy, and they have written, and it is all arranged. And they will be here on Tuesday."

Fräulein Gelsicher heard this piece of news with rather mixed feelings. She always felt more comfortable, breathed more freely, when the Marchesa di Vill' Alta, whom Elena referred to as Zia Suzy, was out of the Province. Although Elena called her Aunt, the relationship was in reality less close —through a Vill' Alta-Castellone marriage two generations before Count Carlo and the Marchese Francesco di Vill' Alta, Suzy's husband, were second cousins. But Italians carry consanguinity to unbelievable lengths, and live up to it; moreover, as the Castello di Vill' Alta happened to be barely a couple of miles from Odredo the two families lived on terms of close intimacy, and Elena and Marietta had been brought up almost together, with much more cousinly feeling than often obtains between real first cousins. Still, there the relationship was, and in Fräulein Gelsicher's opinion it made the relations between Elena's father and Marietta's mother even more deplorable than she would have thought them otherwise. What those relations were she had long been careful, in her shrewd prudence, merely to guess at; but Suzy di Vill' Alta's personality and record left their nature in little doubt. Fräulein Gelsicher's rather rigid Swiss morality had perforce been tempered by a long and observant residence in another social atmosphere to a calm worldly wisdom, which little could shock; she had her own views of what was right, but she did not allow them to obscure a very practical recognition of what human nature was really like, and how it might be expected to behave.    But this particular relation did shock her.    She had been deeply attached to Elena's mother, and knew Count Carlo to have been really devoted to her too; she listened, with a pitying recognition of their curious sincerity, to his frequent and devout references to "my sainted wife."    But the Count was weak and, viticulture apart, silly—it had not been difficult for that Circe of a woman, who could not leave one human being within her reach unpossessed, the governess often thought bitterly, to play upon his weakness, his sorrow and his loneliness, and so to enslave him.    Disapproving profoundly, his part in the affair she nevertheless understood.

But now, really, it was time that it should come to an end. (Liaisons, Fräulein Gelsicher knew, had a way of coming to an end.)    Elena was eighteen, she was getting more and more observant; it was shocking and unseemly to a degree that the slightest risk should be run of her recognising for what it was the state of affairs between her father and the woman whom she spoke of and treated as an Aunt. Indeed it was only a child's blind filial trust and ready acceptance of any state of affairs with which it has grown up that had prevented her, Fräulein Gelsicher felt sure, from recognising it already. She had picked up, as it was, the nickname by which the Marchesa Suzy was known in the entire Province—"The Enchantress"; she laughed her bubbling ready laugh, clear as water, over any fresh instance of some unlucky male falling under the Enchantress' spell.    And now, after several months absence, with Elena by that much older and sharper, they were coming back from Rome, that whole party, a full two months earlier than usual, to trouble the peace of the Province of Gardone. Something ought to be done about it.    Fräulein Gelsicher

had already spent a great deal of time wondering, far more
fruitlessly than was usual with her, what could possibly be
done about it. The only person who would be likely to
have the courage to tackle such a thorny business, or the
wisdom to do it with any hope of success, was Suzy's mother-
in-law, the aged Marchesa di Vill' Alta, known everywhere in
affectionate respect as "La Vecchia Marchesa." The old
Marchesa was very very old, ninety-nine—if she lived till
next September she would see her century out. And she
showed every sign of doing that and more. Her powers of
mind and body were unimpaired to an extraordinary degree.
Her brilliant black eyes, untinged by rheum, saw everything;
she heard whatever she wanted to hear, but quenched unwelcome statements by a sudden and arbitrary deafness; she
remembered everything—including the jewelled knife-hilt
stuck in the broad belt of Murat's green-and-gold hunting
costume—which she wished to remember, and ignored the
rest; her mind still moved like a rapier among such affairs as
she deigned to take an interest in, a rather limited category
which included her own relations, high Italian society, German
royal houses, old lace, diplomatic memoirs and French novels;
but which excluded all social and political movements since
the Republic, Americans, religious thought, and modern inventions of every kind; her tongue still commanded whole
quiverfuls of the most trenchant sentences of appraisal or
condemnation. If La Vecchia Marchesa chose, she could
probably deal with the situation—if not through Suzy, through
Count Carlo. But who or what was to move La Vecchia
Marchesa to such a choice? She must have seen, long since,
what was going on, since at Vill' Alta she lived always in her
son's house; certainly she was not deceived, yet she held her
ancient, wrinkled, bediamonded but still distinguished hand.
How then on earth could she be persuaded to move? There
was no record, in the long chronicles of provincial gossip, of
anything but La Vecchia Marchesa's own initiative having
ever moved her in any direction whatever.

All this passed through Fräulein Gelsicher's mind as she sat at her dressing-table, continuing to put up her hair, while Elena twirled the grey switch, knotting it into fashionable coils (till Fräulein Gelsicher quietly removed it from her hands and put it unfashionably in position on her own head), chattered, and laughed.   When the hair was done, and she could claim her governess's undivided attention, she laid before her on the dressing-table one of the two letters she had brought in, beseeching her, with an impish giggle, to read it.

Fräulein Gelsicher took up the letter—it was unstamped and unsealed, and addressed to Marietta di Vill' Alta.   She knew the writing—it was that of the younger of the Count's two unmarried cousins who occupied the top floor in the house, the Contessa Roma di Castellone.

"What is this?.  It is Marietta's.   I am to read it?" she asked, puzzled.

"Ma si!   Ma si!   You have the writer's permission!" Elena answered, almost suffocated with laughter.   "Read it out, Gela."

Fräulein Gelsicher did as her pupil bade her.   Countess Roma was a foolish woman; like her sister Countess Aspasia an impassioned gossip, but without the self-restraint which restricted the latter lady's communications to the affairs of others—Roma liked to talk about her own uninteresting concerns and doings, and nothing was more likely than that she should wish both Elena and Fräulein Gelsicher to read a letter in which she took an ill-founded pride.


"My dearest Marietta!   Your cousin Aspasia and I have both learned with FONDEST pleasure, the good news of your educational future.   A great opportunity opens before you now, of forming your mind, adding to your accomplishments, and improving your character.   I hope that in everything you will show docility to your new instructress.   The English are a race of considerable learning, I believe, and no doubt your dear mother has chosen for you a woman worthy of your deepest respect.   It is to be hoped that you will not fail to profit by such a chance.   Your cousin Aspasia and I have often felt that you have lacked, in the past, both those full opportunities for study which young girls should have, and any steady model at hand on which to mould yourself. Your Mother's household is so social!   But you will in all probability NOT inherit those qualities which make her what she is, and you may well expect your life, for that reason, to be different from hers.   Indeed I dare almost say that I hope this will be the case!   Beauty is a dangerous possession!!

I embrace you warmly, Marietta cara.

Roma Castellone.

P.S.   Your Cousin Elena is going to the Opera tonight— she has a most expensive dress from Joséphine.   *I* should not have thought this extravagance necessary for a *young girl*, but no doubt Signorina Gelsicher knows what she is about."

A faint flush of annoyance tinged the governess's worn face as she put the letter back in its envelope, but "Very characteristic" was all she said, rather drily.   Elena exploded with laughter.

"Isn't it?   O Gela, I have caught you too!   Isn't it perfect?   Won't it vex Marietta beautifully?"

The governess wheeled round on her stool to face the young girl.

"Elena!   You haven't been doing *that* again?   No, that is too naughty!   You promised me you would give up that silly trick," she said reproachfully.

"For six months!   I only promised for six months, and I haven't done *one* since Giulio's last October!   But what does it matter?   I can write to Marietta tomorrow, before she has time to answer it—she never answers letters for days and days!"   Elena answered airily.   "Don't spoil sport, Gela darling.   Isn't it good?   'I should not have thought this extravagance necessary',"   she read out, and giggled again;

"Gela, you were quite hurt! But you know it is just what they would say, the old cats!"

"You will get into serious trouble one of these days, if you go on with this," Fräulein Gelsicher said repressively. One of her pupil's few, and more disconcerting talents was a quite brilliant gift for forgery. She could imitate any handwriting if she had it before her for a few hours, in the most completely convincing fashion—and, as now, she was equally successful at reproducing the epistolary style of people she knew. For years this gift had been a source of anxiety and annoyance to Fräulein Gelsicher, perhaps the only serious cause of annoyance her charge had ever given her—and she made ceaseless struggles to force or persuade the child to give it up. But the love of pure mischief for its own sake was one of the strongest traits in Elena di Castellone's character, and much as she loved her Gelosia, not even for her could she forego the delight of sitting down to prepare a beautiful and careful forgery of a thoroughly tiresome communication, and then watching, enchanted, the effects upon the victim gradually unfolding themselves. Scolded always, punished sometimes, once or twice really frightened at the unexpectedly serious results of her handiwork, she yet could not stop doing it. It was like a disease, Fräulein Gelsicher said. She, poor woman, as usual got little or no help from the Count in her wrestlings with his daughter on this head; at fifty he had still a good deal of Elena's childish folly in his composition, and when Fräulein Gelsicher came to him with some dire tale of a successful forgery and an infuriated relation, he was more than likely to throw back his great handsome head, and laugh through his grizzled beard till the room echoed. "But it's funny, Signorina Gelosia," he would say, wiping his eyes with his fine cambric handkerchief, when she rebuked him, with privileged severity, for his levity. "You must see how it is funny! Eh, she's adroit, the little one!" and he would go off into fresh fits of mirth.

On this occasion Fräulein Gelsicher triumphed over Elena,

using the green taffeta dress and the necessity for a personal visit to Mme. Joséphine to drive a bargain about the suppression of the letter to Marietta. It was, she agreed, not likely to do serious harm—but her sense of consistency forbade her to countenance it. She put it away in the black russia leather bag, topped with silver, which hung from a silver hook attached to the neat petersham belt that marked the junction between her mauve face-cloth skirt and her mauve-and-white tartan blouse, along with the household keys, her handkerchief, her silver bottle of digestive pills and a slip with memoranda for the day written on it. There was a sentence in the letter which had vaguely worried her, and she wished to read it again. What was it that Elena had written about Marietta's mother, and the tone of that household? As a statement by Countess Roma it had seemed natural enough—from Elena, if she remembered it aright, it was extremely disconcerting. She had no time now, but later she must re-read it and consider it. Putting on her mauve cloth bolero jacket, reaching only to the waist, her mauve hat quilled with ribbon, a grey marabout boa and grey suède gloves, Fräulein Gelsicher went off to do battle on her pupil's behalf with the French dressmaker.

## Chapter Two

THE same Spring sun which had illuminated Fräulein Gelsicher's purple dressing-gown and curling-pins was pouring, on that May morning, into another room in the Casa Castellone, where Giulio di Castellone sat by the window reading Croce's *Estetica*. It lit up the untidy droop of his straight black hair over his high forehead and about his rather unusually shapely head, his delicate ugly profile, and the dusty right shoulder of his shabby serge suit; the fingers of his right hand, curved over the edge of the volume, made a rather beautiful study in shadow on the page, where the black print stood out strongly from the sun-warmed paper. Giulio was twenty-one, but he looked older; his thin sallow face habitually wore a thoughtful or dreamy expression, his shoulders stooped, his young mouth was often set in harsh lines. This morning, that was not the case—there was a look of eager peaceful concentration about him as he read, flicking the pages over with one hand, pushing back his hair when it fell into his eyes with the other—absorbed, satisfied; turning back now to re-read a passage, then turning forward again. / Giulio was tasting one of the purest of human satisfactions—the taking in of a new intellectual conception which, though unfamiliar, is instantly sympathetic to the mind receiving it. / He felt that this was right, this conception of the spiritual faculty in man as fourfold: the aesthetic, that which seeks for beauty; the logical, that which seeks for knowledge; the practical or economic, where will passes into action; the ethical, which strives towards righteousness in action and involves the whole idea of duty and obligation. His own spirit answered the philosopher's thought with a glad affirmative. Yes—and these four, though distinct, were yet one, and of an equal validity; a series, and yet a circle.    And how profound too Croce's contention that that series develops, in individuals as in races, in a certain sequence—first the aesthetic, then the logical or intellectual, only last the ethical.    Croce's insistence on the spiritual value of the aesthetic faculty, and on its being the first to develop in human beings was not, to Giulio Castellone, the startling suggestion that it might have been to a young man in Northern Europe, where an early stressing of the moral aspect, a grim and bleak inculcation of the harshest principles of righteousness even in childhood was still in full force, in those days.    Brought up in a faith where beauty is at least attempted in every form of religious ceremonial, and in a society where a practical rather than an idealistic outlook prevailed, and gaiety tempered all things, including morality, this conception was not strange to him.

But how splendid, how satisfying, the sweep and range of Croce's vision, setting the facts of a small individual experience in relation to a mighty whole; how fortifying to find his, Giulio's, own hatreds and prejudices, as well as his most dear and secret aspirations, given the sanction of clear philosophic expression.    The *ugliness* of any form of evil, his violent sense of the less good, even, as mis-shapen, in some way distorted and crippled—this was right, then!    Putting down his book, leaning forward to the open window to breathe in the fresh Spring air, he propped his head on his hand and thought, carefully relating his own instinctive feelings and ideas to this new theory, as young thinkers do.    He suddenly remembered how as a little boy of eleven he had once protested against going into the *salone* to see Zia Suzy, and when pressed for a reason had mumbled: "She's so ugly."    He had been scolded and derided—what a silly boy!    Everyone knew how beautiful she was.    "To me, she is ugly!" he had insisted stubbornly.    Then he had not in the least formulated his dislike of his Aunt, but now—he tapped the open book— here it was!    Spiritual ugliness—greediness, selfishness.

Austere, unpractical, absorbed in books, Giulio was wont

to pay very little heed to the proceedings of Suzy di Vill' Alta; the gossip of the Province hardly entered his careless ears, and if he heard it, he forgot it—he was very far from assessing her relationship to his Father, or to anyone else, with any exactitude; indeed he thought about her as little as possible. But he had been aware of a vague feeling, lately, that *there* was a point at which something morally disagreeable really touched his life. That is it, he thought now—at least there is moral ugliness there somewhere, and that is why I can't stand her. And seeing Fräulein Gelsicher's neat mauve figure at that moment crossing the street below, on her way to Mme. Joséphine's, he thought ' Gelosia doesn't like her either. I wonder if Gelosia ever reads Croce?' The improbability of this idea made him giggle aloud, a very young boyish laughter; but as he watched the governess disappear round the corner, her head bent to balance her hat against a sudden puff of wind, her marabout boa streaming out behind her—a figure a little elderly, almost a little ridiculous—a sudden feeling of comfort and affection warmed his heart. Fräulein Gelsicher, however much he might tease her and laugh at her, always gave him this sense of comfort and reassurance—and now he felt that he knew why. ' Gelosia has it—*that* beauty,' he muttered to himself. But suddenly he felt that he had read enough; he must get out into the wind and sun, walk and clear his head—these patches and scraps of ideas were no good! Banging the door behind him, he went out.

Down at the great arched doorway, through which a coach could be—and often had been—driven into the inner courtyard, he met the Countess Livia emerging from her apartment on the ground floor. Though Livia di Castellone had been a widow for six years, her tall slight figure was still perpetually clothed in sweeping black, with hints of crepe here and there; her face, once beautiful, now rather pinched and worn, looked out from the austere backward-sweeping lines of a widow's bonnet; there was a curious mixture of resignation and discontent about the expression of her eyes and mouth, a sort of rigid refinement breathed from her whole person. She greeted her nephew with a conscientious show of affection. Giulio kissed her hand perfunctorily, and said "Good morning, Zia Livia. Are you going to Mass?" (It was usually a safe assumption that Zia Livia, when seen issuing from her house, was going either to Mass, or to Benediction, or to hear the Rosary). He did not want to know, he wished he had not met her, but one had to say *something* to people. It was not that Giulio particularly objected to his Aunt Livia, but when he was about to go anywhere or do anything he had a nervous dislike of meeting anyone, for fear of being hindered or stopped. People talked to you, involved you—he never could think quickly enough of the decided word which would set him free; and was liable to get carried off, from sheer irresolution and incompetence, on some horrible enterprise of other people's. Or they asked you questions, to which he never knew the answers! Giulio never ceased to marvel at the things which people seemed to be interested in. What did it matter, any of it?

This morning, as usual, he failed at the questionnaire.

"How unfortunate about your father's waggons," Countess Livia began. "How many is it that are broken?"

"Waggons?" Giulio stared at her blankly. "What waggons?"

His aunt explained about the tragedy, and Fräulein Gelsicher's note.

"I am afraid I know nothing about them," said Giulio, bored and embarrassed.

"And dear Elena's dress. Will Joséphine really have it ready for tonight?" the Countess went on, laying a detaining hand, delicate and small in its black kid glove, on his arm. "Dear child—it would be such a pity for her to be disappointed, would it not?"

Giulio ran his free hand through his hair. "Zia Livia, Elena has already too many dresses!" he said, his voice harsh with nervousness.  "I cannot keep up with them!  Pardon me—I must leave you"—and he bent over her hand again, to kiss it in farewell.

"Your hat!  Giulio, you are not going out without a hat!" the Countess exclaimed, as he straightened himself and took a step towards the doorway.

"Dio Mio!  What does it matter?  Scusa, Zia Livia," he jerked out, and fairly ran through the great arch and out into the street.  Oh, Holy Virgin, what a world to live in! "Waggons!"  "Dresses!"  "Hats!" he exclaimed loudly, as he passed with his rapid stride out of the Via Vittoria and into the broad boulevard, with its clipped avenues of horse-chestnuts on either side, which led out of the town towards the North.  "Dresses!"  "Hats!" he muttered again furiously, skipping aside to avoid a pair of nurses, promenading slowly with their charges in the full fashionable panoply of brightly-coloured tartan print dresses, quilled caps, and long floating ribbons.  What a world to live in! he thought again —when there was the clear world of formal thought to enter into, the hard clean shapeliness of truth to be apprehended, pursued and at last understood.  A steady devotion to that search was surely the only way of living, for a rational creature.  And time was of value—the days, precious as jewels, should be spent in that pilgrimage, not frittered away on dresses and hats!  His face dark with irritation at human irrationality, he walked faster and faster, a thin, hurrying, figure, black hair blowing round his bent head; he only became once more aware of his surroundings when he was well outside the town.

The Province of Gardone forms part of the great plain of North Italy which stretches, roughly, from the Gulf of Genoa to the Adriatic, under the mighty rampart of the Alps.  But that northern mountain wall is not a straight line; it rather resembles a piece of coast—spurs project from it like head-lands, wide bays eat back into it.  And in one such bay lies the Province of Gardone.  On either side lesser mountain chains stand out into the plain, half-enclosing it; only to the South does a soft horizon spread away into the dark heavy haze of a warm climate; to West, to North, to East the eye is checked, well within its range of vision, by a sea of tossing crests, standing up into the sky like the waves of a cardboard ocean. Most of the province, like the rest of the plain, is flat as a board; but a few kilometres north of Gardone the earth, approaching the mountains, begins to ruffle and crumple, as water ruffles and breaks near the shore, into small hills and eminences, with wide spaces between. Out in this direction lay Odredo, Castellone and Vill' Alta, each with its formality of white walls, ilexes and cypresses, crowning some dominating ridge; but Giulio, striding out of the town that morning, still only found himself in the characteristic flatness of the plain, when he at last checked his pace and began to look about him.

He sauntered on, more quietly now; the fit of acute nervous irritation engendered by the impact of Countess Livia's world on Croce's had worn off, and he was able to enjoy what he saw. The flat road stretched away ahead of him, white and straight, bordered on either side by low mulberry-trees clipped into a sort of fan-shape, and planted at intervals; from tree to tree vines were trained in long loops. The mulberry-trees were in fresh leaf, a strong clear green, but along the loops of the vines the little buds and tendrils stood out, delicate and fine as goldsmiths' work in their faint burnished copper-colour, their minute perfection of design. In the fields beside the road the pale spear-like leaves of the maize were beginning to thrust up through the rich black soil; frogs uttered their musical note in the ditches; a swift screamed overhead. The monotonous simplicity and familiarity of the landscape soothed Giulio—he knew this road so well, it was one of his constant winter walks. It was pleasant to see it in this Spring dress. But it had, also, for Giulio, this road, its special associated idea, such as roads near our homes tend to acquire, linked to it by months of solitary musings on its straight stretches; and this idea entered his mind now, un-summoned, as he walked along. It was essential that he should go away and study seriously somewhere, for a couple of years. This reading alone was not enough—at his age one needed lectures, criticism, teaching, the disciplined life of thought. Somehow his Father must be made to see the necessity of it.

It was not at all easy to make Count Carlo see the necessity for things. The Province of Gardone was not exactly a hot-bed of advanced ideas, nor was the Count, viticulture apart, in the least modern in his outlook. He himself had been brought up in the position of a *figlio di famiglia*, the son of his family, comfortably supported under the parental roof, but given no such allowance as would enable him to exercise any sort of independence elsewhere until his marriage. This singular arrangement, almost peculiar to Italian society, which embittered Leopardi's youth a century ago, still seemed to Count Carlo both natural and sensible; and though the name had become out of date even in Gardone, Giulio's actual status remained very much what his Father's had been. He had received a fairly good education, thanks largely to Fräulein Gelsicher's influence; but once this was regarded as complete he had remained at home, spending the little money that he had on books, and his abundant leisure on reading.

At first he had been fairly content, but as time went on, and his increased knowledge showed him more and more clearly his own limitations, his need for a proper course at a University had become an obsession with him. A couple of years at the Sorbonne, or three years at Oxford—that was what he wanted, he thought again now. It would not cost much; he could manage on a very small allowance—less than a third of what would gladly be allotted him the moment he decided to marry. Marriage! He jerked back his head, in a sort of angry disgust—yes, *that* his Father would think per-fectly sensible, that would seem to him well worth while, for his son to marry and breed yet more Castellones! "Spawning!" he muttered, casting a contemptuous eye on the blinking and vociferous frogs in the roadside ditches. "As if there weren't enough of us already, swarming all over the province!" he thought, with a sort of bitter repulsion. "Hasn't Ernest enough children?" But to feed the mind, to breed ideas, to train himself to think, to school his thought into words, something more than his ephemeral sketches of a mood, all that to his Father would seem nothing. He decided that he must talk to Gelosia about it again—she could do more with the Count than anyone.

If only his English were better, he thought, pursuing his idea in the faint encouragement which the thought of Gelosia's help gave him, Oxford would really be the best. He could read English easily enough; but speaking it, and understanding it when spoken—that was difficult. How those two young Englishmen, Roffredo's friends, who had stayed at Castellone last year, had laughed at his English when he tried to talk to them—laughed in fits! He had stuck to it, he had talked to them as much as he possibly could; their amusement was perfectly good-tempered, and *he* didn't care! But that had shown him how difficult the business of lectures would be, if he were to go to Oxford.

Roffredo's name, coming into his mind, again deflected the current of his thoughts. Roffredo was his cousin, Countess Livia's only child, and some five years older than himself— and with his name his image stood up in Giulio's mind: his broad shoulders, his flaming red head, his good healthy mouth, opened in frequent laughter, the air of careless easy dominance that he carried about with him wherever he went. Giulio's own face softened curiously as the thought of Roffredo came to him. He had for this cousin of his the devotion, inexplicable but so common, of the complicated intellectual for the athletic and simple-minded type, which is also physically splendid and morally robust. Mentally the two had nothing in common—Roffredo di Castellone never opened a book that was not concerned with engineering, and seldom indulged in the process of thought at all, unless in connection with the internal combustion engine, now in process of considerable development in Italy; his search for truth was confined to such scientific theories as dealt with the best arrangement of multi-cyclinder engines, and the flash points of various types of spirit.   On such matters he was no fool; he had had one minor invention accepted by a firm in Milan, and was wrestling with another now.   But he accepted with unquestioning readiness and even enjoyment those aspects of everyday life which seemed to Giulio so incomprehensible; and the relative beauty or ugliness of people's souls troubled him not at all.   Of faces and figures, yes!—very much so; but minds didn't interest him.

How much better Roffredo had managed his life, Giulio thought now, as he wandered along between the looped vines and the formal mulberry-trees, than he himself.   He had, apparently without any particular trouble, forced the Countess Livia to let him become an engineer, and to make him a handsome allowance; he lived a completely independent life, and had just spent the whole winter in Paris studying the latest developments in four-cylinder engines.   He had a car —one of the only two cars in the Province; it was only a one-cylinder one, but it had chugged triumphantly about the roads last summer, raising clouds of dust, and terrifying every horse- and bullock-team that it met.   Roffredo—how homesick he was for his face and voice, after all these months!—Roffredo was doing the thing he was made for, and doing it well. Though exclusively concerned with matters which seemed to him, Giulio, of little or no importance, Roffredo himself was not unimportant; he was important in the self-existent independent way in which a fact is important—with the unquestioning, vigorous vitality of some splendid animal or tree. Thinking about Roffredo, he began forgetting his personal envy of his cousin's position, to consider him in relation to what he had been reading that morning.   Roffredo belonged in Croce's third division, the practical sphere of individual

C

action, seeking a particular end, without reference to the universal good or to ultimate standards of right or duty. His activities were what Croce described as "economic". But to this form of action also Croce allowed spiritual validity—so that was all right. Giulio would have hated to feel that Roffredo was, so to speak, outside Croce's circle of spiritual values.

His eye was caught by a group of peasants, sitting under a knot of willows at the edge of a field. There was a woman feeding a baby at the breast; a couple of boys sat beside her, and two or three men lay on the rough grass, eating their midday meal out of coloured handkerchiefs. There was a certain beauty about the group of dark figures, sprawled on the pale ragged winter grass, under the thin green of the budding willows—Giulio sat down on a stone by the roadside and watched them, laughing, eating, and teasing the woman with lively gestures; they looked happy, healthy and contented. He smiled a little sourly, thinking of the Rousseauish idealisation of the simple peasant in some of the books he had read. No one who knew them could put the peasants of Gardone very high in the spiritual scale; they lied, they were sensual, promiscuous, dishonest and idly cruel. Poverty and simplicity they had, but these did not appear to improve them much, for all that the books implied that they were so good for the soul! An idea flicked into Giulio's head as he watched the peasant group. Was it only the things of which one was conscious that affected the soul? In fact, was it the *consciousness* that was important? To those handsome creatures under the tree their dishonesty and sensuality were as natural as breath; did they therefore leave their actual souls unaffected—just as the apparent virtues of poverty and simplicity flowed off them, it seemed, like water off a duck's back? He pulled out a rather bent note-book, and began to scribble away in it, working out this idea, oblivious of time, sitting in the sun on the stone by the roadside.

When he had written to the end of his thought Giulio put

his note-book back in his pocket, and coming out of his absorption, glanced across towards the group that had inspired it. The peasants had gone back to work—the baby alone lay among a heap of coats. He pulled out his watch and looked at it—Roffredo had one of the new watches which you strapped on your wrist, but he, Giulio, had only a heavy old artichoke on a chain! It was past twelve o'clock—then he would be wildly late for *colazione*, he thought, with irritated resignation. Well, there were more important things than meals. But for all that he set out with hurried strides towards the town.

*Colazione*, leisurely meal though it was, was more than half over when Giulio returned. The Count, handsome, urban and urbane in a spring suit of light grey, sat at the head of the table—Fräulein Gelsicher at the foot, Elena on her Father's right. Giulio coming in stood beside his Father, bowed, made a formal apology to him and to Fräulein Gelsicher, and was waved to his seat by the Count with a fine gesture. Umberto, in a white jacket and white cotton gloves, moved round the table waiting, assisted by Luigi, his nephew, a rather awkward youth of seventeen who divided his time between the kitchen, the pantry and the stables, without being a great success in any of them. When his employers were alone at meals Umberto permitted himself a good deal of confidential conversation with them, in a sort of ecclesiastical monotone—at Giulio's entrance he now muttered to the Signorina that as the young Count was so late he had better begin with the nudels, so that Anna might make the young Count a fresh omelette; and on getting her assent bustled out of the room. Giulio, eating his nudels, listened to the conversation of his family. The Count, his napkin tucked carefully in under his splendid iron-grey beard, masticating salad, at once resumed a long monologue on a theory of root-pruning of vines which he had culled from the new French volume; Elena saluted this theme with a minute wink at her brother, brilliant and swift as the turn of a diamond in the sun—he did not however make the response she expected, and after enduring the vines for a few moments she interrupted her Father's scientific flow gaily and brusquely with "Senti, Paparut', do let the vines grow in peace for one moment! Giulio has not heard one word about Marietta."

Elena could take almost any liberties with her Father, especially when she called him by the local dialect word for a father, *paparuto*; the Count, amused, said benignly, "Speak, then, on this great theme!"

Elena, thus unleashed, bubbled out her news.

"Dunque, Marietta is to have a governess!"

"Why?" interrupted Giulio, who was still feeling cross, partly because of his own lateness, partly from his general lack of interest in the concerns of others.

"Dio mio, but to have lessons with her, and be taken about," his sister retorted, not in the least dashed by this chilling reception of her news.  "And senti, it is an English-woman."

For the first time Giulio was interested.  An English-woman in the Province might really help his plans.  Zia Suzy, whose mother had been an American, could of course speak English, but one of her more tiresome affectations, to Giulio, was the pretence that she had almost forgotten it.  He interrupted Elena's elaborations on the probable appearance of the governess by asking:

"When does she come?"

"Tuesday, they all come on Tuesday to Vill' Alta."

"But the governess?"

"Oh, I don't know—soon—perhaps they meet her in Gardone.  But in any case very soon.  Will it not be nice for Gela?"

"That depends on whether she is a nice person," said the Count.

"Papa!  Marietta says Zia Suzy says Princess Asquini says——"

"Says!  Says!  Says!  And the cat said!" said the Count.

"Papa caro! Will you be quiet! Princess Asquini says she knows the family, and they are very *comme il faut*; and the governess is very learned—she has been at Oxford!"

"How at Oxford? Women don't go to Oxford."

" Yes they do! In England now they do since many years! They learn like men. Marietta will end by knowing everything."

Giulio turned to Fräulein Gelsicher. "Gelosia, your nose will be quite out of joint with this colleague of so much learning!" he said.

"Will it not? But since your sister now knows all that she needs to know, this matters less," the governess answered in the same tone. She was pleased that Giulio had recovered his equanimity. The young man was, in fact, considerably exhilarated by Elena's news. If this new governess of Marietta's really was an educated woman, had really studied at Oxford—magical word!—there was no telling what might not come of it. At least he could take regular English lessons with her; his experience of how much schoolroom work went on at Odredo in the summer did not lead him to think for a moment that his cousin's own lessons would be much of an impediment. His imagination lit up—he saw himself on his bicycle flying over daily to Vill' Alta, to spend long industrious hours with a learned woman in spectacles, who would introduce him to the English philosophers, to Locke and Hume and Bentham; coming back laden with books to write English essays, and above all *talking* with the Englishwoman, till his English would be good enough to go to Oxford. He came down out of the clouds when they moved into the *salone*, which looked on to the courtyard, for coffee, and began to cross-examine Elena as to the academic qualifications of the new governess with an interest as marked as his previous indifference had been. Elena could tell him little more—she had shot her bolt of information at once, as she usually did. There remained only speculation, in which, when the Count went off to his study, they indulged delightfully.

Giulio was really very fond of his sister; his ascetic disapproval of most of her interests and pursuits was apt to
disappear in her actual company, when her merriment and
folly, her high spirits and her mischief, above all the thousand
links forged by a childhood spent together, the common stock
of standing grievances and recurring delights, of jokes old and
new and adventures shared, drew him to her in an easy
affectionate companionship which, for all his passion for
philosophical stocktaking, he had not yet begun to analyse.
They sat on together, the pair of them, in the high bright
*salone*, on the spindly walnut settee, exercising their
fancy in wilder and wilder flights of nonsense over the
unknown governess, with peals of laughter. Umberto,
coming in to remove the coffee-tray, shook his head at
them, silently, in indulgent recognition of the inevitable
folly of youth.

Elena eventually confided to her brother her successful
forgery of the morning. Giulio shook his head—he had
been a victim of this gift more than once, and disapproved
of it.

"I thought you had given that up," he said.

"Only for six months! But this was a beauty. I wish
you had seen it."

"Did you send it?"

"No—Gela took it. She might have it still."

As a matter of fact Fräulein Gelsicher was at that moment
in her room, whither she had retired immediately after coffee,
lying—to rest her feet—on the straight armless couch, and
pondering over Elena's letter to Marietta. It *was* rather disconcerting. She re-read the closing sentences: "Your cousin
Aspasia and I have often felt that you have lacked, in the past
. . . any steady model at hand on which to mould yourself."
"Your Mother's household is so social!" "You may well
expect your life to be different from hers—indeed I dare
almost say that I hope this will be the case!"

Indefinite, veiled, prudently expressed as it was, the letter contained a very wealth of possible innuendo; it could be construed as hinting at very little beyond social frivolity, or at almost anything! It was very clever. The question was, how much did Elena mean by it? It was a question that Fräulein Gelsicher could not answer.

## Chapter Three

To be young is always a difficult, dangerous and confusing business—but it can seldom have been so difficult and so dangerous, and above all so confusing, as in England during the first ten years of the twentieth century. Those years were witnessing the earlier stages of a change-over from one social order to another, a change which was completed by the War. The Victorian ice was beginning to break up, but a great deal of it was still fairly solid, especially away from the centre of the stream, along the banks and in the backwaters. Even there, however, the movements of the central current were disturbingly felt. Cracks began to shoot through family life, and the firm Victorian faith in the inevitability of family affection; large chunks of the cruder forms of religious belief broke off and were carried away; ominous shivers ran through the sanctity of marriage, filial obedience, the complacent acceptance of social inequality, and other solid-seeming structures. Above all the moral conventions, those delicate tacit assumptions of what constitutes desirable behaviour, on which each generation stands, were in motion—they shifted under your feet, pushed by some unseen force they tilted sideways, and threatened to plunge you into unknown waters. The greatest disruptive force of all, Sigismund Freud, had not yet fairly got going in England —*Die Traumdeutung* only appeared in 1900, and it was a good many years before these remarkable theories filtered, by way of the psychological works, those little potted abstracts for the general reader, awe-struck conversation, and eventually the novelists, into the general consciousness. All the emotions were still taken at their face value, touched up with a dash of idealism; in those days, in England, sons could love

32

their mothers and mothers their sons without any fear of being secretly disreputable, and the most respectable women would admit unblushingly to having dreamt of root vegetables. But the things one could *not* do, or say, were still a good deal more numerous than the things which one could; and many of the staples of modern conversation in mixed company were hardly even to be thought in secret at the time when Almina Prestwich went off to be governess to Marietta di Vill' Alta.

A few days after Giulio and Elena di Castellone, out in Gardone, were so gaily discussing their cousin's future governess, that personage herself, in her bedroom in England, was occupied in packing, while her younger sister May looked on. The bedroom was full of clothes and luggage. A large black leather trunk, still empty, stood on the once handsome, now rather worn carpet, which bore a disappearing design of maroon roses on a brown and yellow ground; neat piles of underclothing were laid out on the bed, which like so many English beds then was double, and had shiny brass rails and bars and knobs at head and foot. The long mirror door of the wardrobe was open, revealing dresses hanging inside; so were two drawers in the chest of drawers, which like the wardrobe was of highly polished ash picked out with mahogany; the dressing-table, which had a fringed white cover of honeycomb dimity on it, and a fixed mirror, matched them both—so did the washstand, which had in addition a white marble top and a sort of small wall of brown and yellow tiles, representing sunflowers, round the back and sides—so indeed did the four cane-seated chairs which stood round the room with jackets hanging over their backs and piles of tissue-paper on their seats. The furniture of Almina's room was in fact a suite from Maple's, bought some thirty years before and still, after the manner of Maple suites, in perfectly good order despite the lapse of time—doors and drawers closing smoothly with a little puff of air, so closely did they fit, so admirable was the joiner's work. The walls of the room were papered with the Morris marigold, in yellow and white. There was also an armchair. Except for the wallpaper everything in the room was rather ugly, but Almina did not think so—the fad for distemper, plain rugs and rather tumble-down antique furniture had not yet gripped England with any thoroughness; all the things in her room were either solid or handsome, and above all "matched"—she took constant pleasure in the fact that the ewer and basin, and even the lids of the soap and toothbrush dishes bore a design of brown and yellow sunflowers to match the washstand tiles. And she would not really have been wrong in thinking that the whole room gave an impression of pleasantness and comfort, with just enough of a well-worn air about it to mellow it.

"I think we'd better begin on the hats," Almina said to May. "Mother doesn't seem to be coming, and I must get on. But she won't want to see *them*." May agreed, and both girls bent consideringly over the hatbox, a very large square affair in the new greenish canvas, with round projections fastened to the sides, bottom and top. The crowns of the hats were placed over the projections, and then pinned in position, but to prevent conflict between plumes and bows and other lofty erections on the crowns, the hats had to be carefully placed. After some thought—"I should put the green at the bottom," said May.

"Right. Hand it out, will you?" said Almina, taking a box of long steel hatpins with round heads of black or white glass off the dressing-table, and sticking them into the projection on the lid, ready for use. May opened the door of the hat-cupboard, a central compartment of the ash wardrobe, which had more drawers below it, and pulled out the green hat, a huge thing of drooping silky horsehair, the crown smothered in yellow and white roses. She held it up. "It is *lovely*," she said, gazing at it with envy. "Whatever did it cost, Al?"

"It's my best," said Almina, rather repressively. "It was two-and-a-half guineas," she added.

"Gracious! Do stick it on, Al, just for a second, and let me see."

Almina, taking the hat, moved to the dressing-table. It was obvious before she put it on that it would suit her very well. She was small and rather pale, with a great deal of very fine soft hair almost the colour of raw silk—what we now call "ashen blonde" and admire greatly, but which was then called "flaxen" and considered rather dull. In addition she had a neat straight little nose, a neat firm little chin, rather a large pale mouth and large greyish eyes set very far apart under eyebrows much darker than her hair. Today these things would make her the envy of all her acquaintances, but Almina was not considered in the least pretty by her family— not nearly so pretty as May, who in spite of rather rough-and-tumble features had a bright colour, vivid blue eyes, a red mouth, and proper golden hair, which curled by itself. In an age when women had to take what God gave them in the way of hair and complexion girls like May started with a great advantage. Very fashionable married women crimped their hair with tongs, a few dowagers with peculiar reputations painted, Queen Alexandra enamelled her lovely singular face; but among ordinary God-fearing gentlepeople, in town or country, for a girl to have put any extraneous colouring-matter on her countenance would have been unheard-of. Secretly, those whose noses shone bought little cardboard cases containing minute sheets of something called *papier poudré*, which they rubbed over the offending member, usually with most unhappy results; but their mothers confiscated these, if they found them, with a lecture on the appalling effect of getting "talked about"—a calamity which was certain to over-take any girl who was seen with a powdered nose.

Almina's lack of the accepted standard of prettiness did not trouble her quite as much as it would have done most of her contemporaries. She had been to Oxford for three years, and had there become serious-minded and slightly dowdy; she had taken a first in Modern Languages, which had given her a good deal of self-confidence independently of her appearance; she was become ambitious, had views on the economic independence of women, and hoped to have a career. It is true that she did occasionally study her face in the glass, half-critically and half-wistfully—she usually decided privately that her features were really rather good, except for her mouth, and that if her hair *wasn't* as curly and golden as it might have been, at least it was very fine and silky, and there was a great deal of it. And anyhow there were more important things than looks. But now, when she combed up the fine pale stuff before the glass and placed the big green hat on her head, she could not resist a little tremor of pleasure at the image which confronted her. The yellow and white roses brought out the creamy paleness of her skin, making it not a blemish, but something like a beauty in itself; under the soft green of the fine *crin* brim, the pale gold of her hair looked almost lovely. And when she swung round to face May, that young person gazed at her with most flattering astonishment before she said—"Al, it *does* suit you! You really look quite——"

"Quite what?" Almina asked, pleased, and anxious for more.

"Well, nearly beautiful. It's rather like that last picture of Edna May—she had a hat like that."

"You don't think it looks actressy, do you?" asked Almina anxiously. There was no deeper condemnation then for clothes, however becoming, than that they should look "actressy."

"No-o—not that. Only you look so extra nice in it," May reassured her.

"It will go with a lot of things," said Almina, turning to look in the glass again; "the green, and the white, and the white-and-yellow."

"Are they very smart, these people? I suppose they are," said May, "if she's a Marchioness."

"She isn't a Marchioness—she's only a Marchesa—it doesn't

mean the same abroad," said Almina, with fine British depre-
cation of foreign titles.    "But I expect they are very smart—
foreigners always are.    The Princess told Mother they entertained a lot."

"Shall you go to their parties?" May enquired, seating
herself on the bed.

"Look out!   Don't squash my petties!   Not much, I don't
suppose—but I don't really know exactly what governesses
do abroad," Almina said.    "I wish I did know more.    But I
gather I have to take the child about wherever she goes, so I
shall go to children's parties, I suppose, and church, and
things like that."

"You *will* have fun," May said, enviously.

"I hope I shall be able to make a success of it, and do all
they want," said her sister soberly.

"P'raps you'll marry an Italian Count," May was beginning
—her mind always ran to the social aspect of things—when
the door opened and her Mother came in.

Mrs. Prestwich was a woman for whom life over a long
period of years had been a little too much, and her face, under
her smoothly-dressed grey hair, showed it.    Her father had
been a poor but rather popular Baron, of a decent and well-
established creation untainted by trade, her Mother the
daughter of a very minor Welsh peer; she herself, in spite of
the perpetual lack of money in her family, had been brought
up and launched on the world in what still seemed to her the
only normal and proper way: that is to say she had been
presented at Court, had had one complete London season
and one long visit to an Aunt the following year, and had
then lived at home in the country, knowing the whole county
and going to such gaieties as it afforded, in the shape of
croquet parties, archery tournaments and a few balls, till she
married.    Her marriage and subsequent life typified that
gradual swallowing-up of the lesser aristocracy in the middle
class which was such a feature of the latter part of the 19th
century.    Tom Prestwich came of excellent yeoman stock

in the North-country; his grandfather had made a modest, his father a very considerable fortune in trade; the latter kept horses, sent his sons to public school and joined a London club. Young Thomas, who had his full share of the harsh shrewd intelligence which was the birthright of his family, and more than his share of its cool independence, took up medicine, and with success. He had money behind him, and when he met Louisa Heycote, swept her off her feet and married her, he was able to take her home to a largish pleasant-ish Victorian house, in a largish pleasantish garden, on the outskirts of a large and not unpleasant South of England town in which he had already a large and growing practice. There Mrs. Prestwich had spent the rest of her life—there she had given birth to her two sons and her five daughters, the births punctuated by several miscarriages; there she had brought up her children; there, last year, buried her husband; and there, at this moment, Almina was packing her clothes to go out to Italy as a governess.

It was perhaps this last circumstance, more than any other, which had forced on Mrs. Prestwich the full realisation of how far she had failed in her attempts to shape life as she wanted it—which was, after all, only what seemed to her the very modest desire that her children should live as she had lived herself, and be brought up as she had been brought up. She had expected when she married that Thomas's brains and good looks and charm, their easy circumstances and her own social position would make this aim quite easy of realisation. It had in fact proved otherwise, to her surprise and disappoint-ment. Thomas never lost his brains, but his good looks and his charm diminished at a surprising speed; as his reputation increased his leisure for social activities, and his inclination for them, diminished also, and as the expense of educating a family of seven was gradually borne in upon him, his prudent bourgeois unwillingness to spend good money on needless frivolities became more and more marked. Mrs. Prestwich, even at first, had never taken quite the place in society in and round Beamington that she expected, and as the years went on it became more of a struggle.  In a perfectly well-bred way, with a touching and innocent faith in the value and meritoriousness of her efforts, she worked away at her social activities for her children's sake—calling at the right houses in her neat brougham, giving dinner-parties, garden-parties, tea-parties; making correct advances to "worthwhile" people, forming connections; and clinging, just a little, to connections accidentally formed; economising on the house-keeping to contrive the right clothes, more and more for her daughters and less and less for herself.  On the whole she had done very well— the Prestwich family lived in a nice "set"; Almina and May had both been presented, they went to quite a number of balls, and were on visiting terms with several of the county families. But the "set" was a rather more of the town and less of the county than she had hoped; their position needed holding on to, instead of simply happening; there was a good deal of rather careful keeping in touch with her own old friends, of making the best of people, of reminding herself that the So-and-Sos were *really* very nice.  It was, in fact, all very different from the effortless and arbitrary correctitude of her mother's entertaining, in her own youth.

And then Thomas died, leaving his family remarkably ill-provided for.  After the habit of Victorian husbands, his only communications to his wife on the subject of money had been to complain of the size of the cheques he was asked to draw, whether for housekeeping, dress, schools, or pocket-money; but as he always *had* drawn them, apparently without inconvenience, and had never given his Louisa any inkling of what his income was, or how much they could really afford to spend, it was hardly surprising that she, after the manner of Victorian wives, assumed that there was plenty, and extorted all she could in the way of cheques in order to give the children the clothes, the amusements and the amount of entertaining that she felt they ought to have.  After his death she had a rude awakening.  Dr. Prestwich, throughout his life, had lived well up to an extremely handsome income; and except for her marriage settlement and a thumping life insurance, there was little or nothing put by.

There was the practice, which in due course was sold, and sold fairly well. There was also the house, and since largish Victorian houses were already becoming difficult to dispose of, after some fruitless attempts they decided to stay on in it, with a diminished indoor and outdoor staff. The two boys were already earning their own living, but no more; Almina and May had completed their education, but the three younger girls were still at school. Mrs. Prestwich, at last with a grasp of the situation which in all her married life she had never been allowed, found eventually, when everything was settled up, that they would be able to carry on, but every possible economy would be necessary. Almina, for instance, who had had this very expensive new University education, ought to earn something. Mrs. Prestwich had never been really convinced in her heart as to the desirability of the higher education for girls—she thought it made them critical at home, and unfitted them for social life; she didn't care for the tone of most of Almina's college friends, and they were usually dreadfully dowdy. It was Dr. Prestwich, with the firm faith in education of a man who owes much to his own, who had insisted on sending Almina to Oxford. But since she had had the education, she had better make use of it. Mrs. Prestwich knew quite well the use Almina wanted to make of it—to do some research into the early Italian poets and their contemporary history and eventually to write a book about them. But that meant continued expense for ever so long—being boarded with people at Oxford to be within reach of books, or at the best living unremuneratively at home. It would mean skimping on the three little girls, who ought to have their chance. After those miserable wrestlings with figures, on sheets of paper covered with estimates of this and that, poor Mrs. Prestwich, shamefacedly and wretchedly, took her eldest daughter aside and made the admission which the Victorian parent found so unbearably mortifying—that money really was extremely short, and that if she could possibly start earning something, she had better.

Almina, greatly to her mother's relief, took the whole thing very calmly and sensibly. She had been brought up in high principles of duty, obligation and unselfishness—the duty and obligation to express oneself and live one's own life were then not so fashionable as they have since become; in fact the very words connoted a sense of responsibility to others, and especially to one's parents. Besides this, Almina was happy enough to have a spontaneous and unforced affection for her Mother; they had sufficient instinctive sympathy for the relationship to be both easy and strong. She agreed at once, and set about looking for a job. In her heart of hearts she hoped for something reasonably academic, such as teacher in some rather advanced high-school. But her Mother had other views. Among the old friends with whom she had so carefully maintained contact was a certain Lydia Charlbury, who had married a Prince Asquini about the same time that Louisa Heycote married Tom Prestwich. When it was at last settled that Almina was to "earn," Mrs. Prestwich determined that she should earn as much, and in a manner which held as many social possibilities as might be. She wrote to Princess Asquini and invoked her good offices to find a post for Almina as governess in Italy; if one must be a governess, it was both more interesting and less obvious to be a governess abroad. And before Almina's answers to advertisements and consultations had led to any definite offer of a job, Mrs. Prestwich was able to produce the appointment of being governess to the daughter of the Marchesa di Vill' Alta—a high salary, Rome in winter, the country in summer; delightful people, the Princess wrote, in the first society, and a household where "there was always a great deal going on." It sounded perfect, and it was promptly arranged; slightly to Almina's secret dismay, greatly to Mrs. Prestwich's satisfaction.

D

Coming into her daughter's bedroom now, to go through her things and make sure that all was right, Mrs. Prestwich had something of a shock. At the sound of the door opening Almina turned round on the chair towards it; she was still wearing the green hat, over a nun's-veiling blouse which had been white, but had washed to cream-colour. And, as May had been, Mrs. Prestwich was startled by her daughter's appearance. Certainly at that moment, in the hat, Almina looked extraordinarily pretty. Since by the time she went to Italy it would be several months since her father died, and as black in summer was so hot, and presented such difficulties with dust, and moreover as she was to be in the country, Mrs. Prestwich had rather brusquely decided that it would be best to let her daughter go out of mourning, and get an outfit at once which would last a couple of years. But after the months of seeing her in black or black-and-white, which killed her delicate colouring, leaving it cold and crude, the picture now before Mrs. Prestwich was startling. It flashed into her mind that Almina had improved, that after all she might, in the right clothes, be going to be a very pretty girl—and with the thought came a vague disquiet. Tacitly and affectionately, Almina had always been allowed to believe herself plain; if now she was going to be pretty, might not she be rather unprepared for the consequences—for admiration, for advances? Mrs. Prestwich, sending her daughter alone, at twenty-two, among strangers and foreigners, had had some natural anxiety; but she had banked on the girl's plainness as much as on her upbringing to see her safely through. And if one of these bulwarks were removed, it *would* be disquieting. However, she reflected later in the day, it was too late to do anything about it now—you couldn't make a girl believe herself pretty all in a minute. And her upbringing would remain.

At the moment, all she said was: "How nice that looks, my child. But hadn't you better pack it? Have you got everything ready?"

"Yes, Mother. I was waiting for you. It's all here."
She took off the hat and laid it on a chair.

There began the careful process of "going through"
Almina's things. The piles of underclothes on the bed, the
two neat heaps of nightdresses, viyella for winter, cambric for
summer, with their long sleeves and frilled collars, buttoning
down the front to the accompaniment of more frills, the rows
of rolled-up stockings on the chest of drawers, were all
examined by Mrs. Prestwich with minute and anxious care.
Most of the stockings were of black cashmere or black ribbed
silk, but there were a few pairs of the frivolous up-to-date
ones in lisle thread, with lacy openwork patterns all up the
front, in discreet shades of mole and grey—over these Mrs.
Prestwich lingered doubtfully, observing at length:"If you
find these aren't worn, dear, I should put them aside; don't
start on them till you see what other people do."

"No, Mother—I'll remember."

Then the dresses had their turn. Mrs. Prestwich, with a
certain enterprising practicality which always characterised
her actions, had felt it right and worth while to lay out a
good deal of money on Almina's outfit, to give her a fair
start—a policy to which the green hat bore eloquent witness.
She passed her daughter's frocks in review, seeing her in her
mind in each garment; wondering if they were, after all,
exactly what she would need, and of the sort to give her the
reassurance of being "right" in new and alarming surroundings. She handled every one, giving a little discourse on the
sort of occasion on which it should, in her opinion, be worn;
now and then she sighed and said: "I hope it *will* do"—about
some particular garment. Almina listened with admirable
patience. Neither of them, she felt in her heart, knew in the
least if the clothes would be suitable or not; but she was
sufficiently nervous herself about the whole enterprise not to
be antagonised by her Mother's fussing. Her family's attitude
to her appearance had never led her to take an excessive
interest in her clothes, and at Oxford the prevailing concern

with higher matters had made her more indifferent than ever; but she was prepared to believe that in this new sphere they would matter, and therefore she accepted her Mother's outlook, and even shared it. At all costs, she was determined to make a sucess of this governessing job—save money, pay back her Mother for this trousseau, and even perhaps put by enough to keep herself while she worked at her poets later. Her independence beckoned and gleamed ahead of her.

And the moment had its emotional quality too. She was leaving her home to enter an unknown world, and her Mother was doing the last thing she could to equip her for it; exercising for the last time, for who knew how long, that gentle protecting care which had been like sheltering arms round her girlhood. Perhaps for the first time in her life Almina consciously realised the love behind this care, and what it had meant to her; and each time that she said "Yes Mother, I will remember" in her dutiful quiet voice, her heart within her was crying "Darling Mother, I will be what you want, do all you wish. I won't fail you or disappoint you." At the last she did say a little of what she meant. Mrs. Prestwich presently asked to see her jewellery. Almina showed her small possessions—some childish bangles and trinkets, a heavy garnet necklace and ear-rings, rather beautifully set, a little pearl and gold Venetian chain, one or two small pearl brooches of the safety-pin type, presented by godparents for use in bibs, and the inevitable string of corals. Mrs. Prestwich looked them over, and then murmuring— "Yes, I think perhaps—" went away to her room and fetched her own jewel-case, that treasure-house of riches into which Almina and May used to peep as children, with awe-struck delight, when their Mother was dressing for a dinner-party. Something of the old wonder and mystery still hung about the oblong black leather box, with its small key and its velvet trays—Almina felt it again now, as her Mother opened the lid, lifted out the topmost tray, and looked thoughtfully at the contents. At last she took out a brooch, a circle of emeralds and diamonds, and one of the things Almina had always loved most, a pair of bracelets of amethysts linked loosely together with seed pearls, and a pendant to match, with seed pearl fringes dropping from it.

"I think these," Mrs. Prestwich said, "they are young enough, but they are good. For evening, my child, the amethysts—but the brooch you can wear at any time."

Almina was quite overcome. "Oh Mummie darling, they are lovely. I've always loved the amethysts so specially. Thank you so so much." Then she threw her arms round her Mother's neck and kissed her worn gentle face. "I will do my best," she murmured, her face hidden. "I really will."

"I'm sure you will, my darling," Mrs. Prestwich answered, moved in her turn. Holding her eldest daughter, her good trustworthy learned child, in her arms, she felt suddenly that she ought to give her a word of advice, of warning, before sending her off to the continent alone. She sought in her mind for the right thing to say—these things were so difficult. At last—"My child, you will be prudent, won't you?" she said with some embarrassment. "I mean——" she paused. "Always remember to behave like a lady, and you will be all right," she said at length.

"Yes Mother," said Almina, aware of her Mother's embarrassment, which communicated itself to her. She knew dimly what her Mother meant. One was to be careful about kisses and so on. If one was kissed too much, one had a baby—this she knew vaguely. A young man at a dance had once kissed her on the mouth, suddenly, and that had frightened Almina nearly out of her wits; for weeks she had wondered if she was going to have a baby or not. Though she was twenty-two, no one had yet told her how procreation occurred, or children were born, nor any facts about physiology. Like every other natural creature, she had wondered a little; but the only answers that her ignorant speculations obtained had been derived from fiction, and were therefore veiled and confused. *Adam Bede* had given her the data for her fright about the baby. But though Victorian fiction told one a great deal about love, it told one little that was practical about sex; and though she had read widely in poetry not Victorian, Shakespeare and the rest, the allusions which experience finds so broad slipped off the smooth veneer of her utter ignorance like water off a duck's back. She had not had many young men in pursuit of her, and nothing like a love affair; her experience of life was purely literary, and she had not been given the key with which to unlock that literary experience. The parson who prepared her for confirmation had been expected by her mother, after the habit of the time, to tell her what a girl ought to know; but though he was considered rather "advanced" and had embarrassed her mortally, he had left her little wiser than before. He stressed the necessity for purity, without telling her in what exactly it consisted; in a burst of frankness—"Don't let anyone handle your body," he said. That one sentence, which went coiling through her consciousness for months afterwards, was all she had ever been given in the way of practical advice. She was left with a vague sense that though love was undoubtedly the most beautiful and wonderful thing in life, the physical expression of it was impurity, and therefore wrong. All this had not so far greatly troubled her—now, at her Mother's words in this moment of separation, she had for a moment a wild desire to ask her what it all meant; how exactly one was to be prudent, and against precisely what? But she did not ask—such questions were impossible. Embarrassed, she said "Yes, Mother" to Mrs. Prestwich's injunction. And Mrs. Prestwich, like the good Victorian parent that she was, was quite satisfied with her own last words.

It was indeed *very* difficult and dangerous to be young in those days.

## Chapter Four

LA VECCHIA MARCHESA was making her usual morning
progress down onto the terrace at Vill' Alta. She
always emerged, if the weather was fine, soon after
eleven, and took her accustomed seat in a high-backed wicker
chair under the great ilex, with its thick triple trunk—close
enough to the low terrace parapet to be able to use it as a
table on which to place her book, her lorgnette for reading,
her ivory paper-knife, and the wine-glass containing a raw
egg beaten up with a dash of maraschino which Roberto, her
man-servant, invariably brought out to her when she was
settled. Her progress was very slow and extremely dignified,
as befitted an old lady of ninety-nine. First came Roberto,
carrying cushions, a footstool, a rug and a light shawl, opening doors all the way; then came La Vecchia Marchesa herself,
accompanied by Giacinta, her maid, who bore the book and
the other oddments in her left hand, and kept her right free
to support her mistress in need during her passage down the
wide polished staircase. The Marchese Francesco, her son,
and Suzy, her daughter-in-law, had both begged the old
Marchesa for years to let them arrange an apartment for her
on the ground floor—but no, she would not; she persisted in
keeping to the suite of rooms at the west end of the house to
which she had retired when her son married, nineteen years
ago; and every day, at Vill' Alta, downstairs she came, sliding
her old wrinkled ivory-white hand with the huge rings along
the glossy surface of the heavy carved balustrade, putting her
little kid slippers—one after the other, precautiously—onto
each of the wide shallow steps in turn, till she reached the
stone floor of the great hall, with its pale coarse mosaic of
Mars and Venus in the centre, and moved across it to the

door of her son's study. For her age she walked surprisingly strongly, once she reached level ground—just steadying herself on an ebony stick, with a plain smooth ball of ivory for its head. This visit also was a daily ritual—Roberto flung open both the study doors, and announced "La Marchesa di Vill' Alta," more as if he were proclaiming her arrival at Court than in her son's sitting-room; while the small figure, bent awkwardly at the hips but still beautifully upright at the shoulders, passed across the tiled floor.

On this, as on all other mornings, Francesco di Vill' Alta rose to greet his Mother, pushing back his chair; he bowed over her hand, kissed it, and asked how she did, with as much formality as if she were a total stranger.

"Well; well," the old lady replied, with a hint of impatience. "I am always well."

"You slept well?" the son further asked, solicitously.

"Sufficiently. Sleep is for the young!" the old lady answered, with a tiny laugh that was as frail as the ring of fine glass. "And what are you painting this morning, my son?" As she spoke she walked towards a very large table of plain deal, set under one of the windows, from his seat before which the Marchese had risen at her entrance. The table was strewn at both ends with books and magazines, many of them held open with paper-weights, paper-cutters and even other books, displaying illustrations of a botanical nature—in the middle was a block, a box of water-colours, a small jug of discoloured water and a rather ugly purplish flower in a specimen-glass.

"Pipo has sent me this from Brioni"—the Marchese indicated the purple flower. "I am making a sketch of it before it fades. I have revived it with aspirin, but it will not last."

The old lady, now standing by the table, glanced at the plant, which bore a long straggling truss of small flowers, maroon above, discoloured to a greenish yellow below, each on a spindly little stalk. It was very peculiar, but far from pretty. Her tone rather expressed her sense of this as she asked—"And what is it?"

The Marchese Francesco fluttered over the mass of books, peering through thick-lensed spectacles, and took up a small grey paper-covered magazine, on which was printed:

### THE BOTANICAL MAGAZINE
#### or
### FLOWER-GARDEN DISPLAYED

—the cover further informed the curious that this was No. 45 (Price ONE SHILLING) To be continued MONTHLY, that it was "A WORK Intended for the Use of such LADIES, GENTLEMEN, AND GARDENERS as wish to become scientifically acquainted with the plants they cultivate"; and that it was printed in London at 10, Throgmorton Street, for W. Curtis in the year 1792. The Marchese opened it at the place where a slip of paper protruded from the pages, and showed a very delicate and precise reproduction of the flower on the table. "Hyacinthus Comosus" he said triumphantly. "I am sure it is that."

"Giacinta! My glass!" the old lady said. The grey-haired maid, an elderly woman with a sour faithful face, hurried into the room and handed a lorgnette with a long tortoiseshell handle to her mistress—the old Marchesa raised it to her eyes and examined the illustration. "It resembles it," she said. "And where and how does it grow?"

The Marchese Francesco shook his head regretfully, and tapped the page. "It is all in English," he said. "I cannot read it. I must get Giulio to come over and tell me what it says."

The Marchesa laughed her tiny thin laugh again. "Figlio caro, you need not do that any more—Marietta's Anglaise comes today; she can translate it for you."

The Marchese Francesco's face brightened. "I had forgotten," he said. "Excellent! She will be able to translate the whole series to me."

But the old Marchesa was now examining her son's own drawing through her lorgnette. "What do you think of it?" he asked, rather wistfully.

"Molto bene! But why do you spend the whole morning making a drawing, when you have such a good one here already?"—she touched the grey magazine.

"But Mama, you know that I am making my own collection of sketches," the Marchese protested. His mother always tormented him in this way, and after nearly seventy years of it he was still always caught, always hurt; always reassured when, as now, she laughed at him.

"But yes—I know! Francesco, it is charming. Finish it! Giacinta! Take my glass!" And resuming her stick, the old lady, very slowly and carefully, moved back across the room and out towards the terrace.

The Marchese Francesco di Vill' Alta was the eldest of his Mother's fourteen children. He was a tall thin man, with hair already snow-white, and more of a stoop than his mother. He had spent his life as Italian noblemen were rather apt to spend their lives, half in society in Rome, half in giving a vague attention to his very considerable property in Gardone. At one time he had ornamented the diplomatic service, and an appointment in a Northern capital had brought him into contact with his wife, the daughter of a Danish financier and an American mother. Actually, now, the Marchese remembered with more emotion his period of duty in Constantinople, when an expedition into Anatolia had introduced him to *Eremurus robustus* growing in its native habitat. That he would never forget, whatever else grew dim: the great single stalk, springing four or five feet from the dry stony soil, out of its cushion of loose leek-like leaves, the wonderful head of pink flowers, more than a foot long, poised like a blossoming candelabra above the arid landscape. How he had dug, and how vainly, with his knife, seeking to release that prodigious circle of roots, wide as a cart-wheel, embedded so impossibly in the sparse rocky soil, under the blazing sun and the pale glittering sky.

It had been no good, but he had made a sketch; and that first moment of awe-struck vision was one of his imperishable possessions.

Francesco di Vill' Alta might really have been quite a good botanist, but for his weak eyes. These, even with the strongest lenses, prevented him from ever being much good at discovering for himself the smaller and rarer plants; he was obliged to rely on others for that. But people who found a plant which aroused their curiosity either sent it to him, as his brother Pipo had sent the purple grape-hyacinth from Brioni, or took him to see it grow. For a second-hand botanist, as one might say, his knowledge was considerable; and whatever he found he drew—delicate, slightly mannered drawings, accurately and carefully coloured; he had albums-ful of them. People really meant so much less to him than his flowers, which he worshipped with the singular passion of a man who has been, on the whole, a failure with human beings. He was not incapable of affection, or even of devotion—it was just that Life had gradually taught him that *his* affection and *his* devotion were somehow not much good; did not bring in, as it were, the dividend which he vaguely realised that other people got on theirs. Now, when his mother had left the room, he drew his chair up again to the deal table, adjusted his spectacles, dipped a fine brush into the jug of stained water, and went on with his exquisite colouring of the tasselled grape-hyacinth, an expression of supreme and blissful contentment on his gentle intelligent face.

The old Marchesa, meanwhile, went out onto the terrace. Very old people only really see what immediately concerns them—so the old Marchesa never noticed, as she passed down the steps, how the shape of the triple ilex cut like a great dark-green balloon into the clear pale tones of the view away to the North-East; what she did notice, immediately, was whether her chair had been placed exactly right or not, and whether the rugs and footstool were properly arranged. She also noticed Suzy's empty hammock—a brightly-striped gaudy affair with hanging fringes, slung under the tree—with amused disapproval; she thought lounging in hammocks both feeble and slightly undignified. All the same, she made Roberto shift her chair a few inches, so that she could see the hammock without turning her head—she liked being able to look at her daughter-in-law. A decorative creature, Suzy! When she was finally settled, with all her little litter of possessions arranged on the parapet beside her, sipping her egg-nog, the old Marchesa first thought that the egg-nog was very good this morning—she rolled it on her tongue appreciatively; then that it was a fine morning, pleasantly warm—wrapped in her fleecy rugs, her feet and knees were not in the least chilly. Presently she would read—this new book of German memoirs was very scandalous and amusing. Through one of the lower windows of the grey house the white head of the Marchese Francesco was visible, blurred a little by the bright glass with its reflection of the sky, bent in absorption over his painting; from the eastern wing, which projected slightly onto the terrace, came the sound of a violin being played with considerable skill. That, the Marchesa knew, was Paolo, her fourth son, practising his Bach. Paolo di Vill' Alta was a bachelor, and having nothing in particular to do and nowhere in particular to live, settled down in a small apartment of his own at Vill' Alta every summer, making a third establishment under the shallow roof of ridged tiles, with its deep eaves; there he played Bach and studied old manuscript music all day long, occasionally—and very irregularly—occurring for meals at the family table.

Hearing Paolo's music now, the old Marchesa's thoughts, the light straying thoughts of old age, were led to him. Paolo, poor boy! His life was not much good—playing the violin and making his little jokes! No career, no children. But there was more impatience than tenderness in her expression as she sat there listening to the Bach, her little cap of exquisitely fine Valenciennes lace on her snowy head, above her strong old features. Trivial occupations for a man! she thought, playing the violin, or painting flowers. The old Marchesa privately thought both these sons of hers poor sticks, unworthy scions of the family whose name they bore. The Vill' Altas ought to be soldiers, *galantuomini*—it must be the unlucky infusion of the Castellone blood which made them in this generation so scientific, so absorbed in abstractions. The Castellones had always been mad on science— in the 15th century one of them was excommunicated and imprisoned for his scientific writings, which were publicly burnt—whereas the Vill' Altas enjoyed a perpetual dispensation from fasting on Fridays, dating from the 10th century, because the Vill' Alta of that day, by some military exploit, had got the then Pope out of a hole. That was the sort of men Vill' Altas should be—and, a servant at that moment coming out and placing some more cushions in the striped hammock for the Marchesa Suzy, the old lady began to think about her daughter-in-law.

It was really small wonder, she thought, that Suzy should —well, should interest herself! She glanced again at the blurred white shape of Francesco's head through the window —no, he was no man for Suzy! It was not only that he was thirty-five years older than she—at no age would he have been the man for Suzy. He hadn't enough vitality. Suzy was all vitality—it was what one enjoyed about her. The old lady was actually waiting, in a little pleasant stir of anticipation, for the younger woman to come, to warm her with her swiftness of life, merely by lying near her in the hammock. Her relations with her daughter-in-law were curious. She had thought the marriage a foolish one from the start— foreign marriages were always more difficult, and though Suzy was half American, she wasn't even particularly rich. And there was this great discrepancy of age. He would have done far better to marry the Asquini girl when he was thirty, as she had wished him to do. But he had got engaged while he was in Scandinavia, and there it was! When Suzy began to interest herself elsewhere, the Vecchia Marchesa watched with dispassionate attention.    If there had been any serious *incon-venance* she would have disapproved profoundly, would have taken whatever steps she thought appropriate.    But there was not—Suzy was very clever.    She was all affection to her husband, all courtesy, and something more delightful than courtesy to her mother-in-law.    She managed very well. And since no woman of Suzy's temperament could possibly be content or happy with Francesco, the old Marchesa, to whom life had taught an almost unscrupulous realism in such matters, in her secret heart rather applauded her daughter-in-law for the graceful skill with which she kept herself "in health and spirits" as the old woman put it, while making the marriage as much of a success as it had ever been in its nature to be.    She had done no injury to the family, nor to the traditions which it upheld—there was no overt ugliness or roughness, nothing was damaged, there was no fuss.    The old Marchesa hated fuss.    How much better Suzy managed than Pipo's wife, tiresome creature, who was making all this outcry about Pipo's affair with Livia Panelli.    She had had a most tiresome letter from her only this morning.    She was a Russian, though, and they had so little self-control!

Out through the doors onto the terrace came, at last, Suzy di Vill' Alta.    She was a true nordic blonde, with cendré-fair hair, immense grey eyes, and a thick opaque skin of a tone more tender than white, unvarying all over.    Her figure was beautiful, rising to a queenly magnificence of bust and shoulders, above a rounded slenderness below—all her move-ments had the finished grace of extreme sophistication.    It was difficult to decide whether her face was really beautiful or not, and few people bothered to try—it had, in any case, the quality which makes beauty itself interesting.    What was at once arresting about her was the whole impression of finished charm, of a completed work of art, from the elabora-tion of puffs and rolls of her coiffure down to the small cream-coloured kid shoes that appeared below her soft pale dress.

She came over to her Mother-in-law, stooped to give her an affectionate kiss, and said "Good-morning, Bonne-Mama. How well you look" in her warm, caressing contralto voice.

"So do you, my dear Suzy," said the old lady, pleased. Suzy never bothered one with tiresome enquiries about one's health; she assumed that one was well, she said so, and at once one *felt* well.

"Have you had any amusing letters?" the young Marchesa asked, seating herself gracefully on the parapet.

"I have had one extremely un-amusing one from Nadia," replied the old Marchesa. "But my dear Suzy, for the love of Heaven do not sit on that stone without a cushion! You will get piles!"

Suzy laughed. "Bonne-Mama, you will have to stop talking about piles when Marietta's Anglaise comes, or she will be shocked," she said, fetching a cushion from the hammock, and reseating herself on it.

"My dear Suzy, to please you I would do much, but do not ask me to suit my conversation to the ears of governesses," the old woman said, with a little moue. "I am too old."

"You are too perverse, Bonne Mama, that's what's the matter with you! You are quite young enough to do whatever you choose, and you know it!" Suzy returned, with a sort of caressing archness. Ah, that was what was charming with Suzy—she teased one, she caressed one with voice and word and eye; she flirted, one might almost say, with her mother-in-law. It was nice to be flirted with by this graceful gracious creature.

"What does Nadia say now?" Suzy went on, in a different tone.

"Oh, such folly! That she knows that Livia is in Brioni with Pipo, and that if such public humiliation goes on, she will leave him! Public humiliation, indeed! No one but she need know it. Brioni is not Rome or Paris."

"She would do much better not to know it herself," said Suzy tranquilly, taking a gold cigarette-case out of a large gold mesh bag, and opening it. "Bonne-Mama, *vous per-mettez?*" And receiving a bow and wave of permission, she lit a minute Russian cigarette and went on: "But no doubt she has made every effort to find out. Poor Nadia!" She spoke the last words in a tone of real sympathy.

"Do you like her?" the old Marchesa asked, a little surprised.

"Yes, Bonne-Mama, I do—very much. She is *simpatica*, and she is generous and intelligent."

"Intelligent!"

"*Yes*, Bonne-Mama, very intelligent, even. It is only that she has no savoir-faire. And she is full of idealism—she wanted a perfect marriage, and thought that to give Pipo everything was the way to get it. That was silly of her. But she is not stupid."

"It was a ridiculous marriage," said the old lady impatiently. "Pipo would have done far better to take my advice."

"Poor Bonne-Mama! All your sons will marry foreigners, won't they?" Suzy said smiling. "But you know, *mariages de convenance* are going out, even here. People want to arrange these things for themselves nowadays."

"Yes, my dear Suzy, and only look at the *mariages d'incon-venance* they arrange for themselves! Tita Bellini and her Dutchman! They say he gets his money from an hotel! But Nadia cannot leave Pipo like that. It would make a scandal."

"No, it would be unwise. But she is in pain, and people are unwise then."

"In pain! What of it? Is she the first woman whose husband has a liaison? And what did she expect? *Ça arrive, enfin!* But she writes quite wildly. Let me show you her letter." She fumbled in a little bag, very much like the Signorina Gelsicher's, attached to the middle of her person, and produced a thick-looking envelope. Suzy di Vill' Alta took it, and read through the many thin sheets, attentively, a charming wrinkle of concentration between her fine darkened

eyebrows; the old lady watched her, and at the end said—
"Well?"

"I am sorry she bothers you with all this, but she is right
to," the younger woman said smoothly. "She is very
wretched."

"My dear Suzy, I cannot stop her being wretched!"

"Perhaps not. I think you could advise her wisely,
though. I wonder if we should not have her here."

"You really think so?"

"I believe it might be wise. And Bonne-Mama, Pipo is
also stupid! This is partly his fault, you know. I think he
must be scolded! After all, he need not——" she broke off,
with a faint expression of irritation. "Ecco Marietta," she said.

Unlike the very old, when one is fifteen one sees all sorts
of things which do not personally concern one—indeed at
that age impersonal things have an importance, a power to
stir and move the heart which very few human beings then
possess. Marietta di Vill' Alta, pausing for a moment at the
door leading onto the terrace, just registered the picture of
her Mother and her Grandmother sitting there, the pale figure
on the wall, the black figure in the chair; but what she really
saw, with eyes and heart, was what neither of the other two
had noticed—the picture formed by the terrace as a whole.
Vill' Alta stands high, and beyond the terrace parapet the eye
travels clear off into the distance, to pale folds of country set
with pearly white houses and pricked with the dark shapes
of cypresses—in the middle, on an eminence, rises the great
creamy architectural bulk of Castellone itself, creamy save for
the western end, which is painted a hideous maroon—beyond,
blue and clear as flowers, stand the lovely shapes of the
mountains. To the left the dark mass of the great ilex, to
the right the shapely eastern wing of the house cut off the
view abruptly; giving it, by this limitation, a formality of
intention, a pictorial quality that is almost dramatic—it is a
made stage on which to set a play; any human beings on it
take on at once an air of theatricality. To this aspect Marietta

E

was not awake—but to the formal shape of the tree and the house, and the boundless freedom of the view beyond she was. As she stood for a moment, looking at them, she drew in a long breath, as if to inhale their beauty—then, shaking her head, she skipped down the steps, and ran forward to greet her elders. People demanded this tribute—trees and wide views, to which the heart went out of itself, demanded nothing! Marietta preferred trees and views.

She made her two little curtseys, offered her two little kisses, with her warm red mouth in her thin colourless face. If you have seen any of Donatello's youthful St. John the Baptists, you have seen Marietta di Vill' Alta—the thin young neck, the eyes wide apart, the sensitive down-drawing of the upper lip, the soft uncertain fall of hair about a forehead too big and too nobly mature for the rest of the face. The old Marchesa took the child's hand, as she kissed her, and retained it—Suzy was young, but Marietta was younger, too young still to have developed any of those adult perversities which were so annoying; those perversities with which she watched people muddling and spoiling their lives—had watched them, with impatient disapproval, for over half a century. Free as the old woman was from so many of the customary weaknesses of great age, of this one she was not free—of its instinctive tender delight in the warmth of simple affection, such as the very young alone give. She held Marietta's small thin hand, the characterless hand of a very young girl, while she talked to her. Marietta perched on the wall, close to her grandmother's chair.

"Child! Not on the stone! You will get piles!" the old lady cried again.

"Bonne-Mama, you are incorrigible!" Suzy said lazily; "Take my cushion, Marietta—I have the hammock." She moved slowly over and arranged herself in the gay striped affair, her full skirts flowing over the edge, showing hints of filmy lace petticoat, her little cream shoes poised above the fringe.

"Well child, and how are you?" the old lady asked.

"Oh Bonne-Mama, I am so impatient for Miss Prestwich to come! I did so want to go with the carriage and meet her, but Mama said not," said the girl, with the easy confidence which she always used to her Grandmother; they understood one another perfectly, these two.

"She could not go alone, Bonne-Mama, and I really could not rise at that hour," said Suzy. "It was quite unnecessary, also."

"You are always impatient, Marietta, and your mother never—at least never before lunch!" said the old lady, with a touch of mischief. Suzy laughed, but with a slight effort—she always found it easier to get on with her Mother-in-law when Marietta was not there—the old Marchesa doted quite absurdly on the child, would have spoilt her utterly, left to herself.

"Yes, I *am* impatient about her," the girl said eagerly, "I want to see her. I look forward *so* to having a governess! I shall learn so much."

"And what do you want to learn?" the old lady asked, still fondling her hand.

"Languages!" Marietta replied promptly. "I shall learn to read Shakespeare in English, and Goethe in German!"

"Your great-grandmother, my Mother, could read English, French, German, Spanish and Russian. But she always rose at seven!" said the old lady, pretending to whisper. Marietta giggled. "Senti, Suzy," the old Marchesa went on, "of what age is this Miss Prestwich?"

"I have no idea, Bonne-Mama. Whatever age governesses are," replied Suzy casually, putting down a foot and making the hammock swing a little. She knew that her mother-in-law thought this undignified—it was her reply to the early-rising great-grandmother. "Lydia Asquini wrote that she was in every way suitable, and I asked no more. She has studied at Oxford, so she must be very well educated."

The old Marchesa disapproved of women going to college

to be educated, and said so. Governesses at home, masters and classes, perhaps, in Rome, were all that was required for the most ample female education. Marietta and the Marchesa Suzy had to listen to a long account of various accomplished women whom the old Marchesa had known. Suzy hardly heard. She lay smoking another tiny Russian cigarette, and thinking about Nadia, Pipo's wife, and her troubles. Marietta listened politely, but with one ear open for sounds of a carriage on the road behind the house—one could *just* hear it, from the terrace. She would have liked to look at her watch, but that would not have been polite—also, with only one hand free it would not be easy, since the watch, suspended from a long gold chain, was buttoned into a tiny pocket on the breast of her white piqué blouse. It was with a sense of release that she caught sight of two figures coming round the eastern wing of the house. "There are Elena and Giulio!" she exclaimed, and sprang up to meet them.

## Chapter Five

LA VECCHIA MARCHESA watched the three cousins bene-volently as they came strolling along the terrace, Marietta and Elena arm-in-arm and chattering like birds, Giulio looking quite animated. Suzy observed him with raised eyebrows and an air of indolent amusement. She knew quite well that he disliked her, but though this surprised her a little, she never bothered as to the reason, and she was both too lazy and too good-tempered to dislike him in return. The ill opinion of a bookish boy did no harm to anyone. She was however quite prepared to tease him.

"Well, Giulio, this is an unwonted pleasure," she observed, holding out a white and much-ringed hand to be kissed as he approached her. "I thought you always studied all the morning."

"Not always, Zia Suzy," Giulio replied, obediently kissing the hand. "Come sta?"

"He's come to catch sight of Marietta's governess, Zia Suzy," Elena observed mischievously. "Because she has been at Oxford, where the philosophers come from, he hopes she will be a philosopher too!"

"She will be a rather unusual governess if she is," Suzy said.

"On the contrary, my dear Suzy, I think governesses are a race of philosophers—they certainly need to be," said the old Marchesa. "Giulio! do not sit on the stone! You will get piles. Bring a chair—and one for your sister."

"He wants her to teach him English," Elena chattered on, while Giulio fetched a couple of chairs from under the ilex—she was in tearing spirits, as usual. "Shall you mind if he does lessons with Marietta, Zia Suzy? Because that is his idea!"

Giulio was at once upset by this unveiling of his secret plans. "Idiot!" he muttered to his sister as he set down the chairs. "Zia Suzy, I hope you do not believe——" he began, and paused, at a loss how to finish, since this was so very like what he did wish.

"My dear Giulio, if Miss Prestwich can be of any service to you in her spare time, of course I shall be delighted," the young Marchesa said smoothly.

Marietta intervened. She saw that Giulio was vexed, and she hated him to be vexed. "Giulio, come round to the *torrino* and let us watch for the carriage," she said; "Come on."

The *torrino* was a small stone turret, once a part of the earlier castle, which had occupied a site far larger than the present house—it stood some hundred yards away from it, on the opposite side of the building, beyond the eastern wing. The broken masonry had been repaired, a roof put on, and stone seats placed inside, making a sort of small summer-house. It overhung the road, which wound up the hill some sixty feet below; to reach the front door of the house the visitor must either ascend several long flights of stone steps, flanked by cypresses, which rose up from a small gate with a wrought-iron grille in the wall at the foot of the slope, or else follow the road round the shoulder of the hill right up into the village of Vill' Alta itself, with its gaudy-fronted white church and ancient elm-tree—and from there double back along the level, through the great entrance-gates, with the carved stone castles surmounting each pillar, and along the wide terrace which stretched past the whole south front of the house, with its bright formal flower-beds set among the raked gravel, and its carved stone balustrade surmounted with classical statues standing out white against the darkness of the trees which grew on the slope below. Marietta and Giulio, passing through the house, emerged onto this terrace, and walked across it to the eastern end, where a second small flight of steps led down to a path which wound its way through ilexes and olive-trees, up to the jutting rock on which the summer-house stood.    A stone Venus and a stone Mars, one on each side, guarded the top of these steps—the Venus, with a provocative simper, stretched protective hands across her person.    As he passed the last flower-bed Giulio stooped and picked some scarlet geraniums, and going up to the Venus, with a derisive scowl, he stuck the flowers behind her long tapering stone fingers,—the effect was at once ludicrous, and extraordinarily indecent.    Marietta laughed.

"Giulio, you are silly!"

"That makes her look the fool she is," he retorted.  "Stupid creature!   I hate her."

"Povera Venere!   Why?"

He did not attempt to tell her why he hated the Venus, with her feeble unintelligent suggestiveness—he left the scarlet mockery of the flowers on the silly stone, and went on down the steps into the damp coolness of the trees.   He probably could not have explained, even if he had wished to, the shivering contemptuous dislike which any reminder of the feminine aspect of sex aroused in him.   Zia Suzy's perfumes, her lazy use of her eyes, and indolent alluring attitudes, the blatant false modesty of the stone Venus—they were all part of the same thing, a thing which he felt was the enemy of the world as he wanted it.   It was not that he was shocked by sex, as young Englishmen often are—indecency rather amused him than otherwise, and he shared the admirable naturalness of his race, which regards the human body as rather a good joke, or at least as the source of innumerable good jokes; it was more that he felt vengeful towards the female principle, as the foe of the ascetic idealism by which he wished to live.   Walking up to the summer-house to watch for the carriage, still irritated by Elena's indiscretion, his mind turned with relief to the picture he had formed of the woman whom the carriage was bringing—the governess, middle-aged and wise, in whom the female principle was subordinated to learning and goodness, as it was in Fräulein Gelsicher.   Only with more learning than Gelosia had. She would be restful and helpful, as such women alone were.

Marietta followed him. She was quite accustomed to having her questions to Giulio left unanswered, and having to think out the replies to them for herself—weeks afterwards, some chance word of his, often addressed to someone else, would tell her whether she had guessed right or not. Marietta spent a very high proportion of her time in thinking about Giulio. He was one of the few people who were as important to her as trees and views, and rather in the same remote way. His ideas and his opinions had for her now a value, an importance that those of no other human being possessed; places, paths, seats, loved for themselves, took on a precious quality that was like holiness when some memory of Giulio attached to them. So far Marietta had two great loves in her life—Vill' Alta and her cousin Giulio. /She loved, with a child's wistful passion, all the external aspects of her home, clinging to them with youth's haunting desire for permanence; any alteration was agony to her, she mourned a tree cut down as women mourn a lost child. / All the winter, in Rome, where the bright golden light beat on the warm golden buildings, she was homesick for Vill' Alta; walking in the Pincio gardens, she looked wistfully at the unfamiliar beautiful ilexes and stone pines, and longed for the known identifiable shapes of the trees at home —the triple ilex on the northern terrace, the irregular rising ranks of the cypresses beside the southern steps, the gnarled olives round the *torrino*, the squat umbrella pines on the grassy ridge along which one walked to Odredo. The homesick child wrote poems about them—bad, exaggerated little poems, which nevertheless had this surprising quality: that she used the language of a lover heartsick with absence towards her distant home—the grey house, sunrise through the olives, the heart-lifting nearness of the mountains on a day of clear wind.

Within the last year her feeling for Giulio had become less a rival to than an extension of this passion—the two were linked, since it was only at Vill' Alta that she saw Giulio. It is hardly possible to find words to put down secretly and delicately enough the first stirring of love in a young girl—grave, distant, shy and yet intense, a selfless strange enchantment, fed on music, on poetry, on the shape and name of beauty; asking nothing but its own secret life of memory and anticipation; as moving and as remote from actualities as the song of birds. Then, to be spoken to is to be honoured; to serve, a rapturous privilege; to be alone in his company a silencing delight.

Marietta however knew Giulio too well to be readily silenced by his presence, and at the moment her desire to soothe him was stronger than any other feeling. Sitting there, hanging out over the road to watch for the carriage, she said:

"Elena *is* a tease. But you heard what Mama said."

"Elena is idiotic!" Giulio returned, kicking his heels moodily against the stone wall. "She has no idea of what will go and what won't."

"But Mama didn't mind. She said you could work with her. So that is all right, Giulio. It is arranged!" she said earnestly, pushing her grave little face forward to gaze into his, willing him to be reassured and happy. "I shall not do so many lessons, and I shall explain to Miss Prestwich about you."

"She may have her own ideas about your lessons! But teachers usually like to teach," he said, thoughtfully, "and perhaps Gela could coax Papa to let her have a fee, if she does much. I wonder what books she will bring?"

They discussed, in an ignorance as complete as hers about them, what books the unknown Miss Prestwich was likely to bring, and gradually Giulio's spirits rose again, and he began to talk of his ambitions and his difficulties. "You see, Marietta, here it is impossible for me. I can read, but I have no one to ask for explanations. And if I write, there is no one to tell me whether I write sense or not."

"Do you write, Giulio? What sort of writing? Poems?"

F

"Not poems!" His gesture brushed poetry aside. "No, I try to express ideas that I get, from my reading, or from something I see. I suppose you would call them essays."

"Shall you publish them?" Marietta asked eagerly. To her to see her writing in print, over her own name, was an unattainable heaven into which she never hoped to enter.

"I did publish one," Giulio said, half proudly and half nervously, "in a Milan magazine. Roffredo knew the editor and got it in for me. But you must not tell anyone that, Marietta."

"I shall not, I shall not! But Giulio, how wonderful! What was it about?"

"It was called 'Dancing and Life'—it was about how people speak and act in a ball-room, and how they act, those same people, the next day or the day before, with their maid, with the bailiff, with their families. It came into my head after Zia Suzy's big dance here last year. But the idea was, What is the reality of these people's lives—the ball-room part or the other part? You see," Giulio pursued, "usually people would say the normal was the most real, and the dancing part unreal. And for many people perhaps it is so. But for others, it seemed to me, only in the ball-room do they become their most real selves."

He stopped—he had really been thinking about her Mother, and did not care to tell her so. Marietta puckered her dark brows in thought over this.

"Yes—for some that could be so, perhaps. And for others, when they are seeing certain things. Giulio, do you know, this idea of yours is very important!"

"You think so?" he said seriously, surprised and pleased by her response. For such a child she was very sensible and quick, he thought.

"Ma si! One must *know* when one is most one's real self, or how can one live properly? At least *some* of the time, one must be being one's real self, or it is such a waste."

She spoke with intense conviction. Giulio was astonished

at this fervent echo of his own feelings, coming from his little cousin. He looked at her, sitting there, her black plait swinging over her school-girlish blouse, her long black legs dangling under her short skirt; her face was alight with comprehension, the thing he always longed for, and usually so vainly. In a burst of expansiveness, released by her sympathy, he said—"You *do* understand that, Marietta. But how many people don't!" He paused. "Elena, for instance."

"Elena is most herself when she is writing those wicked letters!" Marietta said, with a sudden little grin which made her look girlish again. But then a dreamy seriousness replaced the grin on her small face. This was being wonderful, this talk with Giulio. To be made the sharer of his secrets, to be praised by him for understanding what others failed to understand—what could be more wonderful? This was the height of happiness. "When do you feel most your real self?" she asked him, anxious to prolong the talk, to learn more: "Reading? or when you are writing something?"

Giulio was not sure—and while he argued it out with himself aloud, the girl sat in supreme contentment, her elbow on the back of the stone seat, her chin cupped in her hand, staring out with absent eyes over the flatter country to the South, which was becoming steadily more colourless and indistinct in the noonday heat and haze—nodding her head now and then in emphatic comprehension. She had actually forgotten about the new governess, so absorbed was she in Giulio's ideas and plans, and when a cloud of white dust began to boil up through the trees at the foot of the hill, where the road wound round the corner, it was a moment or two before she paid any attention to it. Down there the trees hid the road itself, but below them it became visible; noticing the dust at last, Marietta twisted round and craned out over the parapet, to catch the first glimpse of the advancing vehicle. Yes, there were the fat white horses, with yellow sweat-stains down their necks and flanks, and the straw

Homburg hat of Tommaso, the equally fat coachman, fore-shortened by the angle from which she saw him. "Giulio! Here she is!" the girl said, in a low excited tone. "Here is the carriage!"

Giulio came and craned out too, over her shoulder. Thoughtlessly, he put a hand on the parapet on each side of her, so that his arms enclosed her; she could just feel the light pressure of his suit against her arm and back—the care-less intimacy of the position made her shiver a little. But Giulio was gazing at the carriage. There was little to reward his scrutiny. Tommaso had thoughtfully taken one of the driving sunshades, a plain affair of natural shantung silk lined with green, and Miss Prestwich had put it up; the summer carriage rug, of striped green and fawn linen, with fringed ends, was spread over her knees—so that all that the watchers from above could see was a circle of fawn above a patch of stripes, with one dark-blue arm, and a hand in a brown suède glove, projecting onto the striped lap. Nevertheless, they watched the carriage in its slow progress up the hill with grave attention. Giulio, who had a natural gift for the por-tentous, spoke at last. "There goes someone who is going to make a great difference to our lives, yours and mine, Marietta," he said solemnly. Marietta nodded in silence. The solemn remark was truer than either of them knew.

But Marietta, even at the most solemn moments, had always an eye to the practical. With a quick movement, now, she wriggled out backwards from between Giulio's propped arms, and stood up. "Giulio! Should we not go down to meet her at the little gate, and bring her up? It is prettier that way—and it will be more welcoming, no?"

Giulio too straightened himself. "Yes, but quick, or we shan't be in time." They set off along the little path, took a short cut through the bushes, cascaded together down the long flights of steps under the cypresses like two dogs chasing the same ball, and reached the small gate just as the carriage drew level with it. So it happened that Almina Prestwich,

who ever since Tommaso pointed out the rather grim bulk of
Vill' Alta among its cypresses on the hill, had been sitting
under the sunshade in the corner of the victoria, hot, thirsty
and nervous, bracing herself to encounter a majestic Marchesa,
as grey and grim as the house, now found herself confronted
by a boy and girl, flushed, laughing, breathless and extremely
untidy, who tugged together at a small wrought-iron gate in a
wall.   The gate had sagged on its hinges, and always stuck a
little; when it opened, it did so with a jerk, and the whine of
iron on stone.   This happened now, and the pair came hurrying through. "Here is the signorina inglese!" said Tommaso,
beaming, by way of introduction.   But at the sight of the
figure in the carriage, small and slight, in a navy-blue coat and
skirt and a broad-brimmed sailor hat, the two eager creatures
checked, in the plainest astonishment.   Only for a moment—
then the girl sprang forward, made a little quick curtsey, and
seizing Almina by the hand cried—"Oh, you are *young*!   But
that is lovely!   I expect I should have loved you anyhow, as
Elena does Gela; but now that you are young, of course I
shall!"

   A little overwhelmed by the warmth of this greeting,
Almina suffered herself to be taken out of the carriage, and
led through the gate, which whined again behind them.   Up
the steps, flight after flight, they went, her new pupil chattering
all the way in voluble explanations, which to Almina's confused mind explained very little.   But Giulio walked silent
behind them, in an astonishment that was tinged both with
disappointment and some other feeling.   This a governess?
This small creature in the youthful clothes and hat?   And her
hair!   Clouds of it, like sunshine—and those great blue eyes
—she was like a child!   Could anyone so young know anything, teach anything?   This was not the sober counterpart
of Gela that he had been looking forward to.   But her eyes
and mouth were grave, when Marietta made some reference
to him, and she turned and looked in his direction—and her
forehead broad and calm.   She might after all be wise, for all

her air of simplicity and innocence.    They went on up the
steps.

At the top Marietta paused.    In front of them, across the
vivid flower-beds of the terrace, rose the house, the grey stone
pale in the brilliant light, a black band of shadow under the
deep cornice, the closed sun-blinds making yellow oblongs
all across the vast front.    Almina looked at it, intimidated.
It was huge; it was dreadfully imposing; it was all that she had
expected of grand and formal—it made the artless simplicity of
the young girl beside her all the more surprising.    Marietta
was pointing out everything, eagerly doing the honours of
her adored home.    "And see, those are your windows, along
at that corner on the right.    And there are two other windows
round the corner, too, so that you look both ways.    Come—
I shall show you!"    And she dragged her along the terrace
towards the eastern end.    As they went, they passed close to
the other flight of steps, where Mars and Venus stood; the
English girl, startled, saw the blazing immodesty of the scarlet
flowers which still decorated the statue.    She turned her head
away, quickly, while an inexorable blush spread over her pale
skin.    How horrible!    Who could have done such a thing?
And to have to pass it with that young man just behind them.
Really, Italians were very—!    She made some remark quickly
to Marietta about the house.    But Giulio, walking just behind,
saw everything—the swiftly averted head, the colour that
spread even over the white neck, under the clouds of sunny
hair, and suddenly he was embarrassed too.    Why had
Marietta brought her that way?    Little idiot!    Why had he
done such a foolish thing?    Discontented again, he followed
the two girls round the eastern wing.

Out on the northern terrace, La Vecchia Marchesa still sat
in her chair, Suzy lolled in her hammock, Elena sat holding
a skein of silk which the old lady was plaiting with her fine
wrinkled hands.    As she approached the group, and during
the introductions which followed, Almina studied these
strangers with whom she was to live with curiosity tinged

with anxiety. In her nervous Italian she answered some imperious questions from the very old lady, the polite and gracious enquiries of the younger one as to her comfort on her journey, the coolly friendly greetings of the other girl, who was, it seemed, the sister of the untidy young man. *She* was not in the least untidy; she wore her white blouse and skirt and trim red petersham belt with undoubted chic—and there was style in the way her dark shining hair was dressed. She looked rather nice, in spite of something slightly ironical in her expression. But the greatest shock was the appearance of Almina's employer, the lady whom Marietta addressed as "Mama". The younger Marchesa was undoubtedly "actressy". Her pretty, rather full face was certainly made up, her eyebrows darkened; her coiffure was inconceivably elaborate. Almina had never seen anyone look like that off the stage—in a private house she hardly looked proper. And her pale dress, all lacy over the bust, was smart enough for Ascot. Or was there perhaps to be a luncheon party? In that case both she and her pupil ought to go and change—she was very conscious of the heat and unsuitability of her blue coat and skirt, and of the white dust which powdered it, mixed with short white hairs from the horses. Sitting rather stiffly on her chair, with these thoughts running in her head, she started slightly when the very old lady tapped her with an ivory paper-knife and said "You speak very good Italian. Where did you learn it?"

"At Oxford," Almina replied.

"How old are you?"

"Bonne-Mama cara!" expostulated Suzy.

"Twenty-two," Almina replied, readily enough.

"Hm! Are you serious?" the old lady next enquired.

Almina was rather taken aback. "I have always thought so—" she began gravely, when the old lady suddenly abandoned her questionnaire, and whipped round on the young man, who had seated himself on the parapet. "Giulio! Do not sit on the stone! You will certainly get piles!"

The young Marchesa exploded with laughter. "Oh Bonne-Mama, how wicked you are!" she said, going over and kissing the old lady. "Come, Miss Prestwich, come to your room. You will want to wash before luncheon."

She swept her off. On the way upstairs she was all charm and kindness, explaining the party—"Elena and Giulio are my niece and nephew—they live next door to us, at Odredo. —My mother-in-law is wonderful, isn't she? Do you know that if she lives till September, she will be a hundred?" The kindness, the charm, the being "taken into" things a little fell like balm on Almina's spirit, tired, nervous and bewildered as she was—in the immense room to which she was finally conducted, she turned to her hostess, in reply to a hope that she would be really comfortable, and said fervently "I am *sure* I shall. Thank you so much." Suzy smiled a little to herself as she closed the door and went downstairs. It would be all right about the little governess—she would be devoted; there would be no trouble with her.

"Well, Bonne-Mama, what do you think of her?" Suzy asked, as she returned to the terrace. "Marietta, go and get tidy for lunch, my child. Your hair is a sight and your blouse is *so* dirty." Marietta went. "Well?" Suzy continued, still looking amused and lighting a cigarette.

"She looks very well-bred, but as a governess, the thing is ridiculous!" the old lady pronounced. "Lydia must be mad!" Suzy burst out laughing again. Her laughter was enchanting—rather high but with a warm quality of mirth in it. The old Marchesa, as if reluctantly, gave a faint chuckle too, as she listened to her daughter-in-law. "No, but it is true," she persisted.

"Oh, Bonne-Mama cara, and her face when you spoke to Giulio! You are a most perverse old woman! No—I think she will do quite well," she pursued. "I know about English girls. They are very serious."

"Her hair is lovely," Elena here put in. "Nearly the colour of yours, Zia Suzy."

"Yes—if she could do it," Suzy said, looking slightly less amused.

"I might teach her to," said Elena.

"It is *her* business to teach," said the old lady, rather tartly. "Governesses need not have fashionably dressed hair."

"We will get Gela to give her some lessons in coiffure, then," said Elena, irrepressibly, "and teach her how to look like a governess. Zia Suzy, we must go, or we shall be late for lunch. Where can Giulio have got to?"

But at that moment Giulio appeared, sauntering round the end of the east wing. The pair took their leave and set off again along the terrace, Elena asking her brother where he had hidden himself. He did not tell her. In fact, as soon as his Aunt and Miss Prestwich had disappeared into the house, he had slipped round onto the South terrace. There, with an anger which he could not explain, he tore out the scarlet geraniums which he had tucked behind the hands of the statue of Venus, and flung them into the bushes.

F

## Chapter Six

THAT first day at Vill' Alta seemed as long as an ordinary week to Almina Prestwich—it was so crammed with new impressions, new people and new things as to be very exciting and exhausting. Her room, in which the Marchesa had left her, telling her that luncheon would be in three quarters of an hour, was highly novel, to begin with. Left alone, she looked round it. There was a large bed, with a high pointed back of carved and painted wood and a rich lace coverlet; a writing table, a high-backed couch, a tall chest of drawers, a cheval glass, three armchairs and several quite large tables—but there was no dressing-table, washstand or wardrobe. Except for the bed and the cheval-glass, it was like a large and richly-furnished boudoir. Moreover, it had three doors in the three corners of the room, besides the one by which she had entered. Cautiously, she went and opened one of them, and stood in surprise. The door led into a very small square room, arranged as an oratory, with a crucifix, prie-dieu, flowers, and a variety of holy statues and pictures. Almina, whose sober Low-Church upbringing had been modified at Oxford into the fashionable High-Church tendency, was charmed with the oratory. She shut the door gently, and tried another. Ah, this was better. Here was the cabinet de toilette, with washstand, dressing-table, commode, and a hip-bath painted white propped against the wall. She noticed with admiration the exquisite quality of the linen on the towel-horse, the vast monograms —S. d. V.A.—on the face-towels and even on the bath-towel, with a coronet above. Here she could wash—but where was her luggage? She wanted her little fitted dressing-case, that awkward square object whose two lids fell back to disclose a vast array of silver-topped cut-glass boxes and bottles, and of ivory brushes and combs—no young lady in Almina's day but carried her toothbrush in a silver-stoppered glass cylinder, her hairpins in a long glass box with a silver lid, her soap in another, and ranged her pairs of brushes and clothes-brushes, one stiff and one soft, behind bands of watered silk, when she set out on a journey. A more futile, heavy, cumbersome and unpractical object than the Victorian dressing-case was never devised by man, or used, as a matter of course, by woman. But where was hers? Thinking that this was rather like Bluebeard's palace, Almina opened the third door. Triumph! There in a third little corner room, fitted up all round with hanging cupboards with sliding-doors, and a glorious array of shelves, was her luggage. She carried her dressing-case into the cabinet de toilette, got out her things, and washed—hurried back to the clothes cupboard, opened her new and exciting suitcase, in which she had prudently put a dress for emergencies, and pulled it out—a bolero and skirt of pale yellow embroidered linen, with a soft white broderie anglaise blouse to go with it. She did her hair and then changed into these garments, wishing, as she did so, that she had got some white suède shoes like Elena di Castellone's. However, her new black glacé-kid ones were very nice, and she put them on. Now, even if there was a lunch-party, she would do, she thought, glancing at herself in the cheval-glass. She looked round her room, so luxurious, formal and pretty, with a sort of startled pleasure—really, this did seem a nice place. But before she went downstairs she slipped for a moment into the oratory, and kneeling at the prie-dieu, prayed with real earnestness that she might not be led away by fashion and luxury, but might serve her employer faithfully, and be of real use to her pupil.

There was no luncheon-party. But it seemed almost like one to Almina when they sat down in the great dining-room with its high painted ceiling—the old Marchesa, the young Marchesa, herself, Marietta, the Marchese Francesco and the

Marchese Paolo, who chose this day to make one of his periodic incursions to the family table. Two men-servants in white cotton gloves moved round the room, handing food which was all strange, and by no means all of it nice, Almina thought. There was a cheese and spaghetti affair at first which she liked, but this was followed by a selection of very odd things fried in batter, and she had no idea what they were—on recognising, finally, an unmistakeable cock's-comb, she was almost too disgusted to finish. Who knew what the other unrecognisable things might be? Almina had yet to learn to appreciate the joys of *fritto misto*. And the next course was worse—large glutinous lumps of something, a-swim in masses of rice and a gravy that was like brown ink, she thought. She was right—she was eating sepia, or cuttle-fish, stewed in its own ink, a favourite dish in the province of Gardone.

Even more disconcerting were the table-manners of some of her companions. The old lady, the young Marchesa and Marietta ate normally enough, except that the old Marchesa, who belonged to an age before table-napkins came into fashion, ignored the fine lace-bordered object by her plate and wiped her fingers, daintily as a bird cleaning its beak, on the table-cloth. But the two men! Both tucked their napkins into their collars at the beginning of the meal, a sensible foreign habit which, being unfamiliar, seemed to the English girl rather ill-bred; she failed to perceive the skill, the really brilliant technique which underlay their manipulation of the spaghetti, that deft movement of the fork by which a lump the size of a duck's egg was coiled round the implement and thrust into the mouth; she only observed, with dismay, the subsequent process of collecting the stragglers by suction. But the last straw was the Marchese Paolo's method of dealing with the cuttle-fish. This gentleman, whose hair was of a thick iron-grey, his skin like old parchment, and his whole appearance of a most delicate distinction, talked steadily during the whole of lunch, in a high and rather beautiful voice and through mouthfuls of food, about Bach's forerunners in the musical world—it was clear even to Almina, who knew little about Bach, that he was a person of considerable knowledge. But when he came to the cuttle-fish, having consumed the solid parts and the rice, still talking about music he swept the fingers of his right hand across his plate, mopping up the ink—sucked them, swept the plate again, sucked them again, and finally, with an air of perfect satisfaction, ran them through his thick hair. Almina was appalled, but no one else appeared to pay any attention. At dessert the Marchese Francesco, who apart from asking his mother as each dish was offered her, if it was what she liked, had made no contribution to the conversation, cut across the information about Bach and addressing Almina, asked her if she could translate a paragraph from an English book for him. He seemed surprised when she said that she could, and relapsed into silence.

But when they had taken coffee, out on the terrace under the ilex, he rose and asked Marietta to bring the Signorina into his room to look at the book. Escorted by Marietta— Almina only realised later that it would not have been strictly *comme il faut* for her to enter his study alone—she was introduced to the little paper-covered volume and the picture of the tasselled grape-hyacinth. He set a chair for her, and stood listening gravely while, after a moment's pause, she read out the whole paragraph in clear Italian. Then he rubbed his hands with pleasure. That was famous! Would she write it down for him? With pleasure, Almina said— with some trouble a space was cleared among the litter on the table, and with a quill pen Almina wrote out the translation. The Marchese held the sheet up close to his thick spectacles and read it—he thanked her with the delighted expression of a child. Almina asked if the tasselled grape-hyacinth grew near Vill' Alta? "Alas, no—in Brioni. The Signorina is interested in wild-flowers?" Very, Almina said: her mother was rather a good botanist, and she collected wild-

flowers herself. "Dunque, Papa, now you will have someone to find flowers for you! That is marvellous!" Marietta
said. "Papa is mad about botany," she confided to Almina
as they left the room, "but he is so blind, he can find nothing
for himself, and I am too ignorant to know what is worth
picking. But with you, I shall learn. Will you teach me?"
Almina gladly promised, thinking with satisfaction and grati-
tude how well it was that her Mother had made her bring her
Bentham and Hooker. To teach this eager-faced nice pupil
to know the wild-flowers would be a charming occupation
on their walks.

Indeed her first concern now was to have a talk with the
young Marchesa; to find out what was expected of her, and to
organise her own and her pupil's day. But this was not so
easy. When she and Marietta went out onto the terrace
again, the old Marchesa had retired to take her afternoon nap,
the Marchese Paolo had also disappeared, and a tall handsome
man with grizzled hair and beard was sitting beside the hammock where the Marchesa Suzy lay, talking to her with great
animation. Marietta checked on the steps. "Oh! Zio
Carlo has come," she said, hesitating; "then perhaps we had
better not disturb Mama."

"Who is Zio Carlo?" Almina asked, firmly—she felt that
unless she made a determined effort from the outset, she would
fall into endless mistakes and confusion among this tribe of
relations.

"He is Elena's and Giulio's father. He is very amiable,
but rather silly," said Marietta, with startling candour.

"Then he is your Mother's brother?"

"Oh dear no!" Marietta replied, laughing—the idea seemed
to amuse her. "He isn't really an Uncle at all. Bonne-
Mama's husband's mother, my great-grandmother, was a
Castellone, so Papa and Zio Carlo are cousins. But we call
him Uncle, because it is more suitable—and Elena and Giulio
call Mama Zia Suzy. We call all the Castellones Uncle and
Aunt—Zia Livia, Roffredo's mother, and—" she giggled

again— "the Sorellone. You will see them all very soon, especially the Sorellone. They are great gossips and very curious—they will come to see you at once."

Almina felt that this fresh lot of names might safely be left till their appearance to be unravelled. "Your Mother is the person I really want to see," she said quietly. "I want to settle with her about your work, and all that."

"Oh yes." Marietta glanced again at the terrace. "But I do not think now is a very good time, as Zio Carlo is there. He comes over most days in the afternoon, you know." She lowered her voice. "His wife, Zia Maria, Elena's mother, died six years ago. He was very unhappy then. Mama has been very good to him; he said so once to me. 'I do not know what I should have done without your dear Mother's sympathy and affection.' That was nice, no?"

Almina made a suitable sound of respectful sympathy, and a face to match. It was nice—it matched her already sympathetic impression of the Marchesa Suzy as a kind person. "Well, since I cannot see her now, I think I will go and unpack," she said.

"Yes indeed—shall I come with you and help?" Marietta said. Almina would rather have been alone, but she felt that this was a good opportunity of making friends with her pupil, and agreed. As they went upstairs, the young Marchesa's clear pealing laugh rang out from the terrace. Coming on top of Marietta's words about her mother and Count Carlo, it gave Almina a slight—a very slight—shock. Its rather complacent gaiety did not quite fit in with the picture of the sympathetic friend consoling the heart-broken widower. But all that was six years ago, she reflected; and laughter did no one any harm. She went on upstairs with Marietta.

The reason for the young Marchesa's laughter had been Count Carlo's incurable habit of getting names wrong. When the two girls came out onto the steps above the terrace he noticed them and said "Who is the pretty creature with Marietta, Suzy?"

"That is her new English governess, Miss Prestwich," Suzy responded.

The Count put up an eye-glass on a riband, and gazed. "Cara, anything less like a governess I never saw," he then observed, turning back to Suzy again. "She has the appearance of being exactly eighteen."

"She's twenty-two, my dear Carlo, and has a University degree," Suzy said, half amused and half impatient—she was already becoming a little bored with the inevitable comments on Almina's youthful appearance. The Marchese Francesco had peered at her through his thick lenses and murmured something about "cosi giovane", and even Paolo, over coffee, had left music alone for a moment to say "My dear Suzy, the governess seems to be of the same age as the pupil."

"Tiens! Well, she is charming—that hair is delicious," the Count now said. "What do you say her name is?"

"Prestwich—and it is not very ingratiating of you to praise her hair to me, lovely as it is," said Suzy, with lazy coquetry.

"Cara e bella! You know that I see no one but you," the Count protested—from long practice he played this particular game with considerable skill and great satisfaction. He bent forward to take her hand and kiss it; then, with a glance towards the steps, checked himself. "Suzy, will it not be—inconvenient—having this young girl here?" he asked, in a different tone. "At that age they see everything, and I am told that the English have no—ma, no comprehension, no savoir-faire. And if this little Postiche is like the rest——"

It was then that Suzy's laughter had pealed out. "Prestwich, my poor Carlo—her name is Prestwich."

He mouthed at it. "Prestveech. It is impossible to say—it is a foolish name," he pronounced. "I shall call her the Signorina Postiche. She will get used to it, as Gelosia has done. But now, cara, tell me—you think this will be all right?"

"Quite all right," Suzy assured him—she would arrange everything. And the conversation went off onto other topics.

Upstairs, the two girls worked away at unpacking and installing Almina's things. The dresses were hung in the cupboards, the stockings and underwear, so carefully checked by Mrs. Prestwich, ranged in drawers, the hats put on shelves. As May had done, Marietta exclaimed over the green hat: "Oh, do put it on and let me see it!" Almina did so. "Lovely! It is lovely! Elena has nothing prettier, even from Madame Joséphine! And on your beautiful hair! Do you know, I think you are so fortunate to have such beautiful hair and such a lovely *teint*," Marietta exclaimed earnestly. Startled and pleased at her enthusiasm, Almina turned back to the mirror. But seeing herself wearing the hat in the glass suddenly reminded her forcibly of the last time she had put it on, in the old comfortable shabby sunflower room at home, with May making admiring comments, and her Mother coming in and giving her that lovely jewellery—and a wave of homesickness and loneliness swept over her; tears stood in her eyes, in the mirror the hat grew blurred and wavered. She took it off, and went on diligently with her task.

The afternoon seemed very long to Almina. She hoped for a summons to tea, but none came. When they had finished the clothes they arranged the books, in neat rows on one of the large tables—lesson books, some solid biographies, English poets, and a few novels: E. F. Benson, Robert Hichens, Mrs. Humphry Ward. Almina showed Marietta the two volumes of Bentham and Hooker, one with illustrations and one with the text, and explained how to use them. Marietta was delighted. At last—"Where shall we work?" Almina asked, when all was done, and they were sitting on the couch, resting after their labours.

"Oh, but in the school-room. I will show you," and she led her off to a pretty room on the same floor, reached by passing through Marietta's bedroom, which was next to Almina's. At Vill' Alta, as in most old Italian country houses, only a small percentage of the upstairs rooms could be entered directly from any corridor—they opened chainwise out of one another, and when the house was full the embarrassed foreign guest, going up late to bed, must generally pass through two or three bedrooms which had already a slumbering or partially-clad occupant. Suzy had very sensibly given the English governess a room which shared with Marietta's a small vestibule, where luggage could be stored and tennis racquets deposited—this already contained a fair litter of Marietta's surplus possessions. Almina duly admired the school-room.

"Yes. It is to the South, so we may find it a little hot," said Marietta, "but there was no very convenient room on the North, Mama thought." (In fact, the Marchesa Suzy had been very careful not to instal the school-room party in a room overlooking the terrace, where her afternoon sessions with Count Carlo took place.) "But if we are hot, we can work out-of-doors, in the shade, no?" Then she passed on to the subject that was uppermost in her thoughts.

"Miss Prestwich, I have something very important to ask you."

"What is it?" Almina asked, surprised and amused at her grave face.

"It is about Giulio, my cousin, whom you saw this morning. Giulio is *molto serio*; he is learned; he wants to be a philosopher—he reads such books! And he wishes to go and study at Oxford. But his English is so bad—if he went, as he is, he could not understand the lectures, nor read the books. And so, while you are here, he is most anxious to study with you also—just English; to read it and to speak it. Not while you work with me, but at some other time. Do you think this could be arranged? Would you be willing? It means so *much* to him!" she said, clasping her hands and looking at Almina with intense gravity.

Almina hesitated. Personally she had no particular objection, especially if the extra coaching were to mean extra fees; but she was a little doubtful of committing herself to such a plan before she knew how much she was expected to do with

her legitimate pupil, and without knowing what the Marchesa
would think of it.

"I think it might perhaps be possible," she said rather
doubtfully, "but I can't really say until I have talked to your
Mother, Marietta. You see we have not arranged your own
work yet—and that must come first."

"Of course, of course. But Mama has already said Yes.
We spoke of it this morning—Elena was stupid, she leapt in
with the plan—she is so headlong and so mischievous! But
even so, Mama said yes. And I know she will leave you to
arrange my lessons as you like! So *do* say you will do it."
Then, seeing Almina still hesitate, the astonishing child went
on: "And you need not be afraid that Giulio will begin a flirt
with you, because he hates girls! He is not like Roffredo.
I think he is horrified that you are young—I saw his face
when you came! He was hoping that you would be like
Gela!" She laughed.

"Who is Gela?" Almina asked.

"Gela is Elena's governess—her real name is Fräulein
Gelsicher—at least she was," Marietta explained, not very
grammatically. "Elena does no lessons now, of course—she
is just beginning to be in Society. But Gela is still with them
—they could not live without her! She does everything.
She manages the house, she keeps Ospedi in order—he is the
bailiff, and he is so bad! But my Uncle is too silly to see it.
And she keeps my Uncle in order too, as much as she can!"
Marietta said, with a giggle. "And for everything for Giulio
and Elena, she is just the one person who does things. She
is so wise, *elle donne des conseils*; even my Grandmother respects her opinion. She looks so old and stiff, and puts on a
severe air—but really she is *molto cara*, and so kind. Everyone loves her."

Almina listened to this account of another governess with
far more interest than she had to Marietta's versions of her
various relations. And as she listened, her heart mounted
within her. From the young girl's odd lively expressions,

and still more from her tone of voice, she gathered a deep impression of the respect and love which the Swiss woman had earned from all about her. If she could do the same it would make this job of governessing, on which she had entered rather against the grain, something worthy of her very best efforts. Inwardly she resolved to do her utmost for this nice child beside her, for the pretty charming woman who was her mother. And beginning at once, she said a little nervously—"Marietta, do you think you ought to speak as you do of your Uncle? It is not very respectful, is it?"

Marietta opened her eyes at her. "Zio Carlo? Calling him silly? But Miss Prestwich, he *is* silly; we all know it. So why not say so? Not to him, of course—except Mama! *She* tells him so, into his face!" She laughed. But seeing Almina still look grave—"If you wish me not to, I shall not!" the impulsive creature said. "I wish to please you in everything!"

"That is very nice—I am glad," Almina said warmly, moved by this admirable disposition in her new pupil.

"And you will see Gela tomorrow," Marietta ran on, "for we are to lunch at Odredo. So then, if you are willing, we can settle with Giulio about his lessons. He will be dying with anxiety about it." And, after further pressure, Almina eventually agreed that, subject to the Marchesa's formal approval, she would be willing to coach Giulio for an hour a day.

Marietta proved to be perfectly right in her prediction that the matter of lessons would be left mainly to Almina's discretion. When the girls eventually went downstairs, Almina managed to catch the young Marchesa, and in Suzy's boudoir attempted to find out what her employer's educational views were. It was not very successful. "Oh, my dear Miss Prestwich, I leave all that to you," Suzy said, lighting, to Almina's astonishment, a cigarette. She and May had very occasionally smoked a cigarette in secret with their brothers; but they were well aware of the impropriety of what they were doing, and carefully concealed the traces of it afterwards by cleaning their teeth and sucking small scented cachous. Girls who smoked were hopelessly "fast"; and as for married women smoking, Almina had never even heard of it. That, again, was "actressy". And here was the Marchesa doing it with the most open coolness. Almina, repressing her astonishment, pushed on with the matter in hand. "How much work do you want her to do?" she asked. "Six hours a day, about?"

"O Dio mio, no! Poor child, she must not be driven like a slave," Suzy said. Three hours in the morning, perhaps, proved to be the young Marchesa's idea, and a little light reading in the evenings. English, she should learn that— she knew a little already; they could study English literature, especially modern literature. The Marchesa preferred modern literature, it seemed. "Her French, you will find, is quite good, but you might also read some French together— memoirs, and so on. Can you teach German?" Almina said she could. "Her Grandmother would like Marietta to read and speak German well—you might also work at that," Suzy said. "The child has some intelligence, but she is very untrained, and lacks application. Make her a cultivated person, if you can, Miss Prestwich. You see she is never going to have any looks to speak of, I fear—so she had better have plenty of intellectual interests." She smiled at the governess. "I am sure you will do this very well. She needs most of all to have her time profitably occupied, you know."

This view of her duties slightly discouraged Almina. But she turned to the next point, with her usual conscientious steadiness.

"There is one other thing, Marchesa," she said. "Marietta says that your nephew, Count Giulio di Castellone, is most anxious to improve his English and to do a little work with me. I told her that I could not arrange anything till I had spoken to you about it. Have you any objection? Provided, of course, that I do not let it interfere in any way with Marietta's work? Naturally, I only want to do exactly what you wish about this."

The young Marchesa laughed a little, blowing out a cloud of smoke. "Poor Giulio!" she said. "He is so ambitious, and so bored, here in the Province. No, Miss Prestwich, I have no objection—pray help him if you have the time. Only he must come *here* for his lessons," said Suzy, suddenly alert, "otherwise it will take too long. But the children all live in one another's pockets anyhow, in the summer." Then she looked very kindly at the young girl. "Are you comfortable, upstairs?" she asked. "You are sure you have all you want?" Almina said that she had. "Shall you be homesick, do you think?" the young Marchesa asked, in a very friendly tone, speaking now in English.

"I hope not," Almina said, smiling. "Marietta is very friendly."

"Yes, she is greatly taken with you. Well, if you *are* homesick, you must come to me and we will have a little talk in English," said the Marchesa. "And you must tell me if there is anything you want." She looked at her. "You look tired," she said, with pleasant concern—and then a thought struck her.

"Tea!" she exclaimed suddenly, looking at her watch. "Of course, you want tea! And it is after five o'clock!" She rang a bell, and gave an order to the servant. "You and Marietta shall always have tea," she said, "in the school-room. I know the English cannot live without it."

Much restored by the tea, and more charmed than ever by the young Marchesa's thoughtful kindness, Almina's spirits had risen a little when Marietta took her out afterwards to see the grounds. They went out through the olives, and came onto the ridge that led towards Odredo. It was a high stretch of wild wiry grass, in which thyme grew—distributed irregularly along it were groups of umbrella pines, and in the open stretches between stood clumps of arbutus, grown to an unusual height, so that their red trunks, with the dusty papery-looking bark, stood out against the dark foliage. The two girls presently sat down. In front of them, through the trunks of the stone pines, the mountains to the North rose, pale and clear in the evening light; their white limestone, touched with the level sunshine, turning them to blue shot with gold. Almina had never seen anything so beautiful, and said so.

"Yes," said Marietta on a deep breath. "It is beautiful. You have no conception how I love this place." Then she pointed out the long building standing up in the foreground. "That is Castellone, where Zia Livia lives."

"Why is one end of it red, and all the rest white?" Almina asked.

"Ah—that is the story! Long ago, one branch of the Castellones had a quarrel with the Vill' Altas, but the rest of the family had not. And they made war on one another. But so that the Vill' Altas should only shoot and bombard at the right part of the castle, those Castellones painted their own part red, so that it should be clear what was theirs and what not. And it has been kept painted red ever since." She paused and laughed. "The Sorellone—Aspasia and Roma Castellone, live in it now. They are the two I told you about. They are spinsters, and great gossips, and so curious, they always must know everything!" "Do you mind my saying *that*?" she asked, turning round suddenly to Almina. The latter had to laugh.

"I will tell you in a week," she said. "When I have met all these people, I shall be able to judge better how you ought to speak of them."

"You won't have to wait a week to meet the Sorellone," Marietta said ruefully. "They will come to look at you long before that."

She was right. When the two girls returned to Vill' Alta to dress for dinner, they saw a small pony-carriage drawn up by the front door. Marietta checked at the sight.

"Per carità!    There they are!" she said in a whisper.

"Who?"

"The Sorellone.    Now they will stay to dinner—you will see!    That is why they have called so late."

Again she was right.    On descending to the great *salone* where the family assembled before dinner, Almina found two strange middle-aged ladies added to the party.    Countess Aspasia was tall and thin, with something martial about her appearance; Countess Roma shorter and very stout, with a rather foolish face and a frequent needless laugh.    And they fully lived up to Marietta's rather unpromising account of them.    After being introduced, Almina heard Countess Roma say, in a very audible aside to her sister—"It is true then—she is quite a *jeune fille*!"    Blushing and feeling slightly indignant (indignation was a feeling very commonly engendered by the Sorellone) she took a chair in a corner, and sat rather in the background throughout the evening, letting the tide of gossip and family affairs flow by her, and thinking how high Italian voices were when a lot of them got together in one room.    The two Countesses were full of information, and their frequent and direct questions showed how they obtained it.    There was a great deal about Roffredo, whose name Marietta had also mentioned.

"And senta, cara Suzy, Roffredo is coming back almost at once; did you know?"    This was Roma.

"And he has taken this small villa that stood empty so long, on the Pisignacco road—so that he can work more freely."

"He is setting up for himself," giggled Roma.

"I advised it," Aspasia said magisterially.    "Indeed, I urged it on Livia.    He is of an age to be—enfin, to be alone, to have some freedom!    Besides," with a meaning glance at Marietta, "it was most unpleasant having all those experiments going on at Castellone.    Loud explosions and reports at all hours—and such smells!"

"Old Alba is to be his cook and look after him," Roma

added, "and he is bringing a chauffeur person, who will also be his man-servant."

Presently Countess Aspasia enquired of the Marchese Francesco how his painting was getting on—he went off and fetched the sketch of the tasselled grape-hyacinth to show her.

"And where does that grow?" she enquired.

"In Brioni—Pipo sent it me."

"Ah. Pipo is in Brioni? Roma, do you hear that? And is dear Nadia there too?" the Countess Aspasia asked.

"No, Nadia is in Rome. She is not very well, and is having some treatment," interposed Suzy smoothly.

"And Pipo is all alone in Brioni? But why should he go *there*?" Roma asked.

La Vecchia Marchesa here took a hand. " Cara Contessa, when my sons reach the age of thirty, I cease asking why they do anything," she said trenchantly. "I regard their lives then as their own concern. Pipo," she added, "is forty-nine."

This disposed of Pipo and his affairs for the time being, and a little flicker of triumphant amusement passed over Suzy's face. She loved seeing La Vecchia in action. Countess Roma now turned her batteries onto Marietta, and began to cross-examine her as to what lessons she was going to do.

"My dear Roma, Miss Prestwich is only with us since luncheon today. She is barely unpacked. You surely did not expect Marietta to start work this afternoon?" Suzy said, in a comic tone of remonstrance which raised a laugh and gracefully covered the rebuff. Almina, watching all these manœuvres, felt with dismay that one would have to be very clever and very ready to live successfully in such surroundings. She also thought with relief, when the sisters had packed themselves into their little pony-carriage and driven off through the warm dusk, that with them, at any rate, she need have little to do. But here she was wrong.

G

## Chapter Seven

FRÄULEIN GELSICHER, after some days of careful observation, was inclined to bestow a tempered approbation
on the new régime at Vill' Alta.   Like everyone else
she had been staggered at first by Almina's youth, and by
what—among the dark Italian hair and complexions—counted
as an almost dazzling prettiness; also she was inclined to feel
that the becoming clothes of Mrs. Prestwich's careful provid-
ing erred on the side of fashion, for a governess.   But she
did not let any of these things bias her natural just and kindly
judgement; she approved of the neat table of hours and
subjects pinned to the schoolroom wall, of Almina's routine
of work from 9.30 to 12.30, walks or tennis in the afternoon,
and an hour or more of preparation before dinner, during
which time Giulio Castellone had his lesson; and she applauded her young colleague's resolute insistence that her
pupil should present herself for work in the morning fully
dressed, and not in a dressing-jacket or wrapper.   She
decided that Miss Prestwich was, in fact, "serious," and told
Count Carlo so, roundly, when he started some rather crude
witticisms about the beauty of "the little Postiche".   She
saw, far more clearly than Almina herself, how difficult the
girl's position might easily become if she relaxed for a
moment that wise discretion which she had so far displayed
—she took occasion, once or twice, to praise her quietly,
when she had observed her refusing the pressing invitations
of some of the young men of the province, who, ignorant of
her exact position, had wished her to join them in a set of
tennis or a game of croquet.   "That is wisely done," she
said; "if the Marchesa herself asks you to make a fourth, of
course it is all right.   And to play with the children is quite

90

another thing." And to the old Marchesa, who rapped out at her one day—"What do you think of Suzy's idea of a governess, eh, Signorina Gelsicher?" she answered with perfect sincerity that she thought the young Marchesa had been extremely fortunate in her choice.

"Choice! There was as much choice about it as pulling a boot out of a bag!" said the old lady. "She has very pretty manners, certainly. Does she know anything?"

"Yes, Marchesa, she knows a great deal; and what is more important, she has I think *beaucoup de fonds*; she is a good conscientious girl, as far as I can judge," the Swiss replied.

"Tiens! Well, I trust your opinion," said the old lady. "I am glad. I wish Marietta to be in good hands. All the same, she is a great deal too pretty. Governesses should not be pretty!" she said, with an amiable chuckle. "Giulio or someone will be falling in love with her."

"I think she is discreet," Fräulein Gelsicher replied.

"Hm! Well, she can't do more," said the Vecchia Marchesa.

One afternoon when Almina had been at Vill' Alta nearly a fortnight, she and Fräulein Gelsicher, with Elena and Marietta, undertook a walk to the village of Macerbo, whose churchyard, set high on a hill, commanded an unusually wide and lovely view—from it, Marietta said, you could look right into the bed of the river Serpiglione, flowing south-westwards across the plain from the mountains. They walked at first by pleasant paths across pastures or through the maize-fields, where every little eminence was crowned with a tuft of acacias, slender and delicate of foliage, and by every stream grew groups of the small poplars, bare save for a long straggling truss of branches at the top, their trunks standing out silvery-white against the distant blue of the mountains. It was a delicious day, hot and bright, with a clear north wind which bent the slender poplars and sent satiny tremors shooting across the flowering grass; the wind affected the two cousins as it does cats, and they were in headlong spirits—

Almina herself felt exhilarated, satisfied after a good morning's work, eager to see later what Giulio would have made of the essay she had set him. She walked in great contentment, unusually alive to the beauty of her surroundings, and the delicious freshness of the early summer's day; in the intervals of her desultory talk with Fräulein Gelsicher, she told herself that she was very lucky to be so happy.

For the last part of the way they had to take to the road, which wound, white and dusty, up the slope of the hill on which Macerbo stood. Another road, coming in from the west from the direction of Verona, met theirs in the square at the top. Along this second road, as they climbed, they saw a white cloud of dust rising, hurtling along at a surprising speed.

"It must be a motor-car," said Elena. "I wonder if it is Roffredo?"

"It must be either Roffredo or the Bianchini's car, because there are no others in Gardone," said Marietta.

"I don't think it can be the Bianchini's," said Elena. "Dino won't let it be used any more. Didn't you hear? It met the dog-cart in that narrow bend in the drive, and killed the horse—and the groom is still in the hospital in Gardone." She laughed—and Marietta laughed too. Almina had not yet got accustomed to the Italian habit of regarding a violent accident involving personal friends as a really good joke, and was slightly shocked by their mirth. When they reached the village, however, the question as to the ownership of the car was soon settled. In the open piazza before the church a small crowd had gathered about a motor and some object on the ground; as the party approached an old woman, with loud screechings, raised the object, revealing it as the corpse of a turkey. Her screeches—it was clear that she was the owner of the bird—were directed partly to the late lamented, partly at a tall vigorous-looking young man with Titian-red hair, wearing a long pale dust-coat like an umpire's, who stood, lighting a cigarette and looking enormously amused, and occasionally remonstrating very good-naturedly with the old woman under the title of Grandmother. At sight of him, both the cousins cried "Roffredo!" and ran forward. Almina and Fräulein Gelsicher, following, saw him greet them with a sort of careless pleasure; then he turned in their direction, saying—"And La Gelosia—" and checked in mid-sentence. "Who is *that*?" he muttered to Elena, looking at Almina.

"That's my new governess, Miss Prestwich," Marietta said.

"She's not your *governess*?" the young man said, incredulous.

"Ma si. E cosi cara," she whispered to him.

"E cosi bella!" he returned, in an undertone, as he allowed himself to be led over towards the two governesses. He greeted Fräulein Gelsicher and suffered the introduction to Miss Prestwich with the same careless ease; then, the matter of the turkey having been liquidated for a few lire, the whole party went into the churchyard. Here more hens and turkeys, to Almina's rather scandalised astonishment, were pecking and gobbling among the tombstones, the photographs set in metal crosses, and the wreaths under glass shades; ignoring these, they walked round the florid whitewashed bulk of the church to the further side, where below a rough stone parapet the ground fell steeply away to the plain. There, sure enough, about half a mile away was the Serpiglione, its broad bed cut deeply into the green landscape, with blue threads of water twining through the bare white expanse of stones—beyond, the plain stretched on, fold beyond fold, the white houses and villages set in it like pearls strewn on crumpled velvet, till the foothills sprang to meet the mountains, and that blue confusion of peaks bounded the whole. Here where they stood they were further West and further North than Almina had been before, and the view had new features. She could now look right into the steep-sided valley through which the Serpiglione cuts its way out into the plain, the exit guarded by a curious isolated block of hill; and round to the East was a mountain she had never seen before, a great blunt-topped

mass rising slightly above its fellows.    The party strung out
along the parapet, the three cousins calling observations to
one another; Almina stood a little apart, looking at the view.
The cool wind lifted the hair round her temples, the expanse
of earth and mountains lifted her heart; that deep-cut channel
of the Serpiglione stirred her, gave a sense of an all-conquering
power, now calm and held in reserve, to be unleashed at the
due moment.    A line of verse, whose origin she had forgotten, came into her mind—"Blown crystal clear by Freedom's northern wind"; it matched her unexpected moment of
exaltation.

Then a flower caught her eye, growing among the stones
of the parapet in small trailing tufts of green, starred with
mauve.    She stooped and picked a piece and examined it; it
was the creeping linaria.    And at that moment Roffredo di
Castellone strolled over and addressed her.

"You collect flowers, Mademoiselle?" he asked, in slightly
American English.

"Yes," said Almina.

"And what is that?" he asked, touching the flower in her
hand.

"Linaria Cymbalaria," she answered.

"Corpo di Bacco!    You are a real botanist!    What a boon
you will be to my Uncle Francesco," he said, with a laugh
which showed a set of very strong white teeth.    Easy and
assured, he let his blue eyes rest on her in a glance of very
direct appraisal.    "You do not look like a learned person,
you know, Mademoiselle," he said.

Almina, disconcerted, blushed a little.    "All the same, I
am; learning is my profession," she said.    And to turn the
conversation—"Signor Conte, what is the name of that
mountain?" she asked in Italian, indicating the big peak with
the blunt summit.

"The Monte Canone.    It is a very good climb by the
western ridge," he said, still talking English.    "Do you
climb?"

"No, I never had the chance."

"Ah, you should. There is nothing like it." He pointed out various peaks to her, telling her their names; presently he said "And do you see that lump of hill at the entrance to the gorge, there where the river comes out?"

"Yes."

"Can you see that there is a building on it? It is clear today—you should."

"Yes, I can."

"That is a fortress—it was built by my great-grandfather, another Roffredo di Castellone," he said. "You see it was by that valley that the Austrians were always coming in, to harry our poor Italy. So he built that fortress—it is a huge place, really—to defend this entrance; he did it entirely at his own—what is the word?—*frais*."

"Expense," Almina said.

"Si—at his own expense. Dunque, the government was very grateful, and offered him all sorts of titles and rewards, but his answer was that he only wanted one reward."

"And what was that?" Almina asked.

"That when he was dead, they should build him into the northern wall, upright, and facing Austria!" the young man said, with a sudden ring in his voice. "So that was done, and there he is, to this day. E bello, no?" he said, looking at her.

"Yes, *rather*!" said Almina with enthusiasm, using the idiom of her day.

The others now came up and joined them—it was time to return. Roffredo offered to drive them back to Vill' Alta in his car, but Fräulein Gelsicher declared cheerfully that nothing would induce her to enter it. "I have no mind to go about murdering fowls," she said. Almina thought it expedient to follow her example, and as the two girls could not go un-escorted, the plan fell through. The car was laboriously ground and started; they watched it chugging dustily and noisily off along the Castellone road, and then set out on their return walk.   And on the way Almina found herself thinking a good deal about that patriotic and romantic figure, the builder of the fortress.   He cast a certain glamour over his descendants—he was, she thought, a most satisfactory ancestor to have.   When Giulio came over for his lesson that evening, bringing one of his laboriously correct but singularly lifeless essays, she watched him, as he read it out, still thinking of the fortress-builder.   Somehow it was not so easy to relate Giulio, docile and extremely shy, with his stoop, his black untidy hair and his sensitive face and hands, to that militant old man as it was Count Roffredo—the body in the wall, still defiant in death, had probably, she felt, owned red hair, white strong teeth, and a manner of indifferent ease.

Roffredo turned up to call the next day at Vill' Alta; when Miss Prestwich and Marietta returned from tennis at Odredo they found him sitting on the terrace with Suzy and the old Marchesa, drinking Madeira.   His manner to the old lady was very attractive, courteous and attentive; to the young Marchesa he was gallant, with the rather artificial and blatant gallantry which Almina was gradually becoming accustomed to see handed out to her employer and Elena by their compatriots.   At dinner the talk was of him.   "It is pleasant to have Roffredo here again," the old Marchesa said to her son. "We missed him last summer."

"He is improved," said Suzy.   "He has more manner."

"He always had a good manner—and how working in a motor-factory can improve it, I can't think," said the old lady. "But he is certainly none the worse.   He is a very fine young man."

"How are his inventions going?" the Marchese wanted to know.

"So-so, I think," Suzy said indifferently.

"He has one—it is something to do with the ignition of the petrol, I think—that is being tested now," Marietta put in eagerly.   "It is something to do with the position of the little points that make the spark, and the metal you use.   And if it goes well, it may be that the N.S.A. will take it.   They are trying it; they are interested."

"And how do you know all this?" her Father asked her fondly.

"He explained it to Giulio, and Giulio told me."

"I did not think Giulio was able to understand such things; his head is always in the clouds," said Suzy lazily, peeling a fig.

"Mama!   Giulio has a very good brain," said Marietta, with slight indignation.   "Hasn't he, Miss Prestwich?"

The old Marchesa fixed her black eyes on Miss Prestwich at this point—the girl was aware of her glance, and knew that she was waiting to see how she would deal with the situation in which Marietta had put her.

"I think he has a gift for languages," she said quietly, "that is all I have had the opportunity of judging, so far."

The old lady gave a tiny nod, and Almina knew that she had passed.   She constantly had the sense, with the old Marchesa, of being given a test question in an examination; it was a little unnerving, but rather to her own surprise, she did not mind it much.   Without knowing why, she found herself both liking and trusting the old woman.

A few days later there was a further addition to the collection of relations which was gradually gathering for the summer, as usual, in the province.   This was the Marchesa Nadia di Vill' Alta.   Suzy had carried her point with her mother-in-law, and had invited Nadia to come for a visit, to see whether something could not be done to improve the situation between her and her husband, the Marchese Pipo. The old lady, while agreeing that it was the right thing to do—how often, she reflected, it was the women like Suzy, and not the rigidly virtuous ones, who saw the right thing to do, and bestirred themselves to do it—dreaded the visit a good deal; her Russian daughter-in-law, with her intensity of emotion, was always fatiguing to her, and in this crisis she was certain to be very difficult.   On the day of Nadia's arrival she was restless and a little irritable—her egg-nog was not right, her shawls were too hot, she did not get her nap in the afternoon, being too fretted to sleep. "You must talk to her too," she said to Suzy. "I cannot do it all alone; that is, I will not," she corrected herself.

"Of course I will talk to her too, Bonne-Mama cara," Suzy soothed her.

The Marchesa Nadia appeared that night at dinner, a tall graceful creature, beautifully built, with black hair parted close and smoothly off one of those square white Russian faces, and immense eyes of a curious pale blue, like glass; she wore the length of her hair in a great plait, pinned round her head like a tiara. This severe coiffure, among the puffs and chignons then prevalent, gave her an archaic look, like a queen out of the past, Almina thought—she was very beautiful. Her hands were beautiful too, long and white; she did not use them for conversational purposes, as her in-laws did, but left them lying, in her lap or on the table, as though they hardly belonged to her—but Almina noticed that they trembled a little, sometimes, even while she talked with a rather feverish animation to the Marchese Francesco. Suzy noticed it too, and sighed to herself—"Dio mio, she is in a bad state," she thought. "I must warn her that she must really control herself when she talks to Bonne-Mama; Bonne-Mama isn't as strong as I thought. We can't have her upset." Like all the rest of the family, Suzy attached enormous importance to La Vecchia Marchesa's reaching her hundredth birthday safely. It was now early June, and the birthday was in mid-September—only three and a half months to go. After they had all taken coffee on the terrace, Suzy, professing concern for her sister-in-law's fatigue after her journey, carried her off to her room. Sitting there, graceful and easy, "How do you find Bonne-Mama looking?" she asked.

"Amazingly. She is wonderful," the Russian said listlessly, walking up and down the room.

"She is not so strong as she looks. Things worry her now—one has to *ménager* her," Suzy said.

"I suppose *I* worry her—my affairs, at least," the Russian said, stopping in front of her.

"Naturally, dear Nadia, she is sorry that you are unhappy," Suzy said, in her warm caressing voice. "We all are. You know that."

Nadia slid her bracelets up and down her delicate arms. "That is the humiliation—everyone knowing, and being sorry for one!" she said bitterly. "However, I suppose she wants to talk to me about it?"

"Of course," Suzy said. "And Nadia, she is worth listening to. She has lived a long time, and she was always a woman of intelligence."

"Sicuro! And not of emotions! Well, I will listen to her, Suzy. But I warn you, I do not think that it will be any good. He will not give up this creature—he is *toqué* about her," Nadia said.

"Pazienza, cara," Suzy said, rising and putting her arms round the beautiful creature—she was always moved by beauty. "See—listen to her, listen gently, will you? She is not strong. And after, you and I will talk. There must be a way. I think Pipo is being *most* tiresome, but we must give him time. Time does wonders."

"Will Time make him love me again? For nothing is any good but that. Nothing, I tell you!" Nadia said passionately. Then her eyes filled with tears; "Oh Suzy, I am so miserable," she said, and put her head down on her sister-in-law's shoulder, and wept.

The old Marchesa's talk with Nadia took place next morning in the former's sitting-room, before she went downstairs. This was by Suzy's wise arrangement. She realised that both were dreading the interview, and decided that it would upset the old woman least in the morning, when she had most strength, and would give her longer to get over it before night, and a better chance to sleep. La Vecchia Marchesa was sitting, fully dressed, in one of the upright chairs she preferred when her daughter-in-law came in—after the usual greetings she motioned her to another chair and said, without any beating about the bush: "Now, my dear, let us have a talk about Pipo."

"Yes, Marchesa. I shall be glad of your advice," Nadia said dutifully.

"That is well—usually advice is more easily given than taken," the old lady said. "Well, I have had your letters, Nadia, and I think I understand the situation. Pipo does not want to give up this liaison at present, I take it?"

The Russian bowed her head in assent.

"But when you are together in Bologna he behaves well—accompanies you everywhere, is properly attentive?"

"Yes—but all that is such a mockery," Nadia said, lifting her head and looking now at the old woman.

"A very useful mockery," the old Marchesa said drily. "Very well, my dear, then it seems to me that the only thing for you to do is to have patience. These affairs do not last."

"Marchesa, I cannot! I have been patient for a whole year, and I am à bout," the younger woman said, with a sort of weary desperation.

The old Marchesa stretched out one of her fine frail hands and put it on the other's knee. "Nadia, will you listen to me?" she said. "You may as well, since you have come all this way to see me," she added, with a little laugh. And as the Russian again bent her head in assent with a slow grave gesture, she went on—"Figlia mia, I think you are looking at this thing in the wrong way. You think it more important than it is. All men, or nearly all, do this from time to time —many women do it too. But the point is that it does not really matter."

"Not matter? That one's husband ceases to love one, gives all his thought elsewhere—this does not matter?" Nadia said, still slowly, still quietly.

"No—it doesn't—not for our purpose,' the old Marchesa said firmly. "We are talking of your *marriage*, Nadia. Marriage is one thing—love is another. They may exist together, but that is a happy accident. Love does not last, not often; marriage does. What matters is that one's marriage should be conducted with courtesy, with amiability—*ma, con decenza*! That *is* of importance. Listen," she went on, as she saw the younger woman move her head restlessly in negation—"I am old enough, now, to speak freely to you about the past. I have had lovers myself—three! At the time, with each, it seemed so very important, his love and mine! And now, at the best I remember them with a little pleasure—of one, I can no longer recollect even his name! It passes—it all passes," the old woman said, in a tone suddenly gone dreamy. The Marchesa Nadia, her interest aroused by this surprising recital, watched her with curiosity —she saw the old dark eyes look far far away, as if into immense distances, and then slowly close.

Only for a moment, however. Then she opened them again, and said, in tones of surprising firmness: "But my family, my children and my grandchildren, my whole life— these are with me still, I who am nearly a hundred! And they are still of value and importance, those things. Even now when I see clearly how little so many things matter, my family's good name is of importance to me still. And let me tell you that in the days when those other things seemed important, I made sacrifices to preserve it!"

"Did you, Bonne-Mama?" the Marchesa Nadia said, with more affection than she had yet shown.

"Yes, my child, I did. Ah, there was one—I would gladly have spent the rest of my life with him, then! He's gone— they are all gone. But I did not, and I am glad that I did not."

"You parted?" Nadia asked.

"Si, we parted. Oh, that was in eighteen thirty-five—the year Mazzini published his first book, the *Fede ed Avvenire*. How wild we all thought him, then!" Again her eyes looked back into great distances, and the younger woman realised, with awe, that she was watching the face of a lover of seventy years ago.

"But now, my child, as to your troubles," the old lady resumed briskly. "It may be that this affair of Pipo's will pass. I think so, myself. They are not really *volage*, the Vill' Altas—they have a strong family sense. But even if you do not regain his love—and that seldom happens—his friendship and his companionship and his respect you can keep, if you will be sensible."

"What do you think I should do, then?" Nadia asked.

"Be patient. Keep quiet. Be amiable, when he is with you," the old lady replied unhesitatingly.

"Let this go on? Make no protest?"

"You have protested, have you not? And has it done any good?" the old woman asked. And as the Russian again made her beautiful weary gesture of agreement—"Of course not," the old Marchesa went on. "It never does. You would have done far better to ignore the whole thing."

"But that would be such utter hypocrisy," the young woman protested. "I could not live a lie to him, when he once loved me."

"You call it hypocrisy—I call it commonsense," the old lady retorted. "What is your own idea?"

"I thought we might separate," the Russian said. "At least, then, I should not be in his house, be with him—always reminded of what is gone!" she said, in a low tone.

"And will that bring him back to you, to separate? Nadia, this is utter folly," the old woman said. "You will make a scandal, destroy your marriage, and injure the child's prospects—and for nothing! That will not help you in the least. No—do as I say—be patient, be cheerful, be a little indifferent. Know as little about it as you can. Above all, say nothing more. I will write to Pipo myself, and tell him to be prudent, considerate—there need be no scandal. Will you do this?"

Nadia sat looking at her hands, which lay, so detached, in her lap. At length, without raising her eyes, she said—

"I will consider it, Marchesa.   And I am grateful to you for all the trouble you have taken."

"If you take my advice, when it is all over you will be grateful for it," the old woman said, as the other rose.  "Ring for Giacinta, will you, my dear?   I want my egg-nog."

## Chapter Eight

"WELL, how did it go?" Suzy said to La Vecchia Marchesa before lunch, when the old lady, fortified by her egg-nog, had installed herself on the terrace.

"She was at least quite quiet," the old Marchesa replied. "That was something to be thankful for. She said she would think it over. But she is full of most strange ideas—when I asked her if Pipo was attentive, ma, behaved properly, when he *is* at home with her, she said that it was hypocrisy that he should do so!"

"Poor Nadia!" Suzy said, with a little sigh.

"We I think are also to be pitied," La Vecchia said, "to have anyone so unreasonable in the family."

"Ah, Bonne-Mama, you must not be too hard on her. Her ideas of marriage are quite different to ours," Suzy said. "I am half American, so I understand all that—Americans think the same about these things."

The old lady gave her a shrewd look. "Well, my dear Suzy, your *americanismo* has not prevented you from fitting very satisfactorily into our Italian way of living," she said; "and very acceptably," she added, with a little smile. "Anyhow, since you understand her, pray talk to her yourself. I am not confident that I have accomplished much."

The Marchesa Suzy tackled her mission that afternoon. After the siesta, when it was cool, she suggested a stroll to her sister-in-law—she had sent Marietta and Miss Prestwich to lunch at Odredo, to be out of the way, with a little note to the Count telling him not to call that day. "You will not be wanted, caro." The two ladies, armed with parasols, strolled gently along the ridge towards Odredo. Some distance along it a little path led off down the slope to a wooden seat, thickly screened behind by a group of arbutus, which commanded the full splendour of the northern view—on this Suzy seated herself, inviting the Marchesa Nadia to do the same. Nadia however dropped onto the dry grass at her feet. They made a pretty group, sitting there, in their flowing pale dresses and graceful attitudes, the dark woman and the fair one—an almost Watteau-like picture of pastoral fashion and perfect tranquillity. The tranquillity however was only apparent.

"Well, so you had your talk with Bonne-Mama," Suzy began, lighting one of her little cigarettes. "How did it go?"

Nadia threw off her broad-brimmed hat onto the grass beside her, dropped her hands into her lap, and sat staring in front of her for a little before she answered. Suzy watched her with a certain anxiety. What was going on inside that shapely dark head? And how extraordinary, she thought, that anyone with so much beauty—for really she was *quite* lovely today—should suffer on a man's account. That face seemed made to impose suffering, not to bear it.

"La Vecchia was—touching," Nadia said at last; "she actually told me about her own lovers, Suzy." She turned her head and looked at the other woman. "It made me wish that I could do what she wants. But it is no good—I can't. I can't," she repeated, in a tone of weary finality.

"Why not, Nadia cara?" Suzy asked kindly.

"Because to me it is all so hopeless," Nadia said. "La Vecchia considers that if Pipo is attentive and polite to me, and respects the *convenances*, and we preserve the appearance of a good marriage, that is sufficiently satisfactory. But to me this is quite horrible, to lie and pretend about it, when there is no love—or no love on one side," she added, in a lower tone. "To live with someone as if you both loved, when there is indifference only, and despair, and hatred—it is abominable! It is not marriage! I will not do it. It is better to separate. Then he can have what he wants—" her tone was of an

H

incredible bitterness—"and I—well, in time I may find peace, alone."

"This is a grave decision, Nadia," Suzy said. "One should think well before doing such a thing."

"I have thought. Dio mio, do you think it has been an easy choice, to give up all the—the love, the hopes, of so many years?" she said, turning her brilliant eyes, swimming in tears, to her sister-in-law. "But I have decided—I cannot change."

"Even if he gave her up?"

"He will not. And if he did, how do I know that he would ever care for me again? I might wait, as La Vecchia says, and we might seem reconciled, and afterwards it might begin again. That would be the last humiliation. No—it must end now. *Cela me déchire.* I can't sleep," she said, in a flat tone of helplessness.

"And the child? Have you thought of Francesca?"

"Thought? Yes! But she can only be injured by living in the infection of such misery. She sees, even now! She asks where her Father is," Nadia said passionately. "She asks why I am sad! Is that good for a child?"

One of Suzy's great gifts was that she could always recognise a fact, and that quickly. She saw on this occasion that there was nothing to be done with her sister-in-law along the lines of argument. Even La Vecchia Marchesa would have to admit defeat this time. The only hope would be to mobilise Pipo—he, if he were willing to break with the Panelli, and brought the lever of passion into play, might avoid a breach; otherwise, she said to herself philosophically, they were helpless. Nadia was a Slav, and could not be dealt with on ordinary Italian lines.

The trouble of course about all these discussions between the Marchesa Nadia and her husband's relations was that they were actually talking about two different conventions of marriage. Nadia, brought up by an English governess in one of the nicest of the old-fashioned Russian country families, held it as axiomatic (as indeed it is generally held in

England) that the only respect-worthy basis for marriage is not suitability, or general and private convenience, or a high probability of a comfortable union, but romantic love. The Vill' Altas took a quite different view. In the society in which they moved, marriages of convenience, though becoming less frequent, still often occurred; and even where the marriage was a matter of choice between the young people themselves, they regarded it, once made, as not wholly their own affair—they accepted unquestioningly the claim of their relations that every marriage in a family was to some extent the whole family's concern; they recognised a certain responsibility, not only to one another, but to their whole circle of relatives.

Now the disadvantage of the English convention of marriage is that it puts a premium on personal feelings. If these alter, the stability of the marriage is threatened; its accepted basis, romantic love, has failed, and the unhappy participants are almost bound in consequence to regard the whole venture as a failure. They are probably wrong—looked at biologically, or as a part of the social structure, the marriage is very likely perfectly adequate or even an undoubted success; an Italian wife, bred up in a saner and more practical theory, would complacently regard it as such, and be a better and a more cheerful wife in consequence.

For it is women who suffer most from this conception, and the worst of this over-personalisation of the married state is that it cuts its own throat. The woman who measures the success or failure of her marriage primarily by the state of her husband's affections is seldom wholly at ease—she is, far too often, secretly taking the temperature of his feelings; the small rubs and checks and difficulties of married life take on a wholly false importance. And the moment that he shows signs of being attracted by someone else, the fat is fairly in the fire. Instead of accepting it as a tiresome, perhaps a most painful, but a very fairly normal state of affairs, which must be left, with patience and good-temper, to run its course, and by no means be allowed to endanger that far more important thing, the marriage itself, she is apt to feel that the foundation of the whole business has gone by the board—and in addition, to suffer the pangs of a quite needless personal humiliation.

Now from these particular distresses the Italian conception of marriage set the woman free. She knew that she had to do her job; bear children, be amiable to her husband and polite to relations. But because she never thought for a moment that romantic love had anything much to do with marriage, its presence or absence did not trouble her on that score—if, as often happened, love came after, and a happy companionship grew, she took it thankfully; but if her husband stepped aside after another woman, provided the *convenances* were respected, and not too much money spent on her rival, she did not feel herself particularly humiliated— the thing was too usual! As for any idea of breaking up her marriage on those grounds, or even regarding it as a serious failure, she would have laughed it to scorn.

Another thing which tended to put the Italian woman in a stronger position than her English contemporaries was the accepted convention that women should go on being admired, treated with gallantry, and even courted after marriage. That shutting-down of all male attention but the husband's, once the vestry door has closed behind the bride, had—and has—no place in the Italian scheme of things; nor had the Germano-British tradition of the subservience of the wife. Her opinions were as much valued as those of her husband, and as freely expressed. This, and the further tradition of habitual courtesy, of being socially adequate and entertaining even within the family circle, added greatly to the pleasantness of marriage—Almina, accustomed to her Father's brusque monosyllables, his lack of response to her Mother's conversational openings, had already noted with surprise, and reported in a letter home, that the Marchese Francesco treated his wife "like a visitor."

Life in Gardone was full of these minor surprises for Miss Prestwich.    And she had another, and a rather more severe one, in connection with the visit of the Marchesa Nadia.    In England thirty years ago the bare possibility of difficulties or disasters in marriage was as far as possible concealed from girls; divorces only occurred among "people one didn't know," unfaithfulness only, and but rarely, in novels, and in the sort of novel one was not supposed to read at that.    Looking back, now, to those days, it is difficult to realise how complete, cast-iron and watertight was the English convention of married virtue, how invisible and incredible anything else; only a study of the minor fiction of the late nineties and the early nineteen-hundreds will adequately bring it home to the modern reader.    And the mass-suggestion of this innocuous fiction, reinforced by the careful silences of her home, had left Almina Prestwich as intellectually ignorant as a child of three of the darker and more unhappy possibilities of marriage. But that day at Odredo, when she and Marietta and Elena were sitting out under the stone pine after lunch, having coffee at the big square stone table which stood under it, she was suddenly and painfully enlightened.    The Count had gone off on an all-day expedition to his estates at Meden, many miles to the East, where he was anxious to put some of his new French theories of growing vines into practice, taking Ospedi, the bailiff, with him; Fräulein Gelsicher had gone too, hoping by her presence to restrain both the foolish enthusiasm of the Count, and the bailiff's unscrupulous rapacity; Giulio had retired to his room to finish an essay before they went out walking.    The three girls were alone, and because they were alone were sewing their under-clothes—those delicate cambric affairs, with ribbons run through slotted embroidery at the waist and round the bust, and broad lace-edged embroidery straps over the shoulders, which they were just learning to call camisoles, and which for the young and fashionable took the place of the woven bodices worn by Fräulein Gelsicher. Rather puffy things, those camisoles were, with a decent fullness over the bosom, produced by fine gathering or by groups of tiny pin-tucks; the ribbon showed coquettishly through thin blouses, but was a terrible job to run in. One carried such work about in large silk bags with hoop handles, or in round flattish sewing-baskets of scented grass, into which the slightly risqué objects could be thrust at the advent of a male relation. The stone table was covered with scraps of lace and embroidery, the resinous shade under the great umbrella pine was full of the hum of insects, broken by fragments of talk and little clear peals of laughter. Presently Elena asked—"And how is Zia Nadia, Marietta? Does she seem depressed?"

"Not particularly," Marietta replied, looking a little conscious.

"There is no sign of Zio Pipo, I suppose?" Elena went on, with a mischievous glance.

"Elena, of course not! You know he is in Brioni," Marietta said, in a tone of faint protest. "He would hardly come just now, besides."

"No, hardly—and leave his cara amoretta! Well, and what are they all doing? Discussing it, up and down?"

"Zia Nadia and Bonne-Mama had a long talk this morning, but naturally I don't know what they said," Marietta replied.

"I wonder how they will settle it," Elena said. "Aspidistra was telling Gela the other day that she believes Zia Nadia means to leave him." (Aspidistra was the cousins' impertinent name for the Countess Aspasia.)

"Surely she could not do that?" Marietta said, looking startled.

"Oh yes, she could. It would make a great scandal, of course, but it can be done. The Tito Serbellonis had a separation—there was a *consiglio di famiglia* and all sorts of fuss, but they got one in the end! Only there, it was *she*," said Elena significantly.

"But could they marry again then? No," said Marietta, wide-eyed.

"Of course not, dunce! One can never marry twice, unless the other is dead," Elena said with a superior air. "Not that that will trouble Zio Pipo!" she added, laughing.

"I think Zio Pipo is horrible!" Marietta burst out, with a sudden passion which startled Almina. "How he *can* make Zia Nadia so unhappy! She is so kind, and clever, and beautiful—such a darling; and she used to be so gay! It is hateful of him, I think."

Almina's conscientious scruples told her at this point that she ought to intervene in this most unsuitable conversation. She knew, of course, nothing about the Marchesa Nadia's affairs, and was greatly shocked by Elena's revelations; casual and elliptical as they were she could not fail to gather the gist of them—and she was scandalised at the open way in which the two girls were discussing a situation which at home would have been a matter for hushed voices and dark hints, even among her elders. However, before she had found a suitable phrase of remonstrance, Elena was off again.

"I, too, think it most extraordinary that he should prefer La Panelli to Zia Nadia. Have you ever seen her? She's a little dark stumpy thing, with eyes like boot-buttons, sticking out, and a snub nose, and no *teint*! Her face is like dirty paper. She is very amusing, and has a comic manner—she is really *gamine*. And she has great chic. But so has Zia Nadia—and she is in addition quite beautiful. Zia Roma says the trouble is that she is too fond of him—though what our Roma knows about men and love, I don't know," she ended, looking delightfully malicious.

"Do men not wish their wives to love them, then?" Marietta asked—and Almina could not tell whether the question was asked in irony or in earnest. That small vivid face was curiously inscrutable at times.

"Ma! Au fond, yes, I suppose so—but they should not show it too much. Men like to be kept dangling," Elena said, with a fine air of knowledge, biting off a thread.

"Elena, do use my scissors—you will ruin your teeth,"

Almina put in; she hoped that this nice governessy phrase would make a break.

"Grazie tanto! Miss Prestwich, do you admire Zia Nadia?"

"I find the Marchesa most charming," Almina replied gravely, "but, Elena, I do not think that you and Marietta ought to discuss her affairs." Gathering courage, she spoke firmly and steadily. "It is no business of ours, and for Marietta at least it is a most improper subject."

Elena looked at her in astonishment. "Improper? But how? Everyone knows that there is this trouble between her and Zio Pipo, and that she is come to Vill' Alta to talk it over with them all, so what harm can it be to speak of it? We have said nothing unkind."

"*I* did not know it, and now I do," Almina said. "I had rather not have heard about it. It is very terrible and very sad, but none of us is in a position to make a useful judgement on the matter, so I think we should do better to be silent about it. The less said about such things the better."

The extreme gravity of her tone and expression, rather than the words of this little homily, impressed Elena in spite of herself. She liked Miss Prestwich, but had hitherto thought her a rather delightful joke. She gave a tiny shrug, now, but then said, with perfect good-temper. "Va bene! Let us talk of something else."

At that moment there was an interruption. "The Three Graces! And all at needlework!" exclaimed a loud cheerful voice—looking round, they saw Roffredo di Castellone bearing down upon them.

"Buon' giòrno! Buon' giòrno!" he said generally, approaching the table. "You too diligent, Elena? What is it? No, let me see!" he said, grasping the shred of cambric, and laughing at her.

"It is two pocket handkerchiefs," Elena said gaily, as he spread it out—the little garment was indeed, in its untrimmed state, sufficiently non-committal.

"Where is my Uncle?" the young man now asked, seating himself.

"He is gone to Meden with Gela," Elena said, "but Giulio is indoors.  Did you want Papa?"

"I did.  Is Ospedi about?"

"No, he is gone too.  We are to grow French wine soon at Meden!" Elena said.  "I will fetch Giulio," and she ran off to find her brother.

"Well, Signorina, have you found any more rare flowers?" the young Count asked, turning to Almina.

"We are going to find some today," Marietta put in. "All sorts of things grow out by the Monte Sant Antonio, and we are going there to see what we can find."

"What, where old Trino lives?  Is he still alive?" Roffredo asked.

"Very much so.  He is Zio Carlo's bird-catcher, you know," she explained to Almina.

"He is the tenth Trino, father to son, to be bird-catcher to the Castellones," Roffredo said to Almina—" that is interesting, no?"

Almina, who had never heard of the profession of bird-catcher, asked if he meant a keeper?

"*Cacciatore?*  No—not that.  He snares the small birds for the table.  You had better take Miss Prestwich to see Trino, Marietta, while you are out there.  It might amuse her."

But when Giulio came down, joyful at the sight of his cousin, and suggested a game of tennis to him, rather to everyone's surprise the young man said abruptly that it was on the whole too hot, and proposed that they should accompany the girls on their walk.  "I should like to see old Trino again," he said.  So the whole party set out, down through the park which lay to the North of the house—not a park in the English sense, with great trees standing formal and noble in rich green pasture, and cropping deer; but a place of rather straggling herbage, with here and there little spinneys and clumps of plantation—larches, willows, poplars—and drifts of tall weeds and tracts of sloes and wild privet. It was all rather untidy, a mixture of the barren and the utilitarian which was rather characteristic of the Italy of those days; but still, in its early summer green, pretty enough, with its weedy lake, overhung with willows, in the middle. Water carts, long narrow wooden barrels slung on wheels, were coming up from the lake towards the house—Elena explained airily that the well was "leaking, or something," so that the water had to be fetched from there. They made a pretty group, the young people, as they strolled along, the young men in their white flannels, the girls in their pale summer dresses and shady flowery hats. Almina's hat was a broad-brimmed thing of white straw, with floating green ribbons—it suited her extraordinarily well, and Elena noticed with sly amusement that Roffredo kept his eyes firmly fixed on it and its owner. Passing through a little wood, Miss Prestwich suddenly darted aside, with a cry of pleasure, to pick a flower—it was the white butterfly orchis, with its delicate straggling blossoms writhing like small white limbs.

"Does it smell?" Roffredo asked her, and took it from her hand. "No, it does not," he said, giving it back.

"Not now, but it does at dusk. If you came here in the evening, the whole wood would be sweet with them," she told him.

"Then will you bring me here one evening, so that I may smell it? Then I shall believe you," he said, standing still and smiling down at her; it occurred to him with sudden force that it would be delightful beyond words to wander through a scented copse at dusk with this delicious little creature, with her face as pale as the flower she held, her great grey eyes, and her hair like spring sunshine. And to engage her attention and keep it for himself, he began to pick every flower and weed he could find, and bring them to her to ask their names—common things like scarlet pimpernel, shepherd's purse, and a small speedwell. With a gravity which charmed him, and

without the smallest hesitation, she identified them all—
*Anagallis arvensis, Capsella bursa-pastoris, Veronica hederae-folia.* At last "I believe she is making them up!" the young man cried—"she cannot know so many."

"At least she is making them up with the correct Latin genders," Giulio retorted.

"You are so ignorant, povero Roffredo!" Elena teased—"you can't even recognise learning when you meet it."

So they wandered on, laughing and picking flowers; Almina found the gay attentions of the two young men very pleasant, so pleasant that for the time she forgot the painful impression which the two girls' talk about the Marchesa Nadia had made on her. Presently they left the park, which was vaguely bounded, here by a broad weed-filled ditch, there by a straggling and indefinite hedge, and emerged onto open pastures; ahead of them rose a little hill, long, low and green—the Monte Sant Antonio. On the top of it they found the bird-catcher's house, a rather tumble-down hovel of grey stone, with quite as much rags as glass in its small windows, and an earthen floor. Almina, with her usual astonishment at Italian manners, thought how impossible it would have been that her grandfather, Lord Portledown, should allow an old estate servant to live in so makeshift a place. Old Trino appeared, a small and rather bent old man, incredibly dirty in person, with brilliant black eyes peeping out of a face that was almost all grey hairs and grime-filled wrinkles—he greeted the cousins with enthusiasm, and was delighted to show the English young lady his whole establishment. Out at the back of the house was a square enclosure surrounded by high hornbeam hedges, clipped and trimmed with most un-Italian neatness—the hedges were double, with a four-foot space between, and Trino explained how he hung his nets between the hedges, and showed Almina the wires, cords and pulleys by which, when the enclosure was full of birds, he could pull one large net along over the whole, through holes in the cottage wall, and then show himself and scare the little creatures into the surrounding nets, to be caught at his leisure. He was not using the nets at the moment, he said; the crop of rape which was to lure the birds into the enclosure was not yet ripe—"But the Signor Conte will be able to have *uccellini* tomorrow," he said triumphantly to Elena. "I am using my lime." And he led them off to a bushy place on the eastward slope of the hill, where small grain was strewn on the ground among innocent-looking twigs. But the twigs had a dark glossy surface; they were covered with bird-lime and firmly pegged to the ground—a hedge-sparrow and a couple of chaffinches were entangled among them, fluttering and struggling, their desperate movements only exposing more of their feathers to the cruel clinging glue. Almina, horrified, turned away—the piteous twitterings and helpless struggles of the little creatures made her feel sick. But the others took it quite calmly—Roffredo touched the lime to test its strength, went to wipe his finger on his handkerchief, and laughed when the linen stuck to his hand, while Elena, always inquisitive, made old Trino show her how he dipped the twigs in the bucket, and the rough brush of coarse grass which he used to spread the viscous stuff on the leaves of bushes where the birds were wont to roost. Trino presently caught the three minute creatures, and with a deft movement wrung their necks. Once all movement in those little bodies was stilled, Almina felt curiously relieved.

They walked back by the other side of the hill, Roffredo pointing out to the party the pink roof of his new villa, just to be seen in the distance through the trees. He was getting settled in, he told them, bit by bit—"when I am properly installed, you must all come and have lunch with me. You will come too, and bring Marietta, won't you?" he said, turning his bright glance onto Almina. A little further on, at a cross-path, he left them, turning off eastward to his house, remarking that he should see them again that night, as he was dining at Vill' Alta—an announcement which caused Almina a sensation of pleasure and expectancy which rather startled her.

He came, looking more arrogant and handsome than ever in his evening clothes. But the evening brought Almina no special pleasure. Beyond a civil greeting on his arrival, he barely spoke to her. She told herself sensibly that this was only natural. She was the governess, and when his elders were present it was right and proper that his attention should all be given to them. But a slight sensation of discomfort persisted—he had been so *empressé* in his manner all the afternoon that the contrast was painful. And his conversation with his hostess went almost beyond the usual gallantry—in England, Almina thought, one would have called it a flirtation. The Marchesa Suzy did her share—she was lazily mocking, delicately provocative, and the young man reacted violently to this stimulus. It made Almina rather uncomfortable. All the unpleasant impressions of the day came back to her as she sat in the high salon—the talk of the two girls about the Marchesa Nadia, which had distressed her more than she realised at the time, the struggles of the little birds among the limed twigs. All the rest of the day, she had not been able to get that picture out of her head—it thrust itself up between her and whatever she saw, unbidden; and now it returned to her with fresh force. She was glad when Marietta's bedtime came, and she was able to escape with her. But her escape was not complete—our escapes seldom are. She went at once to bed, but only to dream all night of herself caught in a limed thicket, her plumage befouled by something horrible which held her fast, while Roffredo hovered over her, smiling his bright imperious smile, ready to wring her neck.

## Chapter Nine

THE final upshot of all the discussions about the Marchesa
Nadia's affairs was a decision to hold a *consiglio di
famiglia* on the matter. Nadia's plan of quietly leaving
her husband, for good, was scouted as utterly improper by
La Vecchia Marchesa; and Suzy had made it clear to the old
lady that further private argument was useless. There remained the question of putting individual pressure on Pipo
to abandon his liaison with the Countess Panelli; but to this
course the Marchese Francesco, rather surprisingly, opposed
himself obdurately. He would neither do it himself nor, he
said, allow it to be done by anyone under his roof. His wife,
on hearing his pronouncement, raised her pretty pencilled
eyebrows—the three of them sat in conclave in his study; his
mother opened her lips to ask him his reasons, and then closed
them again. A possible one had occurred to her—that he
was unwilling to enforce on his brother a standard of behaviour which he had refrained from imposing on his wife.
If the family as a family, he went on, in council, chose to take
that course, well and good. And he did, as head of the
family and at the old lady's instance, write the letter to the
Marchese Pipo announcing that this was their intention. So
the lawyer was summoned, the date provisionally fixed, the
invitations sent out—to the diplomat son, the son who was a
cardinal, the playwright son who lived in Paris, and all the
rest. And Nadia, meditatively bending her graceful dark
head, went back to Bologna till the time came.

Almina's distress over this business had gone rather deep.
She had been charmed by the Marchesa Nadia and her archaic
grace and beauty from the first, and the discovery of those
depths of unhappiness under the fair-seeming surface of this

pleasant Italian family life disturbed her; still more, she was troubled by the airy way in which Elena had spoken of it. She consulted Fräulein Gelsicher about this, telling her what had happened, and blaming herself a little for not having checked the two girls' conversation sooner.

"You cannot prevent them, at their ages, either from knowing of these things or from talking about them, my dear Miss Prestwich," the Swiss said, with a small sigh; "all one can do is oneself to express a just opinion, and so help to form theirs."

"But that isn't easy for me," Almina said. "You see, I have never heard such things talked about. They aren't, at home."

"No—nor much with us in Switzerland," the older woman said. "But here, they are. One must take people and places as one finds them, Miss Prestwich. If Marietta speaks of it to you again, I should refer her to her Mother." She sighed once more, a sigh for which Almina could not quite account. Fräulein Gelsicher was wishing that either girl had a mother who would be of some use in such matters. She was also rather impatient at the English girl's extraordinary innocence; she liked her, she respected her acquirements and still more her uprightness, but the spectacle of a governess who knew so much less of the world or of life than the pupil seemed to her slightly absurd. How like the Marchesa Suzy to have pitched on this pretty inexperienced creature, out of all the governesses in the world!—when what Marietta most needed was a wise firm middle-aged head and hand, to guide her through the distressing complexities of her family circle.

The Marchesa Suzy, however inadequate she might be about governesses, was always at pains to live on pleasant and correct terms with her relations, even those whom she liked least; and in pursuit of this laudable end she set out one day soon after the Marchesa Nadia's departure to call on Roffredo's mother, the Countess Livia, at Castellone. She took Almina and Marietta with her for the drive, exhorting them to put on "something suitable"—Almina interpreted this as an indication for more or less her "best", and wore a frock of pale green silk and the famous green hat.   Sitting opposite her in the carriage, Suzy observed her, thinking— "if she knew how to do her hair, she would be quite devastatingly pretty"; she smiled with rather malicious amusement to think how acutely the Countess Livia would disapprove when she saw her.   Slowly, methodically, the fat white horses trotted along the eight miles of white road which led to Castellone; their white hairs blew back, streaking Marietta's frock of cherry-coloured linen; a cloud of white dust rose behind the carriage, and after its passage settled gently again on the looped vines and mulberry trees which bordered the road, and drifted out over the fields of maize, now getting tall and green.   This generation knows nothing of the peculiar charm of those summer roads, bordered with vegetation white with dust, and the hot smell of dust, of horse-dung, and the acrid ammoniacal smell of the horses themselves. The young Marchesa wore a soft tulle veil, covering the brim of her hat and drawn down under her chin to fasten tightly at the back, to protect her face; a soft cream tussore dust-coat covered her dress—she chided Marietta for not having put on hers, and recommended Miss Prestwich to get one the next time they were in Gardone.   Almina and Marietta, however, did not mind the dust and the horse-hairs; Almina was pleased to be going to see Castellone, so familiar from a distance, at close quarters, Marietta sat watching the pleasant country-side, the delicate groups of acacias on the knolls, the fine slender trunks of the poplars, and beyond them, the line of the mountains.   All that Gardone country is like the backgrounds of early Italian pictures, where behind the Madonna, through some architectural opening, spreads a distance of blue mountains beyond small feathery trees; and Marietta loved it.

The Countess Livia received them in a high cool room with heavy hangings, smelling faintly of damp and of camphor, where they sat on high-backed carved and brocaded chairs, and were offered *petits fours* and dark syrupy Marsala in small glasses—a peculiarly unrestoring form of refreshment after a long hot drive, but the only one ever thought of in ordinary Italian country houses in those days. The Countess Livia, long, thin and black, glanced from time to time at Miss Prestwich with precisely that expression of slightly martyred condemnation which Suzy had expected—it amused her, but could hardly be said to have an exhilarating effect on the party as a whole. Then there was an interruption—the Countesses Aspasia and Roma di Castellone were announced. "Dio mio, I might have known it!" Marietta whispered irrepressibly to her governess—"they must have seen the carriage from the window!"

Their entrance enlivened the atmosphere, all the same. The good sisters had a perfectly sound piece of news. Ernest di Castellone, another nephew of Countess Livia's—he with the smart Belgian wife—had suddenly re-opened the question of selling or otherwise disposing of Castel Vecchio, a small property of the Castellone family lying some miles away to the South, which had been standing empty for years. "Ernest says, if it were done up, some rich American would certainly take it," Countess Roma observed. "What is your view, Suzy? You know so many Americans."

Before the Marchesa could answer, Countess Aspasia intervened. There was a difficulty about the title—before selling the house, it would be necesary to arrange one owner who could be empowered to treat. "But whose is it?" the Marchesa Suzy asked, surprised.

"That is the point—it appears that it belongs in equal shares to eighty-one members of the Castellone family," Aspasia said, with a sort of measured amusement in her tones. "Francesco, Suzy, would be a holder, and I suppose Marietta too. It is very complicated — all the collaterals have a share."

Marietta, her name being mentioned, was encouraged to open her mouth. "Oh Mama, I have never even seen Castel

I

Vecchio! Could we not go there, for a picnic? I should so love to see it."

"You want to survey your property, do you, you mercenary little thing?" her mother said, laughing at her. "I don't know—it is a long way; thirty kilometres at least."

The picnic plan, however, found strong support from the two spinsters. It was years since they had seen Castel Vecchio, they would love to see it again—dear Elena would certainly put them up at Odredo for it, to shorten the distance —"and with plenty of carriages, we could all drive over—rest the horses, see the place, and drive back."

While this plan was under discussion, there was a further interruption. Count Roffredo burst in, exclaiming—"Dio mio, Mama, where in the universe are all my books?"—and then stopped short, finding the room full of people. Only for a moment, however—then he went round the circle, with his usual pleasant assurance, kissing hands all the way, except for the two girls. Marietta at once invoked his support for the picnic plan, and he gàve it enthusiastically—any jaunt which involved driving his car perilously about the Province was sure of Roffredo's approval. Then, with a further enquiry as to the whereabouts of some engineering books which he wanted, he bowed himself out with skilful ease.

What the Sorellone had really come for, however, was not merely to discuss Castel Vecchio, but to learn all they could about the Marchesa Nadia and her affairs, a matter on which the Countess Livia herself was not without curiosity. A polite enquiry from Countess Roma as to the Russian's departure soon produced the desired effect—Livia, with a repressive glance, suggested that Marietta must be tired of sitting indoors, and that she might like to show Miss Prestwich the garden. Marietta dutifully agreed, but once outside the door, far sooner than her governess thought prudent—"Now they will set to!" she exclaimed, "and have it all out. Povera Zia Nadia! Why should they discuss her misfortunes?"

Once out of doors, however, her attention was quickly

distracted. From the lowest of several shady terraces, screened with ilexes and cypresses, and formal with tubbed myrtles and oleanders, they looked out, in the casual Italian manner, over a sort of steading or farmyard, surrounded by buildings, where fowls scratched among waggons, and a couple of bullock-teams stood, waiting to be unharnessed. In one of the sheds a number of women were gathered, and Marietta cried out—"Oh, see, they are taking the silk! Come and look."

They made their way down to the yard. There, in a long open-fronted shed, a dozen or more women and girls were at work, unwinding the raw silk from the still living cocoons of the silk-worms. The two girls watched the whole process. Into shallow pans of lukewarm water, (whose temperature was carefully tested with her naked elbow by an old crone, who greeted Marietta with much affection as "Marchesina") were flung two or three handfuls of the curious little sausage-shaped cases, from a heap on the ground—they floated, covering the surface of the water like little dirty paper balloons. As each pan was ready a woman began very gently stirring and turning the cocoons till they were wet all over—then, with a sort of whisk or brush of coarse twiggy 'gran turco' she began, very lightly and delicately, to half-sweep, half-whip across the surface of the floating mass. Gradually the papery covering disintegrated, and fine single threads of silk began to cling to the brush; she went on sweeping and whipping till from every floating cocoon one of those gossamer filaments clung to the bundle of twigs, in a long fine cloud that reminded Almina of a comet's tail. Now the woman pulled out this tail to a yard or more in length, broke off the brush, made the end of the skein of fibres fast to a small wicker distaff, and then began with a smooth flicking movement of the wrist to wind the silk onto it off the floating cocoons, yard after yard, interminably. The two girls watched, fascinated—all down the shed, into which dusty shafts of sunlight poured, the women stood, turning the distaffs with a peculiar rhythmic movement, very graceful, while the sheeny yellowish filaments grew on them till each woman seemed to be waving a little golden baton. "It's like drawing out star-light and winding it up," Marietta said, her dark eyes alight with pleasure. Almina asked what became of the robbed cocoons, which lay, looking curiously thin and naked, in a growing pile on a cloth on the ground.

"Oh, they are all right—it does them no harm, for the water is of just the heat they like," the child replied—"old Ida sees to that. What are needed to grow, to make more silk-worms, they keep—what becomes of the others I really don't know. Senta, Ida—" and she turned to the old woman and asked her the question.

"The hens have them, Marchesina," the old creature replied, grinning, "it makes them lay."

At this point Count Roffredo strolled up—he had observed them from above and came down to see, as he said gaily, what they were up to.

"It is I who teach Miss Prestwich now, about silk-worms," Marietta said. The young man wandered about, rallying the women in the shed—he slipped a bundle of the loose golden floss off one of the filled distaffs, and gave it to Almina, saying "It is just the shade of your hair." Almina coloured—the women, overhearing, laughed and echoed the remark. But Roffredo was soon bored with the silk-worm shed, and suggested showing Miss Prestwich the garden. Marietta was by this time involved in listening to a long recital by old Ida about the doings of her grand-children—"Yes, go—I follow you in a minute," she said hastily.

So the young man and Miss Prestwich went off together, up into the garden again. Almina was rather acutely conscious that this was by no means what Countess Livia had intended, but comforted herself with the reflexion that Marietta would join them in a few moments. That however was by no means Count Roffredo's intention. He led his companion off along the terraces, out to a part of the garden

which lay beyond the red wing, where the Sorellone lived—
this was wilder, with open stretches of rough grass between
groups of stone pines, and straggling thickets of privet and
arbutus. It was a hot quiet afternoon, with a heavy stillness
in the air suggesting thunder somewhere about; crickets
shrilled wildly in the dry grass, and the loaded sweetness of
the privet-blossom, the fine aromatic fragrance of the sun-
warmed pines came to them in alternation as they walked
along the narrow unkempt paths. A curious disquiet, like
the thunderous overcharged heat of the day, held them both;
they had never been alone together before, and this solitude
was heavy with possibilities of which both were aware.
Almina was at once nervous and excited, and yet full of a
strange physical lassitude—she would have liked, from sheer
weakness, to sit on one of the rather tumble-down wooden
seats which occurred here and there, but was too timid to
suggest it. She was waiting for she did not quite know
what—for something vaguely wonderful to happen, in
which the young man beside her would play a prominent,
perhaps an alarming part. Roffredo was waiting for something too, but in a much more practical way. He knew perfectly well what he wanted—to take the small delightful
figure beside him into his arms, feel her firm supple shape,
and kiss her a great deal, especially at that delicious place
where the fine pale gold of her hair, the little soft strands and
tendrils, melted into the golden-white skin of her neck—all
turned now to an incredible delicate transparency in the green
shadow of her hat. But it was more complicated than that,
too; he liked her enormously, this little English girl, with her
quiet rather definite manner, her surprising botanical knowledge—Roffredo loved precise knowledge about anything—
and a sort of dainty firmness that there was about her altogether. Besides kissing her, he wanted to make her like him,
and like being kissed by him—and he was not at all sure that
she did, or would. Anyhow these things had to be done
nicely, gracefully—had to be led up to; and he found himself

slightly at a loss how to lead up to it with this girl of another nationality—which all added to his sense of tension. While he was making conversation, with unwonted awkwardness, he noticed a flower growing in the grass on the slope above them, a flower with small bluish-purple stars at the top of narrow trumpets. In a moment he was after it, and brought it down to her—"Of course you know what that is?" he said, smiling.

She examined it carefully. "I think it is *Gentiana amarella*, only it is out rather early," she said. "But then of course, it is hotter here."

"Won't you wear it; it is pretty," he said; and Almina pinned it into the breast of her green dress with the emerald and diamond brooch which her Mother had given her. The skein of raw silk was in her way, and he took it from her hand—when she had finished, he held it up beside her hair, smiling, and said "They do match exactly. Your hair is like sunshine—did you know?"

The words were light enough, but the sense of anticipation that had been holding the pair made them heavy with an unexpected significance, like the hot air of the afternoon.

"No," Almina said, colouring.

"But your eyes are grave," the young man went on, still studying her face, "like the day before sunrise. That is beautiful too. Cara signorina"—his persistent glance was half-gay, half-tender—"have you any idea how beautiful you are? I want so much to know."

The directness of this attack put Almina quite out of countenance. "Signor Conte, I wish you would not say these things to me," she protested.

"Why not? Since they are true, and must be pleasant to hear?"

"It—it is not suitable," the girl said, with a rather pathetic attempt to recover her usual self-possessed manner. But it was too hard for her. He was standing so near her, out there in the lonely end of the garden, with nobody about—

surveying her so serenely, so freely, as one might a bird in one's hand—smiling so quietly.   His smile reminded her of something—what was it?   Yes—she remembered; it was her dream of two or three nights before, when she had seen herself as a bird caught among the limed twigs, and he standing over her.   That memory gave the moment an intolerable quality —obeying an impulse that she could neither analyse nor control, she turned away, and walked a step or two forward along the path.

At once he was beside her again.   "Signorina, what is it? I haven't offended you, have I?"

"No—but I would really rather you did not say those things to me," she said, recovering herself a little.

"Because you are the governess?   It always seems so ridiculous to me that you should be a governess at all!   Why are you?"

"Because my Father died, and now we have so little money," she answered.

"I thought your Father was a lord," the young man said.

"No—he was a doctor.   You are thinking of my grandfather.   But he isn't rich either," she said, amused at his tone. "Lords are often poor."

"È vero?   I did not know."   He made some enquiries about her relations, which the girl answered happily enough— it pleased her to talk about them, and she felt that she had safely turned a dangerous corner.   But there she was mistaken.   Her sudden movement away from him had taken him by surprise; it had roused both his curiosity and his instinct for pursuit—shaken him, in fact, out of his rather calculated methods of dealing with her.   To kiss a girl the first time one got the chance was always a mistake, and he had been telling himself so for some minutes past—but now, coming to a seat —"Let us sit," he said; and then, turning to her—"Why did you turn away from me, just now?" he asked, urgently.

Young women in Almina's day, perhaps wisely, never attempted a truthful answer to such a question.   She hesitated a moment. "Because I did not like you to say those things to me," she said.

"But I was not speaking then. I was only looking at you," he protested. "May I not even do that?"—and he bent forward to peer in under the brim of her hat. And as she coloured and was silent, unable to think of a reply, suddenly he took her two hands. "Ah cara, you are too lovely—you must let me look at you," he said, with a sort of half-mocking tenderness. The startled helplessness of her face, now so close to his, was too much for him—forgetting all calculations, he drew her towards him and kissed her, slowly and gently, but with expert mastery.

The girl was too shaken and too inexperienced in such things to attempt any protest, when at last he let her go. "I must go," she said tremulously, getting up. "The Marchesa may be waiting."

"Yes, you must go, cara," Count Roffredo said, springing up too. "Along there—it is shorter. I shall go straight to the car—I have made my adieux. But I shall see you again—soon!" He turned down another path and was gone.

Almina walked quickly back towards the house. In the heaving confusion of her feelings one thought alone stood out clearly—the fear of being late. And where was Marietta? To her great relief, on one of the terraces she came on her pupil, seated on the parapet propped against an urn, one long black leg dangling, gazing out at the mountains—it was obvious that she was making, and had made, not the smallest effort to rejoin her instructress.

"There you are! I thought you were going to follow us," Almina said.

The child looked tranquilly at her.

"I did come up, quite soon," she replied, "but I saw your dress through the trees along there, and I thought Roffredo was probably going to take you for a regular walk, so I stayed here. You're not cross, are you?" she said, slipping off the wall and tucking her arm through that of her governess.

"Roffredo is always amusing, and you see me so much. Where is he?"

"He has gone to his car. But we had better hurry in—your Mother may be waiting," Almina said.

"She will not be. They have plenty to talk about," Marietta said easily. To Almina's relief the child did not appear to notice her failure to take up the question of whether she were cross or not. It would have been a difficult one to answer—she did not herself yet know, in her turmoil of emotions, whether she was glad or sorry that this had happened. She must think it all out later. But on the long drive home she did not really think at all—she sat silent and dreamy on the swaying small seat of the victoria, looking back at that tree-strewn slope below the red wing at Castellone, when now and then a turn of the road brought it into view, as at some strange outpost of a magic realm, a place that did not belong in the real world at all. The horses' hoofs beat out a slow rhythm in her head as she sat, jigging through the golden afternoon countryside, while their white hairs again settled, unnoticed, on her green silk dress.

But the day's emotions were not yet over for Almina. They got in late, and found Giulio hanging about, rather cross —he had brought over an essay to be corrected by Miss Prestwich, and now there was not time. His Aunt charitably suggested his staying to dine, if Miss Prestwich did not mind dealing with the essay afterwards; Count Carlo was also coming over to the six o'clock dinner, and they could drive back together. It was still hot in the school-room when Miss Prestwich and her second pupil repaired there after coffee, and Giulio suggested an adjournment to somewhere out of doors. Almina, tired and with a headache, was glad to agree. The terrace was still occupied by the family party, so they went and sat in the *torrino*, and Almina tried to listen carefully to Giulio's odd English constructions; but all the time, across his words, her mind heard others, and how different! "Ah cara, you are so lovely," and "I wonder if you have any idea how

beautiful you are." The essay corrected, they sat on for a
little while in the summer-house—it was cool there, and quiet,
and Giulio was a silent and unexacting companion. At last
however he broke the silence.

"The day you came, Marietta and I sat and watched for you
here," he said. "Did she tell you?"

"No."

"We were so anxious for you to come, to teach us both,"
he pursued. "We talked about what you would be like. Of
course we expected you to be just like Gela, only more
learned. And when I saw you, just at first, I was horrified!
You were so young. I thought—'How can *she* teach anyone
anything?' Did you see how aghast I was?"

Almina laughed. "No, I was too flustered, I think—it
was all so new."

He looked at her, gravely now. "The reality is no longer
a disappointment," he said, earnestly.

Almina said, with equal gravity, that she was glad. Oh,
that was what was so wonderful about her, the young man
thought, watching her quiet face—her seriousness, her simplicity. So young, so lovely—but she could sit with a man
in an arbour, on a summer's evening, without any smiling or
beguiling or airs or tricks; without consciousness. For all
her youth and beauty she *was* like Gela, after all—learned
and grave and good; the only sort of woman with whom one
could be at peace, with whom one's heart could find a home.
A feeling that was close to adoration stirred in him as he
watched her sitting there, so unconscious and quiet—adoration and yet comfort. "I am so glad you came," he said
suddenly.

"So am I," Almina said, smiling happily back at him. But
she was thinking, as she spoke, of the smell of the privet
and the pines, over at Castellone that afternoon.

On their way back to the house they took the longer path,
which dropped down through olives and cypresses to join the
one which led along the ridge towards Odredo. As they

descended, they saw Count Carlo and the Marchesa Suzy strolling leisurely along this path, talking; they were too far off for their words to be audible, but their gestures made a sort of diagram of their conversation—of a request or affirmation on his side, an amused negation on hers. Something about the intimacy of the whole picture struck sharply on Miss Prestwich's consciousness; it gave her a slight shock. Then, as the two figures moved slowly out of sight behind a group of arbutus, she pushed the thought from her. Italians were always so expansive in their manner—she must not start imagining things.

Giulio however had no such scruples. Coming on top of his meditations about Miss Prestwich, the picture presented by his Father had struck him, too, with unusual force.

"How I dislike my Aunt!" he exclaimed abruptly.

"You should not do that," Almina said, as in duty bound.

"But I do! It is not only that—I disapprove of her," he said vigorously. "She has always been the same—the Enchantress!—she must have a man dangling after her! At her age, it is ridiculous. She makes a perfect fool of my Father. And now it is Roffredo she is after—so Elena says. Certainly it would not surprise me! She was flirting with him enough the other day. It—it is unseemly!" he said, striking his essay angrily against the trunk of an olive-tree as he passed it.

This was more than Almina could let pass. "Count Giulio, I cannot allow you to say these things in my hearing." she said, with a firmness that he had never seen her use before. "*That* is unseemly, if you like. The Marchesa is my employer, and I live in her house—I cannot have her so spoken of."

"That is just what I hate," the young man muttered furiously. "You, of all people! I cannot——" he subsided, obviously struggling to regain his self-control.

"All this is very foolish—you exaggerate," Almina said, with a coldness that she did not quite feel; "Elena is very reckless in what she says, and she does not mean half of it.

You should not pay any attention to her." She was startled and puzzled by Giulio's outburst, and felt that she must rebuke him for it; but she had come to have a warm, almost a motherly feeling for him—his enthusiasm, his difficulties, his eager desire to learn; the same sort of sympathetic affection that was growing in her for Marietta. They both needed so much help, from someone—help which she was happy to feel that she was beginning to give. But they both had this extraordinary recklessness and openness of speech and thought about their elders, which must be checked. Well, she had checked it now—Giulio walked silent and submissive beside her on their way back to the house. But before she slept that night Miss Prestwich found herself thinking a good deal about his words. Coming on top of her own shock at the sight of the Count and the Marchesa, they made a very uncomfortable impression, which she could not wholly brush aside. She remembered how she too had noticed the Marchesa's manner with Count Roffredo the evening after their walk to the bird-catcher's house. Ah, but as far as Roffredo was concerned, it was not true; she knew better! She fell asleep with a smile on her lips.

## Chapter Ten

GIULIO drove back to Odredo with his Father that night in a very angry and dissatisfied frame of mind. Miss Prestwich's firmness had silenced his words, but it was very far from having suppressed his feelings. Indeed it had increased them. She was blind, because her eyes were too pure to see; she was loyal, because that was her nature—so stoutly loyal to a person so unworthy of her loyalty! He felt that he could hardly bear it. He glanced now and then with aversion at the silhouette of the Count's head and beard, as he sat beside him, profiled against the warm starlight—smoking a cigar, humming an air, with every appearance of a man very well pleased with himself; and when his Father asked him some kindly question about his progress with his English lessons, he actually swallowed before replying, as though it required a physical effort to overcome his distaste.

The fact was that the first result of Giulio's feeling for Miss Prestwich, which had been growing steadily during the last weeks, had been to focus his attention on his Aunt Suzy much more closely than ever before. / This often happens—the intensity with which one sees one person suddenly opens one's eyes to others. / For years Giulio, disliking his Aunt, had both avoided her and avoided, as it were, looking at her; since Miss Prestwich's arrival he had been constantly at Vill' Alta, for one thing, and for another had begun to study the young Marchesa with eyes made critical by having a standard of contrast close at hand. And in this new clear-sightedness he had become aware of her flirtation with his Father. So far, he thought it no more than that; but even that was sufficient to startle and disgust him. And this feeling, vague at first, had been crystallised sharply this evening by that sight

133

of them together, when he was walking with Almina.   He
was horrified that *she* should see it too—it seemed a revolting
form of insult to her; and his irritated disapproval had been
turned, by this slight episode, against his Father as well as
his Aunt.

Now Giulio was filial enough to be distressed by this.
Like both Elena and Marietta, and indeed most of the poor
man's immediate relations, Giulio had hitherto slightly, but
on the whole tolerantly, despised his parent; they did not
understand one another in the least, and the boy was often
fretted by his Father's obtuseness about his own plans, but
there had always been a measure of affection between them.
Nothing like this acrid anger and disgust had ever moved him
before, and it made him very uncomfortable.   He spent a
wretched night.   Waking, next morning, in his sun-filled
room at Odredo, overlooking the wide courtyard, flanked
by low buildings—stables on one side, cellars, wine-presses
and store-houses on the other—he went out onto the balcony, and there, drinking his morning chocolate, he tried as
usual to think it all out.   Almost unconsciously, shocked
by his feelings of the night before, he endeavoured to push the
whole onus for them onto the Marchesa.   He was fair-minded
enough to ask himself· *why* he should so much dislike her
flirtations, and found, or thought he found, his answer.   She
was frivolous about Love; even that she could not take
seriously.   If she had had a despairing grand passion for someone, he could have forgiven or even approved it—but not this
laughing lightness.   He remembered his thoughts about the
peasants on the road leading out of Gardone, on the day when
he first heard of Miss Prestwich's coming—that only things
deeply felt affect the spirit.   There was no merit, no value, in
this mechanical reaction to a man's attention, such as his Aunt
displayed with both his Father and Roffredo.

But these meditations did not console him much and, as
was his habit in any distress, he eventually turned to Fräulein
Gelsicher for reassurance and comfort.   He found her in her

room, her grey hair up, but still arrayed in her petticoat and cambric peignoir—to his disappointment Elena was with her, similarly attired, and in a high state of indignation over something. "But I do not *want* them" she was saying, tapping her governess on the shoulder with an open letter. "I tell you, Gela, that I do *not* want them! Neither here, nor at the picnic. And nor does Marietta. They spoil everything, asking and prying; and grumbling! 'Is not this grass damp? Should we not be better in the sun? Or perhaps in the shade? Teh-ha-ha-ha!'"—and she gave a very tolerable imitation of the Countess Roma's foolish laugh.

"What do the Sorellone want now?" Giulio enquired gloomily—he recognised the laugh.

Elena wheeled round on him. "Ma, to come to this picnic that we are to have at Castel Vecchio," she said, pouring out her words even while she kissed him. "And to stay *two* nights here, the one before and the one after! I have had Marietta's note about it only last night, and already this morning they invite themselves! They impose on everyone. Why should we have them? They are bores and mischief-makers."

"You must have them because it is your duty to be courteous and even generous to relations, particularly those who are old, not rich, and like myself, unmarried," the governess said calmly. "Go and write the note, Elena—the servant is waiting."

The girl went up and gave the Swiss woman a little shake. 'You mean creature, Gela! You always use your spinster-hood and great antiquity as a stick to beat me with," she said. "Very well—but I hate it, and I shall get even with them somehow."

"Make it graceful," Fräulein Gelsicher admonished, un-moved, as Elena went out. Then she turned with a pleasant smile and said "Good-morning, Giulio. Can I do anything for you?"

The young man fidgeted about the room for some moments

before replying, picking up the things on the toilet-table and setting them down. At length, coming to a halt in front of Fräulein Gelsicher—"Gela, can nothing be done to stop this business between my Father and Zia Suzy?" he burst out. "It is so—unpleasant."

This was completely unexpected. The Swiss looked at him with concern, and then said, in her usual measured tones —"They are very old friends, Giulio."

"They are not friends at all!" he replied, explosively. "It is a regular flirt! She behaves with him just as she is beginning to do with Roffredo, only more so. Last night we saw them together when they did not know it—it was horrid. It is unseemly, Gela—one's Father and one's Aunt!"

This was so precisely the governess's own view that she found it hard to answer. She wondered exactly how much the boy *had* seen—without knowing that she was rather in the dark. Knowing Suzy, it might have been anything! She said very gravely—"Giulio, if you wish me to listen to statements like this, you must be more precise. Tell me exactly what happened."

"Dunque, Miss Prestwich had been correcting my essay in the *torrino*, because it was so hot; and afterwards—" he rehearsed the small episode. "It was somehow particularly disagreeable, seeing it with her," the boy concluded.

"Did she speak of it?" Fräulein Gelsicher asked, relieved that it was no worse.

"*I* did. I said I disliked Zia Suzy and her goings on. And she shut me up, and said she would not listen if I spoke so——"

"Perfectly right," Fräulein Gelsicher interjected.

"But Gela," the boy went on, more quietly now, "it *is* horrible. It made me feel horrible towards Papa. I do not think it is his fault—it is hers; but I dislike him for it, and I hate that. And it does no one any good, this flirtatious sort of love; it is a travesty. Love should engage the whole energy of the spirit, and teach the soul to use her wings still

more. It aspires, or kneels; it does not flirt and laugh."
He went on in this strain for some time; Fräulein Gelsicher
listened patiently, and now and then she sighed. Giulio
treated her to these philosophical discourses occasionally, but
she had never heard one on love before, and guessed, shrewdly
enough, that Miss Prestwich was at the bottom of it. This
was a complication she had early foreseen; and, once again,
it was the Marchesa Suzy they had to thank for it—getting a
girl like that for governess, with no enquiries! However,
when Giulio had done she merely gave him a few quiet words
on the unwisdom of attempting to judge others without full
knowledge and comprehension. "You will find plenty to
do to manage your own soul, my dear Giulio," she ended up;
"be a dutiful son and an affectionate brother, and leave your
elders alone." And since he had been allowed to say his say,
this rather flat admonition seemed to pacify the boy, and he
took himself off to his work.

Giulio di Castellone was not the only person in the Province of Gardone to spend that morning in disturbing
thoughts. Miss Prestwich woke early, to see the eastern sun
pouring through the olives outside her windows—it streamed
into the room, making brilliant oblongs on the polished floor
—oblongs with a little wavering pattern in them, which
shifted as the leaves outside stirred in the breeze. She lay
watching them, running her forefinger round the edges of the
large squares of lace let into the coverlet on the bed, and
thinking about herself and Roffredo di Castellone. Last
night, what with the changing for dinner in a hurry, Giulio's
essay, and then the fuss he had made about the Count and the
Marchesa, she had had no time to think the whole thing out—
now she must, she must get it all straight.

The emotion of love itself, we are told, does not greatly
vary from age to age; but the preoccupations of those who
love, with regard to it, do change from one generation to
another. Today the main concern of serious young men and
women who find themselves in love is to be sure that their

emotion is a good sound genuine one, and that it is getting a free and healthy expression. They are a good deal less concerned with the social or even with the moral aspect—in fact for them this question of the genuineness or spuriousness of their love has practically become the moral aspect. All this was different thirty years ago. Serious young women, at any rate, in those days had very few doubts about the quality of their own feelings—they assumed their genuineness with touching simplicity. The important question was the nature of the young man's love. Was it "pure"? (If one was sufficiently fond of him, one generally assumed that it was.) Would it lead to marriage? Did one love one's young man more than one's God? (This question actually occurred, more euphemistically expressed, in some of the little Communion handbooks of the period.) In fact the moral and social aspects were paramount. One wondered, after being kissed, "how much it meant", and how to comport oneself.

Almina, lying in bed at Vill' Alta that morning, her yellow plaits hanging down over her high frilled nightdress, her grey eyes serious and absorbed, asked herself such questions as these. The breathless bewilderment, the sort of shivering wonder of those moments at Castellone still overcame her when she remembered them; but she tried earnestly to be practical; to decide, in fact, "how much it meant." And then there was the matter of being prudent, as she had promised her Mother she would. Just what did being prudent, in this connection, amount to? She had better be rather guarded, rather aloof; tell him again, if occasion arose, that she would rather he paid her no more compliments. Prudence could not involve anything so drastic as not seeing him again, which was in any case impracticable. But what about not seeing him again alone? He still talked about that walk to the orchis wood—would that be prudent? The very thought of that made her heart beat in a curious thumping way—no, that would probably not be prudent. It was all so complicated. Perhaps she was exaggerating the whole thing—on the other hand, apart from her being the governess here, there was no earthly reason why he should not pay her attentions, if his feelings were—well, of the right sort! And his words about her position and her parents seemed to show that he recognised this. (Almina, like most young women, tended to fasten on words as her principal witnesses in these secret tribunals.) But what she did not, at any point of this meditation, do was to ask herself exactly what her own feelings were. It never occurred to her that this was the crux of the matter, in regard to prudence and everything else. Quite innocently, about this she quietly set about deceiving herself.

On another point, however, she did try to be honest. After all, she was the governess, and a member of the family was making love to her. That being so, she realised that she ought really to go straight to the Marchesa, tell her what had happened, and ask what she wished her to do? But that might involve her leaving—she had no idea how much or how little fuss such an admission would cause, out here—and then she would be back on her Mother's hands, and all the fearful expenditure on these clothes wasted; when it was not her fault. Besides, the scene she had witnessed the previous evening, and still more Giulio's words about the Marchesa and Roffredo, seemed to make it impossible to speak to her, of all people, on the subject. And yet not to tell her was not quite straight. The oblongs of sunlight shifted across the floor; Graziella the maid came in, bringing her breakfast on a tray—the coffee, the plate of figs, the curious starfish-shaped rolls, with four twisted points, which represented the only form of wheaten bread in the Province, and the funny little pieces of toast, less than two inches square, which were cut out of these rolls; Almina ate with appetite, while Graziella carried steaming cans of hot water into the *cabinet de toilette* for her bath, but still without having reached any conclusion as to what to do. At last a solution occurred to her—when she got the chance, she would consult Fräulein Gelsicher. From her she would certainly get wise and

trustworthy advice.    Braced by the decision she sprang up,
breathed the air at the window for a moment, and then ran
into the *cabinet de toilette* to bathe and dress.

The next few days passed, however, without Almina's
getting any chance to speak privately with the Swiss.    Elena
or Marietta were always about—moreover Fräulein Gelsicher
was unusually busy, wrestling with Ospedi's confused estimates of the probable cost of re-planting portions of the vineyards at Meden, where Count Carlo's best wine came from, in
the new French manner.    She suspected these estimates of
being either extravagant or inadequate, or both, and insisted
on getting them clear before allowing the Count to embark on
the scheme.    Foolish man!—for half what he proposed to
spend on these miserable grapes, the governess reflected, he
could send Giulio away to Oxford, give the boy his heart's
desire, and remove him in time from the dangerous proximity
of Miss Prestwich—who was none the less a danger for being
a good, sober little thing, so far as one could see.    And so it
came about that the day of the picnic to Castel Vecchio arrived
without Almina's having unburdened herself of her secret to
anyone.

The picnic had developed into a monster of an affair.
Except for the old Marchesa, the entire party from Vill' Alta
was going, even the Marchese Paolo; Countess Livia was
bringing Ernest di Castellone's wife, with her small boy and
his nurse, and some neighbours from Macerbo; then there
were to be two carriage-loads from Odredo, including the
Sorellone, who had driven over the previous evening in their
pony-carriage, according to their own unwelcome plan—
finally Roffredo was coming in his car.    But when the carriages began to assemble on the great sweep of gravel in front of
the house at Vill' Alta, between the portico and the geranium-
beds, and the sorting out of parties and allocation of picnic-
baskets began, the Sorellone proved to be absent.    Fräulein
Gelsicher gave a little note from the Countess Aspasia to Suzy
—"Countess Roma is unwell; some interior derangement;

Countess Aspasia did not care to leave her—indeed they think of sending for the Doctor," she murmured to her hostess, with an expression of kind concern on her plain face. Suzy opened the note, glanced at the contents, wrinkled her nose and said "*Tant pis!*" airily—then she went on with her arrangements. "Livia, will you take Paolo with you?"

But when Almina and Marietta were installed in a brake with Tino, Ernest's boy, his nurse, and a vast array of hampers, Marietta muttered to her governess as they drove off—"I wonder what Elena has been up to. Did you see her face as Gela told Mama of Zia Roma's illness? She had on her wicked look." Almina had in fact noticed a peculiar expression of bland attention about Elena when the news of Countess Roma's indisposition was announced, and had wondered what it portended. "Whatever it is, she will tell us as soon as she gets the chance," she replied, in the same tone, "but she would hardly go so far as to make anyone ill."

Marietta laughed. "As to telling us, you are right," she said. "You are getting to know Elena, Postiche!" Count Carlo's nickname had crept round via the cousins to Marietta, and she had begun, tentatively at first, to use it—Almina rather liked it, regarding it as a mark of confidence; but she would not allow her pupil to use it in front of anyone but Elena and Fräulein Gelsicher. While she listened to Marietta's chatter she was wondering rather nervously how much she would see of Roffredo today, and also whether this outing would give her the chance she so much desired of speaking to Fräulein Gelsicher; and in her mind, during most of the drive, she rehearsed the phrases in which she would put her problem before the older woman.

Castel Vecchio lies well away to the South, in the flat part of the plain of Gardone—the cavalcade of carriages, widely spaced because of the dust, soon left the little crumpled hills, crowned with tufts of acacia, behind, and drove through flat fields where the maize and "gran turco" were taking on the yellowish tinge of late summer, and a smoky purplish bloom was beginning to overspread the bunches of grapes, already swollen to their full size, which hung from the vines bordering the road. The castle itself stands on a high hillock or mound, and for more than a hour before they reached it the picnic party could see, first its high square tower, then the great oblong block of the main building, and finally the curtain wall which runs round the entire circumference of the hill. As they drew nearer, they could see that the whole place was considerably more ruinous than they had expected; there were breaches in the topmost battlements of the tower, and great loops of ivy and wild clematis hung from the broken stonework; hawks wheeled and cried about it. There were gaps in the curtain wall too; the Marchese Paolo observed to Countess Livia that it would cost more than all the eighty-one heirs together could put down to bring the place into repair.

However, on arrival, lunch was the first consideration. Rugs were spread and baskets opened on a stretch of smooth turf beside a small stream which wound round the foot of the mound, in half-shade from a group of poplars which crowned the bank above; bottles of wine were stuck in the running water to cool, salad was rinsed out to refresh it, Umberto and Valentino, the Vill' Alta butler, in Panama hats and striped jackets, ran about arranging cold pies, cold roast duck, sandwiches and rolls on tablecloths on the grass. Elena, during the preliminary strollings about, at once gravitated towards Marietta and Almina; she was clearly seething with something which she burned to impart.

"Dunque, here we are, and no Sorellone!" she began, with her delightful giggle interrupting her words. "Isn't that nice, Marietta?"

"What is the matter with Zia Roma?" Marietta asked.

"Nothing! Nothing in the world." Elena's laughter almost suffocated her. "But she thinks there is, and that is the same thing."

"What did you do?" Marietta asked, rather inquisitorially.

"Why, you know what happens if you put a Seidlitz

Powder in a glass of water? Well, if you put one, flat, on the bottom of a certain article, you do not see it at all—but later, you get the same effect." She laughed again. "So, this morning, round comes Zia Aspasia to Gela—'a little bladder trouble, dear Fräulein Gelsicher. I hope it is not much, but I do not think a long expedition would be prudent.' So, there we are."

"Really, Elena, I do call that a revolting trick," Miss Prestwich exclaimed, while Marietta laughed.

"Not at all, Postiche. It was the one way to get rid of them. Their feelings are not hurt, and now we shall have a perfect picnic."

As far as the lunch went, the picnic was as near perfection as need be. Almina remembered long afterwards some of the details of it: the coffee, steaming hot from squat Chinese tea-pots in padded wicker cases, the little squares of butter floating in water in screw-top jars, to keep them cool—mixed with the picture of Roffredo lounging on the grass at the Marchesa Suzy's feet, indulging in rather lazy gallantries with her, while the chequered sunlight played over her white dress and his white flannels, and made broken metallic lights on his red head. She sat rather quietly watching the whole party, as was her habit when "company" was present, and thinking out schemes for getting Fräulein Gelsicher to herself later on.

The meal over, there was a general adjournment to the castle. They climbed the rough track which led to the gate-house, with its arched entrance, and then dispersed themselves over the wide grassy space, probably once a tilt-yard, within the walls. Peasant families had taken up their abode both in the gatehouse, and in the rooms at the foot of the tower and below the long block of the main building; goats and chickens ran about, washing flapped from windows, decayed ironware rusted in corners. It was all rather squalid, and Countess Livia, sniffing delicately, observed to Fräulein Gelsicher that they had far better leave it as it was, to moulder away. But others, including Count Carlo, were enthusiastic for repairing the place; he led the Marchesa Suzy about, pointing out the splendour of the approach and the view, the solidity of the main structure and the possibilities of the great tiltyard as pleasure-grounds. Great beauty the place undoubtedly had. The main building was entered by an outside staircase of stone, with a carved balustrade, which led up to a fine doorway on the first floor; passing in, one entered a chain of great rooms, each the full depth of the building, their high windows looking out over the courtyard on one side and the plain on the other—the last room had a curved end, like the apse of a church, and large oval windows commanding a view to the east. All the rooms had fine floors of black marble and white stone, and magnificently carved chimney-pieces—there were certainly the makings of a splendid mansion here. A stone staircase led on to the upper floors, but only a few of the elders—Suzy, Count Carlo and Ernest's wife among them— had the energy to inspect even the floor immediately above; here the rooms were smaller and more numerous, but still large and of fine proportions. The young people however ranged everywhere, and carried Almina along with them; she saw from a window that Fräulein Gelsicher was firmly anchored by the Countess Livia's side down in the courtyard, and gave herself up to the always exciting pleasure of explor-ing an empty house. On the third floor they found a door through into the tower, and climbed its stone steps, sending the hawks screaming out in wheeling circles overhead, till the lack of a handrail and the ruinous condition of the stonework drove them back; then they scattered through the rooms on the higher floors, calling to one another to look at this and that. Almina stuck closely to Marietta's side, determined to avoid an encounter with Roffredo tête-à-tête. One room at the eastern end had also a small oval window, now unglazed; leaning out of this to see the view, she noticed a fern growing in the stonework below her. It was difficult to reach, and while she lingered, trying to see what it was and wondering whether it was worth while climbing up onto the sill and

trying to pick it, she failed to notice that Marietta had left the
room. She was recalled by hearing the door, creaking
heavily, pushed to behind her—she turned round, and there
stood Roffredo.

"Is it the view or is it a flower?" he asked, coming over to
her.

"A flower," she replied, leaning forward and indicating the
fern. He too leant out to look, slipping his arm gently round
her as he did so; then he stepped back into the room, drawing
her with him, and said—"I will pick it for you in a minute.
But there is a flower I want to pick for myself first—if I may."
And as she glanced up at him, embarrassed and uncertain,
he stood back from her, holding her so that he could look at
her face. "Cara, do you know that ever since we walked
together at Castellone, nine whole days ago, I have thought
of little else but you?" he said, "and of when I should see you
again like this? Have you thought of me at all?"

Now was of course the moment for displaying that prudence
and firmness on which Almina had been resolving for those
same nine days. But with his arm round her, his eyes on
her face, her heart drinking in the sweet flattery of his words,
it was not easy to be firm. And her own good-breeding in
a sense stood in her way—she found it difficult to say anything so abrupt and awkward as "Let go of me, please,"
or even brusquely to release herself. She made one small
struggle.

"Yes, I did—but not quite like that," she said. "Signor
Conte, I really don't——"

"You did think of me too? Then I shall pick my flower,"
he interrupted, with a sort of triumph, and drew her to him
and kissed her again. Held in his arms, under his kisses, a
physical disturbance of such violence overtook the girl as
she had never known before—thought, scruples, prudence
vanished, blotted out by a sort of anaesthesia that was half
bliss, half something terrifying that she did not understand.
Presently the young man raised his head and looked at her

again; her hat, the childish hat held by the green ribbons under her chin, which she had worn on the walk to Trino's, had fallen back; her closed eyelids, the look of drowned defeat on her face, lying so still there on his arm, moved him curiously. "Ah, lovely little one, how I love you!" he murmured, carried away by an impulse of tenderness which surprised himself; and gently pushing her hat further back, he stroked her sun-silky hair. She opened her eyes then, and looked at him in a sort of bewilderment, like a person waked out of deep sleep; he was at once touched and almost alarmed at the effect his kisses had produced on her. "Little one!" he said again, smiling reassuringly. "Come—let us see if we can see Castellone"; and he led her over to the northern window. They could not—beyond the near flatness of the plain the broken country round Odredo was blurred by the afternoon haze into a dim blue confusion. The movement, the little gay discussion as to whether one higher blue bump was Vill' Alta or not restored the girl a little—her sense of reality began to return, and with it her scruples. Pushing her hair back from her forehead, with a gesture as if to sweep some veil away, she moved gently out of his arm, and made one more effort.

"Signor Conte, this makes me unhappy," she said. "I— I think we should stop."

"You are unhappy with me?" he said, moving over to her again, and taking her hand, while his eyes searched her face. "Does it make you unhappy that I love you?"

Those words again! She could not say it—her eyes went down before his.

"No—only, like this——"

He would not have it. "I do not believe it," he interrupted, drawing her once more into his arms. "Little foolish one, it is not true!" Like the bird-snarer's hand, his face came down on hers again; his kisses silenced her words, that secret anaesthesia engulfed her, sweeping away doubts and prudence on a tidal wave which carried her out of all known depths.    When he had gone, slipping prudently away and bidding her not to follow for a moment or two, she leaned again on the stone sill of the oval window, gazing at the view, the fern forgotten, and telling herself in shy secrecy that this was love at last.

## Chapter Eleven

THE Marchesa Suzy di Vill' Alta was not really very fond of picnics. The kind of shoes she wore made her feet ache if she walked much in them, the stays which moulded her figure so elegantly made sitting on rocks or grass uncomfortable; perpetually holding up a parasol was tiring, and without it the sun was ruinous to one's complexion—also in her experience picnics tended to promote, even among the most civilised people, rather anti-social behaviour. She had agreed to the Castel Vecchio expedition mainly out of pure good nature, because Marietta wished it, partly because she had thought it likely that the day would afford further and possibly amusing opportunities for her rather lazy flirtation with Roffredo di Castellone, which was beginning to entertain her a good deal. There was something intriguing about this young man, apart from his splendid appearance; a sort of free detachment, which she always noticed behind his gallantries, was definitely unusual and provocative; in an idle way she felt that she would like to break this down. However, the day had not been a success from this point of view; Carlo had stuck to her side with tiresome persistence, off again on one of his foolish enthusiasms—poor Carlo!—and Roffredo had disappeared into the upper regions of the castle with the children, and been no more seen. By the time the party began to reassemble by the stream for more coffee before the drive back, Suzy was thoroughly bored. She despatched Carlo to summon the young people, and then sat chatting, with mechanical politeness but without interest, to the Countess Livia and Ernest's wife, fanning away the mosquitoes which began to assail the party, as the sun drew westward and the shadows lengthened, and wishing that the others

would come quickly.    Odd that Roffredo should have made
no move to seek her company the whole afternoon, she
thought—if he had, she could easily have detached the Count
and arranged it.    What could have kept him?    When the
younger elements at length appeared, all together in a chattering laughing group, herded by Carlo, she watched Roffredo
more attentively than usual.    In his manner now she noticed,
or thought she noticed, something which she had not seen before,—a subtle air of disturbance, almost of triumph, hard to
define but to her experienced eye fairly evident.    And looking
round the group to find some counterpart of this expression,
her attention was caught by Miss Prestwich's face.    The girl
had a heightened colour; her eyes were absent and dreamy;
though she was behaving with her usual pretty quiet propriety, there was somehow a bloom, a glow about her that
could hardly be mistaken.

The Marchesa Suzy surveyed the pair with a sort of amused
impatience.    Really, Roffredo might have better taste than to
start a flirtation with the governess!    And Postiche, too, with
her mousy ways—could she be allowing herself to receive
attentions on the sly?    That sort of thing would never do; it
would have to be put a stop to, if it were really so.    Her
years of triumphant beauty made it difficult for her to believe seriously in the success of another woman in her own
house.

Suzy's immediate and instinctive method of putting a stop
to it was to apply herself to Count Roffredo.    By a little
ingenious manipulation, a little laughing display of curiosity,
she contrived to arrange that she should drive back to Vill'
Alta in his car.    Seated beside him, she set to work, and the
lively run of her wit, employed on mutual acquaintances in
Rome and Milan and on concerns familiar to them both, soon
brought him back, as it were, into her orbit—made him show
himself, as usual, charmed and amused.    As they drove she
watched his hands on the wheel.    He had very good hands,
shapely and strong, with sensitive square-tipped fingers; she

noticed their strength and beauty, the fine powdering of golden hairs over the backs, and a little shiver of emotion passed through her.   He was very desirable, Roffredo.   She made their talk now a little more personal, and got an adequate response; Roffredo himself suggested prolonging their drive by making a détour to Macerbo to see the view.   By the time they got back to Vill' Alta both were in that slightly emotional state which is ready for the next step, and feels it a pity to stop.   This was the stage at which Suzy usually terminated an encounter, leaving the man unsatisfied; this evening, however, moved partly by her own feeling, partly by her determination to efface the impression of the afternoon thoroughly, she extended to the young man an invitation to remain to an informal dinner.   He accepted, and stayed. During the meal they were a good deal more discreet than they had been on their drive, but there was enough possession in the Marchesa's manner to make Almina distinctly uncomfortable; and when coffee was over the girl was glad enough to plead the excuse of fatigue to quit a field where it was impossible for her to go, so to speak, into action.

In the house her room was still hot, and she felt vaguely restless.   She shepherded Marietta to bed, and then, throwing a scarf round her shoulders, she slipped downstairs, floated like a shadow through the dusk of the hall, treading unthinkingly on the tessellated Mars and Venus, and went out onto the southern terrace; passing round under the eastern wing she went on to the ridge leading towards Odredo. Away to the north-west a warm glow made the stone pines stand out, sharp black mushroom-shaped stencillings against the gold-stained sky; to the east another glow, more silvery, showed where the moon would soon rise.   It was very warm; the summer night was full of fragrances from the thyme in the grass, from the resinous needles of the pines and from the privet lower down on the northern slopes.   She left the path presently, and in the shelter of an arbutus dropped onto the dry grass—leaning back against its red trunk she stared up

at the sky overhead. How lovely it was here, she thought—
and how beyond measure lovely it would have been if *he* could
be here with her. But in the sense he was, still—his words
still rang in her head, the pressure of his hands and lips came
back to her with dizzying force. Oh yes, this was love all
right, the girl thought, feeling her heart beat, feeling the
strangest sensations shake her all over at the memory of those
words and those kisses. Poor child, no one had ever warned
her of the heady magic of sense-enchantment pure and simple,
and she had no previous experience to go on—she took her
body's testimony as the heart's faithful witness. She linked
her very spirit with this untried experience—watching the
great stars, imperceptibly shifting their position among the
delicate pattern of the arbutus boughs overhead, she had a
sudden vision of the wheeling earth, revolving in a universe
whose size made her gasp, but where love, however small,
and linked to this little earth, blazed down the ages, itself a
star. Now this was hers—she shared it; and she told herself
that her love must arise and shine, be faithful and unafraid,
and not let small trials like the Marchesa's manner to Roffredo
dim its glow.

That lady, meanwhile, had been making her own use of
this summer evening. The terrace emptied gradually of its
after-dinner occupants, but even in the gloom under the ilex
where she lay idly in her hammock, rocked by Roffredo, it
was rather raked by the windows of the house, and eventually
she proposed a stroll. They too took the path along the
Odredo ridge. Success with a man always went a little to
Suzy's head, lit up her beauty like a torch; and she was succeed-
ing with Roffredo. As they walked along now, her face pale,
her eyes splendid in the dusk, she was infinitely alluring; her
scent, her warm low laugh, were intoxicating. He took small
freedoms, with her scarf, her fan; she permitted them, laughing
at him while she did so. They came presently to one of the
many seats with which the ridge was dotted, and sat down.
Her hand was stretched along the back, and—"How beautiful

your hands are," the young man observed, looking thoughtfully at it.

"Well, hands are always something!" she returned, with the merry irony which was one of her strong suits. "For an engineer, you are getting quite expressive, Roffredo."

"There are other and perhaps better ways of expressing oneself than in words," the young man answered; he was at once stirred and provoked by her manner and her presence. And, as she merely continued to laugh, with a brusque movement he took her in his arms and kissed her, with a vigour which had an element of temper in it. She neither yielded nor resisted; gave her lips but not her mouth; supple and pliant, she was self-possessed even in his arms. But she was stirred all the same—his youth and strength, his healthy mouth, his off-hand ways woke a deep secret response in her. And when, the long kiss over, she rose and led him back to the house, letting him know amiably that he was a fool and rather uncouth, in her heart she was telling herself that she would let this go on, for a little while at least.

But Almina, crouched under her group of arbutus, had seen everything—seen, in the strengthening moonlight, the laughing gradual approach of her employer and the young man to whom she had just been dedicating her whole love, his hand playing with the end of her scarf; seen, with dismay, the pair settle down on a seat so close to her that she could not escape without being observed; and while she was still debating what to do, seen, with the incredulity of absolute pain, the Marchesa gathered in Roffredo's arms. Propped against the arbutus trunk she stared at the impossible sight, unable to look away—then she hid her face in her hands, and crouched lower, shivering as if with cold, waiting for the sounds of their departure.

They did not stay long. When they had gone, and the last murmur of voices had died away along the path, she sat up and looked about her. The pines, the flecks of moonlight on the pale grass, the great steady stars overhead were the same as half an hour before, but the girl looked at them with unbelieving and alienated eyes.    In particular she stared at the now empty seat.    The shock of what she had seen had been very great.    It was not only her personal feelings which were wounded, at the very moment of their unfolding; all her instincts, all the traditions of her upbringing were scorched by the sudden picture of this double infidelity.    This was far worse than the unknown Marchese Pipo's unfaithfulness to his wife, because it was so much nearer; this was the mother of her pupil, the mistress of the house she lived in—a woman whom she saw daily, who had been kind to her—whom she had seen in the embrace of the man she believed herself to love and be loved by.    Sheltered as her life had been, with her narrow experience, shades and grades of feeling meant nothing to her; they had kissed, with passion, so they must love.    Then what had Roffredo meant that afternoon?    Oh, but she could not remember that now!    It was profanation. She must bury to-day for ever, never think of it again.    This was the end.    She had been imprudent, foolish—oh, but what *did* it all mean? her heart cried against these arguments. Why kiss her, why speak so to her, if he did not love her? Who would not have believed him?    Had she been so foolish?

But the thought of folly and imprudence reminded her of her mother—and with the memory the thought of her life at home, so safe and certain and straightforward, came sharply to her.    Tears came then, of home-sickness almost as much as of misery; she sat for a long time, sobbing, under the arbutus. She was roused by hearing the uncertain chugging of an engine in the distance; that was Roffredo, going home in his car.    The sound brought a fresh sense of misery and humilia-tion, followed by something like anger.    Well, she thought, dabbing her eyes with a soaked handkerchief, she had learned her lesson—she would never be made a fool of again.    And with this frail buttress against the flood of her unhappiness she went indoors.

In the hall she encountered the Marchesa.    The great

L

chandelier was only half-lit on these summer evenings, but even by its dim light Suzy saw that the girl had been crying; her face was very white, surely? A sudden uncomfortable suspicion crossed her mind.

"You have been out?" she said. "I thought you had gone to bed."

"I went up, but it was so hot, I went out again," Almina said.

"Not far, I hope?" the Marchesa said smoothly, but rather repressively.

"Only in the garden," the girl replied; she and Marietta always regarded the ridge as a sort of annexe of the garden. The Marchesa did not, and the reply satisfied her. Wishing Almina a good night's rest, she let her go on upstairs. But as she went into her husband's study to administer her usual goodnight kiss, she remained a little disconcerted. What was Postiche crying about? And she certainly had looked very white.

## Chapter Twelve

THE picnic to Castel Vecchio was the last gaiety at Vill' Alta for some little time. A couple of days later, members of the family began to arrive for the *consiglio di famiglia*. The diplomat son arrived from Brussels with his wife, a lively Frenchwoman who treated the whole thing as a rather amusing novelty; the playwright son arrived from Paris, and sat scribbling at small sheets of manuscript all the time, even, furtively, during the actual discussions; the cardinal son came from Rome, an austere and rather splendid figure, who amused Suzy by showing at least as much concern for the welfare of his little Pekingese as for that of his brother's immortal soul; Nadia came, graceful and silent as ever; Anastasia, the sister who had married a Colonna, came without her husband—he had, she explained to Suzy, no settled convictions on such subjects; the lawyer came, a little withered man with an apologetic manner, which became dogmatic when he felt sure of his ground, as in the matter of settlements; finally, at the very last moment, Pipo himself arrived, lively, breezy and amusing. Before he came, however, Marietta and Miss Prestwich had been despatched to Odredo, to be out of the way. "You see, it is essential that you avoid contact with the leper," Elena observed to them laughing. Almina winced a little at this levity. Her last picture of the Marchesa Nadia had been sitting in one of the high-backed brocaded chairs of the *salone*, on the evening before they left, while the tide of family talk flowed about her, the fingers of her right hand—her hands that were usually so still—moving to and fro, to and fro, over the broad carved arm, with a curious uncertain movement, as if she were feeling her way in the dark. The girl had found something strangely distressing in that one movement of the silent, impassive, beautiful figure; even in her own unhappiness, she could not get the memory of it out of her head.

Meanwhile at Vill' Alta the discussions, public and private, took their slow and formal course, to the accompaniment of long elaborate meals, when everyone behaved as if nothing out of the way were going on, and it was an ordinary house-party. There was a very general concern as to the effect of the unwonted disturbance on the old Marchesa; her health and her appetite and her sleep were almost as much canvassed as Nadia's relations to her husband. In fact, the old lady was really enjoying herself hugely. The tide of human affairs, of family life, was flowing warmly and strongly about her, active and interesting; she found it most agreeably reviving. She liked having all her surviving children with her too, especially Filippo, the cardinal, who had always been her favourite. He had more vitality and energy than any of the others, except Pipo, and more intelligence than he; Filippo was a true Vill' Alta, she thought, watching him contentedly as he sat in her room of a morning—he, alone of all the family, had the privilege of coming to take his chocolate with her before she was up. His noble head had something about it of the fierce intelligence of a Roman bust of the great early period, but made suave by the addition of that strange blend of diplomacy and theology which is the traditional equipment of the sons of the Roman Church; sitting in his scarlet robe, bending to feed Lao T'su, the little dog, with fragments of roll dipped in the chocolate, he would look up at her and make some remark, with a wise smile of intimate understanding that warmed both her heart and her intelligence through and through. Ah, she could have wished him to marry, Filippo, the flower of the flock!—and leave sons of his own sensibility and intellect and energy to carry on the Vill' Alta tradition. Because who was there? Pipo had only his little girl; Edoardo, the playwright, had not married—he stuck faithfully to his French mistress, the actress; and Antonio's boy was a finicking creature, pure French, wholly the son of his mother, and with, already, a tiresome diplomatic manner which sat on him as absurdly as the red coat on an organ-grinder's monkey.    There was only Marietta who was really a true Vill' Alta, among the grandchildren—and she was a girl.    Strange how little they bred in this generation; and she had had fourteen children!    Pipo had been her chief hope— and now with all this fuss, there was but little chance of Nadia's giving him another child.    As that thought came to her, she sighed.

"What is it, Mama?" Filippo asked, at the small sound.

"I was wondering what had come over you all nowadays, that you don't breed," the old lady said a little impatiently; "there's not a child apiece between the lot of you!"

"*I* can't help that, Mama."

"No—more's the pity!"    She twinkled back at his amused smile.    "But Pipo could have had a fine family, if he were not such a fool.    Nadia is strong, and she is a splendid mother; she suckled Francesca for nine months."

"*Did* she?    That was well," the priest said with approval. "But I am not surprised.    She is a good woman."

"She is a very tiresome one," the old lady said, with a return of her usual irritation on the subject of Nadia.    "Why must she make all this to-do?    Her situation is a very common one! Others have put up with it quietly, and borne a family of children to occupy themselves with.    No, no, none of your mortal sin, and what the Church allows!" she went on holding up her little old hand, as her son made as if to speak.    "You know as well as I do, my dear Filippo, that what I say is true. And the Church's rules have really nothing to do with it!    It is a matter of common-sense."

"Mama, you are a shocking bad Catholic, and I ought not to listen to you!" the priest said, rising.    "No, Lao T'su—no more."    He went over, and kissed the little arbitrary wrinkled hand with much affection.    "In this case, the Church and common-sense stand on the same side," he went on, "as often happens! Here Pipo is really in the wrong; and you know it, and so do I, and so does he. And he must put it right—if he can. If you want grandchildren, talk to him yourself, and tell him he must give up this affair. His wife is his wife; he married her; and for good or ill, she is not the sort of person who *can* endure such a situation. I have watched her—she is almost at the end of her forces." His voice suddenly grew stern. "And by *his* act—the wife whom he swore to cherish! No, Mama—he has no excuse; let him do his duty."

From Filippo alone would the old Marchesa have accepted such language. Quietly, almost submissively, she said— "Very well, my son. But will you not also speak to him?"

"I have. I have pointed out his duty. But he respects me little more than you do, Mama! He says"—there was a curious bland smile that was somehow almost painful about the splendid mouth as he spoke—"that I know nothing of the life of a man! You will do better."

"Pipo *is* a fool," said the old lady, with the deepest conviction. And she took occasion to speak to him privately, which she did with her usual ruthless firmness. "Since, of your own choice, you have married such a wife, you must act accordingly," she told him. "No one chose her for you— you did the thing yourself."

Indeed, both in the general conferences—sitting round the great table in the big library, with its huge carved and painted beams crossing the ceiling—and in private talks, the alternatives were set so squarely before the Marchese Pipo that not even his cheerful suppleness could evade them. He must give up La Panelli, or face the disagreeableness of a separation. Suzy, with her usual merciful common-sense, was all for a separation, thinking that it would be, in the end, the best for Nadia's peace of mind; and in this she was supported by the Cardinal. But Antonio, the diplomat, abetted by his wife, was dead against it; so was Anastasia; Edoardo and Paolo, the two bachelors, unexpectedly and to Suzy's mind rather absurdly came out with a united declaration in the same sense; and, more formidably, La Vecchia Marchesa declared herself unalterably opposed to such a course. The Marchese Francesco stubbornly refused to express an opinion; he merely sat at the head of the table, and asked for, and listened to, the views of others. It was impossible to find out what Pipo really wanted; Nadia, whenever addressed, merely repeated very quietly—"I should prefer to separate." But in the end family opinion was too strong for her, or for Pipo either, for that matter. He agreed, with his usual insouciance, to give up his liaison with the Countess Panelli; there was to be no separation. He and Nadia were to return to Bologna together and "try to make it work." Suzy kissed her and wished her well, whispering, "Come to me whenever you want to breathe"; the Cardinal gave her his blessing, formally, and informally murmured—"God be with you, my child," when he bade her goodbye; La Vecchia Marchesa kissed her briskly, and adjured both her and Pipo to have another baby as fast as possible. And Nadia, still gracious, still silent, bowed her head and went away beside her husband. Gradually, unhurriedly, the rest followed, for their various destinations. The *consiglio di famiglia* was over.

Suzy saw them go with mild relief. It had all been a great waste of time, she thought, as she lay in her hammock on the terrace, empty now save for herself and her mother-in-law—it had left everything exactly where it was. Pipo would not change; she knew him too well for that. If it wasn't La Panelli, it would be somebody else. The one satisfaction was that it was safely over without doing Bonne-Mama any harm—she looked better than ever. But how fantastic, really, to suppose that it could change anything, a whole roomful of relations sitting round the table discussing! How could that affect the secret emotions, glad or bitter, of the urgent human heart? The heart took its own way, always. A tiny smile changed the delightful shape of her mouth—thinking of the secret waywardness of the human heart reminded her of

Roffredo.   In retrospect, that evening with him had somehow gathered weight, become more important.   She had set out, half idly, to cure a foolish young man of a foolish infatuation by the surest means she knew; but all through the days of the *consiglio*, talking, caring for her guests, listening to opinions, putting in a word of advice here and there, she had been aware of a secret sense of having a little private hoard of riches in the background which, presently, she could return to enjoy. She had been surprised at the persistence and vigour of this feeling, and its reviving effects on her; surprised too at the kindling vividness of her memory of Roffredo's hands on her shoulders, his lips on her face.   She had not expected to remember them like that.   It was surprising, but it was also pleasant.   And now the *consiglio* was over, and the temporary isolation of Vill' Alta from the rest of the Province—there would be meetings again.   She blew out a cloud of smoke, on a long contented breath, and applied herself cheerfully to amusing La Vecchia Marchesa.

To Almina the move to Odredo had been a relief.   It had at least removed her from the daily necessity of seeing and being polite to the Marchesa Suzy, whose mere presence, since that evening under the arbutus, aroused in her a sort of nervous horror.   She liked the quiet cheerful informality prevailing at Odredo, where the life of the soil, from which the whole great household derived its sustenance, was much more in evidence than it was at Vill' Alta.   Out in the courtyard behind the house the bullock-teams came and went, bringing in wood and water, and meal in squat dusty sacks—the yard was hardly ever without a pair of the great creamy beasts, standing patient-eyed in the shade, chewing the cud, or merely breathing with a strong gentle sound.   On the low terrace above the yard, screened from the house by the growth of pomegranates which sprawled through the white stone balustrade, long shallow trays of coarse muslin were set out, on which the small sweet black plums were drying, turning slowly into prunes under the strong sun.   Anna the cook was busy with jam-making; the two girls and Almina helped to gather green figs for green-fig-jam, and green grapes for green-grape-jelly—Anna made tomato jam too, a preserve to which Giulio was very partial, but which Almina privately thought horrible because of its curious after-taste—what she liked best was the thick sweet jam made from the ripe black grapes, of which Anna was planning a fresh supply later. The Count would come in to lunch, the pockets of his light alpaca jacket bulging with small envelopes, which he would tip out onto plates and sniff carefully; the contents, which were artificial manures recommended for vines, usually smelt frightful, and Elena would scold him freely for such disgusting practices. All this was pleasant to Almina—there was something soothing and steadying about these homely activities. And Fräulein Gelsicher was in herself always a solace and a support. She had now become, so to speak, an indirect one; all question of consulting her on the subject of Roffredo was finished with. That problem, and the dreams which it had fed, were set aside—all that was over, but Almina returned now more earnestly than ever to the governess ideal, to becoming for her pupil what Gela was to Elena. She threw herself with fervour into Giulio's lessons, giving him extra time, making him talk English—with Marietta she made him undertake English readings, all three together, sitting round the marble table under the stone pine.

The fact was that the girl had received a very severe moral shock—and moral shocks are usually far more shattering in their effects than emotional ones. In all these ways her shaken being sought to build itself up again, clinging to work, to simple things and practical tasks, to recover its stability. She took up the pursuit of wild-flowers once more, rising early and going for long walks before breakfast. Though wild-flower hunting had bitter-sweet associations of its own! Wandering homewards, once, her thoughts far away, she found herself unexpectedly in the little spinney where she had picked the butterfly orchis earlier in the year; she remembered how Roffredo had asked her its name, and begged to be taken there at dusk to smell their evening fragrance—it was the first time that he had shown her marked attention.    In a rush of sentimental misery she poked about among the later summer growth till she found one or two of the dead orchis; the frail stalks had given way, but the withered flower heads lay, dry, papery and brown on the dead leaves.    She took one home with her and put it between the leaves of her Tennyson, where the gentian which he had given her that day at Castellone already reposed, carefully pressed.    In Almina's day such rites were quite in order—it did not occur to her, even in her most secret thoughts, to laugh at herself for her folly, or question the merits of an affection so nourished.    But she did thereafter avoid the spinney carefully.

But in spite of this secret weakness, she was steady and consistent in her avoidance of Roffredo.    He came over several times to Odredo, but the cousins made a four at tennis without her, and she always contrived some excuse to absent herself when he was coming.    If he arrived unexpectedly, she gave him the minimum of civil greeting and then slipped away.    She exercised all her small stock of ingenuity to make these evasions look as natural as possible, but the change in her manner with the young Count did not escape the watchful eye of Elena—still less did it escape Roffredo's own notice. Without any clue to the reason for it, the young man was thoroughly puzzled.    Was it coquetry, or an exaggerated prudence, or some real change of feeling?    He had no idea— but whatever the cause, he was equally thoroughly piqued. He had hoped great things from Miss Prestwich's visit to Odredo, where, away from the Marchesa and the need for being gallant to her, he felt more free and more at ease. Roffredo had been rather irritated by the episode on the stone pine ridge.    He had been carried further than he meant; while he had no serious scruples about kissing as many pretty and pleasant women as would let him, he had a private predilection for making love to one person at a time, and a very

shrewd objection to any casual kissings which were likely to
land him in difficulties.   It was not hard to foresee the sort
of difficulties in which one was apt to land oneself by making
love to two women in the same house—that was a thing he
had always avoided, like the plague itself!—and if one was the
mistress and the other the governess, it was worse than ever.
And here he was, practically run into it!   And it was the
governess he cared most about, in this case.   He had not
wanted to kiss Suzy, that night—and his own ardour had
jarred on him afterwards.   Perdition on his feelings!—they
were so wretchedly easily aroused.   But now here she was,
the lovely darling Almina, away from Vill' Alta, with all sorts
of opportunities open before them—and instead of taking
them, she hid herself all the time, the silly little thing.   He
was uncertain, hurt, and helpless.   Could it be only prudence?   If not, what?

   The uncertainty fretted him, and made him think of her
incessantly.   This worried him too.   He was at a crucial
stage with his experiments.   The N.S.A. at Milan had seen
a demonstration of one of his inventions, had praised it, and
suggested one or two modifications—if these could be made
satisfactorily, they held out hopes of taking it.   As a result
he was working feverishly at the villa, often sitting up the
night through, with sheets of squared paper scattered round
him, drinking cup after cup of black coffee, trying to work
out the requisite formulas.   But one wanted one's mind free
for work like that—and often, when he was half-blinded with
peering at figures by lamplight, and dizzy with strain, the
picture of Almina would come swimming in between him
and the paper before him—chilly, prim and elusive, as she
had been the previous afternoon—and he would get up and
stamp about the room, cursing, trying to banish her image,
only to have it slide back again, as soon as he sat down—
tender and yielding, as she had been in that ruined room with
the oval window at Castel Vecchio.   Ah, the sweetness of
her then, with her head sunk on his arm, her closed eyes and

her parted lips—all his! Which was she, really?—the one or the other? Anyhow, she made it impossible to work; and he would go swearing off and throw himself, dressed as he was, on his bed, and fall leadenly asleep.

After one such night, when he had worked later than usual, the light was already beginning to filter in through the slats of the Venetian shutters when he lay down—it fretted his eyes, hot and sore after the night's work, and though he turned on his other side, he could not sleep; into his tired brain, drowsy and uninhibited, crowded visions of Almina—there with him, in the room, in all her delicate fragility—his weary fancy unclothed her, showed her in maddening perfection. He sprang up, at last, unable to endure the torment of these thoughts which he could not control; he would go out and walk—that would put an end to it, and he would be able to sleep. Regardless of the slumbers of Alba, his old housekeeper, he banged open one of the side doors of the villa, and went out.

Outside, the light, which indoors had lanced his eyes with the persistency of arrows, was perfectly soothing—tender, grey and clear; the cypresses round the villa stood up in it like shadows, also grey. He passed through the rather withered little garden, in which Antonio, his chauffeur-servant, tried to make a few discouraged geraniums bloom, and out into the road, where he stood for a moment, breathing deeply—the cool air, entering his lungs, was comforting and reviving. He walked a few yards along the road, and then turned off to the right, where a tiny path led across the pastures towards the Monte Sant' Antonio. Roffredo knew the path well—it had been trodden originally by the feet of smugglers, bringing salt and tobacco in over the mountains from across the Austrian frontier; old Trino, with dark waggings of the head, muttered sometimes that they still used it. Certainly someone used it, for though faint it was still clearly traced in the rough turf, grey now with dew. He followed along the outer fringe of a thick coppice which lay between it and the road; as he walked Roffredo thought idly that he could account for the regular use of the path. In that coppice was a small ruined building, and by it a well or spring, rising in a pool—the peasants credited the well with the power of granting wishes, and went there to make trivial offerings; he remembered seeing fragments of clothing fluttering from the bushes there, from the time when he was a child. No doubt it was such worshippers who kept the path trodden.

Out in the pastures, a light mist lay over the grass; the poplars, just beginning to turn colour, rose through it; while he walked their tops were turned to gold by the first rays of the sun. And now, through the mist, he saw a figure moving ahead of him along the smugglers' path. Roffredo was amused and a little startled—could Trino be right? In the mist he could not see it with any distinctness. He quickened his pace, walking noiselessly on the soft turf—now he was near enough to see that it was a woman; and not a peasant, for she wore a pale dress. A sudden suspicion overtook him—he ran; and as he drew nearer, with one of those sweet pangs with which we salute the impossible joy, he recognised Almina.

All his usual deliberate skill in such encounters forsook Roffredo then. Panting, he came up with her, and took her by the arm. "It is you," he said, as she faced round towards him; and nothing else. They stood so, in silence, for a moment or two, while his eyes travelled over her, up and down, as if to assure himself of the whole presence of her—coming to rest at last on her face, where the delicate colour came and went. At last—"Good morning," the girl said, with the chilly primness she had used to him lately; "Surely you are out very early?"

"Yes, and why? Because of you—because I could neither work nor sleep last night because of you," the young man burst out.

"I am sorry for that—but I cannot help it," she said coldly, walking on again; she carried a little spray of some green plant

in her hand, and raised it to her face as if to smell it, to empha-
sise her detachment.

"Almina, what is it? Why have you changed like this?"
he asked urgently, again catching at her arm.

She moved her elbow to free it. "I have the best of
reasons, which I do not wish to discuss," she said, more
coldly than ever. "Would you please leave me now? I am
going home."

Roffredo was both hurt and nonplussed. "No, I shall not
leave you," he said with angry firmness. "I shall see you into
the Park. Surely you must know that you are most indiscreet to walk alone at this hour, with no one about? The
peasants here are quite untrustworthy—you might be insulted at any moment. You are doing a very foolish thing."

"It is not only by the peasants that one is insulted here,"
the girl said, her lip trembling; her artificial composure was
breaking down under the scene.

"What do you mean? Almina, dearest, darling, I have not
insulted you! What have I said? If I have been rude, forgive me—I have not slept, and I don't know what I am saying," he said, pouring out his words with eager urgency, and
catching at her arm again.

"Not today, no," she said, tears which she could not check
gathering in her eyes.

"Then when? Then when?"

"In England we think it insulting to—to tell a person you
love them, and to—act it, and then to make love to someone
else, on the same day," the girl said bitterly, her grievance
escaping at last.

He stood stock still and stared at her, retaining his hold of
her arm, which this time she had made no move to release.

"Dunque! So that is it!" he said at last. "You saw me
and Suzy?"

She nodded, turning away her head, but he saw two bright
tears fall.

"Cara signorina, I owe you an explanation," he said very

gravely. "Will you allow me to make it? I beseech you to do so—it is important to me." He looked round and saw a pile of logs at a little distance, by the foot of a tree. "Come here and sit for a few minutes," he said, leading her towards it. "You shall hear, and then you shall judge, and act as you please. There!" he said, pulling off his jacket and spreading it on the dew-damp wood.

"You will be cold," Almina said, glancing at his shirt-sleeves.

"No, I shall not." He seated himself beside her. "Now, will you listen to me?"

Again she nodded. Her angry resolution had been shaken by his evident emotion on meeting her, and by his eager words; the thought that she had broken his sleep moved her, and the gravity with which he had made this last request somehow demanded a civil audience. He looked, too, tired and distraught—his eyes were red-rimmed, and there were blue shadows under them on his white skin, which had that transparent whiteness of the red-haired. His usual arrogance was gone—he looked young and serious; at her gesture of assent he looked also relieved.

"That is good of you," he said. "Dunque, you know Zia Suzy—she is—well, very attractive. You have heard that people call her the Enchantress; well, that is not for nothing! And she is a relation; one must not quarrel with relations— and besides, she has been very nice to me. Well, that night, I don't know why—I suppose she felt flirtatious," he said, with a rather engaging flat simplicity; "anyhow she teased me, and I *did* flirt with her. And—it may be less so with women, but you know how it is with men, they are easily aroused—and I am particularly so," he said, with disarming candour—"red-haired people are always the worst for that. And I did kiss her—I do, in such cases! I can't help it. Besides, it was necessary; one cannot do less than is expected of one! But—oh, dear one, lovely one, do try to understand this!—when I kissed you, it was with my heart also—it meant something; and when I kissed her, it meant nothing, except that I was aroused, as I said. Do you believe that?'

She sat with averted head, as she listened. It was all very strange, and rather disagreeable—but it was all of a piece with so much else that was strange, in Italy; it fitted in with things that she had heard Elena say, often. And there was something compelling about his very frankness and sincerity. "Yes, I suppose I do," she said at last.

"Then will you forgive it, and forget it? Almina cara?" He slipped an arm round her as he spoke, and she let it stay; after her days of misery, the comfort of it was so sweet! "Yes, I will forgive it," she said. He drew her very gently and gradually towards him. "And you won't be cruel to me any more?" he whispered; and as she turned her head at last to him, he slipped his mouth onto hers.

"What is the flower, cara?" he asked her presently, when they were sitting quietly, pointing to the little spray in her hand.

"Oh, that is something rather nice—I found it in the copse over there, where the spring is, and the little ruin—Enchanter's Nightshade," she said, holding it up. "I brought it with me for the Marchese. It is not very common and I haven't found it anywhere else about here."

"It isn't much of a flower," he said, taking it from her and examining it.

"No, it isn't out yet—but those buds all open into rather darling little whitish flowers," she said happily.

"Enchanter's Nightshade, did you say? What a curious name. And the Latin, madam Professor?"

"*Circaea Lutetiana.*"

"It should be called *Enchantress's* Nightshade," he said, giving it back to her.

"Why?"

"Because of Zia Suzy." But he wouldn't explain, when she did not follow—he only laughed, and made her renew a promise to come out next morning into the Park and walk with him there. He took her back, past the lake, and parted from her only at the foot of the hill below the house—as she climbed the rough track through the plantation of young larches, smelling sweet now as the sun warmed them, she heard him whistling on his way home.

## Chapter Thirteen

"Ecco, Papa, see what our Postiche has brought you!" Marietta cried, twirling the spray of Enchanter's Nightshade before her father's eyes as he sat at his study table, on their return to Vill' Alta. "Did you ever see *that* before?"

The Marchese Francesco examined the small plant, with its dark delicate leaves, heart-shaped at the base and pointed at the tips, with eager care. "Yes—I know it; it is *Circaea Lutetiana*," he said; "I saw it once in England. But where does this come from? Not from the Province, surely?"

"Yes, it does. She found it herself, the clever thing!—at Odredo."

"Where?"

"In that thicket, by the ruined grotto and the Holy Well." And as her Father looked blank—"O Papa, cara, you go nowhere! It is near Trino's hill. She can take you there one day."

The Marchese Francesco was delighted with his new treasure. He sent for Miss Prestwich, congratulated her, and examined her minutely as to the location and quantity of the plant. Oh yes, there was plenty, she told him, and she could easily find it again, only the bushes were very thick. "But I can go there now and then, and when it is properly out, I can fetch you another piece." As she spoke the thought darted into her head that if she could only manage to let Roffredo know, these expeditions would offer an admirable opportunity for meeting him again. They had had two or three morning walks before she and Marietta left Odredo, and the happiness, the heady sweetness of them had as it were fortified her to face the Marchesa Suzy once more. She had no longer any

170

doubts as to the truth of Roffredo's explanation, or as to his feelings towards her.    This gave her that sense of inner justification which lovers know so well—and, paradoxically, perhaps, the fact of the Marchesa's flirtation with Roffredo seemed to her to excuse her own concealment of her meetings with him.    It was now not only impossible to reveal them— it had become unnecessary as well.

The only difficulty, over which, in her room upstairs, later, she drew her fine eyebrows together in a puzzled frown, was *how* to let him know.    Except for those early walks, she spent practically the whole day in her pupil's company, especially at Vill' Alta; and because that company was pleasant, and there was nowhere in particular to go, she had allowed that one afternoon off a week, stipulated for in her mother's correspondence with the Marchesa, to lapse.    Two or three times lately, it was true, she had asked to be allowed to go in to Gardone to do some shopping—seated in the hot swaying diligence, smelling of straw and horses' sweat, she had gone jolting in to the town, and there made certain additions to her wardrobe, things for which Mrs. Prestwich, for all her care and anxious speculation, had not foreseen the necessity—white shoes like Elena's, and white stockings to go with them; the tussore dustcoat recommended by the Marchesa; a green petersham belt to sew on her silver Liberty buckle, for wearing with her white skirts, and one or two more fine white blouses. These purchases had very nearly swallowed up her first quarter's salary, and were not in fact so necessary as all that— she had made them really, as her secret heart admitted, to be more perfect in Roffredo's eyes.    But they were all good; they would "last", they would "come in later on"—those sacred qualifications of Edwardian wardrobes, so often used, as in this case, to excuse an extravagance.    And till they went to Rome in October, she would really need no money to mention.    But apart from these expeditions, she had almost no time to herself.    She could of course quietly walk out of the great gates beyond the South terrace, cross the white dusty village square with its squat hollow-trunked elm, under which the loungers congregated in a black patch of shade, and post a letter in the Vill' Alta post office; but to begin with that was unusual, since the Castello letters were taken daily in a bag to Sant' Apollonia by a man on a bicycle; and further, the post-mistress took every letter with her own hands, scrutinised the address, and chatted cheerfully with the senders on their reasons for writing—Marietta and Almina, going in to buy stamps, had often watched this proceeding and laughed over it. There was no privacy about village posts in the Province.

The usual commerce in invitations and information was carried on by means of notes. Showers of notes passed to and fro every day; coachmen halted their carriages at the foot of the long flight of steps at Vill' Alta, and their mistresses sat fanning themselves and chatting, while a perspiring footman rushed up with a note; youths on bicycles, with worn broad-brimmed straw hats on their heads and flapping unbuttoned jackets, scattered all over the countryside, bearing notes, wrapped in a piece of rag to keep them clean, in their pockets —waited for the replies, in pointed writing on scented mauvish paper, and bicycled back again. But even the note industry was very fairly public; the Sorellone were not the only ladies in Gardone to go out and interview such a mess-enger, ask him how his master and mistress did, who was stay-ing at the Castello, and where he was going next?—and the youth, unfolding his bit of rag to envelop the answering missive, would display the others, as yet undelivered. "Ma che! one for Carlotta at Macerbo! Aspasia, do you think Suzy can be inviting her to the tennis? She plays so badly." No—notes were not very private either.

It was Roffredo himself who found the solution, and a very fantastic and ingenious one, for this difficulty. On the very day after their return to Vill' Alta he came over to tea and tennis; Giulio and Elena were there too, and afterwards the young people walked back with them towards Odredo. Roffredo had found the moment, fetching himself a glass of lemonade from the table by the court, to murmur to Almina—"Sweetheart, when do I see you again? Properly?"

"I don't know," she murmured back, putting a lump of ice into his tumbler. "I could walk sometimes early; if only I could let you know when. But that is difficult—I don't see how to manage it."

"I will think of something, little love. Grazie tanto, signorina," he said loudly, as Suzy approached.

Now, walking back along the ridge, Almina branched off down a side path, saying that she was going to look for a flower. She had half-hoped that Roffredo would escape and follow her alone, but the whole party came too. Down off the crest of the ridge, the ground was moist and smelt damply of dead leaves; elders and privets grew thickly, their branches stretching across the path.

"Goodness, what an awful smell!" Elena exclaimed suddenly. "What on earth can it be?"

"If this is the scent of your flower, signorina—!" Roffredo mocked, as they all stood still to sniff; there was indeed a strong putrid odour in the air.

"It smells like a dead dog," said Giulio. "Come on, do."

But Almina, stepping carefully in her white shoes, began to range about, pushing and peering through the bushes.

"Postiche, you can't want to *find* it," Elena protested.

"No, but I think I know what it is," she said. "One minute—or you go on. . . . Yes, I thought so!" she exclaimed after a moment; "here you are, Giulio—here is your dead dog!"

They followed her through the bushes to where she stood pointing triumphantly at some tall narrow toadstools, of an ugly greyish white, flecked on the cap with dirty brown—the smell here was almost overpowering. "They are stink-horns; we have them at home," she said.

"Not a romantic subject for nostalgia," Roffredo said, poking gingerly at the largest of the unpleasing objects with the toe of his shoe—it fell over sideways, revealing an unhealthy-looking spongy substance under the domed top. "Pew! it is horrible."

"Come away, per carità," Marietta said, tugging at Almina's arm. "Postiche, you know some nasty things! Don't let's ever come here again."

It may have been that last remark which gave Roffredo his idea. He walked back with Marietta and Miss Prestwich to Vill' Alta, when they had bidden the cousins farewell, and went into the house to fetch his hat and dust-coat. He was gone some time, and when Almina went into the schoolroom that evening to tidy up, she noticed a tiny slip of folded paper sticking out of Marietta's exercise book, which lay on the table. She pulled it out, and read her own name on it, in a round firm writing—with a little pang of surprise and suspicion she opened it. Yes, it was from him. "Country Post-Offices smell frightful, but some are safer than others," she read. "Go and fetch your own letters, in the dogs' cemetery, and be sure to post some!" Laughing at his nonsense, half-frightened at his audacity—for he must have run up to the schoolroom himself, a scandalous proceeding—she carried the note off to her own room, and locked it away in the jewel-box in her little dressing-case. She went down to dinner with a sort of dancing inner confidence, and after coffee ran upstairs, put on thick shoes, and scudded away along the ridge and down the side path to the elder thicket. It was nonsense to come, she told herself—there could be nothing there yet. But all the same she made her way to the ill-odoured spot, and looked about in the dusk. No, not a sign of a note. Then she noticed that the fallen stink-horn, the largest of all, was no longer there. Yes—there it was, broken at one side by Roffredo's foot; but it was standing up again, propped on a twig. She stooped and picked it up— stuck into the spongy tissue beneath the domed cap was another little folded note. She carried it up out of the wood onto the ridge, and leaning against one of the stone pines, read it by the last glow from the west. It was her first love-letter, and though short, it was a satisfying one—ardent, tender and mischievous, suggesting a rendezvous in the Park, early, on the day after tomorrow.    She went back to the house, penned an answer to be slipped into the stink-horn next morning, and went happily to bed, the precious note under her pillow.

This absurd means of communication now secured, and supported by fairly frequent meetings with Roffredo, Almina was able to look on, almost with indifference, at the progress of his flirtation with the Marchesa Suzy.    Not quite with indifference, though; her disapproval of Suzy's behaviour, and a discomfort, which would not be altogether suppressed, at her own concealments set up an underground current of hostility towards her employer, of whose force she was hardly aware.    Turbulent thoughts of criticism, violent inner movements of impatience, disturbed and troubled her.    She struggled against them—with the upper part of her mind she told herself firmly that the Marchesa's behaviour was really no business of hers, and that, though wrong, it was probably only Italian!—and therefore not to be judged by her own standards. (Some of the lessons proper to governesses, so well mastered by Fräulein Gelsicher, Miss Prestwich was undoubtedly learning.)

Others however thought differently.    Elena, whose sharp ironic glance little ever escaped, was by now perfectly well aware of the Marchesa's goings-on with Roffredo, and regisered each manifestation with rather malicious amusement. At the same time she had not failed to notice the young man's manner to Miss Prestwich, nor those minute changes of colour and inflexions of voice which the latter, for all her careful behaviour, could not quite control; in spite of their discretion, she made a pretty shrewd guess at the state of affairs there. She had become rather warmly attached to the English girl; she thought her almost too simple to live, but she liked her all the same, and her liking was strongly tinged with an element of protectiveness, as well as of amusement.    And for all her flippancy and love of mischief, Elena di Castellone, at eighteen, was quite enough of a woman of the world to realise the dangers inherent in such a situation.

"Senta, Gela," she began one morning as she sat sewing and gossiping in her governess's room, "have you noticed Zia Suzy and Roffredo lately?   I think they are getting on rather too well."

Fräulein Gelsicher sighed, put down the slate-coloured thread stocking which she was darning, and looked across at her pupil.   "You are too fond of criticising your elders, Elena," she said non-committally.

"Forse!   But Gela, this is serious—or at least it may be. So forget my youth, and Zia Suzy's great age and inviolable respectability," the girl said, with her irrepressible giggle, "and listen, do.   I *think*," she went on, with unusual emphasis, "that she is in love with him, and means to keep him for herself."

"Then let her—it is nothing to do with you.   And do realise that I cannot properly discuss such things with you," the Swiss said, taking up her darning again.

Elena darted over to her, the skirts of her cambric peignoir flying above her silk petticoat, pounced on the stocking and swept it out of her governess's hand; the polished tartan darning egg fell to the floor.

"Scusi, Gela cara!   But you *must* listen, and you *must* discuss!" she cried, picking it up.   "It isn't so easy as that. I think Roffredo doesn't in the least want to be Zia Suzy's *cher ami*, because he is much too fond of Postiche.   At first I thought it was only a flirt, but now it is more—I am sure of it.   Have you noticed nothing?"

The Swiss did not answer—instead, she asked a question herself.   "Why do you think so?" she enquired, re-possessing herself of the stocking.   "No, it is all right—I can sew and talk."

"Their eyes—their voices!   And they meet; I am sure of it.   Once or twice he has referred to something which happened when he was not there, and we have not seen him since, so that he could not know of it unless she had told him; he has caught himself up, and covered it, but I have seen her face then.    She was afraid."

"When could they meet?    When she was here, she saw nothing of him—she avoided him rather pointedly," Fräulein Gelsicher said.

"I know—at first!    There was some quarrel, I am sure— and pretty certainly Suzy was at the bottom of it!    But the last few days she was quite different to him—and you know she always went for those long walks before breakfast."

"I certainly did *not* know. it, or I should have stopped her! She is far too young and pretty to walk alone.    How do you know this?" the older woman asked.

"Oh, Annina told me, for one thing—and then she brought in that flower that Zio Francesco made such a fuss about, one morning early.    But Gela, the thing is this—what are we to do?    She is so innocent, she is like a child; I don't suppose she realises in the least about Zia Suzy.    But really, I do not like the whole thing at all.    You know, I think Zia Suzy is *capable de tout*, if her own way is threatened," Elena said, very seriously.

For once Fräulein Gelsicher let the criticism pass un-rebuked.    Some profound instinct—for she had never seen the young Marchesa other than courteous and charming— made her think the same thing herself.    If Elena was right, it was a rather menacing situation.    She sighed, and drew out a long thread on her needle, but without speaking.

"I wondered if one should speak to her," Elena said. "After all, she is alone here.    And you know I don't alto-gether trust Roffredo either; he is passionate, and he is rather *volage*."

"It was a mistake her ever coming here," the Swiss said, almost bitterly.    "More enquiries should have been made. Oxford degrees are not everything.    It is not so easy as all that, to be a governess!"

"Oh, Gela darling!" Elena, usually so detached, was

touched by this. She ran across, and gave her preceptress a warm hug. "But what shall we do?" she pursued, returning to her main theme after this brief excursion into the affections. "Should we speak to her?"

"No—leave it for the present. I will think about it," Fräulein Gelsicher said. Then an idea struck her. "Do you think Marietta knows anything about all this?" she asked.

"It is very difficult to be sure what Marietta knows and what she doesn't," the girl replied. "She isn't such a dunce as Postiche about understanding what she sees of people and their affairs, but she notices so little, because she doesn't pay attention—she is always dreaming and looking at the view. And she doesn't say half she knows, besides." She bit off a thread, chose another, and resumed, squinting at the eye of the needle—"I should think that she must have *some* idea about Postiche and Roffredo, at least, boxed up as they are together, all day."

"And about the other—thing?"

"No," said Elena decidedly. "I am sure not. It would never occur to her. She is odd about Zia Suzy; all that is tiresome in her she just closes her mind to. She thinks her nearly perfect, I do believe."

"It is much better that she should continue to do so," the Swiss said. "I hope you realise, Elena, that you must say *nothing* to her about that affair. It would be a crime."

"Ma si! Ma si! Gela cara, I am not eight! Though, you know, I cannot guarantee that she won't see it, one of these days, if Zia Suzy goes on at this rate," the girl said. "But really I am more worried about Postiche. What shall we do, Gela?"

"I shall reflect about it first," the governess repeated.

She did both think and watch during the next few days; and what she noticed, once put on the track, entirely confirmed Elena's impression. The young Marchesa's preoccupation with Count Roffredo she had already noticed with her usual calm disapproval; but this fresh development disturbed her

much more.  She considered the possibility of giving a word
of warning to her little colleague; but the girl's extreme discretion in all her visible behaviour gave small handle for it,
and Fräulein Gelsicher did not like acting on suspicion, or
on the gossip of servants.  The proper person to have
watched and warned was her employer, the Marchesa Suzy—
and she was being far more indiscreet than the governess,
Fräulein Gelsicher thought bitterly.  And the gravamen of
the warning it was impossible to give—that Miss Prestwich
should beware of arousing the jealousy of her pupil's mother
about a young man for whose affection they were rivals!
What an impossible and undignified situation!

In her concern, she thought, as before, of taking La
Vecchia Marchesa into her confidence.  But she dreaded up-
setting her; the hundredth birthday, to which the whole circle
of relations attached an almost superstitious importance was
little more than six weeks off, and the old lady had only
recently undergone the strain of the *consiglio di famiglia*.  In
the end Fräulein Gelsicher decided to leave it for the moment,
and trust to the Marchesa's tact and savoir faire not to let
matters come to a head.  After all, she had always managed
such things very well before.  It was surprising, the Swiss
thought with cold matter-of-factness, that she should be so
careless of appearances this time.

The reason for Suzy's relative disregard of appearances in
the matter of Count Roffredo was simple enough, although
Fräulein Gelsicher did not hit on it—it was largely an impulse
of feminine jealousy.  Having once suspected that there was
something between him and the governess, and having decided to detach him and annex him, so to speak, herself, it
became almost a matter of policy with Suzy to display his
flirtation with her, rather than to conceal it.  In a way, too, it
was a kindness to do it, and stop the silly little thing getting
absurd ideas into her head.  That, at least, was how it began.
She did not bother about it very much—Suzy had a light touch
as a rule.  And she was very well content with life.  Bonne-

Mama was extraordinarily well, and the birthday was now such a little way off, surely she would remain well for those few more weeks. The little governess was quiet enough; she seemed to have taken the hint, and subsided. And she herself was seeing a very satisfying amount of Roffredo. He always accepted her little notes of invitation, and was constantly at Vill' Alta.

But presently a gradual change began to come over the gay contentment of her feelings. Once or twice, when Roffredo had been over to Vill' Alta for tennis, and had stayed on to dinner, they went for a stroll afterwards along the stone pine ridge. Slightly to her surprise, he insisted on taking her down into the shelter of the privet bushes before kissing her. She put this down to the fervour of his feelings, and was not displeased; in fact, he was merely afraid of being seen by Almina. But her seduction exercised its usual power, and he did kiss her, with energy and passion. She was strangely moved by this; she actually trembled in his arms, and asked herself, almost incredulously, if she were really falling in love again at last?

It must be realised that for a woman of Suzy's temperament and experiences the exercise of her powers of seduction and, so to speak, the practice of passion, were almost ends in themselves—an art and a form of self-expression; done as normally, or nearly, as the artist paints or the musician plays. Automatically confronted with a new human being—man, woman, or child—she set about charming it; when it was a man, certain specific results usually followed. To a greater or less degree, he was subjugated; and graciously, skilfully—kindly, really—according to the degree of his infatuation, she let the affair follow its course to its natural conclusion, whether that was a mere flirtation, a passionate interlude, or a regular liaison. But as the musician plays through a variety of uninspiring works merely to keep his hand in, and the artist makes studies of certain effects which he wishes to master, though they will never be completed pictures, so, in by far the

greater number of these affairs, Suzy di Vill' Alta's own emotions were not very deeply involved.    Her capacity for
passion might be exercised, but her peace was not disturbed.

But with Roffredo di Castellone she was beginning to
realise that the case was different.    Sometimes as she lay in
her hammock on the terrace awaiting him, the sight of his tall
easy figure, suddenly appearing in the gloom of the doorway
at the top of the steps brought such a rush of tenderness, of
delighted joy, that she could hardly master it enough to give
him her gay cool greeting.    This was astonishing to Suzy.
And her appearance became of new importance to her.
Secure in her beauty and her timeless charm, she had drifted
into the middle thirties almost without thought, seeing the
harmonious ensemble which she steadily presented to the
world in general reflected back at her in a thousand admiring
glances; thorough and careful, in a business-like way, about
her toilette, she had not seriously considered her looks.    Now
a new imperative need to see herself with Roffredo's eyes sent
her questioning to the great silver mirror with the folding
wings, which stood in the centre of her vast toilet-table, with
its lace-covered top and its white satin flounces.    She sat
there for a long time, one night; she dismissed Agnese, her
maid, as soon as she had unhooked her dress and taken it
away, with a curt intimation that she would do her own hair.
When the woman had gone she sat gazing into the silvery
depths, where her face, softly lit by the candles on the table,
stood out white against the dark liquid background of the
shadowy room, trying to see what Roffredo had seen an hour
before.    The throat was perfect still—she had not *le cou usé*
like so many women—the eyes superb.    But the chin, the
jaw—were they getting a little heavy?    She tilted one of the
wings and examined them from an angle, thoughtfully.    No,
they were all right still.    But the sense of time came to her
as she sat, looking at the picture of a beautiful woman in the
shadowed mirror; she did what she had never done before—
she envisaged the future.    And that brought a sense of

urgency to the present which it had never borne yet. Looking in the glass, she had none of the common fears of its being her last chance to attract a man; but it might well be that she would never again feel so deeply, so joyfully, herself. Then, if this was the last time, now that love was again awake, let her have it in fulness and perfection!—so her stirred heart cried. Slowly, she slipped the chiffon peignoir down off her shoulders, so that the whole white splendour gleamed opposite her, in the heavy silver frame. Yes, let her taste the whole! She closed the wings over the mirror, as if to shut in the picture; shook down her hair, undressed swiftly, blew out the candles and got into bed. She lay there with the sense of a resolution taken—half joyous, half alarmed. Strange how young her heart was still!

Outside, among the stiff black shapes of the stone pines on the Odredo ridge, a man's figure went stumbling down through the bushes to the road. It was Roffredo, finding his way back to his car, after putting another note for Almina under the cap of the next largest stink-horn.

## Chapter Fourteen

HER cousin Elena's recent observations on Marietta
contained a good deal of truth. It was the fact that
such of her attention as was given to human beings at
all was chiefly concentrated on one or two people, who were
really important to her—for the rest, though amiable and
affectionate, she slipped about between human relationships
like a little fish, skimming easily and gracefully, but making
no close or lasting contact. Her relation to her Mother, for
instance, was rather peculiar—Elena had made by no means a
bad shot at it. Her Mother stood in the child's mind like a
sort of statue, dressed, as images in continental churches are
sometimes dressed, in all sorts of rich trappings of perfection
—her beauty, her social skill, her gaiety, her kindness, her
warm laughter. But she was, to her own daughter, ultimately an abstraction; they never reached one another; there
was between them no real intimacy such as existed, holding
fast across their vast disparity of ages, between Marietta and
La Vecchia Marchesa. The two people who really occupied
the child's attention at present were her cousin Giulio and
Miss Prestwich.

Marietta had become surprisingly devoted to her governess. Almina's real love of knowledge for its own sake, her
scholarly attitude to the glory and value of pure learning
(acquired at Oxford, where, thirty years ago, women students
had an attitude of discipleship which would be unrecognisable
and incredible today) answered an untutored but profound
instinct of Marietta's nature. That had been the first link.
Then Miss Prestwich's youth and the honest simplicity which
Elena found so amusing were curiously appealing and

endearing to the young girl. Not yet fully or adequately interested in people as such, her scanty attention, when it was directed to them, found most grown-ups baffling and puzzling; but this simplicity offered no puzzles—it was comfortable and restful. And her instinct—that dog-like instinct by which the attachments of a child are formed—recognised and saluted the real goodness and integrity of the English girl's character; her immature mind, struggling confusedly to shape the values that were to make its world—which is the supreme task of adolescence—was supported by Miss Prestwich's small disciplines and her rigid sense of right and wrong, even when that seemed to her, as to her cousin, so unwonted as to be slightly comic. The bright hot weeks of that summer in the Province were an extraordinarily happy time for Marietta—her intelligence, nourished by the fresh knowledge and ideas which Miss Prestwich provided, grew, expanded, flowered; her feelings grew too, stimulated by the constant companionship of the two people she cared most for in the world—fresh possibilities of intercourse, new points of contact with other minds, opened before her eager eyes. Her world began to take shape—and a safe and happy shape.

But during the last week or so she had become aware of some vague element of disturbance in this happy atmosphere —like the sudden harsh cry, on a day still hot and cloudless, of a peacock, presaging rain. It was the cry of the peacocks at Vill' Alta which put this idea into her head, one afternoon. It was followed during the night by the warning clamour of the bells of all the churches of the plain, and later, at dawn, by a calamitous storm of thunder and hail, which swept down from the mountains, flattening the maize and cruelly battering the just-ripening grapes. (In those days, in the Province of Gardone, hail in the mountains, made known by the telegraph, was announced by a tocsin from every village campanile, to warn the peasants to do all they could to protect their crops.) Marietta, walking out next day and seeing the resulting ruinous desolation, felt again a vague disquiet. With both Giulio and her dear Postiche, she felt that there were things going on which she could not quite fathom.

Her feeling for Giulio was turning imperceptibly into something rather more mature—more watchful, less blindly adoring. She had at first rejoiced in the pleasure he took in Miss Prestwich's instruction, and indeed in her presence; it had seemed a pupilship like her own, and a further link between the two of them. But just lately she thought she had seen traces of another feeling. She could not be sure—the very young are curiously reluctant to trust the evidence of their eyes, and still more to trust the promptings of that sixth sense which, by glimmers or flashes of intuition, informs the unobservant and indifferent as to what is going on about them. Such glimmers were troubling Marietta now about Giulio, and about Postiche too. She was half aware of something at work in Miss Prestwich, something more profound than could be accounted for by what was obvious in Roffredo's manner to her, his laughing evident admiration.

And as the harsh pealing of the bells had followed on the peacock's cry, so confirmation of one part of her hesitant suspicions followed quickly on her first forebodings. On the day of the storm there was to have been tennis at Vill' Alta, and as the sun was shining brilliantly again by the afternoon, a good many people turned up for it, including Elena and Giulio. The courts however proved to be too sodden for play, and the young people amused themselves indoors with charades, paper games, and bean bags, then a very fashionable pursuit, in which small silken bags containing beans were flung from hand to hand down two lines of people, the object being to see which line could transfer its whole stock of bags from one end to the other first. Every large house in the Province kept a supply of bags against such eventualities as this.

Marietta noticed that Giulio was clumsy and absentminded; when the onset of paper games released him from the enforced membership of his team, he disappeared. She

N

slipped out after him, and found him, as she expected, up in the schoolroom, perched on a low settee under the window, a copy-book at his side, reading a book—to her surprise she saw that it was Dante's *La Vita Nuova*. She seated herself beside him, without comment, and looked over his shoulder. Giulio, also without comment, shoved the book in her direction till it rested on her knee, so that she might read too—much of their intercourse was conducted with this wordless ease. He was reading the sonnet in which Dante describes Beatrice's complexion:

> Color di perla quasi informa, quale
> Conviene a donna aver, non fuor' misura ;
> Ella è quanto di ben può far' natura ;
> Per esempio di lei, beltà si prova.

("Of the colour of a rough pearl, such as is suited to a gentle-woman—not too high; she is the most that Nature can do; beauty itself is measured by her likeness.")

Marietta read it, and her light breathing quickened with a little pang of fore-knowledge.

"I had thought I would make a translation of it for her—she likes me to do translations," Giulio said at length—"but it is too difficult, I think." He tapped his teeth with a pencil, meditatively. "It is like her, isn't it?" he said, turning round now to his little cousin. "She has just that broken-pearl complexion, with hardly any colour—and her little air of quality! They say Beatrice was fair, too."

"Yes—I suppose she is like," the girl said, a little hesitatingly. "Only I think Beatrice was more heavenly-minded."

"Why do you say that? Do you think she is earthly-minded?" Giulio asked, in a disturbed voice.

"No no—not that. I don't really know why I said it. Let me think," Marietta said, pressing her small thin fingers over her eyes, a gesture Giulio knew well. "Yes, this is it—Postiche is good, and her mind turns towards Heaven, but she has—she has somehow a lot of links with earth; and

Beatrice—as Dante makes her out, anyhow—had hardly any links with earth at all, except other people's eyes, holding her there."

Giulio considered this.    "That is good and true, what you say about Beatrice," he said at length,; "but what do you mean about Miss Prestwich?"    (Giulio would never use the name 'Postiche',)    "I think she is very much turned to Heaven. What are her 'links with earth'?"

"I cannot say exactly.    But I feel that it is more than just our eyes holding her there!" Marietta said, with a sparkle of amusement.

"If you do not know what you mean, I don't think you ought to say things like that," Giulio said, a little discontentedly.    "I think she is more turned to heaven than anyone I know.    She is so good, and pure, and gentle, and loyal"— he broke off, thinking of his scene with her on the night when they had come on the Marchesa and his Father.    He could not tell Marietta about that.    But the recollection of it moved him strongly, and when he spoke again, his voice vibrated with feeling.    "She is more good than you can know; bad things slip off her spirit; everything that is noble and beautiful finds a welcome and a home in her.    Oh Marietta, you and I have never known anyone like her, and we never shall again!" the young man said, turning dark impassioned eyes on the child.

Marietta sat gazing back at him; in her crumpled white dress, with her long black legs and black plaits, she was a very childish figure, but her face at that moment was not childish— Donatello's St. John the Baptist had given way to the Medusa, her delicate mouth open in a voiceless circle of despair.    And her words, when at last she spoke, were not childish either. "Dear Giulio, do you love her?"

The young man ran his hands through his hair, got up, and walked about the room, with its mildly educational litter; he touched one or two things—the time-table on the wall, Miss Prestwich's black ruler on the table, the flower-press on the bookshelf—and the gestures of his shapely hands as he did so really gave his answer; they so evidently loved what they touched. He came back and stood before his cousin—she had not moved, and sat where he had left her, her eyes all the time fixed steadily on him.

"I don't know," he said slowly. "Perhaps not. I don't know much about love. But she has filled my life, since she came, with—well, with a new meaning; and that meaning is beautiful. I could kneel to her—I want to, sometimes, but it would be silly, and it might vex her. She is so sensible!—and she has no idea, I am sure, how good she is."

Marietta took a deep breath, like a swimmer before a plunge. "That *is* love," she said, with great finality. "One sort—our sort, yours and mine."

"*You* have no sort yet!" he said, smiling—he put out his hand and fondled the dark head. "Little Marietta!"

The young girl, quite gently, moved her head aside.

"It will be my sort, then, when I have a sort," she said, getting up.

"What is the other sort?" he asked, rather dreamily.

"Elena's!" she answered with decision. "And Roffredo's too." She stopped abruptly, as if she had meant to say something more.

"You know a lot! And *hers?*" Giulio asked.

"I don't know which sort hers will be," the child said. "Come on, Giulio, we ought to go down."

"But surely hers will be the same as ours?" he asked, almost urgently, catching her arm.

She twisted it away, brusquely, now.

"I don't know—and nor does she!" she said.

"Marietta! What do you mean?"

"I don't know! Not even that! Giulio, do leave me alone," she cried passionately, and ran out of the room.

Marietta was speaking the truth then. Her instinct had for once outrun her reason, and in the torment of those moments had spoken aloud. Thinking of it, afterwards, she could still find no real grounds for what she had said. But for her

distress she had a definite ground.    It was all too clear that
Giulio's whole soul went out in worship to Miss Prestwich,
and she—little Marietta!—was told so much because she was
too young and childish to matter!    She clenched her small
brown fists at the thought.    To be told, to be his sole confidante, was of course something.    And the fact of his love
for Almina she accepted, as the very young do, in agony and
silence.    Reviewing the waste in her heart, the broken joy,
she thought again of the peacocks' cry and the thunderstorm.
But she could not even rest, unselfishly, in the thought of a
happy future for him.    With sharpened eyes, she watched her
governess on the next day and the next; she saw her calm
friendliness when Giulio appeared, and she surprised the look
on her face when the well-known chug-chug of the motor-car
came in through the schoolroom windows.    Of whatever sort
Miss Prestwich's love might be, it was not given to Giulio!
And with her continental realism, Marietta saw nothing but
misery in store for him.

In her pain, she withdrew into herself more than ever.
Even with Miss Prestwich and the cousins, she became
singularly silent—sometimes apparently lost in thought, so
that she did not always answer when spoken to, sometimes still
and watchful, her eyes travelling from face to face, saying
nothing.    Almina, for all her absorption in her own affairs,
at once noticed this change in her pupil, and redoubled her
normal efforts to interest and amuse her.    She even went the
length, after a couple of days, of asking if she had anything
on her mind?—an effort for a person of her reticence and
shyness.    Marietta raised her eyebrows with a cold stare and
said—"No—why should I have?"    Then, catching sight of
the hurt astonishment in her governess's face, she darted over
to her and flung her arms round her neck.    "Oh, I love you!
But what can I do?" she cried, bursting into tears, and rushed
from the room.    Almina let her be, and made a brew of senna
pods for her that night—so her Mother had always treated
her own emotional outbursts.    Marietta was charming over

the administration of the senna—she sat up in bed, sipping it and giggling, and telling a long lavatory story about how Uncle Paolo had once taken cascara—"but, eating it like chocolate!"—in mistake for something else.　Almina had to laugh, though she was on thorns to slip away to the stink-horns, to see if there was a note to confirm a projected walk for the next morning; she was getting accustomed to the appalling frankness of Marietta and her cousins, and suffi-ciently inured to the water-closet brand of joke to be amused by it.　When the senna was all imbibed she kissed her pupil warmly, told her to stop giggling and go to sleep, and went out.　She did not know that Marietta lay awake for hours, after that, staring with hot wide eyes at the glimmering oblongs of the windows—heard her own light steps on the gravel below, going and then returning; coming upstairs; heard, much later, the little gate down by the road whine on the stone, and other footfalls crossing the terrace—did not know that the child sat up in bed then, straining her ears for sounds in the house to indicate where those last steps went, but hearing nothing—till at last, exhausted, she fell asleep.

Almina took her early walk next morning.　There had been a pressing note from Roffredo, saying that he had news for her, and she fled along the ridge, and dipped down through the larch plantation into the Park with quick light breath, flying colour, and a bounding heart, wondering what the news might be.　Confused thoughts of an open engagement, marriage—some sudden decision of that sort—floated in and out of her head.　She was in no hurry—Edwardian maidens were seldom in anything so practical as a hurry about their love affairs; to love, to wait and dream was good enough, for a long long time.　But an end of concealment would be a real relief; and a new and disquieting urgency in Roffredo's kisses, a rather fierce audacity in his caresses, just of late, warned her startled instinct, rather than her mind, of some subtle altera-tion in their relationship.　She could not know, poor wretched

child, how the freedoms permitted and even encouraged by
the Marchesa's maturity and experience reacted on Roffredo's
much deeper feeling for herself.  Left alone, her shynesses,
her simplicities and obvious innocence might have led him
gently into the paths of tenderness and restraint; but the constant stimulus and incitement of his relation with the Marchesa,
where only the physical was involved, intensified and made
more crude his passion for Almina.

The news, however, was of a different sort.  Roffredo,
having engulfed her in a vast embrace, and told her that she
was looking like Aurora ("whoever she may be, cara!") burst
out with the tidings that he had at last worked out the modifications for his invention satisfactorily.  He could speak and
think of nothing else, and nothing would satisfy him but that
Almina should come to the villa and see the triumphant
arrangement.  Very much against her will, she went with
him—across the pastures, grey with dew still, under the tufted
daffodil-heads of the autumn poplars, on their white slender
stems, and in by the back gate to the villa.  In those days,
to visit a young man's rooms unescorted, in any circumstances,
even at half-past six in the morning, was a dangerously disreputable thing to do, and Almina knew it—she was ill at
ease, and even less capable than she would normally have been
of taking in Roffredo's eager explanations.  From the workshop, constructed roughly on a foundation of greenhouse in
the garden, he led her through a covered passage into his
sitting-room and showed her the plans, set out on the sloping
draughtsman's desk—"See, here—." "The cylinders are now
set so—this makes the whole difference."  But her anxious
eyes strayed constantly from the blue-prints, and the incomprehensible drawings dotted with figures to the door,
fearing at any moment to see it open and old Alba's head
appear round it.  She did however take in, with thirsty
curiosity, all the features of this room where he lived and
worked: the divan in the corner, the printing-frame set in the
South window, with the tracing-cloth still fastened in it

ready to make duplicates of the blue-prints when the sun should be up—Roffredo was draughtsman enough to make his own blue-prints, "though, of course, they will retrace them in their own office if they actually use this thing, because they have their own conventions about details"—the great untidy writing-table, the bookshelves full of technical volumes, the signed photographs of racing motorists on the mantelpiece. The top drawer of the writing-table was open —glancing in, among a litter of papers, she saw a revolver. "What on earth is that for?" she asked, curiously.

"Oh, I carry one when I travel—when I went to San Francisco I was quite glad of it, once or twice!" he answered, laughing carelessly. He took it out, quickly shutting the drawer—per carità! where had he left those notes of Suzy's?— and showed it to her, and the neat mechanism for loading and ejecting; any good piece of mechanical craftsmanship had interest and actual beauty for Roffredo. They lingered long, in spite of her anxiety, for when he had shown her everything he remembered to kiss her again, and both were stirred by his doing so there, in his house, in the enclosed privacy of his room—it was past seven when at last she glanced at the watch in her belt. Nervous, unhappy now, she left; he too looked anxiously all round before they slipped out, hurried through the pastures, and so to the edge of the park. Neither saw— neither could have seen—old Alba, just out of bed, peering through the slats of her closed shutters. But she saw the pretty Inglesina clearly enough, walking away with the young Count.

In spite of the absence of telephones and other modern conveniences, the news service in the Province of Gardone was exceedingly good. There were not only the note-bearing boys on bicycles; there was also the conductor of the diligence, the postman, who practically exercised the functions of a town crier, and the waiting coachmen and footmen at various hall-doors, who held fruitful converse with their colleagues within. By these various means, news flew. On the afternoon of that day, Antonio, Roffredo's chauffeur-groom-factotum, was despatched by Alba to Odredo to request from Anna the cook a good boiling of black grapes for jam. Count Carlo still possessed some vines of the native variety, as well as the phylloxera-resisting Concord grape, introduced from America, with its revolting flavour of black currants, which spoiled the jam as much as elderly connoisseurs, the happy drinkers of pre-1870 claret, hold that it has spoiled French wine. The Concord grape had overrun the province, and good black ones were hard to come by—but the Count had plenty, and Antonio was Anna's nephew. This being so, it was not unnatural that he should confide to his aunt, Alba's confidence to him on the subject of Almina's morning visit to the villa; and no one familiar with Italian country life will be surprised that Anna, in the course of next morning's household colloquy with Fräulein Gelsicher, should have passed this exciting item on to her. It was slipped in very neatly and casually, sideways. "Sissignorina. The jam is made. Alba sent Antonio across yesterday for some grapes, Signorina, to make jam for the young Signor Conte—so I gave him a good basketful. He said the Signorina inglesa from Vill' Alta had been to call on the young Signor Conte before breakfast. I gave him at least twelve kilos, as I thought the Signorina would wish them to have plenty. . . ." etc. etc.

This piece of information upset Fräulein Gelsicher very much. Elena's account of the morning walks, and her own opinion of the girl's character preserved her from worrying over any possible implications of the fact that Miss Prestwich had only been seen to leave the villa, which by direct questioning she elicited from Anna; but, if true, it was quite bad enough as it was. It was madly indiscreet; it was impossible. She must be stopped. Sighing, seated at her toilet-table, the Swiss poked dejectedly at her grey hair, through which one of the brown pads peered coyly, and thought when she could see Almina. Not today—the whole Vill' Alta party was going

to a tennis tournament at Macerbo, which Elena had refused
to attend because she said the play would be too bad.    And
tomorrow would be difficult too, because it was laundry day;
and in addition they wanted, she and Anna, to make a last
brew of grape jam before they got involved in the preparations
for Count Carlo's picnic to Meden at the end of the week.
However, tomorrow it had better be.    The children were
going to Vill' Alta for informal tennis, and she could easily go
too, without any fuss or explanations.    And she must think
tonight, when she was quiet and less busy, exactly how she
could most helpfully talk to that poor child.    For Fräulein
Gelsicher was one of those people who always went behind
effects to causes, and sought to help *there*—it was one of the
secrets of her influence.    And she realised that this was no
casual freak, or piece of outrageous daring naughtiness such
as some girls went in for.    She knew Almina too well for that.
The girl must be head over ears, crazy with love, to have done
such a thing.    And it was that ground-work, that fundamental fact, which had to be tackled; and to tackle it wisely,
knowing all that she knew and Almina did not, she must learn
all she could about it, from the girl herself.    Tomorrow,
then.

But before tomorrow came a fresh perturbation overtook
Fräulein Gelsicher.    Anna was again the source.    Late in the
afternoon they were weighing out grapes together in the huge
vaulted kitchen, to stand, with the loose sugar over them,
disintegrating in vast copper preserving-pans against the next
day's boiling, when Anna, having sent her rough-haired
kitchen-girls flying on various errands, said, finger on lip—
"Signorina, it isn't only the little Signorina who goes to the
young Conte's villa.    There has been also the Marchesa from
over there"—she jerked a thumb over her shoulder; "last
night Antonio saw her, going away.    Nearly midnight!    He
brought back the basket just now, and told me.    *È brutta
cosa, questo, sa!*"

Fräulein Gelsicher listened with more concern than she

allowed to appear; when Anna's recital was over she warned her against repeating gossip, and uttered some strictures against Antonio for reporting things outside his master's house. But she realised fully why Anna had told her, and why the cook regarded this episode as an "ugly thing". Anna, old and loyal, knew all about the Marchesa's liaison with Count Carlo, and accepted it tolerantly; though it had never been mentioned between them, she knew also that "La Signorina" knew of it, and knew that she, Anna, knew. This fresh development was a hit at her master, a disloyalty to the existing order of things—and though Anna, like everyone else, slightly despised Count Carlo, her dogged peasant mind saw no reason in that for being anything but unswervingly faithful to him and to his interests. So "La Signorina" had to be told. And she had also, because the gentry always did these things, to make those remarks about gossip and Antonio. But the remarks did not trouble Anna in the least. Having said her say, she settled her white kerchief further down on her greying hair, screeched a summons to her underlings, as one whistles up a lot of dogs, and went on with her work. That job was done.

For Fräulein Gelsicher, however, the job was only just beginning. This confirmation of Elena's guesses and suspicions—for it is noteworthy that in the Marchesa's case she had no doubts either as to the accuracy of Antonio's statement, or as to *any* of its implications—made the whole thing much more difficult. Miss Prestwich and her indiscretion must of course be dealt with, but it was not much good dealing with her alone—the matter must really be treated as a whole. Like Miss Prestwich, Fräulein Gelsicher had noticed Marietta's curious listlessness and abstraction, these last few days, and it shot across her mind now, with a spasm of real fear, that some inkling as to her Mother's behaviour might be the reason for this change in the child's manner. And that that should go any further, should become a real revelation, was to her strong benevolent goodness simply unbearable. It must be prevented.   But to deal with the thing as a whole was, she felt, beyond her powers.   This, hundredth birthday or no hundredth birthday, was a matter for La Vecchia Marchesa.   Before taking any other step, she would see her. Tomorrow.

## Chapter Fifteen

THE conversation between those two women was, in its way, something of a masterpiece. "La Signorina" had let it be known (by means of Luigi and his bicycle, and one of the enwrapped notes) that she was accompanying the young people to Vill' Alta, and that her visit was primarily a call on La Vecchia Marchesa. This announcement was perfectly normal, since the old lady did not receive an unlimited number of guests, and permission had, so to speak, to be obtained; but while creating no suspicions, it was quite enough to make the shrewd old woman glance sharply at the Swiss when they were seated together in her sitting-room upstairs, where the sun-blinds, lowered against the glare, made the light dim and yellow.

"The children are well? And Carlo?" she asked.

"Very well. But, Marchesa, I am not perfectly at ease about Marietta," Fräulein Gelsicher said. She had decided that this was both the easiest and probably the most efficacious line of approach.

"No? What do you find amiss?" the old lady asked.

"She is pale, and absent-minded, and unusually silent, even for her," the Swiss answered. "For some reason, I think that she is unhappy."

"And have you any idea what the reason may be?" the old Marchesa enquired.

"I know, unfortunately, of something which might be the reason, though I cannot say if it is or not," Fräulein Gelsicher said, gravely. "It is a disagreeable matter, Marchesa, and I make my apologies for the necessity of mentioning it. I do so most unwillingly, but I feel that you alone are capable of dealing with it." She sighed, and straightened her hat.

"Speak out, my good Signorina," the old lady said, rather sharply—suspense always made her impatient. "We know one another, after all."

"Had it struck you that Count Roffredo was on rather—affectionate terms with the young Marchesa," Fräulein Gelsicher said—for all the old lady's encouragement, she found it hard to say what she had come to say.

"Everyone flirts with Suzy," said La Vecchia brusquely. "Of course he does too—naturally I have seen this. What else?"

"If it is a flirtation, it is being carried beyond the bounds of discretion," the governess said, firmly. "The night before last she was at the villa till nearly midnight. The servants are talking. That in itself is not so much, but Elena has noticed it too. And it is possible that Marietta, also, sees something at last. I mean that Marietta sees something," she added hastily, a flush mounting to her thin cheeks at her slip —"and if so, it might be this which is distressing her."

"Hm! Don't distress yourself too much, Signorina," said the old lady, quite kindly. "One can't cook a chicken without pulling out the feathers! How much does Elena know? Does she know about the villa?"

"I think not—Anna told me, and I forbade her to mention it to anyone else. But once talk begins, it is hard to stop it. And Elena is terribly observant." She sighed.

"Elena would have too much sense to speak to the little one about it?" the old Marchesa queried sharply.

"Oh yes. And in any case I forbade her to, long ago," the Swiss said. Then she coloured again—slip number two! But the old Marchesa took these matters with admirable calm. The fact was that she had seen a good deal more than she was prepared to admit to the governess—she had noticed Marietta's pallor and silences, the last few days, and she had observed in her daughter-in-law many minute signs which betrayed, to her experience, something like infatuation. She too had heard the little gate at the foot of the steps whine late at night, and more than once.   She feared that Suzy was getting reckless.   Women did, at her age—and particularly about younger men!   Actually this ventilation of the subject with the good Gelsicher was a relief to her.

"That was well.   And she obeys you still?" she said.

"In such things, yes."

"H'm!   I wish *you* were Marietta's governess!" said the old lady.

"Marchesa, there is another difficulty," Fräulein Gelsicher said.   "I must say that I have seen nothing in her behaviour but the most perfect discretion and propriety, and I do not wish to prejudice her position in any way, for I have a great respect for her, but——"

"Well, what now?" La Vecchia interrupted sharply; "Is that little creature also conducting a flirtation with Giulio?"

"No.   But Elena thinks that Count Roffredo is in love with *her*," the Swiss said.

Old ladies of nearly a hundred seldom whistle.   But La Vecchia Marchesa's expression at this announcement of Fräulein Gelsicher's was the visible counterpart of the whistle of astonishment.   She sat for some moments, in the yellow gloom, looking straight in front of her, with her brilliant black eyes, while her old ivory-white fingers tapped lightly on the carved arm of her chair.   Then—Fräulein Gelsicher was nearly as astonished as if she *had* whistled—she gave her little thin ringing laugh—and went on laughing for some moments. But her face grew sober again, and her minute right hand took a resolved grasp of the ivory knob of her stick.

"Dunque!" she said.   "Signorina, this is folly!   It is *all* folly.   My daughter-in-law is foolish, and Roffredo—if you are right—is foolish, and that little Postiche, as poor Carlo calls her, is no doubt foolish too.   Girls always are!   But"— her voice grew stern—"we cannot have that child upset through their folly.   This must stop.   It must all stop.   I shall speak to Suzy—and to Roffredo too.   That is the major matter; the other thing would hardly upset the child so much."

"And Miss Prestwich?" Fräulein Gelsicher asked. She was relieved that the old Marchesa was taking the thing so well, and that she was at last going into action, but that unseasonable laughter had disturbed her, and she wanted to know where she stood, and where her young colleague stood, too. If possible, she wished to suppress the business about Almina's visit to the villa; she had not seen it herself, she felt sure it was an isolated occurrence; and a certain fellow-feeling, an obscure instinct of professional solidarity made her desire to protect the girl from the consequences of a situation in which she assumed her to be very little in fault, if at all.

The old lady looked keenly at her. "You say you have seen nothing indiscreet?" she asked.

"Nothing," the Swiss answered stoutly. "Quite the reverse."

"So—that is also my impression. Well, if she behaves, probably she can stay. It is not *always* a girl's fault if men fall in love with her," observed the old Marchesa, ironically. "I shall warn Roffredo to leave her alone. Though, mind you, a more idiotic arrangement than to have such a creature as governess! And both houses full of young men. But you should speak to her—a light word! She is well brought up; probably she realises that nothing of the sort can be countenanced. You are, in the circumstances," she leant lightly on the last three words, "the best person to do this."

Fräulein Gelsicher agreed. The wealth of implications in that phrase "in the circumstances", tacitly accepted between the two women, gave the full measure of their mutual understanding of the whole situation.

"As for Marietta," the old lady went on, after a pause—and on the name her voice lost its businesslike brusqueness, and became almost wistful—"all we can do, I think, is to watch, and see. If you are right, and if there is no further cause for her—" she checked, for once, to find a word—"*malaise*" she finally pronounced, "she may forget it all. Have you her confidence?"

"No. Miss Prestwich has."

"Ecco! There you are!" said the old lady almost angrily. "Impossible! In any case," she continued, after a moment's thought, "it would be cruel to send Prestwich away now; the child loves her." Again there was that softening of the old voice. "No—you do your part, Signorina, and for the rest, I will deal with it. Will you ring the bell?"

But when Giacinta had summoned Roberto, and he had escorted Fräulein Gelsicher downstairs, the old lady sat for a long time in the golden-shadowed room, thinking. What an imbroglio! Three-quarters of a century of ironic observation of human follies had made her very much awake to the element of comedy in such a situation. At the same time she was sorry for Suzy. She was fond of her, and she knew that these things go hardly with women at her age. And Roffredo —she knew it well—was very attractive; the old woman's experience recognised at once in him a dominant sexual quality, over and above his physical splendour. One could not wonder at Suzy. But—the old face hardened—she had got to behave, now. Suzy had had her day—and a long and agreeable day, too; now it was the child's turn. "I won't have her sacrificed," the imperious old creature said to herself. "My darling, my treasure!" No—at any cost she must be saved from such a moral shock. She sat on there, quietly resolved; she would tackle Suzy, finally and completely. There was no great hurry. After nearly a hundred years of life, time does not seem so short, nothing is so pressing. She would take a quiet moment, when she herself felt strong; she *was* a little troubled with her breath, just now. Tomorrow Suzy had some party, and the day after there was Carlo's picnic to Meden—but after that, some time. Now she was going to rest a little. No suspicion that events might move too fast for her and her arbitrary decisions troubled her mind. The old eyes slowly closed.

When the Vill' Alta carriage drove into the square at Pisignacco two mornings later, Suzy, seated under her parasol,

O

surveyed the scene with amused satisfaction.    She was in good
spirits, and was looking forward to the day.    For one thing,
Roffredo was to be there, and she had reached the stage when
merely to see him, even among others and in a crowd, satisfied
a thirst that now would seldom be stilled.    But probably she
would also see him alone, and she proposed in any case to
contrive to drive back with him from Pisignacco in the
evening.    The Odredo picnic to Meden was an annual event,
much looked forward to in the Province, where picnics played
a large part in the life of the community; it was one of the
most romantic and exciting of these excursions, because it was
so far away, and the scenery, in among the steep foothills of
the eastern range was beautiful and thrilling after the plain.
But the expedition was a considerable undertaking; the distance and the rough mountain roads made it unsuitable for a
good many of the local conveyances, so there was always a
general rendezvous at Pisignacco, where a re-shuffle of
passengers took place; a rough brake, generally used for
the conveyance of goods, was sent down from Meden to meet
the party and take some of them on.    So at this moment the
Sorellone's pony-carriage was being trotted homewards by a
small boy, and the Casertas' heavy tumbril-like barouche was
majestically leaving the square, to return and fetch their
owners in the evening; Roffredo's car was being shoved into
the inn yard among an enthralled crowd of onlookers.    The
square was full of carriages bright with parasols, glossy horses
and shining harness; baskets were being carried about, greetings exchanged, and people hustled into vehicles with loud
cries, only to be hauled out of them again and made to sit
somewhere else.    Suzy ejected Almina and Marietta, who
were to crowd into the Meden brake with the other young
people; she collected Dino and Carlotta di Caserta for herself,
and added Countess Aspasia di Castellone, with a few low
lazy words.    Marietta and Almina joined Giulio, who had
walked from Odredo, on the church steps, where they stood
looking down on the scene—the black shadows under the

arcaded loggia of the town hall, the pale tones of the houses, originally well-built and even noble, but now shabby and decayed, their fine fronts broken at street level by the sunblinds of small shops.

"I *like* Pisignacco," Marietta announced suddenly.

"Why? It's a dirty smelly little place," said Elena, who had joined them. "Come on, the brake is ready—let's get out before the crush."

"It smells of the past—it is old and lonely," Marietta said, wrinkling her small nose as if to catch the odour of antiquity, and following her cousin through the crowd to the brake. There they piled in, much squashed together—Roffredo contrived to sit between Almina and Olivia di Caserta, a lovely little thing of seventeen; this meant knees touching under the striped linen rug, and once or twice he managed to touch Almina's hand too, stroking the palm with his fingertips, while he joked, with a perfectly blank face, with Giulio opposite. Almina had not so much control—the soft urgent movement of his fingers in the curve of her palm sent little shivers running all through her body; she was afraid of her too-ready changes of colour, and turned her head over her shoulder to look out behind her. What she saw was worth looking at. Soon they were in among the hills, and the valley narrowed; the slopes were densely clothed with a growth of young sweet chestnut, now turned to brilliant yellow—they moved in a golden world, under a blue heaven, with a lively chattering river keeping them company on their right, whose deep pools were blue too where they caught the sky. Almina at last put both her hands outside the carriage rug, to enjoy all this enchantment without those disturbances set up by Roffredo's touch—this brought her a reproachful pinch on the knee, but she paid no attention. When they got out, he contrived to murmur in her ear—"Cara, I must do my duty now, but after lunch, will you walk with me?" She nodded. "If it's possible."

At this picnic, Suzy had no responsibilities—it was Fräulein

Gelsicher's task to see that lunch was correctly set out on the terrace before the sub-bailiff's house; she was free to wander round the village with Roffredo, stared at with astonishment by the dark-faced round-headed inhabitants, who curtsied with guttural greetings, and to go and look at the waterfall. The Count was busy fussing about the wine—they were to drink white Meden wine, from the best slopes, at luncheon, and after were formally to inspect the site for his new experimental vineyards, to be planted in the French manner; this, for him, was the *raison d'être* of the picnic.   Walking with Roffredo now, enjoying her temporary freedom, Suzy thought of Carlo.   Poor Carlo!—with his vines and hopes and experiments, his futile gallantry.   Under the compulsion of her feeling for Roffredo, she had latterly modified her relation with him, on various excuses, and his slightly fatigued acceptance of her denials had shown up to her, at last, her old liaison for the poor thing that it was.   Looking covertly at the young man beside her, with his youth and vigour, his abrupt hawklike swoops of mirthful comment, his grace and his laughter, she sighed with happiness, thinking how wonderful it was to have this splendour for her own, to hold his devotion.   But—her thoughts turned back to Carlo—she could not, would not, withdraw her friendship and interest so abruptly; these were what he really needed from her, and he should keep them.   She even took a new subtle pleasure in being what Carlo wanted, as perfectly as possible, for Roffredo's sake—and when the time came, after lunch, to make the tour of the vineyards, she put up her parasol, and with a gallant gaiety walked about on the hot rough earth of the terraces in her thin small shoes, asking questions, showing interest, being what was wanted, with exquisite and easy skill.

But after a time she became aware that Roffredo was no longer there to mark the perfection of her performance.   The party, trailing round in the heat, became thinner and thinner, till besides herself and the Count only Fräulein Gelsicher, the Sorellone  Dino di Caserta, who grew vines scientifically too, and Ernest's little boy (who came because he liked picking and eating the grapes) were left, apart from Ospedi and the sub-bailiff, who stood respectfully about in the background, and answered questions when applied to. Suzy's interest began to flag then—she noticed how hot and sore her feet were, and how rough and nubbly the ground; but she held up heroically till the grateful moment when Fräulein Gelsicher suggested quietly that they had seen enough—all the proposed new part—and that the gentlemen might go on alone if they wished to examine the high slopes further on. So they retired to the little meadow by the stream, fringed with wild raspberries, where coffee was to be drunk, and sat on rugs in the shade.

Fräulein Gelsicher had her own reasons for this adjournment. She had counted on a chance at this picnic of speaking to Miss Prestwich. But as Almina had sought in vain for an opportunity to speak to Gela at Castel Vecchio, and failed to get it till too late, so now the Swiss sought vainly for her colleague. The young people had scattered over the golden hillsides, on the ploys proper to youth at picnics—picking wild raspberries, flirting, looking for a view—and though she walked up slopes and down, and enquired of those she met, she found no trace of Almina. Even when the party gradually reassembled, tired, hot, and ready for lemonade or coffee, there was no sign of Miss Prestwich, and it was presently observed that both Giulio and Count Roffredo were missing too. And suddenly—it might have been due to Fräulein Gelsicher's obvious fussing—Suzy's suspicions flared up again. Though tired, she had been so happy and serene, waiting there by the musically-flowing water, thinking of the drive back and the evening at Vill' Alta, remembering the pleasure of the morning stroll—now it was all turned again to poison and pain. With unusual energy, she declared gaily that they must be found, those three wanderers—let there be a search! And no great enthusiasm showing itself—indeed to her annoyance Elena went so far as to observe languidly that they all three had watches, and would doubtless come in good time—she set an example by rising herself and starting off—it was cooler now, and pleasant to walk!—escorted by the Count.

"Misfortune on her!" Elena muttered to her governess. "Now she may find them!" And she herself set off too, in the direction where she had last seen Roffredo and Almina, seeking a hilltop whence they would get a view.

But it is hard to find a view on those wooded hills of Gardone. The growth of young trees clothes them to the very top, so that when one has struggled up a wood-cutter's path, at the summit one finds the leafy roof still over one's head, and curtains of foliage draped all round. This had happened to Roffredo and Almina; in vain, holding her hand, he had tugged her, laughing and breathless, up various tunnel-like wood-shoots, walled with the dark stems and floored and canopied with gold—at the top there was still nothing to be seen but the golden pattern of the leaves against blue sky—her face, he said, laughing and kissing it, was the only view! Still hopeful, lost in the delight of each other's presence, they had rambled far from the point where they set out, and it was Suzy and not Elena who at last found them. Was it blind chance, or some sharpened subconscious faculty which led her to take that high path near the waterfall? Anyhow there, where the roar of the falling water drowned footsteps and voices alike, walking a little ahead of the Count, she came on them. They were sitting in a hollow far below the path, leaning against a rock—at least Roffredo so leant; the girl half-lay with her head on his shoulder, her face upturned to his, utterly surrendered, while with his free hand he played with her hair, arranging a yellow chestnut-leaf in its paler gold, trying it this way and that. The tender absorption of his gestures, the utter rapture of her upturned face told a tale of mutual passion so clear that it could not be mistaken.

At the sight Suzy stopped dead. She reached out and

touched the nearest tree, as if to support herself—her other hand hung limp and inert.  She felt cold and slightly sick. She opened her mouth, but no sound came out of it.  Count Carlo, coming up behind her, said "Cosa è, cara?"—and she realised that he had seen nothing.  Suddenly she knew that he must not—that *no one* must see this sight which was her private humiliation.  She turned and faced him, manœuvring him back along the path.  "It is no good going on," she said; "the path stops at the waterfall.  Let us go back,"—and she pushed him gently ahead of her.  She must do this now, what was necessary; try not to think, to feel, till later.  "Let us go down," she said, when they had retraced their steps some distance—they took a downhill path, and when they reached the bottom, safely out of sight of the hollow, she stopped again.

"Call, Carlo," she said.  "They may be somewhere about. Forte! Because of the torrent."

But when the Count lifted up his voice in a brazen bellow, she turned aside and again leant for a moment against a tree. In imagination she saw the sound reach that lovely idyll in the hollow, saw that blissful group torn apart by the summons from a forgotten world—saw the last eager clinging kiss.  Oh no, she could not bear it!  How was she going to bear it? How dared he?  How dared she?  As the first shock passed, anger and torment woke in her.  The Count shouted again— and this time there was a faint answering cry above the distant roar of the waterfall.

"Bene!  That was Roffredo.  I wonder where he was, that we did not see him," he babbled cheerfully—then, as she did not answer, he looked at her.  "Cara, you look pale," he said with concern.  "Are you well?"

"I am tired," she said; "it was so hot in the vineyard. Come—let us go back; they will follow."

They did turn up, eventually, where the rest sat drinking coffee by the stream, but separately—Miss Prestwich first, carrying a bunch of wild-flowers, Count Roffredo a few minutes later.  Giulio, who alone had found a view, having scrambled to a distant rocky summit, had already re-appeared; so had Elena.    That young lady noted the separate arrivals and the wild-flowers with amused approval—"Postiche is coming on!" was her inward comment.    Fräulein Gelsicher was not quite sure what to make of it.    But Suzy eyed the flowers in the English girl's hand with real hatred.    Artful little creature! she used every ruse to protect herself and cover her duplicity.    And when the girl civilly offered to take away her cup, she refused coldly, saying that she had not finished, though the cup was manifestly empty.    The icy tone and obvious rebuff were observed by Elena with a faint lift of the brows—"Dio mio, did she see something, I wonder?" she thought to herself—"Then there *will* be broken plates!" But she was unable to keep her entertained but watchful eye on her Aunt much longer—the carriages were ready, and everyone was marshalled into them.    Was it by accident that Roffredo rode this time with the Casertas and the young Marchesa, or was she determined to keep him under observation?    Elena could not be sure; Roma had come babbling up to her at that very moment with some giggling pointless communication about Giulio and Olivia di Caserta.    Silly creature!    The brake drove off.

But on its return to Pisignacco it was at once evident that something had gone wrong.    The occupants of the carriages which had already arrived were standing about, looking slightly disconcerted and irritated, as people do when a contretemps occurs at the end of a day's pleasuring.    The Caserta tumbril and Countess Livia's victoria from Castellone had both failed to arrive, it appeared, and there were now not nearly enough carriages to take the party home to their various destinations.

This muddle gave Suzy her chance.    She had resolved during the drive that she must deal with Roffredo at once. Even now she could hardly credit the fact of his defalcation—she clung to the belief that it was a mere fancy, and that if she applied her full powers, she could yet win him back to her;

but her stormy resentment and her terrible anxiety alike could bear no delay. It was all quite easy, she said—if Count Carlo would give the Casertas and the Marchese Francesco a lift, sending the former on to Macerbo, the Vill' Alta carriage could take back the Castellone party. "The children can perfectly well wait here a little, if Fräulein Gelsicher will stay with them, till we send something back to pick them up—and Roffredo will give me a lift, will you not?"

He would, of course—and so it was settled. The carriages rattled away out of the square, and Fräulein Gelsicher, Elena, Giulio, Marietta and Almina were left to wait, and to amuse themselves as best they could.

To the end of his life Giulio di Castellone remembered that evening at Pisignacco. The sun had set, and a glow from the West lit up the worn façade of the church—the square was full of shadow, and a hot smell of dust mingled with cool breaths of damp air coming up from the river. Elena and Fräulein Gelsicher settled down on the church steps, on cushions which Elena resourcefully borrowed from the sacristan. But Giulio was in a mood of exaltation, engendered by his climb and by the beauty he had seen that day—he insisted with unwonted firmness on taking Miss Prestwich down to the bridge to look at the church from there. And having once detached her from the others, he was in no mood to part from her again. They wandered rather aimlessly through the almost empty streets of the little town, their feet stirring up the still-warm dust, which gleamed pale before them in the twilight; pausing now and then to contemplate some old fragment of building, an arch, a staircase, or a stone balcony, embedded as it were in the more recent architecture—half-seen in the deepening dusk, these objects took on a fresh beauty and importance. But it was one of those rare hours when everything has beauty and importance. Giulio talked continuously, as Almina had never heard him talk before, on the meaning of life and the significance of beauty—moral and intellectual beauty as well as the beauty of things seen; some barrier was broken down in him, and his heart poured out. He never spoke of his immediate feeling for her, but, unaware still of that, she realised that his soul was being spread before her, and it moved her. Half drugged with love—for Roffredo had been more articulate than ever before, that afternoon in the hollow among the chestnut-trees, she was yet reached in her dream by this spiritual emotion, and answered with vital comprehension. In spite of his insistence, she had never yet read Croce, and did not recognise the source of much of what he said—and yet it was not pure Croce, it was Croce made living and his own by the boy's recent experience. Both spoke, out of their ultimate depths of being, words which they hardly recognised as theirs; yet they had a truth beyond what is reached as a rule in daily life and speech.

To and fro, up and down they went, on the white dust in the shadowed streets, under the strengthening shining of the stars—and now and again, oblivious of onlookers, they crossed the square. Marietta had not joined the others on the church steps—seated alone in the shadow of a pillar, under the loggia of the town hall, she watched them pass and re-pass; she could barely see their faces, but something about their rapt unobservant movement, like that of a sleep-walker's, told her quick intuition what was taking place. She watched, and when they were out of sight still brooded on them, in agony and exaltation. "Oh, for once he has what he wants," she murmured to herself, as they moved out of sight up a side street.

Elena watched them too. She was amused and a little surprised, but her interest was wholly concentrated on the Suzy-Roffredo aspects of Miss Prestwich's affairs, and Giulio's feelings had entirely escaped her observation. Sitting on the steps of the church, munching Biscottini Delser, those nasty little over-sweet marzipanish affairs of Austrian importation which were the nearest approach to a biscuit then obtainable in the Province—"How bored she must be! I am sure Giulio is talking philosophy to her," she observed airily to her companion—no fatigue, or miscarrying of plans, could check Elena's use of her eyes and tongue. And getting no response —"Gela," she began again, "did you notice how unpleasant Zia Suzy was to her at tea? Do you suppose she saw something? Because if so, there is going to be trouble."

"I cannot tell," the governess replied wearily; "but if there was anything to see, it was most unwise."

"Poor Gela! You *are* tired. Pazienza! The carriage will be here in no time." Then she was off again. "Anyhow, I think *she* is unwise, to seek a tête-à-tête with Roffredo at this moment! She was angry, and Roffredo has a temper too. It would not be a good occasion to *lui faire la scène.*" She chuckled a little. "I wonder how they are getting on." She chattered on, but Fräulein Gelsicher paid little attention. It was true that she was very weary, and her feet hurt terribly, after all that walking about in the heat; she was discouraged by her failure to get in her talk with Miss Prestwich, and more alarmed than she cared to admit at the possible repercussions of this first open indiscretion on the girl's part. She must see her tomorrow, whatever happened. Meanwhile she was really too tired to think about it any more tonight. Oh, her feet! She sat dejectedly in the starlight, and thought about her corns.

## Chapter Sixteen

"DUNQUE, she committed suicide! Yes, with this revolver. They found her in her room, in the morning. It seems Zio Pipo telegraphed at once, but you see your Father and Mother and everyone was at the picnic, so they only heard last night, when they got back. Giacinta would not let a telegram be given to La Vecchia, so in the end Valentino opened it. I believe he sent a telegram to say Zio Francesco was away—so Roma said."

"But are you *sure*? Mama only said that she had died suddenly," Marietta said, still incredulous.

"Perfectly sure. Roma told us so only just now, at luncheon. She said she had heard it all from Zia Suzy."

"Yes, they were here this morning—we saw the pony-carriage out of the window," Marietta interjected.

"Well, there you are! I suppose Valentino let it out, and they will have heard something at Castellone, and come hurrying over to sniff it all out!" said Elena, inelegantly. "But Zio Francesco *has* gone to Bologna, no?"

"Yes, he went this morning. To be with Zio Pipo, and to see about the funeral, and all that, Mama said—she came and told us. But she has to stay with Bonne-Mama, because of the shock. And she said I was to wear *this*," Marietta said, indicating her white frock and black belt and ribbons, "'till she could see about proper mourning. And that we were to come out for a walk. So we came. I am glad we met you." She sighed—her small face was far from glad; a puzzled frown drew her delicate brows together. "It is better to know things, though they never think so." She sighed again. "But *why*," she went on after a moment's pause—"Elena, why should she do this, now? That is what I do not under-

212

stand—I thought it was all settled, after the *consiglio*, and that Zio Pipo was to give up that other, and they were to be happy again."

The two cousins and Miss Prestwich were sitting under one of the pines on the Odredo ridge, on the dry grass. Miss Prestwich and her pupil, obediently taking their walk, had headed for the park at Odredo, where there was more shade and more privacy than on the roads; but half-way they had met Elena, and settled down to discuss this shattering piece of news. Almina had been told no more than Marietta, and was greatly shocked by Elena's tidings—at this point, however, she felt that she must intervene.

"I do not think we had better discuss it too much, do you, Elena?" she said gently.

"Oh, nonsense, Postiche! Why not? Marietta is not a baby, though they always think so. She would have been bound to hear it anyhow, quite soon. There will be a tremendous lot of talk, and I expect it will be in the papers— Zia Roma said there would have to be a police report. The police had been—there was a letter as well this morning from Zio Pipo, and I believe she saw it; anyhow she heard what was in it. Zio Pipo was actually away that night, when it happened. As to *why* she did it," Elena went on, " I don't suppose we shall ever know, unless she left a letter. They do, sometimes. Roma hadn't heard of one, though. I suppose she felt that it was all more than she could bear," she pursued, thoughtfully, "and that there was no other way out for her. There *are* situations that cannot be supported."

Almina was struck by Elena's words. She remembered with sudden force her last sight of the Marchesa Nadia—the last she would ever have, now—seated in that chair; the cease-less movement of her fingers over the carved arms, and the sort of despairing immobility of the rest of her figure. She was saddened by the death of that beautiful gracious creature, and pained to think of the misery and hopelessness which must have brought her to it, little as she could envisage them.

Marietta sat silent for some time. At last—"Povera Zia Nadia," she said, in a tone of indescribable sadness. "I suppose I shall have to wait to understand. No, don't explain any more, Elena—I don't *want* to know!" she said, with sudden passion. "Postiche, can't we go home, now?"

"You are very changeable," Elena said—"a moment ago you wanted to know."

"Yes—but not now. Elena, I am not cross—forgive me! But it is too difficult," the child said, her face working. "Oh, Postiche, *can't* we go?" She burst into tears.

Fräulein Gelsicher, less than twenty-four hours before, had said to herself that 'whatever happened' she would speak to Miss Prestwich about Count Roffredo on the following day; and La Vecchia Marchesa, two days earlier, had also promised herself to deal faithfully with Suzy on the same subject as soon as the Meden picnic was over. But the Marchesa Nadia's suicide was just one of those happenings, entirely outside human calculation, which prevent the carrying out of their intentions except by very determined and remorseless people. There was no real reason why Fräulein Gelsicher should not have contrived to see Almina, but the difficulty of intruding on the stricken household, the fear of being thought to come collecting gossip, like the Countesses Aspasia and Roma, and the general concern—which she shared—as to the effect of this shock on La Vecchia Marchesa combined to make her feel it impossible for the moment. As for La Vecchia Marchesa herself, for the time being the news put everything else out of her head. Of course she had to be told, and Suzy undertook this task, despite her private preoccupations, with her usual courage and insight. "Bonne-Mama cara, I have terribly bad news for you, from Bologna," she had said simply, after she had sat with her for some minutes in her room. (She had risen early on purpose, and had Giacinta waiting outside with brandy and sal volatile.) "It is about Nadia."

"She has left him after all?" the old lady asked.

"Yes—for ever." She waited to see the effect of this announcement, and remained silent through the old lady's first outburst of irritation. Her silence at last drew La Vecchia's attention. "Where has she gone?" she asked, rather tremulously, a fresh idea dawning on her.

"She is dead, cara," Suzy said, gently.

The old lady stared, at first incredulous, then with comprehension.

"*Elle s'est suicidée?*" she asked, taking refuge in French from the bleakness of fact.

"Yes—quite quickly. His revolver. She did it well—it must have been over in a second."

"Ma! She had courage, anyhow!" the old woman said. "But how needless! Was Pipo there?"

"Not that night—he came back next morning, soon after they found her. Francesco has gone to him."

She spent most of the morning with La Vecchia, listening and discussing—psychology was little known then, but a shrewd instinct told Suzy that the best way to minimise a shock was to let anyone talk it out, on the principle of sucking the poison from the wound. The main burden of La Vecchia's observations was the folly and impatience of young people, who always attached such senseless importance to things that happened, and would never wait to let Time bring its own solutions. By lunch-time, however, Suzy had the satisfaction of seeing the old lady reasonably tranquil; she ate a good meal, and settled quietly down for her siesta. She had stood it far better than anyone could have hoped.

But Suzy was one of the very determined and remorseless people, who carry out their plans regardless of the strokes of fate; and in this case the stroke of fate actually played into her hands. Her drive home with Roffredo the previous evening had been a humiliating failure. She had begun by rallying him, with as much tact and gaiety as she could summon, on the subject of Miss Prestwich; but the tact and gaiety were thin to start with, and wore thinner against his stiff chilly refusal

to discuss her at all.    They had just avoided an open breach,
but she had done no good whatever; she had said far more than
she meant, had come near indeed to giving herself away
completely—and she reached home entirely lost, at last, in
jealous fury.    It was her first failure, and to fail in competition
with one's own governess would be galling to any woman at
any time—to do so, as Suzy did, just when her heart was stirring into flower at the touch of late passion was a peculiar
cruelty.    Before Roffredo set her down, at her request, at the
little gate at the foot of the steps, she had decided to get rid of
Miss Prestwich, and at once.

The news of her sister-in-law's suicide really helped this
scheme.    She realised, with an added sense of jealous irritation, Marietta's devotion to her governess—to send her away
while the child was in the house would mean scenes and difficulties of every sort.    But confronted with a *fait accompli*,
there would be less trouble.    The same applied to Francesco;
he too was sometimes tiresome about demanding incon-
veniently precise explanations for a course of action, and
stubborn in his refusal to do what he did not approve of, as
in the recent case—she had never quite followed his reasons
there—of bringing pressure to bear on Pipo.    But Francesco
was now gone, for three or four days at least, and the old
Marchesa, at her instance, was keeping her room—she had
only to remove Marietta, and all would be easy.    And the
tragedy offered an ideal excuse for getting Marietta out of the
house for a few days.    At the very time when the three girls
were discussing the news out on the stone pine ridge, Suzy, at
the heavy ormolu escritoire in her boudoir was writing a note
to Fräulein Gelsicher, asking her if it would be convenient to
have Marietta to stay for a few days, alone?    "This house is
no place for her at the moment," she wrote, "and I am constantly occupied with the Marchesa.    She has stood it mar-
vellously, but she will need great care.    But Miss Prestwich
had better remain here, I think—there is so much to be done;
so many notes, and the flowers, and I have the mourning to

see to." She paused for a moment, after writing that, with suspended pen—that list of occupations for Miss Prestwich might look unpleasantly like a lie, later—and Suzy was always careful to cover her tracks. No—for she could let it be understood afterwards that the governess's association with Roffredo had only come to her knowledge *after* she had made all these arrangements. She finished her letter, sealed and directed it with a firm hand, and gave orders for it to be sent to Odredo precisely at five o'clock, when Marietta would have returned for her English tea. And when the old Marchesa had finished her nap, and was fortified by a little glass of Marsala, she went and told her what she proposed. La Vecchia was pleased—it was a good idea to get the child away, and it showed a concern for the little one's well-being which was rather unusual on Suzy's part. She praised her daughter-in-law. "That was well thought of."

So it was settled, and Marietta went off the following day immediately after luncheon. Suzy was in a curious state of nervous tension till she had gone; it was as if she realised obscurely that the real danger, the most profound opposition to her will lay concealed in that small childish figure. She watched the little girl's farewells to her governess with a keenness of impatience which surprised her. "Goodbye, cara Postiche," the child said. "In two or three days, I shall see you again—and that will be all the nicer! Oh, à rive-derti!" she cried, and flung her arms round Miss Prestwich's neck in a long straining hug. Even when the carriage had rolled out of the great entrance gates, Suzy did not feel really secure—she went up to her room, telling Miss Prestwich to remain in the house, as she would need her presently; and it was only when, three-quarters of an hour later, she heard it return and go round to the stables that she felt safe to embark upon her task. In the interval she now sat, now walked up and down, bracing herself to the coming interview—marshalling arguments to convince herself (and others) of the right-eousness and necessity of her action, arranging phrases. She felt curiously shaken and insecure, whatever she did with her mind—it was probably the shock of Nadia, she told herself impatiently.

Miss Prestwich spent that three-quarters of an hour very differently. The Marchesa Nadia's death had sobered her— it had not quenched her private joy altogether, but it had somehow put it out of focus; moreover it had revived her conscience, and this took effect in a newly-kindled desire to do right, to help, in every way that she could. Whatever the Marchesa Suzy might do in the way of flirtations, she had never been anything but kind to her, Almina, and she was after all her employer—she was in trouble now, she had looked quite white at luncheon. The girl had noticed that the flowers in the dining-room and the *salone* were not very fresh; she slipped out to the big flower-pantry leading off the hall— yes, as she had expected, the roses and sweet peas had been brought in by old Ugolino, but no one had done them. She set to, carrying out the faded vases, re-arranging them, and carrying them back; that would be a help, the Marchesa loved the flowers to be perfect. Happy-hearted, she worked away, glad to be of use—it was in the flower-pantry that Suzy found her when she came down in search of her, and the girl turned a bright expectant face on her employer as she came in.

"Will you come up to the schoolroom, Miss Prestwich— I wish to speak to you," the Marchesa said.

Almina followed her upstairs. She was a little surprised to get no commendation for her activities—the Marchesa was usually very generous with the kindly word of praise or thanks —but she was still in her happy mood of humble helpfulness when, in the schoolroom, the Marchesa turned about and faced her.

"Miss Prestwich, I must ask you to leave my service," she said.

Almina stared at her, stupid with astonishment.

"To leave?" she faltered.

"Yes. You will hardly need to be told why."

The girl had turned very white—at the last words the colour rushed into her face. She struggled with herself a moment, and then said, with a painful effort—"I should like to be told why, Marchesa."

Suzy tapped on the floor with her foot—she had determined on an icy self-control, but at this show of firmness her temper began to rise.

"When a governess conducts an intrigue with a young man in her employer's house, and absents herself from her duties in order to enjoy his society, it is usual to dismiss her," she said, with bitter coldness.

Almina, with the misguided shrewdness of youth, seized on the weak point in this indictment.

"May I know when I have absented myself from my duties to receive Count Roffredo's addresses?" she asked, choosing by instinct that particular and most wounding phrase.

Suzy stepped back as if she had been struck.

"At the picnic," she said, speaking with difficulty in her effort to control herself. "When you should have been in attendance on my daughter, you were in his arms! It was very well thought of, to return separately, and with flowers in your hand!—but everyone is not quite a fool! You were seen."

For some reason, at that Almina's resistance crumpled. Suzy thought that it was the consciousness of guilt; in fact it was the real hatred in the older woman's tones which broke her down—she had never in her life heard those accents before, and they appalled her. A sudden realisation of what this meant rushed over her—severance from Roffredo, though bitter, was the least of it; it was the return home, in disgrace, at the outset of her career; the failure of her desires of helping Marietta, being another Gela—the crumbling of all those bright hopes and aspirations, her Mother's sorrow. She began to tremble all over; she put out a hand to the table by which she stood, to steady herself. Oh, she *must* do something! This could not happen. With an effort which left her almost breathless, she forced herself to an attempt at submission, an appeal to the woman whose fault, she deeply felt, was so much greater than hers.

"Marchesa, I have been in the wrong," she said, struggling to speak steadily. "I know that I ought to have told you, long ago, that Count Roffredo was paying me attentions. But there were—there were special difficulties," the poor child said, stumbling over this impossible aspect of the affair. "And I did once try to end it. But he would not accept that —and then it began again. And apart from my being in this position, there is of course no real reason why he should not —care for me. But I know that I did wrong not to tell you. But except at Meden, that once, I have never let it interfere in any way with my duties to Marietta—never. I have constantly been with her, and tried—oh, even out of lesson hours, I have tried so hard to help her, to make her happy!" She fixed her eyes, now, on the Marchesa's face, in an intense appeal. "So, if you could perhaps accept my apologies, and——"

Her voice died away, broken against the older woman's stony silence, the cruel blankness in her eyes. Nothing she could have said would have shaken the young Marchesa's angry resolve; but her words about having tried to end the Roffredo affair, and Roffredo's having insisted on re-opening it woke fresh tortures of jealousy in Suzy's heart. The thought that while she had been (however delicately and skilfully) taking the lead, keeping the thing going, the girl had been seeking to stop it, and yet been ardently pursued, was little short of agony. For she could not but believe it—the girl's face told her it was true. Well, she would do it no more!

"I cannot alter my decision," she said coldly. "You must leave."

"When?" Almina asked, with white lips. She had realised that there was nothing to be done, even before the Marchesa spoke.

"At once. The carriage will be here at six to take you to

the diligence.    There is a train from Gardone to Vienna at eleven."

Almina looked helplessly round the room, with her litter of possessions—then at the clock on the bookcase.    It was already half-past three.    She would barely have time to pack, she thought; even in such moments, the practical exercises its tyranny.    Then, as the Marchesa turned towards the door, another thought struck her.    Money!    She had very little left—not enough to take her to Vienna, far less back to England; those unfortunate purchases of extra clothes to please Roffredo's eyes had left her small exchequer very bare. Tears came into her eyes at the thought of them.    She forced them back, swallowing hard; she must get this, at least, arranged.

"Marchesa!" she said, rather hoarsely.

"What is it?" Suzy asked, her hand on the door.

"My salary," the girl said.    "There is a month owing, and I——"

"When a person is dismissed for impropriety, it is not usual to pay them any wages," the Marchesa said, in cold level tones.

"But you cannot!—there has been no impropriety—you can't do this!" the girl stammered out.    "I—I have no money to get home with!"

"You should have thought of that before you started on this intrigue—it is no business of mine," the other retorted, turning the handle of the door.

Almina darted across to her, desperate now, and seized the handle too.

"You have no right to do this," she cried.    "It is wrong— it is dishonest!    I have a right to my month's salary, at least. I must have money to get home with."    She was almost beside herself.

Suzy had of course meant from the outset to pay the girl her wages, and indeed whatever was necessary to get her home—her one desire was to be rid of her.    But that unlucky honesty of Almina's about her attempts to end the affair had made her so angry that she lost all sense of reason. And the girl's desperate words now angered her still more. She would *not* be so spoken to—dishonest! She would teach her a lesson. She shook her hand off the knob. "Let me pass, please. I have nothing more to say. But remember that young women who have lost their character have *no* rights."

Almina stood staring at her, her chest heaving with her difficult breath. "This—this is wickedness!" she said, almost in a whisper. "I haven't lost my character. You want to take it away, out of jealousy! Because he loves me, and he doesn't love you! I saw you and him, too!—after Castel Vecchio. It is worse with you; you are married. *I* have a right to love him."

At that, Suzy's full fury, with difficulty held in check till now, blazed out.

"Be silent! This is insolence!" she said. "You will go, and you will go unpaid. Creeping and stealing out at night, to see him, and if you could not do that, to spy! You have admitted your relation with him, and that you concealed it. If you were to speak, who would believe you—the governess who tries to seduce a rich young man? And you boast to me of your success! You are disreputable! Fawning and wheedling, doing the flowers!—so helpful always! Faugh! Go!" She went out of the room, shutting the door with a sharp snap behind her.

Almina remained standing where she was, looking at the painted panels of that slammed door. They were painted a deep cream, with faint gold lines on the mouldings, and small golden sprays in the angles of the panels—she saw all these details, in those moments, with intense clearness; she even traced the outline of the nearest spray with her finger. Her stunned mind involuntarily sought to anchor itself on some visible object; by *seeing*, she tried to shut out the tones of that harsh voice, uttering horrors which still rang in her wounded ears. She had never before met real hatred or cruelty; she was frightened by it—frightened, and completely crushed. Presently she left the door, and began, wearily and mechanically, to collect her things and carry them into her own room; she pulled out her boxes and started to pack. She did it badly —her hands trembled so that she could hardly fold her dresses, and tears which she could not check constantly blurred her sight. They fell in showers on the green dress which she had worn that day at Castellone, when she and Marietta watched the women at work on the silkworms, and Roffredo took her for a walk and told her, for the first time, that she was beautiful—on the white hat with the green ribbons, which he had so often pulled off that he might play with her hair—every dress had some gay or tender memory of him attached to it. Even bitterer was the other memory of that glad packing at home, so full of hope and expectation; May's eagerness, and her mother's love and care. But she went on, in a sort of blind haste—it was as if the need to be ready by six had mesmerised her. And such a horror of the young Marchesa now gradually took her that she wanted only to be gone—gone away, beyond all risk of seeing again that frightening face, distorted with fury, of hearing the terrifying hatred in that voice. What to do she had no real idea, but she must *go*—and so she must be quick! She was really near to hysteria before she had finished.

It was only when she was seated in the carriage, driving down the hill, that she began to think seriously what to do next. She counted her money—only forty-five lire; she had had to give a shamefully small tip to Graziella, who had always been so helpful and kind. The diligence, with all that luggage, would be five, dinner would be five—where could she go, or stay, with thirty-five lire? She *must* do something. The thought of going to Odredo and appealing to Fräulein Gelsicher for help darted into her mind—but Marietta would be there, and Elena, and Giulio; she could not think how to contrive to get hold of Gela without being seen by some of them; and to face them, with all her luggage, dismissed in disgrace, was more than she could bear. They too might think her wicked and shameful—they might already have been told; and who, as Suzy had said, would believe her word, the governess's, the stranger's, against that of a relation —married, popular, secure? Ah, there was *one* person who would believe her, and only one: Roffredo! He would believe, because he *knew*—he would help her. He had money, would help her to get home. She would rather not have had to ask him, of course—but in her helplessness and despair he, with his love, stood out as her one saviour. She must go to him, somehow.

The carriage pulled up. It was the diligence stop. Fat old Tommaso climbed down, unstrapped the luggage, and set it among the dusty weeds by the side of the road; he did all this extremely slowly, arranging and re-arranging it, coiling his straps afterwards with meticulous care. Tommaso had orders he did not like—to put down the Inglesina and her luggage at the cross roads at 6.30, and then to return. The diligence would not come till ten minutes to seven, and a pretty signorina like that ought not to be left alone by the roadside, just now at the vintage-time, in particular, when so many of those rascals of peasants were tipsy. Why she was leaving so suddenly he did not know, but she was a pleasant Signorina, always with a kind word—there was no harm in *her*, he would swear. So he dawdled over the luggage, and then turned his horses round very slowly, leading them; and after that he said the flies were a curse of perdition, and spent more time choosing some boughs of acacia, and biting off the thorns, and fixing them under the absurd straw hats which the animals wore on their heads. At last he had to go, but if the diligence were punctual, there was only five more minutes to wait; he wished Almina good luck, flourished his whip, and trotted off.

The diligence was however *not* punctual—it was ten minutes late. Almina, seated on her luggage by the roadside, watched for it anxiously. A man came striding along through the white dust—his bare arms and legs were stained a deep red to above the knees and the elbows, as if they had been dipped in blood; with his dark face and rough hair, in the low light, he was a frightening sight. Almina started at first; then she realised that he had merely been at the vintage, pressing out grapes for wine. He said "Buona sera," but left her in peace, to her relief. Then a teamster came by, perched on his loaded wain—he saw her, smacked his lips, and made a vulgar gesture. She turned her head away, and suddenly felt a sharp pain across her neck—the teamster laughed loudly; he had flicked her with his whip. Trembling with shame, anger, and helplessness, she sat perfectly still—mercifully he drove on. Oh, would the diligence never come?

It did come, at last, rattling and swaying round the bend, and drew up at sight of a passenger. The conductor took up her luggage, and asked "À Gardone?" Almina nerved herself to ask her question—could they leave the direct road to Gardone and make a short détour along the Pisignacco road, to set her down at the Villa Gemignana? The driver and conductor looked curiously at her—the young Conte di Castellone's house? "Yes," Almina said, nervously aware of their scrutiny. The two men consulted together, while she waited in painful anxiety. Well, it might be possible, but it was off the proper route, do you see, and it would cost extra, with that copious quantity of luggage. How much? Well, it would be seven lire. This was outrageous—frankly blackmail, but Almina agreed, sighing with relief. Fifteen minutes later the diligence deposited her and her luggage at the door of Count Roffredo's villa.

## Chapter Seventeen

SINCE the completion of his work on the new invention, and the despatch of the blue prints to Milan, some days before, Roffredo had been rather at a loose end. The news of the Marchesa Nadia's death had reached him—as it had most people in the Province—in the course of the previous day; this prevented him from going to Vill' Alta, which in any case he felt small inclination to do at the moment, after his unsatisfactory drive home with the Marchesa Suzy from the Meden picnic. That drive had been more than un-satisfactory—it had been rather unpleasant. Suzy had—well, she had practically shown her hand, and it was not a hand that he was prepared to play. And he had been forced to do something like showing his—a thing Roffredo never cared to do unnecessarily, where women were concerned. But Almina he was anxious to see—for his own sake, and to find out whether there had been any "repercussions" on her as a result of the drive. He rather feared it—Holy Virgin, what these women were when they were roused! Look at Nadia, delicious creature that she was—first all that colossal fuss, the *consiglio di famiglia* and the rest of it, and now committing suicide! And for what? Pure jealousy! But he guessed that under the shadow of that tragedy Almina might be both unable and disinclined to meet him for a day or so—and though he had slipped a sympathetic and enquiring little note into the last remaining stink-horn last night, he had not been surprised to find it, still untouched, when he went this morning. Sweet little thing, he hoped she would be all right! Anyhow this business of Nadia would presumably keep Suzy quiet for the time being.

But when Antonio came into the room where he was sitting

waiting for dinner, idly turning over the pages of an American engineering magazine, and said that a Signorina was at the door and wished to speak to the Signor Conte, he sprang up with a prophetic pang of suspicion. "Che Signorina?"

"Quella Signorina inglese, da Vill' Alta," Antonio replied.

"But bring her in! Corpo di Bacco, don't leave her outside!" And without waiting for the servant, he strode to the door.

One glance at the girl standing there, with her white face, and her luggage on the path beside her, told him the whole tale, or most of it. O Gesù in Paradiso, *what* a bitch!

"Come in, cara," he said gently—"come and sit down. No, leave all that—he will see to it. Antonio! Bring some brandy and soda—quickly!" He led her in, and set her down in the big armchair; took off her hat, the straw sailor which had so impressed Giulio with its youthfulness the day she arrived at Vill' Alta, and threw it on the divan. He stooped and gave her a quick kiss before the servant returned. "Don't talk now, little love," he murmured—"wait till you have drunk something—you look half-dead."

"It is the money—I have no money," the girl said in a low breathless tone, turning her grey eyes, which looked immense in the dead whiteness of her face, up to his. "But you will lend me enough to get home with, won't you, Roffredo? You see without money, I can't do *any*thing"—her voice sank away, on the last words, into the tonelessness of complete despair.

"Oh, may she rot in hell for ever!" the young man murmured, very softly, to himself. The servant just then bringing in the tray, he poured out a good stiff brandy-and-soda, and gave it to Almina. "Drink that, sweetheart—it will do you good. Yes, of course I will give you money—whatever you need!" He stood looking down at her, as she sat there, gulping over the unwontedly fiery drink, with the signs of tears on her small white face, and wondered exactly what beastliness Suzy had used to her; it was clear, even to his inexperience, that she was pretty well at the end of her tether.

"Now," he said, when she had taken most of it, "tell me. Has Suzy turned you out?"

"Yes," she said.

"Because of me?"

The girl blushed deeply.   "She said so."

"How did she know?"

"She said we were seen at Meden.   She said that I absented myself from my duties to be with you," the girl said, her lip beginning to tremble.   "And you *know* that isn't true!"

"Don't worry, cara," he said, taking her hand and fondling it—"here, finish this!   Now," he said, putting down the empty glass—"go on telling me—I want to get it quite clear. Did she say who had seen us?"

"No—but I think it must have been she, from her words."

He considered.   "Very likely—it was that old clown Carlo whom we heard calling.   I daresay she was with him, and they may have seen us before they called.   Carlo is always full of tact!   It might have been someone else, though.   Well, what else?   Did she give any other reason?"

"No—only that."

"And what is this about money?   Has she not paid you?"

"No."

"How much was owed to you?"

"Only a month.   Even that would not have been enough, except for third class."

"But this is monstrous!" the young man said, his indignation rising.   "She should have given you your salary and your fare!   What excuse did she give for not paying you?"

"She said," the girl began—and stopped.   "She said one did not pay people who are dismissed for impropriety," she whispered, and hid her face in her hands.

"Oh Holy Virgin and all the Saints!   This is too much!" he exploded.   "She, with her amours in all directions, mistress to her own husband's cousin!   She must be insane!" He fumed up and down the room.   "One can sue her for this! I will not have it." Then he noticed Almina again; the sight of her crushed figure brought him back to the question of her immediate needs. He rang the bell.

"Tell Alba that we shall be two for dinner," he said, when Antonio came. "Let her make something extra—an omelette or something."

"Sissignor Conte."

"And there is no hurry—she must do it decently," he said, looking at his watch.

"Sissignor Conte."

When the man had gone he went back to Almina's chair, knelt down beside it, and put his arms round her. "Dearest little one!" he murmured, kissing her. She turned and clung to him, as she had never done before—that trembling eager clasp told more plainly than any words of her feeling of shipwreck and despair. "I must be wise for her—she's used up," he thought, as he smoothed her hair. "It's the devil of a kettle of fish, though! Suzy's a tough customer, with her position, and people are so accustomed to her escapades that denouncing her wouldn't do much good. And of course we *have* been meeting—only the mornings, it's true, but who's to prove it? I wonder who *did* see us at Meden?" His thoughts ran on—angry as he was with Suzy, the practical issues were clear to his mind. Roffredo was extremely practical about any matter while he gave his mind to it—the trouble was that he seldom gave his mind to a thing for any length of time; some other idea, entering, could easily drive it out—also to tiresome things he seldom gave his mind at all. Now, however, while he stroked Almina's hair, he thought hard about what she had better do. Really, for her own sake, it would be best if she were to go. She had not *quite* good enough a case to take on Suzy, especially as he, Roffredo, was her main witness. He was not such a good one! He would get her money for her, though, if he had to go to the Marchese Francesco to do it. But any return to Vill' Alta was impossible, and there would be no hope of her finding a place

anywhere else in the Province—Suzy would see to that!—
had seen to it, really, with this shameful dismissal.

"Cara, what do you want to do?" he asked, raising her face
so that he could see it.

"Oh, I must go!" she said, letting go of him and sitting bolt
upright. "I *must* go! If only I can get the ticket. Have
you enough money? I shall send it you at once when I get
home."

"I have *plenty*," he soothed her—he pulled out his case and
showed her a thick pad of notes, and drew a handful of gold
pieces from his pocket—in those days there were gold pieces
all over Europe. "We can get whatever ticket you want, and
you shall have plenty in hand. But senta, cara, when do you
want to go?"

"Oh, tonight! I must go tonight! The express goes at
eleven," she said, again with that sort of wildness of energy
which betrayed her shaken nerves.

"You are sure you are equal to it?"

"Oh yes, perfectly. Besides, where could I be? I have
nowhere to go—I can't stay at an hotel alone."

This was all true enough, and Roffredo agreed to it.
"Very well—I will drive you in to the train," he said. "But
there is plenty of time—it's barely eight yet. We will have
dinner together quietly, and you shall rest a little, and get up
your strength. Come—do you want to wash? See to your
hair? Dinner will be ready in a moment."

They dined, after some delay, rather well. Old Alba had
a passion, like that of love, for her task—moreover she had
the native Italian genius for flavours and improvisations, and
doted on the young Count. And she was seething with excitement over this development. What in the world was the little
Inglesa doing here, with all her luggage, at seven o'clock at
night? The young Marchesa over at Vill' Alta had the hand
in it, for a certainty—she was up to no good! Alba was as
well-informed as Antonio over Suzy's nocturnal visits to the
villa, of which there had been more than one, and even more

*au fait* with her other affairs.   So she cooked the best possible dinner, to celebrate this excitement.   And Roffredo, feeling that Almina needed all the support she could get, opened a bottle of champagne, as well as the red wine which stood on the table; he made her drink both, and constantly re-filled her glass.   While Antonio was in the room he spoke on indifferent topics.   "I sent off my plans last week to the N.S.A.," he said—"the very day you were here."

"Have you heard from them?" Almina asked.

"Only the acknowledgement.   But I may hear any day now. It will be a great thing for me," he said earnestly, "if they take this idea.   I shall be assured then of a future in the industry— a real stake in it."   He talked on, with a sort of glowing practicality very characteristic of him, about the future of the motor industry, which he envisaged purely in terms of engines, and of flying, which he conceived in terms of horsepower and revolutions per second.   In fact this absorbing subject, while it lasted, very nearly drove Almina's troubles out of his head.   He even ordered another bottle of champagne to drink to the success of the invention.

But towards the end of the meal, when Antonio had retired, leaving the dessert and coffee on the table, all the young man's tenderness and concern returned.   Almina had comported herself during dinner with what seemed to him a peculiar perfection—sitting very quiet and formal, eating extremely little, but obediently drinking what she was told; listening, mostly in silence, to what he said, but occasionally raising immense eyes to his face, and making some appropriate remark—to herself and her own troubles making no reference whatever.   This extreme stillness of manner, instead of her usual youthful animation, gave an added depth, a sort of tragic quality to her beauty.   He saw her almost with astonishment—love had already made her more lovely, but pain had made her wonderful.   It was hard to have to lose her, just at this moment—it was not going to be easy to part!   He stretched a hand across the table and took hers, looking at her suddenly with deeper eyes—perdition! how lovely she was.

"Come into the sitting-room, cara," he said abruptly. "We shall be more comfortable there." She rose and went in to the other room, moving with great dignity, very slowly and carefully; he followed, bringing the glasses and the last of the champagne. Let them make the best of these last hours, he thought, already a little reckless with the amount of wine he had drunk, a little dizzy with his mounting passion, as he set down the glasses and bottle on the writing-table; he went over to where she stood by the mantelpiece, and took her in his arms. "Oh, you lovely, you darling," he murmured, and covered her face with kisses.

Almina's great deliberation and dignity of movement were actually due to the fact that she found it very difficult to move at all. A curious lassitude, which she did not in the least understand, had come over her—her limbs were strangely heavy, as if she had lead, not blood, in her veins; on the other hand her head had an odd lightness about it—she seemed to be somehow remote from her surroundings; the table, the peach on her plate, were at a great distance from her, Roffredo's voice came to her from far away, and was moreover slightly dulled by a soft continuous rushing sound in her ears, like the noise in a sea-shell—even her own words seemed to distil themselves, of their own accord, from her mouth. They did this very slowly and carefully; and when she rose to go into the other room those curiously stiff limbs of hers made their own motions, also very slowly and carefully; but somehow they were dissociated from her, she was independent of them and they of her. She had in fact drunk a great deal, and she was in no case to resist it. She had had nothing to eat since lunch at 12.30 (for she had been far too hurried and distracted to think of tea) and in the interval she had passed through the fiercest emotional upheaval of her whole life. The brandy-and-soda, administered with the best intentions by Roffredo, had revived her, but it had also gone directly to her head—it left her without appetite, but very thirsty. So she ate very little, and drank a great deal.

And let no one be surprised that she did not at once recognise the symptoms of intoxication. How should she? Young women in her day seldom met with alcohol; the helpful experience, now so universally obtained at sherry and cocktail-parties, did not exist for her. Nothing was drunk before meals by anyone, and by girls, very little at them. There was an immense amount of wine about—sherry, white wine, claret, champagne and port appeared at quite ordinary dinner-parties, but it was not good form for girls to drink them; that, too, was "actressy", and hostesses looked askance at a young woman who took more than a polite sip of champagne on special occasions. Nothing had surprised Almina more, in Italy, than to see Elena and Marietta calmly drinking wine at lunch and dinner, even though they usually mixed it, after the custom of the country, with water. In time she had learned to follow their example, but a glass of the light country wine took no effect, and there was nothing to warn her of the results of mixing brandy, red wine and champagne, in considerable quantities, on an empty stomach. And her distress and confusion of mind were anyhow so great and so unprecedented that they would in themselves have accounted for almost any unusual sensations. "I must be very tired, tireder than I knew," she thought, finding how hard it was to walk into the sitting-room.

But when Roffredo came and took her in his arms, she found that in this prevailing remoteness one part of her being was still awake. He was being good to her, taking care of her—in this strange revelation of cruelty and despair, which had turned her universe upside down, he stood firm, her one anchor, her single link with the old safe world of affection and kindness. She clung to him, for that. And he loved her. That was of enormous importance, now that the shadow of disgrace had for the first time impinged on her own life, her own person—his love stood, a bulwark between her and the loss of her self-respect. And she so loved him! So, with even more fervour than in those moments which had startled him before dinner, she turned to him now, returning his kisses with a sort of involuntary and helpless simplicity and ardour.

That innocent abandonment robbed Roffredo of the last remnants of his wits and his self-control. She was too exquisite, like this—too unbelievably marvellous; at once yielded and passionate. "Come to the divan, cara," he murmured into her mouth. "Come!" He led her across the room, and then lifted her bodily and laid her down on the heaped cushions. Prolonging the perfection of her mood, in spite of her protests he gave her yet more champagne, took more himself. But at last he set the glasses down, and returned to her. Lying there, enveloped in his caresses, that strange anaesthesia which had sometimes frightened her before returned. But now it was at once more powerful and less frightening. And she was leaving him—soon, in an hour! She might never see him again. That, almost her last conscious thought, gave poignancy to her love—she could not, in these last moments together, love him enough—her darling, her Roffredo. But the anaesthesia gradually overcame her altogether—remotely and yet burningly, her body was aware of his hands, her yielded mouth of his; she was aware too of an incredible impulse towards him, and yet of a complete passivity and surrender. This was all utterly unknown, unheard of, incomprehensible—and as its mighty strangeness increased, her awareness of it lessened. Consciousness, at last, faded away—to be torn, when quite out of reach, by a furious and intimate pain. Then absolute blankness.

## Chapter Eighteen

THERE was a slat missing in one of the green sun-shutters outside the window on the east side of the sitting-room at the Villa Gemignana. Through the gap thus formed the early sunlight streamed in, making an oblong bar of light which reached to the opposite wall; in its passage across the shuttered room it touched various objects, making them stand out with a clearness which was almost startling in the greenish twilight—three squat inkpots on the top of the draughtsman's desk standing in the window, the projecting corner of the printing-frame, in white unvarnished wood, rather dirty, and the two champagne-glasses on the table, in which it turned the liquid, still and bubbleless now, to a weak gold; finally it struck the wall above the divan and rested, a bright rectangular shape, on the pink distemper. This bright shape struck the wall rather high up when it first entered the room, but as the time passed it crept steadily downwards and sideways, till at last it reached the divan itself. When it touched Almina's face it disturbed her, and she woke up.

She did not at first realise where she was. She was conscious that her head was aching with extraordinary violence, so that the bright sunshine was painful—she shifted her position to avoid it, and shut her eyes again. The change of position brought on a strange swimming giddiness—she seemed to be spinning round and round. She changed her position again, more than once, seeking to find one in which she could feel steady, feel still. Then she opened her eyes once more, and looked about her in a sort of dulled confusion, peering through the dim light, while her senses slowly awoke. Surely this was Roffredo's room? But why did she feel so sick? It was more than feeling sick—she felt *ill*, deathly ill; so ill that that in itself frightened her. And the swimming giddiness did not stop. Then she saw the champagne bottle on the table—the bar of sunlight was touching it now, lighting up the gilt foil on its shoulders. That brought back, instantly, the memory of last night. But what was she doing here still, with the sun shining, in daylight? The effort of thought made her head ache worse than ever, and her mouth was extraordinarily uncomfortable—there was a sickening taste in it. But she was to have caught the train last night! Startled, beginning now to be frightened of something besides her sense of illness, she sat bolt upright—and then saw her clothes over a chair.

Nothing in Almina's life or training had prepared her to meet such a moment. Her inexperience offered no concrete explanation of what had happened, and the views in which she had been brought up no excuse. She simply found herself, without any warning, in a situation of horror so impossible that her mind could not face it. For some time she lay quite still under the rug, trembling a little now and then. A sound outside roused her to the necessity of getting dressed before anyone should come, and, hurriedly, she began to do this. But when she tried to stand the giddiness and nausea overtook her again, and her shaking and uncertain hands made the process a slow and difficult one. She felt acutely thirsty—a glass of water was what she craved for. She even went over to the table, thinking that she might drink some of the stale champagne; but when she got there, some vague associated memories produced a violent recoil—she left it untouched. Now her mind, still numbed with shame and bewilderment, began to work a little, but slowly, and only on immediate things. She must go, somehow. But where was Roffredo, and how was she to get to the station?

Then the difficulty of putting up her masses of hair without mirror, brush or comb suddenly absorbed her. Her luggage must be somewhere about, but she dared not try to find anyone to ask for it. She could not bear to see anyone, anyone!

Except Roffredo. She found her hairpins in a little jade cup on the table, but her hand was shaking so that she spilt them, and had to pick them up—stooping made the pain in her head almost unendurable. And raising her arms to put up her hair brought the giddiness and the feeling of illness on again so violently that she had to sit down. Tears of help-lessness and despair ran down her cheeks. She found her handkerchief on the divan, wiped them away, and went on wrestling with her hair, while that bewildered shame invaded her more and more completely as, slowly, her mind grew clearer. If only she had some water to wash her face, it might stop this appalling headache! But though she knew her way to Roffredo's room, where she had washed the previous evening, she could not bring herself to adventure outside the door. And where *was* Roffredo? And she was still without money, she thought desperately, and it must be getting late—the sun was high and strong. She found her watch on the table, but it had stopped. Mechanically she wound it, slipped the chain over her head and buttoned the watch into the little pocket on her blouse.

There was a sound of slippered feet shuffling along the passage. Almina stood and listened, trembling. Then there came a tap at the door, and old Alba pattered in, carrying a tray with coffee and rolls, which she set down on the writing-table, saying "Buon' giorno, Signorina" very cheerfully. She went and threw open the shutters, letting the sunshine stream broadly into the room, and set a chair before the tray, glan-cing at Almina with a sort of cheerful inquisitiveness the while. Oh, she did look bad, poor little thing! Well, it was no good making a sour mouth at her because of what had happened last night. The young Count should not have given her all that champagne, or taken so much himself either, for that matter. She didn't look at all *that* sort!—she looked frightened to death, like a lamb in a butcher's yard.

"Let the Signorina take her coffee—it will do her good," Alba said, drawing back the chair invitingly.

Almina never moved—she stood, in her little blue coat and skirt, with her badly-arranged hair, staring at the old woman. At last:

"Where is the Signor Conte?" she asked, nervously.

"Gone, Signorina—gone to Milan! He had a telegram this morning, early, early—they brought it out from Pisignacco. This Compagnia has taken his invention, Antonio tells me—these things, I don't understand them, I! But it shall be very important, it seems. So he went with Antonio in the car; he was dressed and out of the house in a small quarter-of-an-hour; and just caught the express at Gardone."

"Did he leave a note for me? A letter?" Almina asked, rather wildly.

"No, Signorina."

"But he *must* have done! He would not have gone without." She twisted her hands together. "Are you sure?"

"Certain, Signorina. There was no note." ·

The girl's face, white already, turned whiter. Her mouth worked. At last—"Did he leave some money?" she asked, very low.

"Veda, Signorina, he was in such a hurry," the old woman said. "He thought of nothing, sicuro, but of the good news about the invention, and catching the train. He was sent for, the Signorina sees. She knows what the Signor Conte is, when he is excited—everything, everything is forgotten!"

Again Almina stood still, saying nothing. It seemed to her that there was nothing to say. So he had gone, and left her here in his house, like this!—she shuddered from head to foot—and had not even thought to leave some of all that mass of money he had shown her last night. *Now*, how could she leave? What could she do?

"Let the Signorina drink her coffee," Alba said again, with practical concern. She poured out a cup, and then took the girl by the arm and led her to the table. Almina took one mouthful, and then pushed back her chair.

"I should like to wash," she said.    "Where is the luggage?"
In this nadir of despair and shame and confusion her instinct
suddenly turned to this simple thing—one washed before one
breakfasted.    Alba fetched her dressing-case, took her in to
Roffredo's *cabinet de toilette*, and brought a can of hot water;
there the girl washed her face and hands, and put up her hair
properly.    And there, having done this, without warning she
was violently sick.    She felt better after that, and cleaned her
teeth with relief; she drank a glass of water, too.    Then she
went back into the sitting-room and drank her coffee, cup
after cup, till she had drunk it all.    That revived her slightly;
and pushing the tray away across the writing-table, she put
her elbows down on the cleared space, and took her head in
her hands.    She was aware of the need to think quickly and
clearly as to what to do next, but it was extremely hard to concentrate, and moreover every attempt at thought was obscured
by an obsessing sense of shame and hopelessness at the idea
of what must have happened the night before.    *Adam Bede*
and the Victorian novelists had given her no data for envisa-
ging it, but they had given her a strong generalised notion of
the fact at which, shrinkingly, she guessed, and of its social
consequences; she knew, in that generalised way, that she was
"ruined", "fallen".    And the knowledge crushed her.    The
night had made true those accusations of the Marchesa's which
she had so bitterly resented for their injustice the day before.

Her one impulse was to escape from the scene of this double
disaster; but Roffredo's cruel carelessness in rushing off without remembering to leave her any money made that impossible.
And *now*, she could hardly take his money!    That would be
like—she pressed her hands desperately to her eyes, as if to
shut out the intolerable thought of what that would be like.
"Oh, OH!" she moaned aloud, in the extreme of horror and
misery—the sound was like a tiny scream.    She got up, unable to bear the very position in which that thought had
touched her, and walked up and down the room.    Alba had
not bothered to remove the champagne bottle and glasses, nor

to tidy the rumpled divan; with the true Italian mixture of insensitiveness and casualness, she had let them all be. They could be done later. If the Conte and the Signorina had spent the night like that, they had—what did it matter to her? But Almina's eye lit on them, and she shuddered again, from head to foot. She suddenly remembered her dream, the dream she had had after their visit to Trino, of herself as a bird, held fast among the limed twigs, her plumage soiled and befouled—in the confusion of her mind this image presented itself to her with almost violent clearness. She *must* get away from here, out of this house! But where? But how? "Oh, if only I could see Gela!" she said, just above her breath. She sat down again to consider this possibility. If she walked to Odredo, which was simplicity itself, surely she could get hold of Anna or Annina, without facing Umberto at the front door, and ask them to bring Gela down to her, without risk of seeing Elena or Marietta. Oh, Marietta, her darling pupil! At the thought of her, of all she had meant to be to her, of the child's loyalty and love and need, for the first time tears came with real freedom—she put her head down on her hands and sobbed.

But the thought of Marietta also brought back an overwhelming sense of her own disgrace. As she *now* was, she could not go to Gela, even, for help. If she had found it too difficult yesterday, when it was only the disgrace of being dismissed, how could she do it now, when—when—when she was ruined? "Oh, if only I *had* gone to her yesterday, and not come here!" the poor little creature sobbed out—"oh! OH!" Why had she not? Why had she not had the courage? Why had she let such small things distract her from it, or even large ones, like the general distress over the Marchesa Nadia, which had somehow made it seem so much more difficult?

At the recollection of the Marchesa Nadia a new idea struck her. She lifted her head, and sat staring in front of her for a long time. She had suddenly remembered what Elena said, when they were sitting on the stone pine ridge, the three of them, and discussing it—"There are some situations that cannot be supported." Oh, it was true! And now she too was in such a one. And the Marchesa Nadia's way out was the only way. The thought came to her like an illumination —the only thought that had so presented itself during this morning of baffled helplessness and misery and confused despair. Slowly, she stooped down and pulled open the drawer of the writing-table. Would he have left it there?

Yes, he had. And because he had shown it her so thoroughly, on that morning when she had been so happy with him, and yet so afraid of being seen by the servant—oh, mercy! she had been afraid to be found there then, walking, dressed! And now! But because of that, she knew exactly how to work it. She took the revolver out, opened the magazine, found the box of cartridges in the drawer, loaded it, and clicked the magazine to. Then she put it on the table beside her and sat looking at it. The head, or the heart? Or did you put it in your mouth? She shuddered a little, at that.

The impulse to suicide is a curious thing. Those who have experienced it, and survive, usually agree that it really would appear to be a sort of madness, so complete is its domination; the restraining bonds of religious training and family ties are swept away and forgotten. At such moments as those through which Almina Prestwich was passing, there is no moral argument—the only questions are "Can I?" and "How?" When these are settled, calm comes. It was so with her. Her wretchedness had been so absolute that this decision, and the prepared means to carry it out, brought her real relief. She was quieter now, and her head a little clearer; she thought more quietly. What had she to do first? The idea of writing to Roffredo came to her, but she put it aside. It was useless. He did not need a farewell, or he would not have forgotten all her need and gone off like that; and—and he would not—. She did not finish that sentence in her mind. But she did not want to send reproaches either; that was useless too.   There was something wrong about the whole thing—his love, her love; she wrinkled her fine dark eyebrows, trying to think, in this strange new calm and clearness, what *had* been wrong with it.   It had seemed—her mouth quivered a little—it had seemed all right; it had seemed perfect!   But that didn't matter either, now; she need not puzzle it out.   It hadn't been what she thought, but she did not know how she could have told that it wasn't.   Let it go. There was one thing though that she must do—one person with whose love there had been nothing wrong!   Tears blinded her as she opened another drawer and pulled out some paper on which to write to her Mother.

That letter to Mrs. Prestwich took her a long time.   It was as nearly impossible to write as anything could be.   Faced with the task of framing the actual sentences, the difficulty of concentrating returned; her head ached, her words and thoughts surged forward and then slipped away again, eluding her.   And she was interrupted at every sentence by memories which shook her, by unbidden pictures which sprang out in her mind of her Mother's face, of little past kindnesses—and then of her incredulousness at this news, her disappointment, her worry, her bitter sorrow.   Now conflict and argument did enter—but mostly under this curious guise of pictures. And she found it impossible to envisage her return, as she now was; she could see her Mother's distress at her death, but she could not see any picture of herself living again at home, after what had happened.   Her life at home—it had in any case receded and become far away, during this time abroad; now it seemed to her that it had vanished, perished completely, stolen from her by Roffredo's act.

All the same, the writing of that letter nearly shook her resolution.   In any other room, probably it would have done so.   But here, whenever she raised her eyes, searching for a phrase, they lit on either the champagne-bottle, still standing on the table with its peculiar day-time air of rakish dissipation, or on the divan, with the crumpled cushions and rug—

and each time that she saw these things, she shuddered a little, and set her small jaw firmly, and went on with her task.

It was done at last. She sealed up the envelope, addressed it, found a stamp in her purse and put it on. She took another sheet of paper and wrote on it in Italian—"Please put in the post"; and placed it and the letter together on the table in front of her. That was everything. Now it had come. There was nothing else to wait for. She picked up the revolver, and examined the catch and the trigger, still with that same curious calm clarity of mind in which she had as it were floated ever since she took her decision. It struck her suddenly that this detached calmness was rather like the odd remoteness in which she had eaten and moved the evening before, only without that sea-shell rushing in her ears. She put the revolver down again, at that, with a little shiver of disgust. She must have been drunk, then, though she had not realised it. But she was sober enough now, she thought, irritated by the memory; the only thing now was to remember the Marchesa Nadia, and how well and swiftly she had done it —to choose exactly which way, and then to keep her hand perfectly steady, and make no mistake. Her hand was not very steady—she held it out to see; but it was better than when she had spilt the hairpins. And she could prop it on something. Very well, then—which place? The temple, under the left breast, or the mouth—pointing well upwards?

There was a sound of voices outside—Alba was speaking to someone. Antonio, or one of the trades-people, no doubt. Well, she would wait a moment till they had gone—there was no violent hurry. Alba had been shuffling about all the time, doing things in Roffredo's room next door, so the girl paid no particular attention to steps in the passage. She sat at the table, the letter and the revolver in front of her, still in that state of almost dreamy calmness, when without warning the door opened, and the Countesses Aspasia and Roma di Castellone walked into the room.

*Chapter Nineteen*

IT has already been said that the news service in the Province of Gardone used to be extremely good—very nearly as good as it was at the same period in the West Highlands. The Countess Aspasia had her coffee and rolls brought to her room every morning at ten minutes to nine precisely by Maria, the fat, cheerful, inconsequent personal maid of the two sisters; this hour was dictated by the fact that it was the earliest moment at which the Castellone baker could be induced to deliver the fresh hot rolls which Aspasia regarded as indispensable to her breakfast. Countess Roma only had her coffee taken to her at nine, and was generally still in bed, but Countess Aspasia was always up, her hair already done in a rather squashed-looking grey bang across her forehead, with coils going up and down the back of her head, and her toilet in the familiar silk petticoat and cambric dressing-jacket stage. Her petticoats were invariably of grey and white tartan taffetas, and her dressing-jackets, more coquettish than Fräulein Gelsicher's, were flounced with Valenciennes edging. On this particular morning Maria was five minutes late, and Countess Aspasia, rather irritated, had begun to polish her nails, a task usually carried out after breakfast. When the servant appeared, she upbraided her brusquely, but entirely without heat. Maria apologised, also without much conviction, and then broke headlong into the morning's news—it was her custom to serve up any fresh items, so to speak, along with the coffee. Yes, she was late, but the baker had been so long telling her, and then the postman had come! The diligence driver was the baker's wife's cousin, and lodged with them in Castellone, and last night when he came home he told them—let the Countess figure to herself!—that he had picked up the little Signorina inglese from Vill' Alta, with all her luggage, at the cross roads. "She was waiting there, alone, la povera!" And she had asked him to take her round by the young Count's villa. Which he had done—yes, and set her down there, baggage and all. At seven in the evening. And—Maria carried on with a rush, dreading an interruption, as her mistress made a clicking sound with her tongue—at this moment the postman came, so they spoke all three together. The postman had already called at the Villa, and had spoken with "quella vecchia"— so Maria described the ancient Alba—because of the telegram; and the vecchia told him that the young Signorina was still there, asleep! Maria, her eyes like saucers, made a dramatic pause at this point.

"*What* telegram, fool?" the Countess enquired.

"The telegram from Milano. It was sent out from Pisignacco. And the young Conte went off at once to Gardone in *quella macchina*" (so the Province at large invariably described Roffredo's car) "to catch the express to Venice. He took it. He is gone to Milano. But the Signorina remains."

Countess Aspasia rose at that moment to an enormous height in her servant's esteem. Without comment, she observed—"If the postman is already come, where are the letters?"

Maria had forgotten the letters in the thrill of all this news. Babbling "subito", she fled to fetch them. Left alone, the Countess Aspasia took a turn down the room, which like most Italian rooms was large and rather bare; at the further end she paused and spoke aloud: one sentence—"This is some of Suzy's work!" The moment Maria returned with the letters, she flung them, without so much as a glance, on the table, and ordered the pony-carriage to be brought round in a quarter of an hour. Then, leaving her coffee untasted, she strode into Countess Roma's room.

"Up! Up!" she cried to her sister, who still lay in bed,

reading a French novel; curling-pins clasped her rather sallow forehead round like a belt of machine-gun cartridges; the frilled cambric sleeves of her nightdress fell over her hands, which were covered with white cotton gloves—her white hands were Countess Roma's chief vanity, and she habitually slept in gloves to keep the blanching cream on them during the night.

"Cosa è?" she asked, rather resentfully, closing her book and slipping an ivory paper-knife between the pages.

"I shall tell you as we go—we must start in fifteen minutes for Roffredo's house. I have ordered the pony-carriage," Aspasia said—and regardless of Roma's babbling protests and plaintive demands for enlightenment, she scourged and harried her into her clothes and through her toilet, saying constantly—"Leave that!" "You can do that later!" about all but the most vital operations. Aspasia thoroughly despised Roma in most respects, but that strange family link, forged by blood and common ties and a common life, which so often exists between elderly sisters made it inconceivable that she should undertake such an enterprise as this without her. Cross, uncomfortable (because Aspasia in her hurry had laced her stays too tight), "practically starving" as she bitterly protested, Roma was at last got into the pony-carriage, a low-hung affair, and the sisters drove off, their flowered hats nodding incongruously above their grey heads in the bright morning sunshine, as the little vehicle bumped over the cobbles of the Castellone street. Aspasia of course drove, and Roma made her usual ineffectual protest—"I might sometimes drive, at least!" Once en route, Aspasia briefly re-told Maria's tale. "Suzy has been up to some of her tricks, for a certainty," was her comment. "Quella piccola is not the sort to go staying at young men's houses for nothing. Prrt!"— she flicked the pony, who though rather ancient still had spirit enough to shy at a goat which came wandering down the road, and flourished her whip at the goat.

"But what are we to do?" Roma asked, straightening her

hat, which the lurch of the encounter with the goat had set askew.

"Ma, at least see what the position is," Aspasia replied, "and find out what has happened. I heard that Suzy had sent Marietta to Odredo without the little Postiche, and I wondered why. She is deep! There may be plenty to do!" she added significantly. "Anyhow, at least, we shall *know*."

Knowing was one of Countess Aspasia's deepest passions, and this hurried drive had been undertaken partly out of the mere desire to be first on the spot in such a major scandal. (She would have made an admirable modern reporter.) But there was more to it than that. No serious amount of love was lost between the poor, forceful, highly intelligent spinster, with her plain face and her awkward figure, and her much richer, beautiful and successful kinswoman, whom, as half an American, she inevitably regarded as something of a parvenue. Sustaining a perfect outward amity, reluctantly conceding all that must be conceded to the Marchesa Suzy in the way of kindness and savoir-faire, in her presence unwillingly submitting to her charm, Countess Aspasia nevertheless nourished a profound distrust of her relation—as Elena and Fräulein Gelsicher also did, and on as slight grounds. She felt that Suzy had it in her to "play anyone a bad turn"; and mixed up with all her other motives for this jaunt was a secret hope that a chance might be offered her, quite correctly, "*de lui contrarier d'une façon ou d'autre*" as she expressed it to herself. But she said nothing of this to Roma; Roma was too untrustworthy—she gabbled. To her she merely speculated, very agreeably, on Suzy's possible actions and motives—"You remember the other day at Meden, when they were late for tea, how she dragged that wretched fool of a Carlo off to look for them! That's pretty—to drag the old *amante* off to help her to find the new one!" She gave a harsh cackling laugh.

"But do you think they were together? They came back separately, as I told you before," Roma argued.

"Chi sa? But which would *you* take for a walk, the cow or

the calf, if you were a young man?" Aspasia asked, with true Italian relish of her own coarseness. And she laughed again, and whipped up the pony.

But there was no laughter in her face when she walked, twenty minutes later, into Roffredo's sitting-room at the Villa Gemignana, followed by Countess Roma. With one sweeping glance she took in the whole scene—the champagne-bottle, the tumbled divan, the girl sitting with a white, rather dazed face at the writing-table, the stamped letter and the revolver before her. It was such a diagram of tragedy that she really needed to ask no questions at all. With a swift pounce she snatched up the revolver and put it out of reach. Then she turned to Almina.

"So that was the idea!" she said.

The girl had risen, slowly, and stood looking at her, while an appalling expression came over her face—that of the human being who is in complete uncertainty as to what horror to expect next. It is an expression not often seen by civilised persons, except during modern Colonial wars; but like the champagne-bottle and all the rest, to the Countess Aspasia it told its own tale. She went round to the girl, took her by the shoulders, and set her decidedly down in the chair again.

"Have you had some coffee?" she asked, indicating the tray.

"Some—enough."

"Va bene. Ring!" she commanded Roma. When Alba came, she curtly bade her remove the coffee and the champagne-bottle—"What disorder!" she commented acidly; while the woman did so, she folded the rug and beat up the cushions on the divan, and told Roma to sit there. In the restored decency of the room she then drew forward a chair and sat down beside Almina. Without a word, without a gesture of kindness, she had nevertheless made an intention of benevolence perfectly evident—that unstrung, disintegrated look began to fade a little from the girl's face.

"Now, tell me what has happened," she said firmly. "Why are you here?"

"I had no money—and I thought Count Roffredo might lend me enough to get home with," Almina answered.

"Tchk!" Countess Aspasia clicked her tongue. "You were dismissed, then? For what?"

"Because I—because I had received the attentions of Count Roffredo," the girl answered.

The Countess Aspasia sniffed. "And why had you no money? Was no salary owing to you?"

"Only a month."

"The Marchesa did not pay this?"

"No."

"And her reason for paying you nothing?"

The girl struggled before she spoke. "She said it was not customary—in the circumstances."

"What circumstances? Speak up—I can't hear you. Dismissed for impropriety? Così! And was that true?"

"No!" the girl said, bursting into tears. "It wasn't! And she said that I neglected my duties to Marietta to be with him, and that was also untrue. I did not—I would not. I loved her."

Countess Aspasia nodded to Roma, registering agreement. Then she resumed her cross-examination.

"When *did* you see him, then?"

"Before breakfast—we walked."

The older woman burst into a lough laugh. "Dio mio! Venus is not in the ascendant at such an hour! Was that all?"

"Yes. I—I did conceal it," Almina said. "He said he loved me, and I believed him—" there was a peculiar intonation of disillusionment on the last words. "But I considered that he had a right to, and I to let him—" again a nod of agreement passed between the sisters—Miss Prestwich's family connections were perfectly well known in the Province—"except for being the governess, here."

"How, being the governess?" Countess Roma asked.

"Roma, do me the favour not to interrupt! It is evident!"

But Almina answered the interruption. "Since I was in the position of governess, I should have told the Marchesa. I know it. I thought of it. But at first I was not sure, and by the time I was—I thought I was, I mean—" her lip quivered—"it—it had become very difficult to do that."

Roma was irrepressible. "Because you suspected that *she* too was interested in him?" she asked, her round eyes goggling with interest in her fat face.

"I saw them," the girl said simply.

The sisters exchanged glances which contained whole salvos of comment.

"Where?" Aspasia snapped.

"On a seat in the garden"—the girl turned her head aside, as if in distaste.

"H'm! Well, that did not make it precisely easy for her," Aspasia observed to Roma. "But you still went on meeting him, after that?" she asked, turning again to Almina.

"No!" the girl said, almost violently. "I did not! I would not see him again—I kept away from him. I was angry. But one day I met him, by accident, when I was walking alone, looking for flowers, and he stopped me, and he would know why—why I had changed to him; and at last I told him. And then—" she stopped. Even at that moment some deep instinct made her hesitate so to give away another woman as to proffer Roffredo's own explanation to her.

Countess Aspasia had no such hesitations. "Well, then what? How did he make you change your mind?"

"He said"—she paused for a phrase—"that—the other—was only civility; that it was necessary; but that it meant nothing. And I—I thought it was true."

"Without doubt it was true!" Countess Aspasia said, as much to her sister as to the girl. "What did I say to you, Roma, as we drove here?" She turned to Almina again. "Dunque, after this explanation you continued to go for these early walks? And how did the Marchesa in the end find out?"

"She said we were seen at Meden. I think she saw us herself. Marietta was with Elena and the little Caserta girl, so I went for a walk with—him." Almina said. This cross-examination was painful, but in a way it was a relief too, to get everything admitted at last, to a third party; and in any case she was too exhausted to resist—she was wax in Countess Aspasia's rather ruthless hands.

"Were you kissing, when she saw you?" Countess Roma interjected, greedily.

"Of course they were kissing! Did you imagine they were playing chess?" Aspasia said impatiently. "It is exactly as we thought—she saw them there when she went with Carlo. And then she got rid of Marietta, to have the coast clear—and now this!" Then she started on a fresh tack. "How did you get here?"

"By the diligence—I paid him to come here, so that I might try to borrow some money."

"The carriage took you to the diligence?"

"Yes."

"And Tommaso waited till it came?"

"No—I had to wait a little," the girl said, flushing—even after all that had happened since, she did not like to recall the memory of that wait by the roadside. Countess Aspasia observed the flush, and guessed at the cause. Never mind, that could wait—she would get that later. "Suzy must be mad!" she said to her sister, briefly, and went on with her main line of inquiry.

"So you came here to borrow money? And would Roffredo not lend it you?"

"Yes—he said he would," Almina said, tears gathering again in her eyes. "He had plenty, he showed it to me; and he said he would drive me in to the express at Gardone at eleven. But we had dinner first, as there was plenty of time." She stopped.

"Well, and then what happened?" Countess Aspasia pursued, remorselessly.

But Almina had used up practically all the strength and self-control she had left.    She struggled with rising sobs, tried to speak clearly, but without much success.    "I don't know—we drank a great deal of wine, and then we came in here—and I really don't remember—don't remember—."    The sobs became convulsive, strangled her voice, shook her whole body; she put her head down on the table, holding it with her hands as if to hold in the sounds by force; but they gained on her, grew louder and louder, till they broke on the screaming note of violent hysteria.

Countess Aspasia dealt with this collapse with perfect competence.    She pushed the girl's head down between her knees, sent for water, did whatever was necessary, keeping up meanwhile a steady commentary to her sister.    "Ma, it is perfectly clear, what has happened last night!    And then this telegram came, this morning, and he rushed off, forgetting her, the money, everything!    Alba said she asked if he had left any money.    That is Roffredo all over!"

Countess Aspasia was of course perfectly accustomed to that peculiar bird-wittedness, that volatile irresponsible hopping from one interest to another, from one enthusiasm to the next, which is such a marked characteristic of her countrymen. But in this case it actually roused her ire.    Putting a fresh damp pad on Almina's forehead, as she lay where they had placed her on the divan, deep sobbing breaths still painfully leaving her chest, she continued—"But this is rather too much, to leave her so!    And indeed to seduce her!    She is not of that type."

"What is to become of her?" Roma asked.

"I shall take her home with us, to Castellone," Aspasia pronounced magisterially.    "For a month at least—until we see! We cannot send her back to her Mother like this—she is an old friend of the Princess Asquini's!    It would make an appalling scandal."

Roma looked slightly aghast. "Suzy will not like that at all," she observed. "Is it wise, Aspasia?"

"My dear Roma, if you believe that after *this* performance Suzy will sing at all loudly, I think you deceive yourself," Aspasia said. "When her own behaviour has been of such an *inconvenienza*, she can hardly criticise the actions of others. She must have been quite out of herself to do such a thing. Leaving the girl alone on the road! Certainly that will have been by her orders. Though I shall find that out from Tommaso. No—I shall do it. You will see that La Vecchia will agree." "Besides, it is a work of mercy," she added righteously, as an afterthought.

She presented the same bold front, later in the day, to the Countess Livia, Roffredo's mother. The return to the red wing at Castellone of the pony-carriage, with Miss Prestwich as an extra occupant, did not pass unnoticed either in the central portion, occupied by Ernest's wife, or in the further end, where Countess Livia lived; nor did the subsequent arrival of all Miss Prestwich's luggage in Roffredo's dog-cart, driven by Antonio. The baker and the postman had of course not confined their absorbing communications to Maria, and both the other establishments were seething with excited but uninformed comment by the time the two flowered hats, accompanied by Almina's straw sailor, were seen nodding up the steep approach to the red front door behind the pony. And even while Countess Aspasia, with her usual strong common-sense, was getting Almina put straight to bed in a pleasant room at the North-east corner, looking out onto the mountains (nearer here than at Odredo or Vill' Alta) Countess Livia was putting on her widow's bonnet and a flowing crêpe-trimmed silk mantle to walk the ninety yards along the terrace in front of the long building, from her own front door to that of her cousin by marriage.

Countess Livia had disapproved violently of Miss Prestwich ever since the day when Suzy took her to call at Castellone, and so enjoyed watching the widow's reaction to the governess's green silk frock and the green and yellow hat; she felt her to be "a thoroughly unsuitable person", and had lost no opportunity of saying so ever since. And now, armed with the flying rumours, with her characteristic brand of rather sour piety she endeavoured to remonstrate with Countess Aspasia on her incredible action in bringing "that young person" to Castellone, "practically under my roof". It was true, as she said, that she could hardly believe her eyes when she saw Miss Prestwich descending from the pony-carriage.

Countess Aspasia was quite unconcerned. "Yes, I have brought her here," she said, "I considered it right to do so. For the present, she remains with me."

Countess Livia's ears were almost as difficult of credence as her eyes.

"*Remains* with you? My dear Aspasia, this is very extra-ordinary. Do you wish to give your countenance to such behaviour? May one ask for how long she remains?"

"She remains for at least a month. By that time it should be clear whether Roffredo has given her a baby or not," Aspasia replied, delighting in the embarrassment she was causing. "And if you wish to know, my dear Livia, the sort of behaviour I do *not* countenance, it is that of a young man who, when a girl in desperation (as a result of gross injustice and ill-treatment) goes to him to borrow money to return decently to her home, uses her distress as an opportunity, first to make her drunk, and then to seduce her. *That* I do not countenance. Do you?"

Disconcerted was a mild word for Countess Livia's reaction to this attack. "How do we know that she went to borrow money?" she said, still flushed by the less bearable parts of Aspasia's speech. "And how do we know that he seduced her?"

"That is what we shall know, for certain, in a month; per-sonally I have no doubt of it, but you can ask him, if you like, when he comes back from Milan," Aspasia said, inexorably, "He should know, unless he was himself too drunk to recollect! As to her going to borrow money, I know it. I have seen Alba, remember."

Routed on this front, Countess Livia tried a flank attack. "In any case, I hardly feel that you ought to have her here among us all. Suzy would not have dismissed her without cause."

"No, she did not. She had an admirable cause—jealousy of her own governess! Did you know that Suzy constantly visited our dear Roffredo at night? Late—leaving him towards midnight? Bella cosa, no? Very creditable to Suzy! As to Roffredo, *there* I say nothing; when a young man flirts with a woman ten years his senior, one knows which to blame! But do not seek to shuffle off *their* misdeeds onto that unfortunate child. I warn you that I shall not lend myself to it! Suzy was seen there, remember."

This onslaught completely undermined the remaining shreds of the Countess Livia's morale. Clearly there was nothing to be done with Aspasia. And though she was not a clear thinker, she did realise that the less the Countess spread her knowledge of Roffredo's part in the affair (which, according to her usual practice, she had made complete by enquiry on the spot) the better for herself, Roffredo, and everyone else. Partly to achieve this end, partly to cover her retreat, she sighed, and said that it was all most distressing. "But the important thing is to prevent La Vecchia Marchesa from hearing of it. It would be a serious shock for her—anything might result! Remember, the birthday is in three weeks, now. We should be careful not to let the story get about, cara Aspasia."

Countess Aspasia had already thought of la Vecchia Marchesa. The old lady was one of the very few human beings to whom she accorded her whole-hearted respect and liking.

"Lo so," she said briefly. "I shall not tell her unless I must. But I do not guarantee that she will not find it out for herself. There is not much that escapes *her*."

*Chapter Twenty*

COUNTESS ASPASIA was quite right about La Vecchia Marchesa. Very little did escape her, at any time. And though she sometimes conveniently failed to hear what she did not wish to hear, her ears were preternaturally keen for all those things which others desired to keep from her—it was as if their very wish for secrecy sharpened their voices and carried them direct to her brain. (Everyone who has lived with very old people will recognise this singular and exasperating trait.) On the morning after Almina's dismissal the old lady, against Suzy's wishes, suddenly decided after all to go downstairs that day. No, she felt perfectly well, and go she would. The fact was that she was thoroughly bored upstairs. But because she had taken this decision rather late, she had her egg-nog in her sitting-room, after she was dressed. The door into the little lobby beyond, which more or less shut off her apartments from the rest of the house, was ajar; in this lobby Giacinta and Roberto were getting her rugs and cushions together, in preparation for the transit downstairs, and discussing in lowered voices the absorbing news of Miss Prestwich's flight to the Villa Gemignana and her annexation by the Countesses Aspasia and Roma, which by various channels —notably the belated sending of a note written to Suzy by Ernest's wife, and carried on a bicycle by a Castellone garden-boy—had reached Vill' Alta a short time before. The old lady, sipping her egg-nog, presently became aware of their voices, speaking with unusual animation; she caught the words "Signorina" and "Villa" more than once, and then Roffredo's name—tilting her white head to the angle at which she could best catch the sounds, sharpening her attention with a great effort, she now heard a whole phrase, in Roberto's voice, incautiously raised in his efforts to convince Giacinta of the truth of the latest development: "It is true, I tell you; the two old Countesses have taken her to Castellone! Giacomino saw them before he started, arriving there, with our Signorina.

"Giacinta!" the old lady called sharply.

The maid hurried in. "The Marchesa wishes?"

"Shut the door!" the old woman said. When the maid had done so—"What were you and Roberto tattling about outside?" she demanded imperiously.

Giacinta smoothed her black silk apron and looked blank. "Nothing of importance, la Marchesa."

"Where is the Signorina Prestwich?" the old lady asked.

"Non so," Giacinta replied.

"Giacinta, you might know by now that it is no good lying to me," her mistress said calmly. "Why has the Signorina gone to Castellone with the two Countesses? When did she leave here?"

This evidence of knowledge defeated Giacinta. She saw that further refusal to speak was hopeless, in spite of the Marchesa Suzy's injunctions to keep the departure of the Signorina from the old Marchesa for the present, so as not to cause her any fresh disturbance so soon after the ill news of the Marchesa Nadia's death.

"Last night, about six," she said.

"How did she leave?"

"In the carriage."

"And went where?"

"To the diligence, credo."

"E poi? Speak up, woman—what is all this about the Conte Roffredo's villa? You had plenty to say to Roberto about it!"

By such means the old lady prized out of Giacinta all that the servants knew; once forced to speak, indeed, Giacinta gave the tale with a certain discreet gusto: the rumour of Miss Prestwich's having gone to the villa and dined there—no, she had not gone in the carriage, the diligence took her round that way—Count Roffredo's hurried departure for Milan early this this morning, and Roberto's latest report from Castellone that the two Countesses had gone over to the young Count's and brought her back, luggage and all, to Castellone. When she had heard it all, la Vecchia Marchesa, without comment, sent for Tommaso. While she awaited him she thought over the maid's story with a certain discomfort. It looked as if Suzy had been most unwise, and her recent conversation with Fräulein Gelsicher gave her a clue to one reason for this lack of wisdom. Aspasia was shrewd—she would not have taken the girl in unless she were satisfied that there was a good deal to be said on her side. There was something behind all this— something which had not come out. Why had the girl gone to the Villa and stayed the night? It was not like her—she was a perfectly *rangée* little thing.

Her meditations had carried her so far when Tommaso was announced. He stood, fat, sheepish, but extraordinarily sturdy, twisting his straw Homburg round and round in his blunt red hands. The old Marchesa dealt with him shortly. He had taken the Signorina to the diligence the previous evening? Yes. Not to Gardone? No. By the Marchesa's orders? Yes. He went nowhere else? No. In all good faith, merely to establish one aspect of the servants' story, which she did not yet wholly trust, the old Marchesa then asked—"You saw her get into the diligence, yourself?"

Tommaso twisted his hat more violently than ever, and shifted from one fat foot to the other. "Marchesa, no," he brought out at length.

"Ma come? You did not leave her alone by the road to wait? Dio mio, you know your business better than that!" the impatient old woman broke out, in genuine surprise and irritation.

Tommaso's embarrassment became pitiful to see. "Si, la Marchesa. E vero, la Marchesa. But we were rather early, the Marchesa sees—and the young Marchesa had wished the carriage to return in good time. And the Marchesa will understand that the diligence was rather late—" his voice trailed away into a wretched silence. Tommaso knew as well as anyone else the disreputable nature of the instructions he had received; it was unheard-of for a coachman to leave a lady waiting by the roadside if, as seldom happened, she were using the diligence at all.

The old Marchesa took it all in. Her mouth drew together in an almost bitter line. "Va bene—that will do," she said quietly. When he had gone she rang her bell again—a little silver object which stood on a small table by her chair.

Giacinta reappeared. "Comanda la Marchesa?"

"Inform the young Marchesa that I wish to speak with her."

"It will be the *colazione* in ten minutes," the woman said, exercising the habitual freedom of controversy with their employers so common among Italian domestics. "Will the Marchesa not first go downstairs? Roberto has all ready."

"Roberto can wait. The *colazione* can wait. Have the goodness to do as you are told," the old lady fairly snapped. Tommaso's evidence of Suzy's venomous folly had made her really angry. But when her daughter-in-law came sweeping in, graceful, finished, beautiful, an expression of concern on her charming face, the old woman felt a pang of real pain for the suffering that could have made her so mis-translate her proper rôle and purpose in life, could have betrayed her into behaving in this crude and cruel way. That it was a betrayal of the *willed* personality she never doubted. But no pain or pity could ever turn la Vecchia Marchesa from a course which she felt to be necessary.

"Figlia mia, is it true that you have dismissed Miss Prestwich?" she began, without any preamble.

Suzy blanched a little. Obviously Bonne-Mama had found out somehow. "Yes, Bonne-Mama, I have. It was necessary," she said in her charming caressing voice.

"Why?"

"She was carrying on an intrigue with Roffredo; it was needful to put a stop to it. Livia would have expected this of me—and in any case, she could not be a good influence on Marietta, in the circumstances. She admitted that it had been going on for some time, and that she had concealed it from me," the young Marchesa said smoothly. "I feel sure you will agree with this, Bonne-Mama."

"It is possible," said the old lady drily. "Though I myself should have considered Marietta's feelings rather than Livia's. The child loves Miss Prestwich. But one may agree with a course of action without agreeing as to the means of carrying it out. Was it not rather sudden? And if it had to be done so hastily, could not the carriage have taken Miss Prestwich to Gardone, at the proper time?"

"Vedi, Bonne-Mama, that is so late for Tommaso! And the horses had already been to Odredo in the afternoon. Besides, in the circumstances I really did not feel called upon to show her quite the attention that would be shown to a guest."

"H'm. That might still have been preferable to her going to dine at Roffredo's, and spending the night there," the old lady said.

No word of this had of course reached Suzy's ears; she was the one person to whom nothing would be said on the subject. She drew in a sharp breath, and stood looking down incredulously at her Mother-in-law. At last with an effort,—"Well, that speaks for itself!" she said, very slightly shrugging her shoulders.

Again that sharp sense of pain and pity assailed the old woman. Whatever she might think of her actions, she admired, even in this moment, her daughter-in-law's graceful self-control. But she had to get this matter cleared up, even if it meant breaking down those skilful elegant defences. There was still that something behind, and she was sure now, from her whole manner, that Suzy knew it and meant to conceal it, whatever it was. A suspicion, which caused her an ever deeper discomfort, was gaining on her as to the possible nature of that something.

"I am not sure *what* it speaks for," she said.   "It puzzles me
—it is very unlike her.   Why do you suppose she went there?"

"Ma, to see him, of course.   Surely it is evident?" the
younger woman said, a note of scornful bitterness creeping
into her voice at last.

The old woman looked keenly at her.   "Did you part in
anger?" she asked.   She was getting there—she was nearing
the clue.

"Naturally, it was not a pleasant interview," Suzy answered,
trying to speak lightly again.

"How?"

"Bonne-Mama cara, how could it be?"   Really, the old
lady was being most tiresomely persistent and uncompre-
hending.   "She tried of course to justify herself."

"But did you part with mutual courtesy, or in anger?
Suzy, I wish to know," the old Marchesa repeated steadily.

"To some extent in irritation.   She was insolent," Suzy
said, a little colour coming into the warm matte pallor of her
face at the recollection of that scene.   "Does it matter?" she
asked, a little wearily.

La Vecchia had nearly got there.   They had quarrelled,
then, face to face!   "You remembered, in your irritation, to
pay her her fare?" she said, "to see that she had plenty of
money for the journey?"   There was actually a note of
anxiety in her voice.   *Was* it that?

Suzy moved to the window and adjusted the fastening of
the sunblind.   For an intolerable moment she stood there,
with her perfect figure in her black dress, and her soft elaborate
fair head silhouetted against the glowing yellow oblong of the
window; while her hands wrestled with the fastening, her
mind wrestled with the impossible admission—she saw it now
as impossible—that she had got, in a moment, to make.
Seated in her chair, the old woman watched her, again
feeling that pain—only now the pain was almost physical;
unconsciously, she put her hand to her left breast, to what
seemed to be the seat of it.

Slowly Suzy turned round, a bitter blank defiance in her face. But when she saw the position of that small frail hand on the little black figure, the consternation in the old woman's eyes, her expression altered. With a swift impulsive movement she went over and stood close to the old Marchesa's chair.

"No, Bonne-Mama, I did not," she said. "I—" her face worked for a moment. "I lost my temper completely, and I—I never went into it properly with her." Even now she could not admit that she had been asked for money by that desperate child, and had refused it. She had been a fool! She might have foreseen all this. "I regret it very much," she went on after a moment. "I was in fault."

The old Marchesa looked steadily at her. She could see it all now—Miss Prestwich's actions, Suzy's actions, and the reasons for them, were quite clear; in Suzy's case, in particular, her mind and her own experience pieced the whole thing together. But what a betrayal! Oh, how foolish young people were! *Suzy* to do such a thing as this!

"My child, you were," she said very gravely. "This was most discreditable folly. Really, it is madness!" she said, her sense of the impropriety of the whole affair gaining on her, and surmounting her pity. "I do not know what evidence you had against Miss Prestwich, but nothing short of *flagrante delitto* could justify such behaviour! The girl is of good family, remember, and recommended by personal friends. And to send her away like this, at no notice, and without money—it is insanity!" She paused—she was not aware of fatigue, but somehow she felt the need to wait for a moment before continuing. "You will have to pay her a quarter's salary, and her fare," she said then, firmly.

"Si, Bonne-Mama—I recognise that. I will," Suzy said. She paused for a moment and then said—"But where is she? Is she still there?"

"No. By some means which I do not understand, it seems that Aspasia heard of it, and went this morning and fetched her. At the moment she is at Castellone."

That had to be said. The old Marchesa was divided between her desire—an unwonted one for her, on the whole—to spare Suzy's feelings, and her strong instinct to check and upbraid folly, which of all things she hated, wherever she met it. That conflict was making this conversation—yes, fatiguing *was* the word, after all. But Suzy's involuntary expression of dismay at hearing that Miss Prestwich was still in the Province, on the *tapis*, and in the hands of the Sorellone, the most redoubtable of gossips, brought her pity to the fore again. She would help Suzy as far as she could.

Again her daughter-in-law roused her admiration by her self-control. With a light movement of face and shoulders, as if somehow burying her concern, she said quietly—"Then we had better send the money there."

La Vecchia Marchesa considered in silence for a moment. "I think," she then said, "that I will ask Aspasia to come and receive it on her behalf. That seems to me the most suitable course. Will you hand me my writing-board, my dear?" She did not say, what was very much in her thoughts, that by this means she might learn more precisely how matters stood —all sorts of uncomfortable possibilities stood round in her mind like menacing figures; she had heard only the barest outline, and Suzy had not been at all expansive with her. There might be worse to come, Roffredo being—well, what she knew her young countrymen to be with women. Nor did she give expression to another idea, that if she spoke with the Countess Aspasia it might be possible to set some sort of limit to the sisters' tongues. But Suzy—it was the one flaw in her self-control during the whole of that difficult scene— made it clear that this contingency was present to her mind also. Handing the blotting-board, with paper and envelopes stuck under its dark green Morocco corners, to the old lady, she asked—"Did Roma go also to the villa?"

"I believe so. Now I shall write this. And after all, Suzy, I think that I shall not come down to luncheon. It is late, and I am a little tired," the old lady said.

La Vecchia Marchesa's courteous note brought the Countess Aspasia over that afternoon in Ernest's wife's smart brougham —the pony had done enough that morning to make it certain that he would be intolerably slow on the eight-mile stretch between Castellone and Vill' Alta. But the Countess Ernest took no sides in the affair, and found Countess Aspasia better company than most of Ernest's provincial relations; she was charmed to lend her brougham and her cockaded coachman. (Like so many Belgians, she affected English manners, and even in the Province of Gardone put her coachman and footmen into hot dark liveries and cockades.) Countess Aspasia was quite ready to go, and in any case, La Vecchia Marchesa's requests were regarded in the Province as something in the nature of Royal Commands. But she left Roma behind this time. Roma was not asked, and, as she pointed out, someone should be there to keep an eye on "quella piccola". "Do not let *anyone* see her," she said: "let her sleep. Do not, Roma, chatter to her." And with Roma's indignant protests in her ears, she set off.

The old Marchesa received Countess Aspasia in her own sitting-room. Suzy was not visible. La Vecchia had not attempted to beat about the bush in her note. "I understand that Miss Prestwich is staying with you," she had written. "There is some money still owing to her which in the hurry of her departure she did not take. I think possibly to procure you a satisfaction in affording you the opportunity of receiving it on her behalf." Garlanded like a sacrificial calf, with civil phrases behind and before, there stood the meat, the admission of error, plain and bald. It was for such a manner of dealing that Aspasia so profoundly respected the old Marchesa. And it simplified the course of the interview considerably. A fat envelope lay on the little table beside the old lady, an earnest of what was to come. But neither was sure quite how much the other knew—Aspasia, for instance, though she had made a guess, was not certain whether Miss Prestwich had been dismissed with the old Marchesa's sanction or without it—nor what line each was likely to take; accordingly, their opening moves were made with a certain circumspection. After the Marchesa had thanked Countess Aspasia for her goodness in coming, and Countess Aspasia had said what a pleasure it was, and how deeply distressed she and dear Roma had been at the news of the Marchesa Nadia's death, and how well, in spite of it, the Marchesa looked; and had asked when dear Francesco would return, and learned that he was coming back tomorrow, Wednesday— and after a little glass of the syrupy Marsala had been offered and accepted, they at last made a beginning on the subject in hand.

"So Miss Prestwich is with you, Contessa?" the old lady began.

"Yes, Marchesa. She is not very well," Aspasia replied, blandly.

"Suzy has had occasion to dismiss her," the old lady said, gravely, "but in all this confusion about Nadia, it was done in some haste, and mistakes were made." She, for her part, did not know if Countess Aspasia had heard about that disastrous and culpable business of the carriage. She took up the envelope. "Here is a quarter's salary in lieu of notice, and the month that was owing, and a full fare back to England, with all expenses. I think that that meets all obligations." Countess Aspasia took the envelope, and signified assent. "And now, my dear Contessa," she went on, "I do not know if you agree with me, but I am inclined to feel, much as I personally like and respect the girl"—she leaned a little on the word respect—"that the sooner she leaves the Province, the pleasanter for her, and indeed for everyone." She spoke with perfect friendliness, but with a certain decision.

"In other circumstances, dear Marchesa, I should be entirely of your opinion," Countess Aspasia answered; "but, owing to this unfortunate mistake"—and she too leaned a little on the word—"a state of affairs has arisen which makes me regard it as desirable that Miss Prestwich should remain with us for a

S

certain length of time." She looked squarely at the old
Marchesa, and the old Marchesa looked back at her. Better
make sure, the old woman thought; and she said aloud—
"Might I ask what those circumstances are, Contessa? I have
great confidence in your judgement, as you know, but at
present I am a little in the dark."

"But certainly, Marchesa. Being without money, except
for a few lire, and unable therefore to travel, Miss Prestwich
—unwisely perhaps, but she was in a situation of great distress
and difficulty—went to Roffredo with the intention of borrow-
ing some. He had declared an attachment for her, and she
relied on him. Beyond his deserts, as it proves. He did
agree to lend her the money, and to drive her to the station,
but as she left this house five hours"—again she leaned on the
words—"before the express was due, there was unfortunately
a considerable interval of time to wait for it, during which he
gave her dinner, and so much wine as to render her practically
unconscious, I gather. In any event, she spent the night at
the villa with him." She paused.

"I see," the old lady said. It was black enough. "And
how did you hear of it?" she asked. There was no doubt
more to come.

"My chattering servant told me when she came with my
coffee, thanks be to Heaven!" Countess Aspasia said—"that
she was there, and that Roffredo had gone galloping off to
Milan on the morning train. It seemed to me distinctly out
of the ordinary, to say the least, and I decided to look into it.
Mercifully I did not delay! I took Roma, and we drove over
at once. We found that unfortunate young woman sitting in
Roffredo's room, with his revolver loaded, and a sealed letter
to her Mother in front of her. That letter saved her life—
without it, we could not have been in time."

The old Marchesa heard her in silence. Only her small
wrinkled hand travelled up to her left side—that curious pain
again! Suzy's betrayal of her better self had been deep
indeed, had almost plunged them in disaster. And that un-

happy little creature, with her pretty face, her graceful good manners, and her devotion to Marietta—to have brought her to this!

"That," Countess Aspasia pursued firmly, "is why I think it desirable that Miss Prestwich should remain with us for the present. Indeed at the moment she is quite unfit to travel; the shock—*both* shocks," she said with emphasis, "have affected her severely. I have had the Doctor; he has given her sedatives; he thinks she will do." She paused, and then said—"Do you agree that this is the right course to pursue, Marchesa?"

"But certainly!" the old lady said, with energy. "We have reason to be extremely grateful to you, my dear Aspasia. You have averted a tragedy. *One* tragedy, anyhow," she amended. "As to her remaining, you are perfectly right; she cannot go home." She considered, tapping the fingers of her left hand on her knee, so that the diamonds winked briskly, even in the shaded room. "You are satisfied that she really *did* go to Roffredo in order to borrow money?" she asked, rather sharply.

"When she woke in the morning and found him gone, leaving no note, she *asked Alba* if he had left no money! To that point she was reduced!" Aspasia said; for the first time she allowed the bitterness of her indignation to come into her voice. "I am satisfied that she went for no other reason. Dear Marchesa, consider her situation! For this dismissal was wholly unexpected. She would hardly have cared to go to Odredo for help, in the circumstances—and to whom else could she apply?"

"È vero—è vero," the old woman murmured, half to herself. Again she considered. Then she raised her white head and looked straight at the Countess Aspasia, her black eyes full of intelligence, and spoke briskly. "Contessa, this is an unhappy business," she said frankly. "Something must be allowed to Suzy for the distress of Nadia's death—she was very fond of her; fonder than I was! I found that intensity very fatiguing!—and for the shock of finding this—entanglement—going on in her house. For I gather Miss Prestwich admitted that it had been going on for some time. But it was not well handled—not well handled!" She paused. "We are all very much in your debt. You have saved us from one disaster. As to the other, we must hope for the best. The first time is often—in somma, nothing results! I could have wished that some other shelter could have been found for that poor child, but—let it be. It is most good of you. But— for *her* sake—the less said the better. I feel this strongly!" she said, with great energy.

"Marchesa, I agree," Aspasia said. She meant it—she was, as always, disarmed by the old Marchesa's courage and frankness. But for all her intelligence and clear sight, she never recognised the ungovernable quality of her own tongue; it never occurred to her that her concurrence now meant exactly nothing, and that in her heart she fully intended to spread this superlative story far and wide.

"As to Roffredo—" the old lady went on. "I have no patience with him! Though he is no worse than all the rest. What did he need to rush off for, like that?"

"This invention! It seems it has been accepted. Roffredo has no stability, in any case," Aspasia said, dismissing him. She rose.

The old lady rose too. Then another idea occurred to her. "That letter," she said. "What became of it?"

"I have burnt it," Aspasia said.

"You are perfectly right. Do not let her write to her Mother about all this—there is no necessity, for the present," the old lady said. She held out her hand, and for the first time that afternoon she gave her little, old, detached, wise smile. "Goodbye, my dear Aspasia. I think we understand each other."

But when the Countess Aspasia had gone, she sat for a long time in her chair, singularly conscious once more of that pain of whose origin she could not be sure. Was it only in her heart, or physically in her breast as well? What an imbroglio, what a foolish, needless, wretched business it all was. O Suzy, Suzy! She thought of Miss Prestwich, with her bright face and ardent devotion to her task and her pupil—and she thought then of Miss Prestwich's pupil herself, her loss, and her horror if she ever learned the truth of all this. "My darling, my treasure"—the severe old lips shaped the tender words; and a tear, bright as the diamonds on the hand she still held to her heart, slipped down the deeply etched lines of her cheek. Then, quite suddenly, still sitting in her chair, she dropped off to sleep.

## Chapter Twenty-one

O N that same Tuesday afternoon, Elena and Marietta, after the siesta, were sitting out by the round marble table under the stone pine at Odredo, Elena sewing, Marietta faithfully and laboriously ploughing her way through *Pride and Prejudice*, a dictionary by her side. It was very hot; the scent of the larches on the slope below, with its curious sweet tang, like the smell of apples, came up to them and mingled with the strong resinous scent of the stone pine —by the track leading down to the park a group of young plane trees stood out in the afternoon sunshine, their thick yellowing leaves so motionless that it was as if they were embedded, beyond power of movement, in the solid golden air. Once or twice Marietta laughed. "What is it?" Elena asked at length.

"Questa Elisabetta! She is so sensible, it comes out as comic," Marietta said. "Oh, I wish Postiche was here!" She pushed the book away, and sat looking in front of her.

"Is there something you do not understand?"

"Yes—lots! None of it! I can't make them out. They love, it says, and they seem to suffer; but it is all done by writing, and bowing, and clever words, and thinking in your room! That is part of love, no doubt," the child said thoughtfully, "but surely there is also more. This Darcy shall be a galantuomo, I gather; would he not *sometimes* take her in his arms?"

Elena laughed. "You want Postiche to expound love *à l'anglaise?*" she said.

"I suppose. Oh, I want her for everything! I do miss her so," the child said simply.

"You've only been away from her twenty-four hours, and you will soon have her again," Elena said sensibly.

"You are like Elisabetta!" Marietta replied.

A peacock's harsh cry, distant but loud, rang through the still air. Marietta sprang up.

"There it is *again*!" she said. "I wish they would not."

"You are absurd," Elena said, good-temperedly. "What harm do they do you?"

"I don't like them—they make me think of destruction and disaster," the child answered sombrely. "Oh, there's Gela! Good."

Fräulein Gelsicher's spare figure was indeed visible, sheltered by a green-lined tussore sunshade, crossing the hot space of gravel between the shade of the tree and the house. Elena welcomed her with her customary vivacity.

"Gela, it is time you came! Marietta is fussing about the peacocks again. You remember how silly she was about them yesterday afternoon? Now she says they are a presage of disaster!"

"I did not say they *were*—I said they made me think of it," Marietta said, still seriously. "Oh!"—as the long-drawn melancholy cry came again, she put her small brown hands to her ears. "Shut up!" she said menacingly, to the direction of Vill' Alta.

Fräulein Gelsicher however did not embark, with her usual friendly readiness, on the subject of peacocks. Her face was serious and rather drawn. "Elena, I should like to speak to you," she said, with unusual gravity in her voice.

"*I* will go! *I* will go! I am sick of sitting still!" Marietta cried, and moved off towards the ridge that led to Vill' Alta.

"Marietta! You are not going far, are you?" Fräulein Gelsicher called after her.

"No—nowhere in particular," the child said. Responsive to some unspoken hint in the voice, she turned back, and made towards the house.

"She must not go *there*," Fräulein Gelsicher said, also

moving her head in the direction of Vill' Alta, as she sat down.

"What is the matter?" Elena asked.

"A very—a most distressing thing has happened," the governess said. "We have all been too late. I ought to have spoken yesterday, or even the day before; but with the Marchesa's death, it seemed so difficult"—she spoke as much to herself as to Elena. "And La Vecchia Marchesa too, it seems, did not—" She broke off, and sat looking distressfully at the pointed toes of her tight shoes, slightly dusty from the gravel.

Elena rose, took a wicker foot-stool, scooped up her governess's thin slate-coloured ankles with one hand, and with the other pushed the foot-stool under her feet. Then, returning to her chair, "Do stop blaming yourself, Gela, and tell me what has happened," she said.

"Merci, mon enfant. In the ordinary way it is not a thing I should wish to tell you," Fräulein Gelsicher said; "but with Marietta here, I think I must, for I shall need your help."

"Is it about Suzy?" Elena asked calmly, taking up her sewing again.

"Not exactly. Partly. She has dismissed Miss Prestwich," Fräulein Gelsicher said.

"How monstrous!" Elena exclaimed. "What on earth for?"

"I do not know. I have heard nothing from there. But —Elena, *would* you be quiet and listen?" Fräulein Gelsicher said, almost imploringly, as the girl made an impatient movement. "Remember, it may not be—it may sound worse than it is, for I have only heard through the servants. But it seems that she was sent away last night, and without much money; in any case, she persuaded the diligence driver to take her to Roffredo's house."

"The *diligence*? Where was the carriage?"

"It appears that the carriage took her only to the diligence stop," Fräulein Gelsicher said, unhappily.

"That woman!    All right, Gela—I will be quiet.    Go on."

"Roffredo certainly meant to take her on to the night train, because Antonio was told to get out the automobile," Fräulein Gelsicher pursued, "but naturally he gave her dinner first, and—" she stopped, her face full of wretchedness.

"He kept her there and seduced her, I suppose?" Elena said, in the calm tones of cold fury.    "Brute!    I told you he wasn't to be trusted.    And I told you Zia Suzy was *capable de tout*. Now we *see*!" she said, getting up and walking up and down. "Now we see her as she is!    And *that* is why Marietta was to come here, to be out of the way—but Postiche must stay, to help with the flowers and the letters!    Oh, la ——!" she used an unprintable word.    "And all *this*, with Zia Nadia, her own sister-in-law, lying unburied, hardly cold!    *Quelle ordure!*"

"Elena, Elena, do not speak so loud!    Try to control yourself!" the governess said, firmly.    "You will be of no help unless you can behave reasonably."

"Where is she now, the poor little thing?    Is she gone, or does he keep her there still?" the girl asked abruptly.

"They are both gone.    He had a telegram from Milan, about his invention, and went off very early; and she, it appears, is gone to Castellone."

"To Castellone?    Why on earth there?"

"The two Countesses drove over and fetched her, soon after ten, in the pony-cart.    How they came to do so, I can't say," Fräulein Gelsicher said, in a tone of weary bewilderment.    "But they did—and there she is."

Elena first stared, then broke into a laugh.

"The Sorellone to the rescue!" she said.    "That is perfect! They *would*!    They know everything, always.    And Aspidistra would adore such a chance of putting a spoke in Suzy's wheel.    I don't blame her!"    Her face grew sombre again.

"The important thing, and that you can help me in, is to keep it from Marietta," Fräulein Gelsicher said.

"That's impossible!    It will resound all over the Province, especially since the Sorellone have taken a hand in it."

Fräulein Gelsicher sighed. "True. But we must try, at least for the present. She is in mourning, and we can remain very quiet. Consider the effect on her!"

"Zia Suzy might have thought of all that before! Oh, the poor little worm! I can't imagine what she will feel," Elena said. "And that wretched harmless little Postiche!"

"Remember, Elena, as to Miss Prestwich, it is all guess-work—about last night; we *know* nothing."

"Oh no! And we don't know Roffredo! And it is only occasionally that two and two make four!" the girl broke out impatiently.

The governess sighed again. "I thought that perhaps I would ask Countess Aspasia if she could come over and see me," she said. "Then I should learn the facts, and it might be easier."

"I doubt if you get any facts to make it more bearable for Marietta," said Elena. "Still, try."

"Very well. I will go and write the note," Fräulein Gelsicher said; and rose, and resumed her green and white sun-shade, and walked back to the house.

Marietta, restless and listless, had roamed off to the back yard, where she first watched the wine-pressing going on for some time; the Count was there, in an alpaca suit, super-intending operations. Then she amused herself by feeding a pair of the bullocks with carrots, and stroking their soft creamy noses. She felt slightly puzzled and uncomfortable. She missed Postiche, and she did not *quite* see why she had been sent to Odredo without her. When Zio Ascanio died, three years ago, she was not sent away. And Postiche had promised to write *every* day, and she had not written yet. She could easily have sent a note over this morning! She was still vaguely concerned, too, about Postiche and Roffredo—whenever she began to think about Postiche, she could not help thinking also about *that*. She had a curious feeling that so long as Postiche was with *her*, she was safe—but now they were parted, and she experienced a vague disquiet on her

governess's account.    And what was this which had so upset
Gela?    She had looked as if something awful had happened,
just now.

It occurred to her presently that she had not been in to the
house for over an hour; the post was due, and there might be
a letter or a note from Postiche.   Her feet winged by the
thought, she flew across the yard, up on to the terrace where
on her last visit the plums had been drying, swung over the
balustrade and ran in by the back door.   In the great flagged
passage outside the kitchen a group of maids were clustered
together, whispering and nodding in eager conversation; they
fell silent at her approach.   She went through the heavy doors
into the hall, with its huge painted beams, and carved and in-
laid chests standing between the high square-barred windows;
Umberto was at the front door, in earnest conference with the
postman—at the sound of her feet he turned, saw her, and
made a warning gesture.   They too stopped talking.   And
there was no letter.   Marietta turned away and went upstairs,
tears of disappointment welling up in her eyes.   Oh, she *did*
so want to hear from Postiche!   She did so *want* Postiche!
It was cruel of her not to write.   No—it was not cruel—she
would never be cruel.   There must be some reason.   But
what was it?

To reach her room she had to go through Elena's.   The
door was open, and she walked in.   Annina, Elena's and
Fräulein Gelsicher's maid, was in close conference with the
laundress, who had brought up some clean linen; they did not
hear her light feet on the carpet, and she caught some words—
"Yes, at the villa; and then they took her to Castellone,
and—"   When the women saw her they started, and broke off
in mid-sentence, with an obvious air of confusion.

"Who has gone to Castellone, Annina?" Marietta asked,
half idly, half irritated by this universal air of mystery.

"Oh, no one of importance, Marchesina.   I was talking to
Marta," the maid replied, laughing foolishly.

"*That*, I saw," Marietta said, rather haughtily, and went on into her room. There she went over to the delicate marquetry escritoire and sitting down, wrote to Miss Prestwich. It was a dull little letter, describing every one of her actions since they parted; none of her vague disquiets, and hardly any of her secret longing got into it—just three sentences at the end: "I wish you were with me. Nothing is very nice without you. I do not think Mama can really want you so badly as I do!

I embrace you tenderly

Marietta."

That evening, when the two girls went to bed, Marietta assailed Elena. "What are the servants whispering about? They are all chattering together, and when I come, they stop, and look like fools. And Gela had that long talk with Zio Carlo after dinner. Is something wrong?"

"Not that I know of," Elena said. "Look, would you like me to brush your hair?"

"Oh, thank you. But I can. Elena, I do not want to pry," she pursued, fixing her great serious eyes on her cousin's face, "but surely if the servants can know it, *I* can."

Elena again assured her that it was nothing—"Servants are always chattering; they think of nothing but their lovers! Here, they are not like your Darcy and Elisabetta!" she said. Marietta laughed at that, but she went to bed with an unsatisfied look on her small face.

Next day a number of things happened. The Sorellone duly came over, in response to Fräulein Gelsicher's note, but so late that they had to be asked to remain to lunch. Countess Aspasia was annexed by Fräulein Gelsicher and carried off to a small sitting-room downstairs, where the latter heard, for the first time, the full story of Suzy's reckless cruelty and its consequences. She sat with a face of misery, thinking, once or twice, how appallingly right Elena had been in her bald surmises of the day before. Both her mercifulness and her good sense were forced to approve Countess Aspasia's action; but,

like the old Marchesa, she felt that it added to the general
difficulty and complications.    How, for instance, was she to
keep Marietta away from Castellone, if the child once learned
that her beloved Postiche was there?    And some further news
which the Countess brought added to this feeling.    After
giving a full and dramatic account of the affair—Aspasia was
a born *raconteuse*—she proceeded—"And imagine, Roffredo
is now back!    Yes, it occurred to him suddenly, at Milan, the
featherhead! how he had left her, *plantée*, at his house; and for
all that his invention has been accepted, he turned straight
round and came tearing home by the night express!    He
arrived this morning on the same train as Francesco.    Si, si,
Francesco is back too; the funeral was yesterday.    She is
under the earth now, povera Nadia, and Pipo will be able to
carry on his amours in perfect freedom!"    She laughed her
harsh cackling laugh.    "Anastasia has taken the little Francesca, for the moment; she came to the funeral, and carried her
off to Rome the moment afterwards."    She paused to draw
breath.    "But, cara Signorina, imagine what Roffredo has
done!    The moment he heard from Alba where the little one
was, he got into his automobile and rushed over to Castellone!
Ma si!    That is why we are so late.    The pony was at the
door, we were about to start, when we heard quella macchina!
And in he came, quite distraught.    He must see her—and
here was her money!    He *had* left it after all, on the mantelpiece—yes, yes, the notes were under a vase, but of course no
one saw them.    I told him that he was a little late, with this
thoughtful kindness!    And that she now had all she needed."

"Did he see her?" Fräulein Gelsicher asked.

"Dio mio, no!    She is still in bed—it has been a great
shock; the Doctor will not let let her rise at present.    He
gives her soporifics.    She lies dozing most of the time.    I
told Roffredo not to bring that noisy machine over again, disturbing her with the sound.    Indeed, I told him a number of
things!    And then, just as he was leaving, looking like a
whipped puppy"—again she gave a little laugh—"who should

come in but Livia!    I thought we should never get off.    She too had heard the automobile, and came trailing across.    I suggested that they should perhaps repair to *her* house for their conversation!    And she took the hint.    Livia is furious —I heard her beginning as they went.    Our young Roffredo has not had a very pleasant morning!" she concluded, and laughed again.

Meanwhile Elena had been left to entertain Countess Roma. Now Roma had received strict injunctions from her sister not to touch on the 'affaire Prestwich' with either of the young girls, and it is just possible (though far from certain) that if Elena had been ignorant of it, she might have done as she was told and held her peace.    But Elena, naturally, began instantly to ask questions, and well-informed questions at that; and finding that she already knew so much, Roma was delighted with the liberty which she felt this gave her to tell all she knew.    She had already disobeyed her instructions on the previous afternoon, when Aspasia had gone to Vill' Alta to see the old Marchesa; making some excuse to look in on Miss Prestwich, and finding her awake, though drowsy and unguarded with the drug, she had "chattered to her", and to some purpose; she had amongst other things extracted from her the full story of her departure from Vill' Alta, the solitary wait at the diligence stop, and the vicious insult of the teamster with the whip.    And all this she now passed on, with a wealth of detail, to the girl.    She also, under pressure, confirmed Elena's shrewd guess as to what had happened at the Villa Gemignana, to which indeed the revolver episode, eloquently related by the foolish woman, bore its own sufficing testimony.

This ill-considered loquacity of Countess Roma's had far-reaching results, as ill-considered speech is apt to have.    The petty details of Suzy's cruelty, and the depths to which it had borne the English girl carried Elena's indignation, already vehement, beyond all bounds of reason, prudence, or justice. Her lively mind at once flew ahead to schemes of vengeance;

in the meantime she was so angry that she quite lost sight of her duty to her neighbour, in the persons of Marietta and Fräulein Gelsicher. She sat seething all through lunch—a difficult meal, with four out of the six persons present bursting with one subject, which owing to the presence of the two others could not be discussed. The success of Roffredo's invention, however, and his return from Milan, were considered by Countess Aspasia to be suitable matter for general conversation and, initiated by her, were liberally dealt with: even hung on to, as people do hang on to a subject in such circumstances, to avoid awkward silences. But after coffee, when the Sorellone had driven off in their little pony-carriage, and Fräulein Gelsicher had retired for her afternoon rest, Elena was in no state to resist the second onslaught made on her by Marietta.

The young girl's vague suspicions and fears had deepened during a morning which, for her, had been rather wretched. There had been no letter, no note from Postiche in reply to her outpouring of the previous afternoon, and a suggestion to Fräulein Gelsicher that she and Elena might walk over to Vill' Alta to see her had been vetoed with a brusqueness which surprised her; moreover the two separate confabulations before lunch, between Countess Aspasia and Gela, and Elena and Countess Roma, had not escaped her observation. And the servants' whisperings had been even more pronounced than on the previous evening—"she", "the Young Conte," "the villa", "Yes, to Castellone" had recurred so often that she was now, putting all these things together, definitely convinced that something was up, and vaguely suspicious that it might concern her darling Postiche. Accordingly, as soon as the two girls were alone, she turned firmly on her cousin

"Senti, Elena, I think you must tell me now what the matter is. I know there *is* something, with all these conversations; besides, if there were not, I should be allowed to go across to Vill' Alta, and also Postiche"—her voice fell away a little—"would write to me. So now—what is it? If you do not tell me," the child said, very quietly, "I shall go to Zio Carlo. I shall be able, easily, to get it out of him, for he will make mistakes. And I *must* know."

This demand put the match to Elena's superfluous store of gunpowder. She had all along believed that it would be impossible to keep the thing from her little cousin, and now that her suspicions were aroused, the game, she considered, was up. And her anger at Roma's tidings obscured any lingering compunction she might have felt. Briefly, baldly, she poured the whole thing out—Postiche had been dismissed, the day before yesterday, and without enough money to get home with; she had gone to Roffredo to borrow some—"he was in love with her, you see"—and he had promised it, but he kept her there all night, and in the morning this telegram came, and he had rushed off to Milan, leaving her, everything! "It seems he did leave some money for her, but in a silly place, where it was not found. And then the Sorellone heard of it, as they alone would, and went poking over to see what was happening, and took her back with them to Castellone, and there she is." Some belated feeling of compunction, aroused by the expression on the child's face, made even Elena slur over the night at the villa, and suppress the revolver.

Marietta listened to the tale in complete silence, her face once more that of a small Medusa. Her silence continued for some time after Elena had finished; she sat looking, not at her cousin, nor exactly away from her, but over her shoulder, as if what she had heard were set out in the distance beyond Elena's head, and she was reviewing it there. At last, speaking with a great effort, she said "You have not told me *why* Mama dismissed her."

Again Elena's anger got the better of her judgement.

"Ma, because she found out that Roffredo was in love with her. She saw them at Meden. And she wanted him for herself, you see," Elena explained with airy crudeness. "She *said* it was because Postiche was carrying on an intrigue with Roffredo! But there cannot have been much in that, or La

Vecchia would not have made her send all that money to Postiche, yesterday. No, the real reason was the other thing —I have seen it for a long time, and so has Gela; and Aspidistra is convinced of it too." She paused; the extreme whiteness of her little cousin's face made her, belatedly, regret her words. "Marietta, I am sorry to say this," she said more gently. "But it is true, and you may as well hear it from me, for you would be bound to learn it sooner or later," she added, with an unwonted movement of self-justification.

Only four days before, when the three girls were discussing the Marchesa Nadia's suicide, Marietta had said "It is better to *know* things." She had not then learned that knowledge can be both an intolerable burden and a crippling wound. She was to learn it now. This information which she had so determinedly demanded from Elena was like a blow between the eyes—it is true to say that her mind staggered under its impact. It had so many ramifications and implications, this set of facts: her dual loyalties, to her Mother and to Miss Prestwich, were plunged into violent conflict; recoiling, she saw an abyss opening almost under her feet, which had seemed of late to stand so firmly and gladly on the safe ground of love and goodness and a new happy comprehension of life. She would lose her Postiche, that was certain, to whom she owed so much of this fresh feeling of confidence and security; in a sense she realised that she had lost her Mother too. Her mind sought to grapple with these calamities, and then as it were fell back, appalled by their magnitude—for a moment she covered her face with her hands. But she quickly raised it again—even at this moment she was determined to understand, to *know*; and there were lacunae in Elena's narrative, all was not yet clear.

"And why?" she asked in a strained little voice, "have they taken her to Castellone? Why did they not let her go home, when the money came?"

About this, too, Roma had been greedily precise, confirming Elena's first swift and knowledgeable guess. And again the violence of her anger about the whole thing robbed Elena of the restraint she might at another time have shown in dealing with Marietta.

"Ma, they will keep her for a month, to see whether she is going to have a baby or not," she said, with her usual incisive bluntness; "you see, she spent the night there with him.    He made her very drunk," she added in extenuation—"I am sure it would not have happened otherwise, with Postiche."

This time Marietta did not look away, at first.    She sat staring at Elena's face, as though she had seen a monster issue from her mouth.    Then, quite suddenly, she dropped her head between her arms on the marble table, and broke into low but violent sobbing.    "Oh, Miss Prestwich!" she murmured between her sobs.    "Oh, my dear dear Postiche!    That is why you did not write!    Oh, OH!"

Elena was seriously disturbed by this result of her reckless handiwork.    She rose, and put her hand on the child's shoulder.    "Marietta, cara, do not cry so," she said, for once uncertain what to say.

After a moment or two the girl raised her head, checking her sobs with a violent effort, and looked at her cousin.

"That was not really Mama," she said, speaking very fast. "Not to do that!    That is not like her—it is not *her*!    Either there is some mistake, or she was under some obsession.    That is *not* Mama, Elena."

"No, cara," Elena said soothingly—though in fact she felt that it had been precisely Suzy.    But Marietta's reactions to the whole business had frightened her.    "No," she said, and stroked her shoulder again.

Suddenly Marietta sat very upright.    "Elena, Giulio must not know!    Not *that*," she said, with immense emphasis.

"Not what?"    For once Elena was entirely at a loss.

"Not about—Postiche.    And Roffredo.    He *must* not! He must *not*!" she said, her voice rising to a high strained note.

"Very well.    But why not?"

"Because—he loves her.    So much—not like Roffredo!

It is with his soul. Elena, promise me that he shall not know this!"

"Cara, from me he shall not. And I will tell Gela, and she will tell Papa. It ought to be all right—Giulio talks to so few people, and he does not listen," Elena said consolingly.

"You promise?"

"Ma si, I promise! But how did you know this?" Elena asked, her invincible curiosity even now emerging, with the true Italian detachment from the misfortunes of others. She was quite unaccustomed not to be first in the field of local love-affairs with her sharp guesses.

Marietta did not trouble to answer. Having got Elena's promise, which she knew she would keep, she sat again staring in front of her. At last she got up.

"You see that I was right," she said.

"About what?" Elena asked.

"About the peacock's cry. Here is disaster." She turned away, and went slowly indoors, leaving her cousin staring after her.

*Chapter Twenty-two*

ELENA was quite right about Giulio's normal inattentiveness to what went on around him. He had been completely oblivious, for instance, to the general atmosphere of mystery and gossip in the household during the previous twenty-four hours. But he did occasionally pay attention to matters which concerned people whom he cared about, and during lunch he had registered, with real pleasure, the fact that Roffredo had been to Milan, had had his cherished invention accepted, and was now returned. It occurred to him that he had not seen Roffredo since the picnic at Meden, and that it would be extraordinarily pleasant to see him again. Accordingly, in the middle of the afternoon he set off, with his long mouching stride, to walk to the Villa. He told no one where he was going; it was not Giulio's custom to advertise his movements, and indeed there was no one about to tell, since Fräulein Gelsicher was resting, the Count was out in the yard watching one lot of wine being piped carefully into barrels, and Elena and Marietta were talking under the stone pine. Unwarned and unwitting, he strode off across the Park to meet his private tragedy.

Roffredo was delighted to see him. His morning had been fully as unpleasant as Countess Aspasia had delightedly deduced—verbally trounced by her, angrily upbraided by his Mother, and realising that this would be the general attitude for some time to come, he had retired, half hurt, half sulky, to the Villa. He felt a strong need for sympathy from some one, and saw small chance of getting it. After all, he had not done any of this intentionally; he had simply been overtaken by the situation—by both situations. He had really meant to take that darling little thing to the train—he adored her, when

284

all was said. But he had drunk so much, and she was so adorable—well, there it was! He *was* like that. And next morning when the telegram came—well, again, it was the crowning of two years of work, of research and struggle, of what had for so long appeared to be fruitless calculation and experiment. Surely at such a moment, if ever, a man might be pardoned for losing his wits a little? And it was hardly his fault that she had not found the money—in his hurry there had been no time to find an envelope, write a note. It was only by a combination that all this had happened. And he was bitterly sorry. But no one seemed to believe that, nor even to be willing to listen to his explanations.

So he was charmed to see Giulio. He took him into his sitting-room, which was pleasantly cool in the afternoons, offered him Marsala and brandy-and-soda, both of which Giulio refused, took a brandy-and-soda himself, and showed his cousin, on the tracing-cloth, the salient features of the new invention. And then he threw himself back in the armchair in which Almina had sat to drink her brandy, and embarked upon his own troubles. Giulio was always interested, always sympathetic and affectionate, even though they cared about such different things, and though in some ways he was almost more like a girl than a man—one could count on Giulio.

Blowing out a cloud of smoke, "My Mother," he began, "is a most difficult woman, sa. It is impossible to make her understand the most obvious things; she has her own *parti-pris*, always, and she will not even listen to what one has to say."

"What will she not listen to this time?" Giulio asked, sympathetically—he could readily believe in any amount of tiresomeness on Countess Livia's part; he himself always found her *poco simpatica* to a degree.

"Oh, this business about the little Miss Prestwich. You know that Suzy has dismissed her?"

"What? No, I did not know it. No," Giulio said in some agitation, which he at once strove to conceal. With everyone but Marietta, he was as shy as a girl about his feeling for Almina.

"Yes, she did.   A couple of days ago.   And without much money.   So the poor little thing came here to borrow some," Roffredo went on, affecting an airiness he did not really feel.

"Why did she come to you?" Giulio asked, with nervous abruptness.

"Well, because—in somma, we were on very good terms," Roffredo said, with great naturalness.   "And of course I was delighted to let her have whatever she wanted, and I promised to drive her in to the train, because that miserable Suzy would only let the carriage take her as far as the diligence."

"She is gone, then?   Gone back to England?" Giulio interrupted.

"No—in a way I wish she were!   That is the devil of it. As you know, the night express does not leave till eleven, so I had to give her dinner first; and she was so upset at being sacked, that to cheer her up I gave her champagne."   Roffredo began to feel rather expansive; this reconstruction of his actions, this establishment of the purity of his intentions to someone who would listen sympathetically was giving him the peculiar satisfaction that it gives to us all.   He sat looking up at the clouds of smoke which he exhaled, as he talked, and so did not notice the peculiar tautness which was coming over Giulio's expression.   "One way and another, we both drank rather a lot," he pursued, "only she was so quiet with it that I did not realise how much effect it was taking on her.   And when we came in here afterwards, she was so adorable, *tenera e appassionata com' è mai stata*, that I lost my head altogether, and we never went to the train at all.   What is it, Giulio?" he asked in slight surprise, for his cousin had risen from where he sat on the divan and was standing in front of him.

"She spent the night here, with you?" Giulio asked, in a voice perfectly quiet, but with a curious vibration in it.

"Yes—here, on the divan.   She is divine, like that!   I had not in the least meant to, but you see I am very much in love with her, and I think I was probably rather drunk myself. Anyhow——Giulio, per l'amor di Dio, what is wrong with you?" he ejaculated, as the young man caught him a swinging blow on the side of the head.

"Stand up!" Giulio said——"stand up, stand up!" Roffredo was in any case rising to his feet, too utterly astonished even to be angry. As he got up his cousin came at him again, his face now quite distorted; Roffredo parried the blow, and then caught his wrists and held them firmly——he was by far the more powerful of the two. "I won't fight with you, Giulio," he said. "What *is* all this? What the devil is wrong?"

"Let me go—don't touch me," Giulio said, panting. "Wrong? You ask what is wrong? When you did *that* to her? When she came to you for help, you made her drunk, and then took her for your pleasure! She, purity itself! Oh, God in Heaven! Let me go!" he said, his voice rising almost to a scream. "Take your hands away! Don't touch me! I hate your hands—I hate to see you! Let me go!"

"Giulio, caro, how could I know? I am terribly sorry— unspeakably sorry, but do be reasonable," Roffredo said. "I have told you that I regret it for her sake; it was not meant— and I regret it more for yours." He still held his distracted cousin by the wrists, as gently as he could; Giulio's struggles, which the other resisted as little as possible, drew them now in this direction, now in that, so that the two young men seemed to be performing a sort of agonised waltz round the room. "I had no idea of this," Roffredo went on, endeavouring to say something soothing. "I thought you never cared for girls."

"Girls! I do not. She is not as others! But to you she is; just a girl, one more instrument of your foul enjoyment. O, how I hate you. *Will* you let me go?" Giulio cried, almost beside himself.

"Yes, if you will go quietly," Roffredo said. "Here, you can come out this way." He let go of the other's wrists, and walked calmly ahead of him to the door leading through to the workshop, opened it, passed on, and opened the further door into the garden. The quiet steadiness of his tone and movements did something to calm Giulio—he followed, making no attempt at any further onslaughts. At the garden door Roffredo turned. "Giulio, I am *sorry*," he said simply; "I wish you could believe it."

His cousin ignored the appeal. "Where is—she—now?" he asked, gulping a little over the pronoun.

"At Castellone. They came, the old Sorellone, yesterday morning (hearing, God and they alone know how! that she was here) and fetched her away. She stays there, for the present."

There were other things that Giulio could have asked— why Miss Prestwich should be staying at Castellone, why Suzy had dismissed her. But the very sight and presence of Roffredo was so horrible to him that his one wish was to be gone. "So," he said and turned and strode off down the path.

Roffredo walked slowly back through the workshop into his sitting-room. There he wiped his forehead, poured out another brandy-and-soda, took a gulp of it, and lighting a fresh cigarette, threw homself down again in the arm-chair. Perdition!—that *was* a scene! Who could have guessed such a thing? Giulio in love with her! If he had only known, he would not have said a word, he thought gloomily. Poor lad —and now he was gone off like a bear with a sore head. He put up his hand to his own head, and felt the bump rising just in front of the temple, where his cousin had struck him.

Even on Giulio, it appeared, one could not always count.

Giulio himself, meanwhile, strode away, walking as fast as his legs would carry him. Anything, anywhere, to get out of sight of that house, the scene of her degradation! As soon as he could he left the road, dreading to meet anyone he knew, and took the little smugglers' path across the pastures. In his distress of mind he walked at random, and the small thread of the path as it were led him forward, past the Monte Sant Antonio, with Trino's house set like a lump of rock on the further' end, beside the formal oblong of the hornbeam hedges, and out into the country beyond. Here the ground was drier and more broken; watercourses with crumbling banks intersected it, and the pastures degenerated into rough indefinite herbage, set with bright wild-flowers—the boy's heart contracted as he recognised some of the things which Miss Prestwich had brought home, named and rejoiced in. She had so loved them, bright and innocent as a flower herself —and now she was soiled and broken! Every thought of her was torture, let his mind turn which way it would. As he crossed a rise, still walking with that agonised speed, the long line of Castellone rose into view, on its ridge—it was as if it rose to hit him in the eyes. He checked his pace, stopped, and stood staring at the maroon-coloured eastern end. She was there, somewhere, in some room—feeling what? thinking what thoughts? He moaned, and covered his face with his hands. But some strange pitiful impulse drew him on towards it. Some distance from the village he crossed the road to Gardone, along which the Sorellone had driven the day before on their hurried expedition to the villa, and vaulted over the low stone wall which surrounded the whole Castellone domain. He climbed the slope beyond, over the dry brittle slippery grass, between the silvery trunks of the cypresses, until he struck a path leading along the level towards the house; he followed it round the curve of the ridge till he came in sight of the blunt maroon-coloured mass, with its blank bright windows and crenellated battlements. (It was, though mercifully Giulio did not know it, the very path along which Roffredo had led Almina on the day when she was taken to call at Castellone, and he first kissed her and told her that she was beautiful.) There, in the shelter of a group of laurels, the young man stood, gazing at those blank anonymous windows which sheltered the entity he cared most for in the world. His thought tried to pierce through them to her—he imagined her sitting, lying, speaking, praying, in tears—and every image increased his own torment. For one wild moment he thought of going to her—forcing his way in, taking her hand, declaring his love, his worship, his silent steadfast adoration. But the thought of the Sorellone quenched this impulse; he saw them too, Roma with her greedy shameless curiosity for all that touched on love or sex, Aspasia with her harsh ironical phrases, her merciless cackling laugh. Giulio had at all times the shy young man's timid hatred of elderly spinsters, and now he could not face them. He shivered at the thought of Almina—small, reticent —defenceless in their hands. Distraught afresh, he turned and hurried away, back along the path, down the slope, over the wall, and off across country towards Odredo.

The whole lay-out of Giulio's character, his type of interior life, made this particular blow fall on him with especial weight. By nature and inclination he had at first so to speak jibbed at the female principle in general; having been conquered by the female principle in the person of Miss Prestwich, and having by her been introduced, as it were, to love, his cast of mind then made him, sub-consciously, jib at the physical side of it, and stress its ethereal and spiritual aspects—less clear-sighted than his little cousin, he would have the object of his devotion to be "heavenly-minded", and of a dazzling purity. To a preconception and an attachment such as this, Roffredo's story was a peculiar agony. The pain and shock of it would have been great to any sensitive young man, for the first time in love; to Giulio they were crushing. He was accustomed to live by his mind, and his mind was quite unable to deal with this thing. He could find no reason for it, no sense or hope in it anywhere. Every thought of Almina—her past, her future, her love of Marietta, her help to him, his own work, his love—led back, as it were, to the divan at the Villa, darkly illuminated for him by Roffredo's phrase, whose very tones rang in his head—" she was *divine*, like that." And his mind found no means to counteract or allay or banish the torture of that thought; it seemed to run all through him, awakening sensations which filled him with disgust and shame.

His tormented mind drove his hurrying body homewards even faster than he had come. It was getting late, now, and the sun was very low; the hollows were damp pools of chill air, into which he descended; on the rising ground between them a sudden warmth, held by the vegetation from the full heat of the day, met him in waves, bearing the sweetish dusty smell of the ripened maize. At the time Giulio was not aware of noticing any of these things, but for years afterwards he hated that smell, when he met it on dusty paths at sundown. As he approached Odredo his pace slackened. He felt that he could not endure to see anyone, and yet he also felt that he could not bear this misery alone much longer. Climbing the track through the larch plantation from the Park towards the house, the thought of Marietta beckoned to him—to her, it would be possible to pour out his wretchedness; she had a trick of understanding, little and young as she was. And if he did not speak to someone, he felt as if some tangible part of him within would crack or break. As he came up onto the terrace he saw her; like a visitation from Heaven, sitting, already changed for dinner and alone, by the marble table under the stone pine, in her high-necked white dress, with her black shoes and stockings, and her heavy black sash. Heavenly visitations sometimes appear in very curious disguises; to Giulio di Castellone that childish figure brought an incredible sense of—really *soulagement* is the only precise European word. He went over to her.

She looked up and saw him. She realised at once that, somehow, he had heard. She rose very quietly, walked round the table to him, and slid her little thin arm, in its ridiculous puffed sleeve, through his. "Come and walk, dear Giulio," she said. "Come along the ridge."

On the stone pine ridge, tonight, there was a new scent. Along the southern brow, at the Odredo end, a straggling hedge (which in the Italian manner sheltered nothing and divided nothing from anything) extended for a couple of hundred yards—a hedge of a curious rambling shrub, stiff enough to stand upright, but throwing out long trailing branches like a rambler rose, each branch set close with small stiff leaves, green above, below of a whitish silver powdered with minute lustrous bronze spots, and bearing small thick-set creamy flowers, also specked with bronze, which exhaled an extra-ordinary fragrance, something between orange-blossom and mignonette. Miss Prestwich had been charmed with this plant even before it flowered, and had endeavoured to find out its name, but none of the family knew it, and Gino, the old Odredo gardener, referred to it vaguely as "quel rampi-cante." It had just come into flower, and the sweet heavy scent loaded the air on the whole ridge as the cousins passed along it. They walked for some time in silence. It was Marietta who spoke first. As they approached one of the seats—"Giulio, I know," she said.

He stopped and turned to her, then.

"I feel that I *can't* bear it," he said, with a curious simplicity. "I do not see how I am going to bear it. I told you—you know what I feel about her. And now she—he—" a sort of spasm contracted his features. "I loved him, too, you see," he said irrelevantly.

"Who told you?" Marietta asked.

"He did. I went over to see him, to congratulate him. And he then told me—quite lightly, as if it were a small thing! —what he had done. I do not really understand it—why she was sent away, and so on. But this was quite clear, what happened between them there. He said they were both drunk!" the young man said, in a tone of agonised distaste. "But she—if you think what she must also feel! I do not see," he said again, "how one *can* bear it."

She had loosed his arm when he turned to her, and stood now in front of him, her eyes on his face. "Darling Giulio, I know," she said again. "Oh, I am sorry. It is no use trying to tell you how sorry I am. I too, you know, love her. But I feel—oh, that somehow it is not real, all this; that it has nothing to do with *her*."

"What do you mean?" he asked.

"A person who is tipped out of a boat and drowned has not committed suicide.   It is like that."

"But they are drowned just the same," he said, wearily.   He moved over to the seat as he spoke, and sat down on it; he felt suddenly very tired.

She followed him, and sat down too.

"Yes, but their soul is not the same," she pursued.   "In Purgatory, to that degree it stands upright—it was not cowardly—it did not surrender to despair.   There is that difference.   And in this—she may have loved him, indeed I think she did; but *that*, without being married—she would not have done it."

As she spoke, there slipped into Giulio's mind the recollection of his thoughts about the peasants, months ago now, when he walked out of Gardone on the very day that he first heard of Miss Prestwich's coming to Vill' Alta.   He had thought about it again since, more than once, but he had never really settled to his satisfaction whether or not it was true that only *conscious* experiences affect the soul.   That seemed to be also Marietta's idea.   But the thought slipped in and slipped out again—for the moment something else had caught his attention.

"Why do you think that she loved—him?" he asked—he could not easily speak Roffredo's name.

"I just think it—it was my impression," the child said; "I do not *know* it."

"*He* said so," Giulio muttered miserably, half to himself. Then, stung by the recollection of his cousin's complacent tone as he said "We were on very good terms", he turned on her, suddenly furious.   "You said yourself that day at Vill' Alta, after the thunder, that you did not know of which sort her love was—like ours, or like his!   Why did you say that? Did you know something?   That she was going with him then, perhaps?"

The child remained perfectly steady.   "No.   I knew

nothing, and I don't know anything now, but what you know. That she went there that night to him, was—was Mama's fault," she said, with a quivering mouth. "She had no money. That, I *can't* really understand! But it seems it was so. And I do not really know much about any sort of love—except that they *all* seem to make people either cruel or miserable! I said that, that day, because—I did not know, I just felt that she might love differently to you. But Giulio," she said earnestly, the tears standing in her eyes—"of whatever sort Postiche's love may be, remember that she is *good*. You know that. Hold on to that."

For the moment he seemed to listen to this, and to be quieted by it. "Come back, now," she said, rising and tugging gently at his arm—"come on, Giulio." That they would be late for dinner was in her mind, but she did not speak of it. He came with her, obediently, and they walked back through the overpowering sweetness distilled by the flowering hedge. But suddenly he broke out again. "She is good, yes, as you say—but she has been dishonoured, deflowered, as if she were of the lowest! Nothing can alter that, nothing, nothing! That is *done*; that is so." He spoke like a person in a violent passion—his hands were shaking, his mouth worked, his face was very white. Marietta was frightened by his state. She made no further attempt at argument or consolation; murmuring all the time "Come, dear Giulio; come; come on," she led him into the house by one of the garden doors, and upstairs, and into his room. As they reached it, the great bell which hung outside the house above the courtyard clanged out its deep musical notes, announcing dinner.

"Stay here," the child said. "You can have something upstairs. I will find Gela. Stay where you are." And she flew off in search of Fräulein Gelsicher.

She met her just leaving her room. "Ah, you are dressed —that is right," the governess said pleasantly.

"Gela, can you come back to your room for a minute? Yes, I know we shall be late, but I must speak to you," the child said, pulling imperiously at her arm.    After one glance at her face, the governess agreed.    In her room she drew down the long embroidered bell-pull, saying "Wait a moment"; the resultant tinkling was followed almost instantly by Annina's entrance.

"Tell Umberto to ask the Signor Conte and the Contessina not to wait—we shall be down presently."    Then, as the door closed behind the maid, she turned to Marietta.    Elena, with her customary impulsive frankness, had already made a clean breast of her revelations to Marietta, and had also imparted to her governess her little cousin's injunctions on the subject of Giulio; to her surprise (and slightly to her annoyance) Fräulein Gelsicher had shown herself perfectly aware of this further complication.    She had wasted no time on blaming Elena; she enquired carefully into Marietta's reception of the news, sighed, poked at her hair, and said—"Well, Giulio at any rate we must shield if we can," and left it at that.    But she was quite prepared for severe distress on the little girl's part, and this sudden application did not surprise her in the least.    Fräulein Gelsicher had a very sound sense of values; dinner, though normally at Odredo it was fixed as a Median law, was of secondary importance at a moment like this.

Marietta's first words did surprise her, however.

"It is Giulio," she said.    "He has heard.    He went over to Roffredo, just to congratulate him, this afternoon, knowing nothing!—and Roffredo told him.    And Gela, for him it is *fear*ful.    He loves her so, you see."    She poured her words out in a swift cataract, with the light delicate emphasis she always used, which made her speech so charming. "He is almost ill with it—he is quite wild.    When he told me, I said what I could, but really he hardly hears.    So I have taken him to his room and told him to stay there. He cannot come down—he is not fit.    I think you should go to him."

Fräulein Gelsicher studied the child's face.    She was rather touched and moved by her concern for Giulio, in the midst of her own distress, but she said nothing about that.    She went straight to the main point.

"Did Roffredo tell him—everything?"

"About the seduction?    Oh yes," the child said with a sort of matter-of-fact hopelessness.    "Just the one thing he should *never* have known.    And he cannot bear it.    Please go to him, Gela.    I think he should have a sleeping-draught."

"Yes, I will go," the governess said.    "And you, my child —you will go down to dinner?    This is all very distressing for you, too."

Marietta turned away.    "Oh yes, I will go.    I am all right," she said, in a rather unsteady voice.    Then she turned towards the Swiss again.    "Only Gela, please do not send me back to Vill' Alta just yet," she said, speaking now with great intensity. "I feel I *cannot* go there just now.    Mama—this is all through her, this misery for so many!    I do not understand it, really" —she put up her two hands to her small closely-brushed dark head and held it.    "Giulio—and Postiche herself!    And Gela, Postiche is *good*!    I have been with her so much, I know her better than anyone.    Roffredo may have flirted with her and made her love him to some extent, but she would never have been immoral.    About that I am certain.    Mama did not know her as I did.    Oh, I *do* not understand it!" she said again.    "But you will let me stay?"

"Yes, you shall certainly stay for the present," Fräulein Gelsicher assured her.    That distracted gesture of the child's hands, coupled with the self-restraint, the pitiful effort at loyalty of her words, gave the governess the measure of her distress and conflict.    "You shall stay—indeed we shall be very glad to have you, my child," she said, and hurried along the passage to Giulio.

## Chapter Twenty-three

ONE might really compare those three houses, Castellone, Odredo and Vill' Alta, during the days that followed Miss Prestwich's dismissal, to three anthills, flung into a feverish intensity of activity and busy stirring movement, as by the careless poking of a child's stick, by the Marchesa Suzy's action. Suzy herself was almost as surprised as a child who pokes an anthill for the first time, by the results of her thrust. She had dismissed a little governess, of whose behaviour she disapproved—however mistaken the manner of it (and she was forced to admit that the manner had been mistaken), that was really all; and lo, those dull orderly mounds of earth were instantly covered with seething life—different generations ran to and fro, antennae waved as ant took counsel with ant, measures were taken, grubs (Giulio and Marietta) were protected, an ant-like moral fervour reigned. (Ants, as the author of the Book of Proverbs long ago noticed, are highly moral creatures.)

All this fuss was really rather a severe shock to Suzy. To begin with, she felt that it was out of all proportion to the small and simple fact; but it was the attitude to herself which surprised and pained her most. In the whole course of her pleasant and successful life she had never encountered open disapproval, let alone reprobation—now she did, and she did not like it at all. The Marchese Francesco, on his return from Nadia's funeral, instantly noticed Miss Prestwich's absence, enquired as to the cause, and asked a tiresome number of painfully precise questions about the reasons for her dismissal; he liked the pretty sensible botanically-minded little governess, and made it perfectly clear, in the upshot, that he thought the reasons inadequate and the dismissal a mistake. He, like

U

Bonne-Mama, was quite besotted about Marietta, and set what
seemed to Suzy an absurd and exaggerated importance on the
fact of her devotion to the little English girl.    Bonne-Mama
herself, though she said very little, had made her disappro-
bation of the whole thing perfectly clear; that tiresome old
woman, Aspasia, by championing the girl's cause and taking
her to Castellone for this prolonged stay was making a fool of
her, Suzy, before the entire Province—though really it could
hardly be regarded as *her* fault if the silly little creature had no
more sense than to go and get herself seduced.    Livia had been
to call, upset, indignant, and reproving, terrified lest "quello
lord", Miss Prestwich's grandfather, should suddenly turn on
them and demand that Roffredo should marry the girl.    (Lord
Portledown, so odd an adjunct to a schoolroom, had from the
outset loomed portentously in the eyes of the Province of
Gardone; Livia had always felt that a governess who was
connected with a title must be, apart from those clothes of hers,
"a thoroughly unsuitable person".)    And then had come the
news, yesterday, that Giulio was now ill, or as good as ill,
owing to *his* infatuation with Miss Prestwich.    It really seemed
as if the wretched girl had turned everyone's head!    Giulio,
Marietta and Roffredo—Suzy's eyelids flickered in a little
spasm of pain and distaste at that last thought—all so ridicul-
ously attached to her; and even with the others, Francesco,
Livia, and actually Bonne-Mama herself, it was as if this little
foreigner had upset her, Suzy's relations, had as it were ousted
her from her secure and unchallenged place in their affection
and esteem.    It was almost incredible.

She was sitting in her boudoir, on the Saturday morning
after that disastrous Wednesday of encounters, thinking of all
this, when Valentino the butler brought in a note on a salver.
She took it with a little tremor of the pulses, a slight change of
breath; she knew the writing—it was from Roffredo.    When
Valentino had gone she opened it, half eagerly, half in fear for
what it might contain.    Roffredo had played her rather a bad
turn, too, by advertising his attachment to Miss Prestwich, in

what circumstances had turned almost into a public seduction. But Suzy was too Italianised to take a serious view of this lapse, and too much in love with him not to be ready for a resumption of relations if he showed the smallest inclination for it; she had suffered from his silence, from not knowing what view he took of her part in all these events, and what she feared, as she opened his note, was a curt expression of vexation and reproach on his part.

But her fears were unfounded. The letter was not like that. "Cara Suzy," it began. "How annoying all this is! I am afraid that you must have been having all sort of *embête-ments*, and chiefly through my folly. I admit that I lost my head completely the other night, and behaved like an idiot. I am a good deal ashamed of myself, and I beg you to forgive me. Do you? And to prove it, will you let me see you? Do—I need to so much; and if I saw you, I could explain everything. It would not I think be very wise for me to come to Vill' Alta just now, nor for you to come here; but will you meet me on Sunday evening in that little ruin by what they call the holy well, in the little wood? You know the place I mean—it is close to where the smugglers' path crosses the road. The ruin is not far in—the bushes are rather thick, but perhaps that is all the better! About a quarter to nine. Do not keep your carriage—I will have the dog-cart to drive you home in. And I will have a rug and cushions there, so that you need not spoil your pretty clothes!

"Ah cara, I want to see you so badly!

"*Ti bacio le mani e* ——!

Roffredo.

"P.S. Do not on any account send an answer—it is far more prudent not to. I shall be there, waiting for you, in any case.

R."

The female heart is a strange thing. Suzy di Vill' Alta, with eighteen years as a reigning beauty behind her, breaker of scores of hearts, known to the whole Province as The

Enchantress, read this precious epistle with tremulous happiness and quivering soft hope. So perhaps he found that he did care for her, after all, more than he knew; that he could not do without her. Anyhow this meeting would give her another chance to make all come right, to secure his love and fasten him to her; and she was too accustomed to success to feel very doubtful. "Oh, caro," she murmured—and because his words, his very writing were so absurdly precious to her, she put the letter to her lips before she hid it away in her escritoire between neat bundles of receipts. Her thirsty curiosity about Roffredo moved her later to ask Valentino who had brought the note. He could not say—there was some slight mystery about its arrival. It had not come to the front door; it had apparently been left by some peasant children who came to collect the daily milk allowed to their mother by the Marchesa. When the servant had gone Suzy smiled again—Roffredo was not a very neat intriguer! She sent no answer.

On that same day, at lunch at Odredo, there were *uccellini.* Old Trino had been active, and the small bodies of singing birds, spitted five in a row on silver skewers, appeared as a second course, resting on a yellow bed of polenta; they looked hardly bigger than bumble bees, and each side of the breast afforded a bare mouthful. Count Carlo ate his skewerful with relish, praising Trino; Fräulein Gelsicher took hers with her usual careful attention to the quality of the cooking; Marietta waved the dish away with tears in her eyes, recalling Miss Prestwich's horrified dislike of consuming larks and goldfinches; Elena, as she ate, suddenly started out of an absorbed silence with a half-checked exclamation and a quick laugh— she finished the meal with a sort of dancing sparkle of some private satisfaction showing about her eyes and mouth.

When lunch was over she pounced on Fräulein Gelsicher. "Senta, Gela, that poor little Marietta is still very mopish. I think we ought to do something to amuse her."

"We cannot do much, while she is in mourning," Fräulein Gelsicher replied.

"Not socially—but get her out more.    I have thought of something."

"What is that?"

"Why, you know this flower that Postiche found in the spinney?  Zio Francesco has never painted it yet.  But I know the place, and I thought we might get him to come over tomorrow, and do it on the spot, and then have a little picnic there.    If he comes, you need not bother to; you can be with Giulio.    But it would make a little change for her."

Fräulein Gelsicher thought this an excellent idea.    She commended Elena for her thoughtfulness, and broached the scheme to Marietta.    The child was not at all enthusiastic; in fact, so far as her listlessness and courtesy permitted she opposed it.    Yes, she would like to see Papa, but need they go *there*?  But Elena, with lively and cheerful persistence, bore her down; Zio Francesco would so enjoy it, and it was a pretty spot.    She got her way—the note was despatched, the Marchese Francesco sent a delighted acceptance, and on Sunday, after *colazione*, he arrived in the brougham with his paintbox, sketch-book, camp stool and all the rest of his plant. The two girls, with the picnic-basket, joined him, and drove off along the Pisignacco road to the spinney; there they unloaded their effects, and sent the carriage back to Odredo to rest the horses.

It was another of those hot still September days which are so frequent and so lovely, in early autumn, in the Province of Gardone.    The little copse of tall young ash and poplar-trees, with a thick undergrowth of hazels and elders below was drowsy with the hum of insects and the warm winy smell of the ripe elderberries, which glistened, where the sunlight pierced the green gloom, like glossy black beads set on invisible plates.    Elena, poking and hunting with swift efficiency, soon found a plant of the Enchanter's Nightshade growing in a spot sufficiently open to permit of the use of the camp-stool; there she installed the Marchese Francesco, and in a short time he was completely absorbed, sitting in perfect contentment, now leaning his white head forward to peer through his thick-lensed spectacles at the modest little object, now straightening up again to transfer his observations to the sheet of rough whitish paper.  Marietta, who had wisely provided herself with a rug and a cushion, settled down a little way away with *Pride and Prejudice*.

"Why on earth," she said to her cousin, "have you brought a mackintosh to*day*, Elena?  It is so hot and fine."

"I thought it would do to sit on; it is very old," Elena replied, airily waving the object, which was in fact antique enough.  She did not however sit on it—still waving it, she wandered off round the end of the copse, in the direction of the smugglers' path, and disappeared.

The hot half-hours passed.  The Marchese painted, Marietta read a little, but spent most of her time lying on her stomach, her chin propped on her hands, gazing at the sunlit insects which moved in a mazy spinning pattern among the bushes, or watching the ants, the long thin-legged spiders and the small beetles which ran about between the grass-stems.  She was still very unhappy, and on this particular afternoon she was unusually aware of her unhappiness.  To be free to idle away the hours on a rug at the edge of an unfamiliar wood was normally, for her, to be filled with an active delight; but today this sweet impersonal pleasure in the shapes of plants and the innocent activities of insects and the fall of light was taken from her.  Her mother's action was a pain which she hated to contemplate; it had outraged her sense of justice, and forced her, for the first time, to make a moral judgement on the Marchesa—and this judgement inevitably roused strong feelings of resentment and indignation on Miss Prestwich's behalf.  The child's loyal spirit suffered from this.  About Miss Prestwich, too, her feelings were all pain and uncertainty. She missed her terribly, and longed to see her, to express her love and sorrow, and comfort her; but a fine instinct, born of her traditions, told her that for the moment this somehow would not do, for either of them; it would cause more pain

than it would give relief.    But her mind worked distressfully at the subject of Almina's disaster.    Brought up among
Italian outspokenness, and for months of the year in the
country, she had a perfectly adequate working knowledge of
the physical facts of life—among the peasants about her, desire
and promiscuity, and the physical results of desire and promiscuity were everyday matters, and hardly more disturbing
than the breeding of animals.    This was the first time that
those things were brought, so to speak, into the ambit of her
moral consciousness; on them, too, she was now forced to make
a moral judgement.    She realised that most of the people about
her, while laying the blame for what had happened primarily
on her Mother and Roffredo, nevertheless tacitly assumed that
by that night at the villa Miss Prestwich had been, in some
very outstanding way, depreciated—that both her virtue and
her social value were greatly diminished by it.    And because
this had happened to someone whom she loved and knew well,
Marietta began to question the actual grounds of this depreciation—(as devout Church-people in England, when their
daughter finds herself married to a lunatic or a confirmed
drunkard, begin to question the grounds of the Church's attitude towards divorce).    She could not feel that those grounds
were either very logical or very just—her mind recurred again
and again to the idea which she had expressed to Giulio on
that day when she first heard the story, that the thing was an
accident, and therefore without moral importance as far as Miss
Prestwich was concerned.    Consequences there might be—
and it was the possibility of the baby, she supposed, and the
resultant disgrace which made them all think like that.

Giulio's attitude in particular distressed her.    He was still
very unwell—overwrought, sleepless and acutely miserable.
This in itself would have troubled her, but she felt very definitely that it was caused, and aggravated, by his morbid
physical horror at what had taken place.    All that business
about being dishonoured and deflowered she simply could not
see the sense of.    It was the spirit that counted, and if the

spirit was upright and unconsenting, the body's misfortunes seemed almost irrelevant. Anyhow they could not have the crude importance which Giulio attached to them. Up till now Giulio and she had always been in agreement about most things. Why in this case would he persist in tormenting himself to death with this perverse and inconsistent attitude? Of course he was jealous, but he could have been jealous, she told herself, without *that*. She recognised that his feeling was a sort of extension of the depreciation idea; and as so many grown-ups held that, it was understandable that he should hold it too. But it was worse with him, and was doing him actual harm; until he stopped feeling like that, he would go on being ill. And she could not see how to stop him.

It was a heavy set of problems for a fifteen-year-old to tackle single-handed. But so far her feelings were so much involved that she shrank away from any discussion of them, even with Gela or Elena. She lay on the rug all that afternoon, thinking round and round the whole thing, chewing a grass now and then, waving her legs when a horse-fly settled on her calf, and coming back, always, to the despairing thought that, under whatever obsession, her Mother, her own Mother, had been both wrong and cruel.

She was interrupted by the Marchese Francesco. Having finished his painting of the Enchanter's Nightshade, he came over to her; he was thirsty, he said, and what about their picnic? Marietta, glad of any distraction, sprang up, and asked where Elena was? The Marchese had not seen Elena. Marietta called—called again and again—there was no answer. "Where can she have got to?" the child said, in surprise. "Well, never mind, Papa—let *us* at least eat and drink"; and she unpacked the picnic basket, and set out the padded wicker teapots of coffee and milk, and all the rest of the simple meal. "Let me see your picture, Papa," she said when they were seated, and examined the painting of the flower. It was as beautiful and careful as all the Marchese Francesco's flower-paintings, and rather more elaborate than usual; the Enchanter's

Nightshade stood, with a frond of dog-mercury for neighbour, and a low-drooped truss of elder-berries in the background. "Good, pretty—it is exactly like," she said. The Marchese beamed through his thick lenses, and patted her hand—"I am delighted that it pleases you, piccolina," he said. He peered at her, then, rather wistfully. "You are all right at Odredo, with your cousins? You are happy?" he asked.

The child sprang up, and threw her arms round his neck. "Oh Papa *caro*," she said, hugging him, her face hidden—"oh Papa caro! Yes, yes, I am quite happy. They are good to me—all of them."

He held her to him and kissed the top of her head, which was all that she presented to his face. "That is well. And you—well, you must be a good child," he said, with a rather pathetic mixture of embarrassment and affection. "That is all you have to do, remember, my little one. Presently," he cleared his throat, "we shall make some nice arrangement for you. But just for the present—well, you generally *are* a good child," he said, and kissed the thick black hair again.

Greatly to the relief of both, at this point Elena appeared; her arrival shattered the tender difficult moment. She looked hot and rather dishevelled; her hands were stained with earth and there were earthy marks round the bottom of her white dress. "Oh, I am thirsty!" she exclaimed, plumping herself down on the rug. "Zio Francesco, am I late?"

"Very late," Marietta replied for him. "What on earth have you been doing?"

"Excavating!" Elena replied promptly. She had, she explained, been making an examination of the little ruin in the wood.

"I wonder you did not hear me call, then," Marietta said. "I shrieked and shrieked."

Elena supposed, pouring out coffee and drinking it, that she had been too busy to notice. She spoke again of her thirst, and said how hot it was. She was right—although clouds were now coming up and obscuring the sun, under the overcast sky the air was closer and more oppressive than earlier in the day. "It might thunder," she said.

The brougham drove up, and they bundled in their effects and took their places. Just as they were starting—"Your mackintosh! You have forgotten your mackintosh!" Marietta exclaimed, looking round.

Elena looked vaguely about. "It must be somewhere," she said, and they drove off. But when the two girls were put out at Odredo there was in fact no sign of it. Elena was quite undisturbed. "I must have left it in the wood," she said. "It doesn't matter—I can fetch it another day. It was so old and dirty, the rain will do it good." And she laughed.

Suzy di Vill' Alta too had watched the darkening sky with anxious eyes that afternoon. Rain would wreck the rendezvous, to which she attached a passionate importance—mackintoshes and thick shoes were such desperately unromantic and unbecoming things, and one could not sit on cushions in a ruin in any comfort during a thunderstorm. But there was no sign of rain when she set out about a quarter past eight; it was cloudy still, but very warm, and she was able to go, as she had hoped, in the filmy dress of black Spanish lace, very transparent and graceful, with wide floating sleeves, trailing skirts, and loose flowing draperies everywhere; the frail black made her fairness both fragile and wonderful. She threw a flimsy black chiffon wrap over all this, and went, eager as a girl, down the long flight of steps to the carriage;—she generally used Agostino, the young groom, for night work, and did so on this occasion. Leaning back in the corner, as they bowled smoothly along the white road, pale now in the failing light, she closed her eyes, rehearsing in her mind, for the ninth or tenth time that day, the precise tone and shade which her manner to Roffredo was to bear when they met—the degree of coolness and detachment, the hint of reproach and—guided, naturally, by his reaction—the transitions by which aloofness was to slide into accessibility, and accessibility into that touch of responsive passion which, so far, had never failed to kindle

his.   Ah but, she sighed to herself, finding small tremors
running all over her, she must keep herself well in hand; it
was dangerous, it put one terribly at the other's mercy to be
so much involved, so moved, oneself.   She lit a cigarette to
steady herself, and sat listening to the sharp rhythmic noise of
the horses' feet, her lovely pallor lit at intervals by the tiny
red glow, in the shadows of the carriage.

At the spinney she got out, and dismissed Agostino; he
turned his horses precisely where old Tommaso, earlier in the
afternoon, had turned when he brought the Marchese Francesco
and the two girls in the brougham.   When the carriage had
disappeared round a bend of the road, Suzy began to make her
way into the wood.

It was very dark in there.   Dusk was already fallen, and
the overcast sky made the gloom deeper still, even out on the
road; in the thick shadow of the trees and bushes it was almost
pitch dark.   Suzy had a rough idea of where the little ruin
was, but it was years since she had been to it.   She began to
push her way cautiously through the dense undergrowth, trying to avoid too much damage to her frail clothes; but in the
darkness she could really see nothing, and boughs and leaves
pushed against her, sprang back and whipped at her arms and
face.   Really, Roffredo might have chosen a more convenient
place, she thought, turning round to free her wrap, which had
caught on something; fumbling awkwardly with the invisible
obstacle, she comforted herself with the thought that in a few
moments, at most, she would be with him, being restored and
commiserated with; hearing his voice, touching his hands—
and then, presently, knowing the penetrating wonder of his
mouth on hers.   She pushed on.

But what was this?   A spray of leaves touched her arm,
cold and damp—she drew her arm away, but the spray stuck
to it.   Startled and disgusted, she put out her left hand to free
her right, and touched another bough, which also stuck; stepping sideways to avoid the revolting contact with this invisible
nastiness, she found that the whole of the left side of her dress

was caught—when she moved she seemed to be pulling half the wood after her. It was incredibly disgusting, this unseen slime which clung to her clothes and hands; sickened, she tore at her dress to free it, but the flimsy lace and chiffon stuck obstinately to the leaves and to her hands; as she stooped to draw her skirts away, a damp spray caught her full in the face —and that too stuck.

At that she screamed—not very loud. "Roffredo!" she called—disagreeable as it was to be found in this state, she must get him to help her. She pulled the loathsome spray from her face, breaking the twig, and wiped it off her hand onto her dress—it stuck there, but she could not help that; feeling for her pocket handkerchief, she listened, with a thudding heart, for his reply. There was none. When she wiped her face, the handkerchief stuck to it. Shuddering with disgust, she called again, louder—"Roffredo! Here! Help!" Still not a sound came but the note of a sleepy bird, which, startled by her cries, went whooping away through the wood. It was very extraordinary—the ruin must be quite close, and she had been careful not to be too early; he must have heard the carriage on the road, and know that she was there. She called again and again, louder than ever, forgetting all caution in her disturbance—what *could* have happened to him? It wasn't possible—an icy pang of fear and anger went through her at the thought—it wasn't possible that he had failed to come? And in panic at the idea she called again, her voice strained now with anxiety—"Roffredo! Here, quick! It is not a joke! Help! It is I—Suzy." This time not even a bird answered; the high notes of her voice were followed by absolute silence.

It was probably the realisation that he had really not come, that something had gone fatally wrong with the meeting which precipitated Suzy's collapse. With the curious incredulity which always accompanies a disappointment as bitter as that, she felt that she *must* reach the ruin and see for herself whether he was there or not; for an instant the pain of his absence almost made her forget the nightmare of the sticky boughs, and she started wildly forward again. She was actually quite close to the ruin, though in the dark she could not see it, and just on the edge of the gummy area; if she had gone back to the road then she would have escaped with a ruined dress. But she went on, and soon she was hopelessly involved. A bough, swinging back after her passage, caught her on the bare nape of her neck, and clung there; as she backed desperately to break it and free herself, another caught her hair, and pulled out the elaborate mass of puffs and curls; the loathsome stuff was everywhere—on her hands, on her clothes; and every part of her dress stuck and clung to some other part. In the darkness this suddenly became a horror that could not be borne—she lost her head completely, and began to run this way and that, screaming, calling for Roffredo, and struggling frantically among the sticky bushes. The experience of actual horror is like a sort of insanity; once a human being really surrenders to it the mind quickly loses its control, not only of the body but of itself, and a sort of dementia supervenes. This happened to Suzy now—she ran and screamed in that black thicket like a mad-woman.

Even before this happened, she had forgotten the very existence of the well—plunging wildly, in her frenzied efforts to escape, now in this direction, now in that, she came on it without warning in the darkness, and pitched in head-foremost.

The so-called well was not of any great depth; it was only a pool, a couple of yards across and three or four feet deep, with mud at the bottom and mossy remnants of masonry round the edge, but there was enough water in it to soak Suzy from head to foot. The shock of the cold plunge brought her to her senses to some extent; when she had struggled to her feet, and stood holding on by the bank, dripping and shivering, for the first time she attempted to think what to do next. She could now see the little ruin close in front of her, a solid black mass among the shadowy dark shapes of the trees; she thought she remembered that it was quite near the edge of the wood on that side, and that if she went straight out past it, she would come onto the smugglers' path. After some unsuccessful efforts—for Suzy was not athletic, and the sides of the pool, though low, were steep and slippery with moss—she managed to struggle out onto the bank. She made her way to the ruin, and felt round it with her hands—it was too dark to see, but there was no sign of rugs or cushions; dry sticks, dead leaves, earth and broken fragments of stone were all that her searching fingers touched. With a little choking sob she left the place, and pushed out through the bushes behind it. The slimy stuff was here too, but on her wet dress and hands it no longer stuck. Now she was clear of the wood, and here was the smugglers' path; she turned right along it, and soon reached the road.

Here she paused, and again considered what to do. From where she stood to Vill' Alta was nearly five miles, a longer walk than she had attempted for years, even when stoutly shod and prepared for exercise; now she had only her soaked and flimsy evening shoes, and she felt weak and exhausted. But she had told Agostino not to come back, as Roffredo had suggested, so that now she was left without any means of return except on foot, unless she applied to Roffredo for a lift —the villa was only a few hundred yards away. But that she could not do. Turn to him now, after he had treated her like this! she thought, with an angry sob—no, never. And supposing that there was some mistake, that she had misread the date, how fatal to let him see her in this state—her clothes ruined and clinging to her all over, her hair pulled down and dripping with wet, her hands and face scratched—she could feel the scratches—and dirty with water and that foul slime. It must be bird-lime—the thought suddenly occurred to her —but how crazy of old Trino to put it in such a place, and in such quantities. She must speak to Carlo about it. But— her thought went back to Roffredo again—no; anything was better than to let him see her like this, with all that was at stake between them. And she began to walk along the road in the direction of Vill' Alta, hobbling rather in the clinging constriction of her wet clothes, her high-heeled shoes turning over now and then in the rutted dust; as she walked, she thought of this meeting, of how carefully and gladly she had prepared and beautified herself for it, of the sweetness of reconciliation and tender joy she had hoped it might bring, and the tears, unseen and unheeded, ran down her stained face.

The road seemed endless.   The severity of her experience in the wood had left her almost exhausted, the plunge into the pool had made her cold; her teeth began to chatter, and though she tried to hurry, in fact she walked very slowly indeed. Once or twice she stopped to rest for a few minutes, leaning against a roadside tree.   After what seemed to her an immense time she reached a cross-roads; she realised with a shock that she was only at the diligence stop—there were still nearly four more miles between her and home.   She began to wonder if she could do it—besides feeling cold, she now felt ill as well.   But there was nothing for it but to persevere, and she struggled on.

Soon after the diligence stop a fresh misfortune overtook her.   She heard footsteps approaching, and then a burst of song—a man's figure loomed up in the darkness, which here on the road was not so deep as it had been in the wood; he lurched unsteadily as he walked.   Suzy stepped off the road, hoping to escape observation, but she was not quick enough; the peasant saw her white arms and her dark figure, reeled across to her, and made to embrace her, with a coarse endearment.   She stood her ground, trembling, and bade him begone, firmly—but he caught her by the shoulders and planted a winy kiss on her neck before the dampness of her clothes and hair struck through, with a shock, to his fuddled senses. "By God, she's all wet!   By God, it's a perditioned mermaid!" the drunken creature shouted, recoiling in tipsy horror, and lurched off down the road, calling on the Saints to protect him. Suzy's shock and fright were even greater than his; she scrambled madly through the looped strands of the vines that bordered the road, and hid herself in some bushes in the meadow beyond. There she cowered, trembling and shivering violently; it was a long time before she could bring herself to venture out onto the road again. And even then, every time she heard or thought she heard a step—and several more peasants passed, for the vintage is a time of work at a distance, and of revelry afterwards—she left the road and hid. And each time that she did so, she found it harder to get up and go on again, walked with more difficulty. Her homeward progress was very slow indeed.

## Chapter Twenty-four

AGNESE, the Marchesa Suzy's maid, had been in her service for many years, and was far too well-trained, and too much accustomed to her manner of life to be worried by her absence at night for a reasonable length of time, still less to raise what she called a how-do-you-do about it. On such occasions she dozed, fully dressed, on a couch in the small room adjoining that of her mistress—where by day she sewed, washed gloves, and pressed out scarves and dresses—till such time as her employer should return; Suzy frequently told her that tonight she need not bother, but Agnese had learned to sleep well, if lightly, on the couch, and felt more satisfied if she was at hand in case she was wanted. On this particular Sunday evening she was unusually wakeful. She never really liked it if the Marchesa was not returning in her own carriage; the fact of her mistress keeping a manservant up half the night seemed somehow, to Agnese's ideas, to confer a certain respectability on the whole proceeding; moreover she was a little anxious because on such a cloudy evening, threatening rain, her employer had persisted in going out with no better protection than that thin chiffon wrap. So she roused up constantly to strike a match, look at her watch, and then go and peer out of the window. The Marchesa Suzy was seldom very late, and this evening she had gone out early; by midnight Agnese was distinctly surprised that she had not returned. By twelve-fifty she was anxious; she lit the lamp, did up her stays and re-fastened her bodice, and sat listening near the window. By one o'clock she became certain that something was wrong, and after some hesitation, she tiptoed off presently to the servants' quarters and roused Valentino. Valentino came shuffling out, sleepy and cross, into the passage, with an old dressing-gown of the Marchese Francesco's over his nightshirt—he was a taller man than the Marchese, and his bare shanks, knotted with varicose veins, projected some distance below the faded flowered silk. "What is it?" he asked. "Is the Old One ill?"

"No, but She has not returned."

"Well, there is nothing to worry about in that, is there?"

"Yes there is. It is past one. She is never so late as this."

Valentino yawned, stretched, and then scratched the back of his neck. "One is sometimes delayed," he said. "Who took Her?"

"Agostino—but he was sent back. And it is *much* later than usual. She is never after the midnight and a half."

Valentino yawned again, hitting his mouth with the flat of his hand, and then scratched once more, this time his head. "What should be done?" he said.

"Send for Tommaso. We could seek her."

"Do you know where she went?"

"I can find out." Like all ladies' maids, Agnese was perfectly familiar with the various hiding-places in which her mistress believed her more private correspondence to be securely concealed, and while Tommaso was sent for she slipped off, candle in hand, to the boudoir, and ferreted among the receipt files till she came on the latest note from Count Roffredo. She read it, replaced it, and returned. Tommaso, shirtless, and wearing a discarded livery top-coat over a pair of ancient trousers, had been produced, and standing there in the passage, the three servants embarked on a sort of *consiglio di famiglia* on their own account. Agnese, armed with the information that the Marchesa had gone, not to the villa but to the ruin in the wood, was emphatic that she must be sought— "She is not even under a roof!" Tommaso was more doubtful; the orders to Agostino about not returning had been precise—"and if one goes against orders, and arrives at an awkward moment—well, that is not very suitable!" Agnese was persistent—it was far later than usual, it was altogether too late, and the young Signor Conte was "unreliable as a squirrel." "Look how he left our Signorina, on that occasion!" In the end she had her way; Tommaso hustled off to put the horses to, Valentino routed out the cook to get water heated—"She will be frozen after all these hours, in that thin wrap!" the maid insisted; and Agnese herself collected a cloak, scarves and rugs, and slipped down with them to the stable. She made the old coachman light and bring a stable lantern, and they set off.

It was by now a quarter to two, and even Tommaso was beginning to be infected with some of the maid's anxiety. As he drove along he peered into the shadows beyond the two faint yellow circles of moving light cast by the carriage lamps. He had put on a shirt and a proper coat, but, per Bacco, the night air was cold! She would not be too warm, la Marchesa, by this time, unless she were in a house. He whipped up his horses.

They came on her about a mile from Vill' Alta, out on a level stretch of road, with no trees near it but the low clipped mulberries supporting the roadside vines. Agnese, who had her head out of the carriage window, saw her first, before the carriage lights reached her—the white arms against the shadowy black figure, on the pale road. She was staggering along with the uncertain steps of complete exhaustion—when she saw the lights coming she made a feeble effort to leave the road and creep through the vines; but the ditch was too much for her—she fell, and lay where she fell. As the carriage drew up Agnese sprang out, lantern in hand, and ran to her; when she reached her side, she almost recoiled, so shocked was she at what the lantern-light revealed. The Marchesa's face was ghastly: white, scratched, and dirty, and ravaged with those peculiar deep marks which are left by fatigue, exposure, or a violent emotional experience—she looked twenty years older than when she had left the house a few hours before. To the maid's horror even the thin wrap had vanished, and much of the frail dress itself was torn away, leaving the neck and arms quite bare; what was left of it was damp and clammy, as was the pitiful hair, which hung down loose and wet, with no pads, or puffs, or curls left anywhere. All this was alarming enough, but when she tried to get her into the carriage, her mistress's state alarmed the servant still more; she was icy cold to the touch, and shivering violently—when Agnese tried to raise her to her feet she collapsed again, moaning, and asking to be left alone; she seemed to have no strength or wits left. Agnese shrouded her in the cloak, but had to get Tommaso to leave his horses and help; between them they managed to bundle her into the carriage. There Agnese muffled the chilled woman still further with the rug, and sat chafing her icy hands while Tommaso drove on till he found a lane's mouth to turn in. "Hurry, you—she is cold as a corpse!" the maid said in a piercing whisper from the window, as the horses backed the vehicle awkwardly out into the road again. Tommaso had seen enough to make him realise the need for haste; he took the level stretch and the lower half of the hill almost at a gallop. But when he came just below the house he slowed down to a walk, and at a walk drove in along the drive—pulling up just short of the house—"It won't do to disturb the Old One," he said in an explanatory whisper; "Which door?"

Uncertain whether Valentino would have opened the front door, and anxious as Tommaso to avoid any noise or commotion which might disturb the old lady, Agnese plumped for the back, in the *cortile sporco*; and perhaps for the first time in her life Suzy di Vill' Alta came into her own house by the servants' entrance. Valentino was hanging about, dressed now after a fashion; he also had at last come to feel a certain anxiety, as two o'clock came and passed; he muttered to Agnese, as she stood in the back passage, supporting the muffled figure of his mistress, that the cook had taken the hot water to the Marchesa's room.

"Help me to get her upstairs, and then get some brandy, quick," Agnese hissed back. "These stairs—it is quicker."

Supporting her on both sides, they took her up the back stairs to her room, and put her on the couch. "Now the brandy—and Apollonia must fill some hot bottles," Agnese said, going with him to the door to be out of ear-shot.

"She is ill?" Valentino asked.

"I fear it—don't undress, you, and tell Tommaso to stay up a bit. We may have to send for the doctor."

"What has happened?" Valentino asked.

"How should *I* know? But she is wet as a drowned cat, and chilled to the bone! Be quick with that brandy," the maid snapped, fairly pushing him out of the door—she closed it, however, very gently after him.

In those days personal servants in the country in Italy were rather good at first aid. Living, as a rule, far from any sort of medical help, they had to be. Agnese was. She pulled off all her mistress's wet clothes, wrapped her in a fleecy dressing-gown and blankets, and sat her in a chair; then she fetched a foot-bath of warm water and set her feet in it, making it gradually hotter and hotter with additions from the great brass-bound hammered copper cans, with their double spouts and brass lids, which Apollonia the cook had brought up. When Valentino came with the brandy she demanded mustard, and while he fetched that she gave the Marchesa a good tot of the spirit, mixed with hot water. She put the mustard in the foot-bath, and the stone hot bottles, presently produced by Apollonia, in the bed; she kept the cook to help her, and between them they sponged the Marchesa's face and hands, and did their best to dry her hair, one or other of them continuously plying her with the hot brandy the while. To their astonishment they could not get her face and hands clean, even with soap and water—some darkish sticky substance was all over them, and gummed her damp hair into matted masses here and there. The cook, puzzled, bent and sniffed at the wet head. "Santa Vergine, it's bird-lime!" she whispered. Agnese sniffed too. "It's true!" she said. "In the name of all the Saints, what can have happened?"

But she did not attempt to ask. She would not have thought it correct to do so in the cook's presence, and she realised also that it would be of no use. The Marchesa sat limp and dazed in the chair, submitting to all their ministrations, "like a baby or an idiot", as Apollonia said later downstairs—only once or twice she said "Grazie, Agnese," in her usual courteous tones, though it was clear that she hardly knew what she was doing. The mechanism of habitual graciousness persisted through exhaustion, illness and dulled senses. This moved the maid strangely; tears came to her eyes. "Niente, niente, la Marchesa," she murmured fervently, each time she heard those automatically spoken words. At last she and Apollonia had done all they could—the Marchesa lay in bed, still wrapped in her dressing-gown, with the bottles pushed to a suitable distance; her hands and feet were much warmer, and her partly-dried hair wrapped in a towel; she seemed sleepy and quiet. Agnese sent a message by Apollonia to say that Valentino and Tommaso need not sit up; she would do so herself, and there was in her opinion no need to send for the Doctor—she thought the Marchesa would do, now. Excited, seething with unsatisfied speculation, the seniors of the Vill' Alta household retired to bed.

But in the morning it was quite clear that the Marchesa Suzy would not "do". One glance told Agnese that, when she slipped in at about 8 a.m. to look at her mistress. She was still more or less asleep, but she was shifting restlessly in the bed, and breathing heavily; her face was flushed, and a hand which she flung out above the bedclothes was burning hot when the maid touched it. Agnese's experienced commonsense needed none of those glass thermometers, silly little breakable things, which the young Marchesa so constantly used on the Marchesina, to tell that here was high fever. She fetched an underling, sent her for the Marchese Francesco, and told him brusquely that the Marchesa was ill. The Doctor must be fetched—not the one from Pisignacco, but the good one from Gardone. (The Pisignacco doctor was a sort of cross between an apothecary and a vet, and Agnese, with a certain experience of Roman doctors, rated him at his true value.)

The Marchese Francesco was rather fussed, as he always was by any sudden emergency calling for decisive action.   He stood fiddling with the tassels of a more recent edition of the dressing-gown in which Valentino had appeared during the night, and then asked what was wrong with the Marchesa?

"She went for a drive yesterday evening, without a proper wrap, and took a chill," the maid returned, blandly.

The Marchese bent and peered at his wife through his spectacles, and then addressed her—"Cara, come stà?"

The Marchesa opened her large eyes, and stared full at him; then her face took on a look of horror, and she said in a small voice, but with an extraordinary intensity of expression, which gave it the piercing quality of a cry—"Roffredo!  Help!  It is not a joke!  Come!"

Those brief sentences, obviously spoken in delirium, sent the Marchese Francesco flying.   Agostino was sent on horse-back to Gardone for the doctor, a garden-boy was despatched to Sant' Apollonia with a telegram in the same sense.   (There was always a slight uncertainty in the Province as to which of these methods would prove the quicker, so in cases of grave emergency people used both.)    And when her breakfast had been taken to her, he sent to beg an audience—it really almost amounted to that—of La Vecchia Marchesa.   Unlike his brother Filippo the Marchese Francesco had not, so to speak, the run of his Mother's room in the early morning; but the habit of a life-time was not to be broken—to her, in any trouble, he had always hastened, and to her he hastened now. Not even to his Mother had Francesco ever spoken his heart about his wife; the old lady had often wondered how far his placidity about her vagaries was due to indifference, how far to sheer obliviousness of them, and how far to a sort of resigned tact.   But there could be no mistake about his dis-tress and concern at that moment.   Suzy was one of those fortunate women who are never ill, and the old Marchesa had to go back to the hours of her confinement, before Marietta's birth, to find a parallel for her son's present misery of anxiety. It seemed to her to be of exactly the same quality now as then, eighteen months after his marriage, and with a flash of surprise it occurred to her that perhaps after all Francesco, in some deep corner of his shy and incompetent heart, still loved the beautiful creature who, through all her adventures, had never shown him anything but graceful affection and courteous consideration—at least in little things, she amended to herself. And the old Marchesa knew how much fuller life is of little things than of big, and how no amount of righteousness over great issues, valuable as that may be, can by itself really replace the daily sweetening of life by just such small unfailing kindnesses. It might be, she thought, studying her son's disturbed face, as he sat by her bed, his eyes, behind those masking lenses, fixed on her face in a pathetic appeal for reassurance and support—it might be that he loved Suzy still, and needed and longed for something more than she gave him, even though what she had given had been enough to keep love alive. It struck her suddenly that Francesco was getting to be an old man, a thought which had never occurred to her before. (To La Vecchia Marchesa the world was filled with incredibly youthful and immature people.) With unwonted warmth she comforted him, praised the Gardone doctor's skill and Suzy's superb constitution, and promised to see her as soon as she was dressed.

The doctor arrived soon after eleven, and took a serious view. It was an acute congestion, it might develop into a pneumonia. There must be expert nursing—and two Moravian Sisters were telegraphed for from Padua; it was further than Venice, but the doctor had a high opinion of the hospital and nursing there. (Such a thing as a lay trained nurse hardly existed in Italy then outside Rome, where a handful of English ones drew immense fees.) And then he asked a number of questions as to the origin and onset of the illness. The Marchese Francesco repeated Agnese's story of the drive and the thin wrap. The Doctor shook his head. That might account—but so sudden and so sharp an attack looked more like some severe exposure or acute chill, such as might be caused by a wetting. The old Marchesa here intervened. The illness had only manifested itself this morning, the young Marchesa was already too ill to be questioned, she herself had as yet had no time to make enquiries. When the Doctor came again in the evening, she would probably be in a position to furnish him with such information as was *necessary*—she emphasised the word a little—for the conduct of the case. In the meantime his instructions should be followed, and she wished him a very good morning. The determination of her speech and manner fairly swept him out of the room; the old Marchesa belonged to a generation which regarded doctors as a slightly superior sort of chemist, and treated them accordingly.

But when the dog-cart had been despatched with the prescriptions to Gardone, and the Doctor's more immediate instructions carried out, the old lady sent Giacinta to sit with the young Marchesa, and commanded Agnese's attendance in her own room. She privately agreed entirely with the Doctor's view that such an attack was not likely to be caused merely by a chilly drive, and she was determined to get to the bottom of the matter. That Suzy had gone out last night she knew, that it was to meet Roffredo or Carlo she guessed—she suspected the former, since an attempt at explanation and reconciliation was a fairly obvious move on either side. But she knew nothing more; the servants' prudent manœuvres had been so successful and so silent that nothing of the nocturnal comings and goings in the house had reached her ears. When the maid appeared she dealt with her with something more than her usual unhesitating firmness.

"Agnese, your mistress is gravely ill," she said. "It is essential to know exactly what has caused this malady. You must tell me *everything*, do you understand? Everything that you know."

"Yes, la Marchesa. It is not dangerous, the Marchesa's illness?" the maid said, in an anxious voice.

"It is indeed dangerous," the old lady answered, brusquely. "Now tell me, at what hour did the Marchesa return last night?"

"Something after the two hours, la Marchesa."

"Did you see her?"

"Yes, la Marchesa."

"Did she seem well then?"

"La Marchesa, no. She was wet and cold, very cold."

"Wet? It has not rained! How came she to be wet?"

"I don't know, la Marchesa. But she was wet all over and already drying again; her clothes were all torn, and there was something on them, and on her hair and hands—bird-lime, credo."

The old lady listened with a grave face. "Who drove her last night?"

"Agostino, la Marchesa."

"Send him to me."

"La Marchesa, he is gone to Gardone for the medicines. And he did not bring the young Marchesa back. She dismissed him, early, early."

"Who did bring her back, then?"

"Tommaso, la Marchesa, and I. When the Marchesa did not return, I grew anxious, and took the carriage, and we found her and brought her home."

"Found her where?" the old lady asked sharply.

"On the road, la Marchesa, between here and Odredo. Walking along, stumbling and falling, without cloak or wrap, her hair all down and her face dirty! Oh, my poor mistress!" —and the maid began to cry.

"She was alone?"

"Quite, quite alone! And in such a condition! We had to carry her to the brougham—she could hardly stand," the maid sobbed out, fairly letting herself go at last.

"Stop snivelling, and keep your wits in your head!" the old

Marchesa said sharply.    "What did you do for her when you
got in?"

"Wrapped her in blankets, la Marchesa," Agnese replied,
obediently wiping her eyes, and sniffing—"and set her feet in
hot mustard-water, and gave her brandy; and then put her to
bed, well wrapped and with plenty of hot bottles.    She slept,
and I hoped she would be better this morning."

"You did well," the old lady said briefly.    She considered
for a moment or two, tapping her old hand, her usual accompaniment to thought, on the arm of her chair.    There was
something extremely peculiar about the servant's story.    Then
she looked hard at the maid, who stood, still sniffing and
dabbing rather furtively at her eyes, before her.

"Agnese, have you any idea where your mistress went last
night?"

"Yes, la Marchesa."

"Where then?"

"To meet the young Signor Conte."

"How do you know this?    Was there a letter?"    (The old
Marchesa had not lived for ninety-nine years among Italian
servants for nothing.)

"La Marchesa, yes," the maid said simply.

"Bring it to me."

So Roffredo's epistle was fished out once more from its
resting-place among the receipts, and put into la Vecchia
Marchesa's ancient hands.    She dismissed the maid, and read
it, sitting alone; when she had finished it she, like Agnese
sniffed, but with a different intonation.    Then she took her
morocco-cornered writing-board, and indited a short note, in
her fine spidery old writing, and despatched it, and waited,
using her bright old wits on this extraordinary set of facts, but
without, it must be confessed, much result.

That note brought Count Roffredo over soon after *colazione*.
She received him in her own sitting-room.    The young man
entered with, as she rather grudgingly conceded, an extremely
good manner—courteous, slightly chastened, almost submis-

sive, but without any underbred signs of being ill at ease. She looked at him consideringly, while he kissed her hand, seated himself at her bidding, and enquired after her health— no, she did not wonder at Suzy.   He was young, but he had that quality, belonging neither to age nor youth, nor even to greatness of intellect, which makes some men's mere entry into a room a matter of importance to those in it.   A difficult gift for the possessor; difficult as beauty.   Marietta, she thought, who would not have beauty, would have it too. But at the recollection of the unhappiness that this young man's recent actions must ultimately bring on Marietta she hardened her heart against him.

"What time d. <sup>?</sup> Suzy leave you last night, and where?" she asked abruptly.

The young man looked at her in apparent astonishment. "I did not see the Marchesa Suzy last night," he said.   "I have not seen her since the Meden picnic."

The old lady eyed him, as he afterwards said, like a monkey. "So—but you expected to see her, I presume?" she asked.

"No, I did not—I had no reason to expect that pleasure," the young man said, politely and quietly, but as if a little at a loss.   A civil liar, anyhow, the old lady said to herself.   But her quick irritability began to mount.   Taking the letter from a little bag at her waist, she handed it to him, saying—"And you did not write this either, I suppose?" with fine sarcasm.

The young man took it and read it, from beginning to end, and then looked up at the old lady with a grave and rather bewildered face.

"No, I did not write it," he said firmly.   "I have never seen it before in my life."

The old Marchesa looked full at him, and he looked as steadily back at her.

"So you deny it?" she said, coldly.

"Most certainly I do," he said, with vigour.   "I have never in my life invited the Marchesa Suzy, or anyone else, to that ridiculous ruin—and since the picnic at Meden I have neither seen the Marchesa, nor held any sort of communication with her. And I should perhaps tell you that I was by no means in the mood to write her such a letter as this—" he tapped his fine hand sharply on the outstretched paper. His face had grown surprisingly angry. "I *am* penitent, I *am* ashamed of what happened the other night—but not towards *her*! But for her unwarrantable treatment of that unfortunate girl, I should never have been in the position to 'lose my head and behave like an idiot'!" He shook the sheet of paper angrily before the old lady.

"So—you put the blame on Suzy for your behaviour?" the old Marchesa said, getting angry in her turn.

He checked at once, and his manner changed.

"Not wholly, Marchesa," he said gravely. "I know that what I did was inexcusable, and I regret it bitterly. But to this extent I do blame Suzy, that she dismissed that wretched girl without a shred of justification. Once for all, and to you, I wish to say this. I was in love with her, and we did meet— but only out walking, before breakfast—of all times!" the young man said, with a disarming inflection. "She would never do anything else—never for an instant would she neglect Marietta, or her duties. And for Suzy to allege impropriety, and dismiss her on these grounds without money enough to get home with, to turn her into the street—it was unpardonable!" He spoke steadily, but now with a sort of restrained vehemence.

His anger, and still more his championship of Miss Prestwich, convinced the old Marchesa as nothing else could have done that he was in fact *not* the author of the letter which he still held. But his last speech sent her off on another tack.

"Do you want to marry her?" she asked.

He looked slightly taken aback, and sat for a moment, obviously thinking.

"*Now*, no," he said at length. "If we had been left alone, if the thing had been allowed to run its course in peace, I think very likely I should have wished to. But this would give us a bad start.    I should feel that I had been compromised into it, the Province would probably be odious to her, let alone Rome, and she—she is sensitive and proud; she would feel all her life that I had done it out of pity.    It would make it too difficult.    English, too!    That is of itself a difficulty." He looked hard at the old face opposite him—it was as if she were somehow drawing out of him secret truths of which he had never before been aware.    "I shall never be able to be very thorough as a husband," he said, with a curious simplicity. "I must make an easy marriage, with a wife who knows all the ropes and will do three-quarters of the work.    An Italian, with her own resources—and a clever one."

The old Marchesa looked at him for a long time in silence, with a very curious expression on her face.    It was not like a monkey, this time—there was an odd softness in her look. But at length—"Roffredo, I had no idea that you had so much common-sense," she said drily.    Then she reverted to the matter in hand.    She took the letter from him, and looked at it again.

"Very curious," she said, examining it.    "So it was a trick. H'm!    Someone has been behaving very badly.    Suzy went to this precious rendezvous, and somehow got wet through; and she had to walk home, alone.    Today she is ill.    Had you heard this?"

Roffredo had not heard a word.    He expressed proper concern, asked all the right questions.

"The Doctor comes again this evening," the old lady said. "I am afraid it is grave, but we shall know more then."    She looked at the letter again.    "But who can have written this?"

"Who?    There is only one person in the Province who could have written that," the young man said, energetically— "and naturally she will have had her knife into Suzy over all this; she was devoted to Miss Prestwich.    Of course, it is my cousin Elena."

## Chapter Twenty-five

LA VECCHIA MARCHESA was not as familiar with Elena's
activities in the matter of forgery as might have been
supposed. Fräulein Gelsicher was deeply shamed by
them, and had always done her utmost to prevent accounts of
them from getting about; and the awe in which even Elena
stood of the old Marchesa had been sufficient hitherto to protect the household at Vill' Alta from any direct attacks, except
occasionally one on Marietta—about those the little girl
giggled subsequently with her cousins, but held her peace to
her elders. The Sorellone had once been victimized, but
about such things the victims themselves are wont to be rather
silent; it was therefore a well-known joke among the younger
branches of the Castellone clan, but was more or less confined
to them.

When Roffredo had gone the old lady read the letter again,
carefully. The handwriting was a perfect imitation, the
phrasing diabolically clever. It was just what one might
have expected a young man to write, in all the circumstances.
With the curious detachment of the very old, she even paid
the document the compliment of giving her little dry chuckle
over it. But it was essential to find out what had happened,
for Suzy's sake and Francesco's, and she despatched yet
another note, this time to Fräulein Gelsicher, demanding that
Elena be sent over in the carriage immediately to see her.

Fräulein Gelsicher was slightly mystified by the note, but
at once did as she was asked. Elena was not; the news of the
Marchesa Suzy's illness had reached Odredo, by the usual
channels, during the early afternoon, and the usual futile
efforts to prevent Marietta from hearing of it had been initiated—efforts more futile than usual, since Count Carlo was

plunged by the tidings into a babbling distress. In her secret heart Elena was slightly dismayed; she was also full of curiosity as to what had happened; but she was equally full of a certain determination. She put on a neat frock, tidied her hair, and set off, without comment, in the carriage.

La Vecchia Marchesa was inclined to think rather highly of Elena. She did not put her on the same shelf as Marietta, but she liked her trimness of appearance, her liveliness, her uncomplicated fearless sagacity, her rather *méchante* wit. When the girl had made her curtsey, tendered her rosy blooming cheek for the routine kiss, and seated herself, with a twitch of her white skirts and the correct side-by-side emplacement of her white shoes (young girls in Italy thirty years ago were not encouraged to cross even their ankles) the old lady regarded her, far from inimically, for a moment before opening fire. Yes, she was a proper Castellone—full of spirit, fine and well-set-up; a fit cousin to Roffredo. How that flimsy creature Carlo came to have such a daughter! However, discipline had to be administered, and facts established. She set to work, with her usual determination.

"My child, I have sent for you to ask you some questions, which you will have the goodness to answer accurately," she began. "On Saturday my daughter-in-law, Suzy, received a letter, purporting to come from your cousin Roffredo, inviting her to meet him last night at a certain ruin in the little wood near his Villa, by what I believe they call the Holy Well. The letter urged her to dismiss her carriage, as he would bring her home. She went, and sent the man back. What happened there, I do not know—and as she is now gravely ill, indeed in delirium, it is impossible to find out. But Roffredo, whom I have seen, denies all knowledge of the letter, and I am inclined to believe him." She paused, and looked steadily at her great-niece. "Do you know anything of it?"

"Yes. I wrote it," Elena said at once.

"You did! And may one ask why you did such a thing?"

The girl looked at the formidable old lady with a level gaze. "Yes, Bonne-Mama," (Elena and Giulio, like Marietta, used the familiar title.) "I will tell you. I did it because I was not at all pleased with Zia Suzy for the way she treated Postiche. Indeed, I have not been pleased with her for a long time! I hated to see her always having her own way, tormenting people and making them her slaves, and being perfectly successful with it—still praised, still admired! Even Papa! Oh yes—I have seen that quite clearly, just lately; she has had him too! It is not what I like—one's own Father made a fool of in that way! Anyone can see what poor Papa is—weak as water; but because she is dull here, and must have a man, she takes him, and keeps him on a string! It is not dignified for him—or for us, me and Giulio." She paused, as if gathering her forces, and then looked straighter than ever at the old Marchesa, who listened to this outburst in complete silence. "And when it came to downright cruelty to that poor little creature, who is as innocent as milk, I would *not* let it go unpunished! Do you know that she sent her away *without money?* All this going to Roffredo and being seduced is quite directly the fault of Zia Suzy; unless she was in desperation, Postiche would never have gone near the Villa. Roffredo is a fool and a brute—he has *no* self-control; I blame him too —but if that wretched little thing has a baby, the real responsibility will lie at Zia Suzy's door! And what a way to behave, sending her only to the diligence, and having her left there alone! Do you know that a peasant came by as she waited, and struck her with his whip, across the neck?" Her always high colour had risen, her superb brown eyes blazed, the ring of her words was almost splendid. "So I said to myself that *she* too, Zia Suzy, should be left on the road alone; and know what it was to be insulted, perhaps, by peasants, as she had chosen should happen to a girl, almost a child, and a foreigner at that! *That* is why I wrote that letter."

The impact of youth's independent standards on maturity,

the recognition of the child as a person, and a person with quite marked views of his own, always comes as something of a shock, even to middle age. To great age, when the protagonists gaze at one another across the gap of two or more generations, the shock is sometimes more startling still. Across that gulf of time the old Marchesa now gazed at Elena di Castellone, with feelings, quite simply, of absolute astonishment. This young creature, barely out of the schoolroom, had thought this whole business out, assessed it, judged it, and most vigorously acted on her judgement. What startled the old woman most was what Elena said about her Father and Suzy. She herself, holding the accepted standards of her class and her day, had serenely tolerated the liaison, since it involved no open breach, no violent disturbance of the *convenances*; this girl of eighteen now sat there and told her to her face, not only that she was aware of it, but that it infringed the dignity of herself and her brother. This was quite a new point of view to the old Marchesa—it had never really occurred to her that Elena and Giulio *had* any dignity, let alone any views on the morals of their elders.

But great age, oddly enough, finds it far easier to bridge the gulf of two or three generations with tolerance and comprehension than middle age does that of one. Middle age has all sorts of vested interests to defend—its authority, its dignity and its personal life, on all of which youth's clear-sightedness and independance of outlook may painfully impinge. Old age is less concerned with these things—its personal life is becoming remote; the dignity of age can look after itself, and the old care the less about authority, since they bear no real responsibilities any more. Great age has only one serious vested interest—warmth: physical warmth for its old bones, the sunshiny warmth of affection for its old heart. So it was not really surprising that the old Marchesa should rally rather briskly from the shock of Elena's outlook. Here, within an hour or two, were both she and Roffredo, the pair of them, vigorously assailing the character and actions of Suzy, her favourite daughter-in-law; and, in Elena's case, energetically reprobating a manner of life, a set of standards which she herself had always thought, within certain limits, perfectly admissible. But with the curious detached adaptability of age, she was able to make a swift mental adjustment to the new point of view. The fundamental honesty, accuracy and justness of her mind rose to recognise, and even to salute not only the sincerity but the justice of the girl's speech. Yes, she was right—it was undignified for them, and unfair to them. About the rest, at bottom, Elena was right too. The old lady felt a sudden respect for the girl's instinct for righteousness, violently and even wrongly as she had expressed it.

But for the moment she left all that. She had still to get at all the facts.

"So—you wrote it. And Roffredo knew nothing of it. And you arranged for her to go home alone, on foot. But how came she to be wet through? It did not rain. Agnese says that on her return she was soaked to the skin and covered with some sticky stuff, like bird-lime."

Elena looked at the old Marchesa with round eyes.

"How she got wet, I don't know, unless she fell into the pool," she said. "There is a pool, just by the ruin. But the bird-lime I arranged myself. I did not mean to, at first—I meant only to let her go, and hope to find Roffredo, and not find him; and to have to walk home alone. You see, I know quite well that it was only out of jealousy that she dismissed Postiche; because she wanted Roffredo for herself, as well as Papa—or perhaps instead of him!—and she had found out that he was in love with Postiche." She paused, her colour vivid again with indignation; there was a ring of scorn in her young voice. "But on Saturday, we had *uccellini* for lunch, and that suddenly gave me the idea of the bird-lime—to put it on the bushes round the ruin. So I made Gela invite Zio Francesco—he is so blind, he sees nothing, and poor little Marietta is always so moony!—and while he painted the flower, this Enchanter's something, and she read and moped,

I ran across to Trino and got a bucket and a brush, and put it all over the bushes."

The old woman glanced at the fresh face opposite her with something very close to awe, tinged with comic appreciation. This was something like an *intrigante*!

"So this invitation to my son, to paint the flower, was purely for that—to give you the chance to lime the bushes?"

This time Elena blushed, but she answered steadily.

"Yes, Bonne-Mama."

"H'm!" said the old lady.   She looked at her niece, with her bright black eyes, and her head cocked on one side, with something of the half-wise, half-ironic expression that one sometimes imagines in the bright eye of a small bird.   "And do you think that was a pretty trick?" she asked, in a perfectly amicable voice.

Elena continued to blush.

"No, Bonne-Mama," she said, still with her ready frankness. "I believe it might have been better if I had not had *that* idea."

"So do I," said the old lady.   "That was rather an ugly joke.   I think you have too much intelligence to play such tricks as that."

Elena said nothing.   The old lady looked thoughtfully at her.

"Well, my child," she said at length, "I am glad you have told me everything plainly.   It seems clear what happened— poor Suzy will have got all gummed and entangled with this substance, and must have fallen, in the dark, into the well. That explains why she was so wet.   And now she has pneumonia," the old lady said, as if to herself, with a sudden simplicity of sadness in her voice.

"Bonne-Mama, for *that*, indeed I am sorry," Elena said, impulsively.

"My child, I believe you.   And that, you could not foresee. But now listen—I have something to say to you."   She sat silent for a few moments, tapping with her hand on the chair-arm; and Elena sat silent opposite her, her eyes fixed on the old lady's face. The absence of direct reproof had rather disarmed her, and she was cooling down after her outburst— she was somehow quite prepared to listen.

"I see," the old lady went on at length, "that it is perhaps natural that you should resent Suzy's relation to your Father. Very young people believe that their parents belong to them; and parents believe that their children belong to *them*, too. They are both wrong! No one belongs to anyone else, though one may attach others, by good fortune, or by one's own affection." She paused, and her old eyes looked far away. "But actually," she resumed with one of her little bursts of briskness, "I believe this relationship has brought him both comfort in a genuine grief, and a sympathy which has given him real happiness. There has been that side of it —which you have perhaps overlooked! Men are very oddly made—you, who observe so much, might consider this aspect also! Your Father cared too deeply, I believe, for your Mother to wish to marry again; but he required relief—they all do—and Suzy gave it to him. If you had thought a little further, had looked beyond your own feelings, this might perhaps have occurred to you."

The honesty and directness of the old lady's words moved Elena as much as they surprised her. She too sat silent for some moments, looking at her lap—then she raised her large brown eyes to the old lady's face.

"Bonne-Mama, I do see that," she said. "But with one's own Father and one's own Aunt, one does *not* like it! Is that wrong? I wish very much to know what you think. Giulio and I have both felt it—unpleasant; and Gela is too loyal—in somma, she will not discuss it, and I understand that she cannot, with us. But I feel—somehow, a second marriage would be different. That too I might not like, but I should feel it differently. Is that just silly, selfish?"

Posed with this question, with a directness equal to her own, it struck the old Marchesa suddenly what an abnormal conversation this was to be taking place between herself and a girl of eighteen. But abnormality *per se* is often met by the very old with a strange equanimity.

"No," she replied. "It is not wholly selfish; at least, it is quite natural—selfishness *is* natural," she said, with a dry smile. "But the family has claims, in such a case; I, in my time, have acknowledged them." And as she had done when talking to the Marchesa Nadia, she first looked far away, and then closed her eyes. She opened them again, quickly, and went on—"I should have seen sooner that this would not do." (It was clear to Elena that now she was talking to herself.) "No—it will not do. It must end." She sighed. "I hope it does not end forcibly—my poor Suzy!" And she went on murmuring something, vague sounds of tenderness, of which Elena could not catch the words; but the sense—of anxiety and loving distress—the girl did grasp. She bounced up off her chair, and kissed the old lady. "Bonne-Mama, I *am* sorry —about this—and you. I did not mean to hurt you and cause you this anxiety."

The old lady returned her kiss. "My child, playing Providence is generally a dangerous game," she said, with a return of her briskness. "Sometimes one must do one's part, arrange things; but vengeance, at least, is best left to the Lord God. It is said that He has a taste for it!" she added, with one of her sly looks. Then, abruptly, she changed the subject. "How much does Marietta know of all this?"

"About Zia Suzy's illness?"

"No, the rest—Miss Prestwich and her dismissal, and Roffredo; and also about her Mother's part in it all. Does she know anything?"

"Yes—she knows most of it; about Roffredo and Zia Suzy certainly—about Papa, I think not," Elena said.

The old lady looked vexed. "Could this not have been avoided? I thought the Signorina had more sense."

"It was not Gela's fault. It is mine, if anyone's. I told her," Elena said. "But she was picking up so much from the servants anyhow that she must have heard it in time.    And also Giulio flew to her, mad with despair, after he had seen Roffredo and heard about Postiche from him, and poured out the whole thing."

"Why should he tell *her*?    And why was he mad with despair?"

"Oh, he tells Marietta everything—they are thick as thieves," Elena replied, with a slight return of her usual airiness.    "And Giulio, you know, is head over ears in love with Postiche, so for him this is all awful.    He is in a most miserable state; he will not eat, he does not sleep, and he cannot work, or read, or do anything.    We do not know what to do with him; Gela is at her wits' end."

"And Marietta?    How does she take it?" the old lady asked anxiously.

"She is *very* unhappy, I think," Elena answered.    "She never says anything, you know—or very seldom.    But she loved Miss Prestwich, and believes in her, and I think she has not liked what Zia Suzy did.    And that will have hurt her too.    For her, really, it is worse than for anyone, for she has two affections spoilt," Elena said, with her customary brief assessing of the situation.

The old lady tapped on her chair.    Then she asked Elena to give her her writing-pad, and indited her third note that day, summoning Fräulein Gelsicher to visit her next morning; and gave it to Elena, and dismissed her.    When the girl had gone, she sat again, thinking about the whole thing.    The onslaught of youth on maturity made her feel more tender and protective to Suzy than before.    But—really that young girl, Elena, was right.    Youth had its claims.    It was time that this business of Suzy and Carlo should stop.    Indeed, for Marietta's sake, Suzy's activities of that sort must really all stop.    And remembering her interview with her son that morning, she thought that it was perhaps the case that he too, the ageing husband, had some claims which now deserved consideration, as well as youth.    Poor Francesco, he had not had much out of life! His flowers!—and even that passion had been used by that impertinent little monkey, Elena, to bring about his wife's discomfiture and illness, perhaps her death. Youth was very unscrupulous, the old lady thought. But the thought of Suzy's illness suddenly spurred her—she must go in a moment and see how she was, poor Suzy—gay, delightful, affectionate Suzy. She was a little tired, after so much talking with these definite violent young creatures, who all seemed to find it necessary to shout at one! But she must go. She rang her little bell for Giacinta; she liked the maid's escort for all expeditions about the house. But by the time the maid slipped noiselessly in, the old lady had fallen into one of her sudden sleeps.

Fräulein Gelsicher was actually exceedingly glad to receive the old Marchesa's summons. Ever since that unlucky Wednesday of encounters and revelations she had been longing to take counsel with La Vecchia Marchesa; but her hands had been so full with Giulio, and the general relations of Odredo with Vill' Alta were become so peculiar, that she had lacked either the time or the courage to seek an interview. So she welcomed this opportunity eagerly. Marietta too was occupying her thoughts a great deal. The governess's perceptive and affectionate goodness, coupled with her professional preoccupation with female youth, had made her realise far more clearly than Elena the extent to which the little girl was suffering, both from the moral shock of her Mother's behaviour and from the calamity which had overtaken Miss Prestwich. But besides this, the child's insight into Giulio's feelings, revealed in several conversations after that first one, had given away to the Swiss woman's experienced penetration something of the nature of her feelings for him. And instead of brushing this aside as girlish silliness, she recognised, with serious concern, how much it added to the load of pain and problems which now rested on those little thin shoulders. About Marietta, too, therefore, she would be glad of the old Marchesa's advice. She saw no easy outlet for her. To return and live with her

Mother, with some other governess substituted for the one she loved so much, a perpetual reminder of her loss and the reason for it; watching, with eyes sharpened by this bitter experience, the manner of her Mother's life—that was not going to be so easy. And that Mother, aware of her scrutiny and the reasons for it, and as the girl grew older increasingly irked by this watchful presence—how was she going to treat the daughter whose personal life she had always affectionately ignored, even when things were at their best and easiest between them, and she could rest secure in that blind aloof childish deference and dutiful affection? Really, the Swiss woman thought, as she drove next morning up the long curve of the hill below the great grey house, the best thing the Marchesa Suzy could do now would be to die! That would resolve several major problems at a stroke—Marietta's future, Giulio's and Elena's relations to their Father, and, no doubt, a good many private preoccupations for Count Roffredo—not that she wasted much sympathy on *his* worries.

It seemed, on her arrival, very much as if the Marchesa Suzy were going to gratify her impious wish. The doctor's brougham was at the door, and moved away across the sweep towards the flower-beds to make room for the Odredo carriage; upstairs she had to wait for some time in the old lady's boudoir, since the Marchesa, as Roberto informed her, was with the doctor in the young Marchesa's room. When the old woman at last appeared, walking in leaning on her ebony stick and escorted by Giacinta, it was with a grave and anxious face.

"Yes, she is very ill—terribly ill," she replied briefly to the governess's enquiries. "It is an exceedingly severe pneumonia. She has of course a wonderful constitution, and that gives some hope; and the two Sisters seem excellent. We shall not know much till Sunday or Monday—the crisis, the decision, should be reached then." She gave a tiny sigh. "Meanwhile, I thought that you and I ought to have a little talk," she resumed. "Elena tells me that Giulio is in a very bad state—indeed Suzy mentioned something of the sort—and that it is because he is so deeply attached to Miss Prestwich. Is that true?"

"Perfectly true, Marchesa. Poor boy, he idealised and worshipped her—he who never looked at a woman before! —and this affair at the Villa has been a fearful blow to him. I really do not know *what* to do with him," the Swiss said distressfully, mechanically straightening her hat; "young men are really outside my province! I have greatly wished to ask your advice. He eats next to nothing, and hardly sleeps; he has given himself over to this sorrow in the most complete way, and unless we can do something, I cannot foresee what the end of it will be. It is eating into his mind."

"It was the greatest folly ever getting that poor girl here," the old lady said irritably. "However, that is the past. He must have distraction," she said, decidedly.

"Pardon me, Marchesa, but if you mean social distraction, he will not take it. He will not see anyone if he can help it, except me and Marietta—for whom it is not good to listen constantly to his misery."

"No; he must go away," the old lady said. "Is there nowhere that he can be sent?"

"I do not know," the Swiss said doubtfully. "His great wish has always been to go to Oxford to study—that is why he was so anxious to learn English with that poor girl. But I have never been able to persuade his Father to agree to it."

"Carlo is, and always was, between you and me, a fool," the old lady said energetically. "But now, he *must* see the necessity. I shall speak with him—it must be arranged. There is money enough?" she asked.

"Oh, for two or three years at Oxford, certainly," Fräulein Gelsicher said. "Marchesa, if you could get this settled, it would do more for Giulio than anything else. I believe it would cure him."

"It *shall* be arranged. Now tell me, how is that little

thing, Marietta? All this is very hard for her. And Elena tells me that she knows all about it?"

"Yes, Marchesa. Giulio made her his confidante. That is a most extraordinary child," the Swiss said, in a rare burst of enthusiasm. "Her patience, her wisdom with him!—and her silence and self-restraint about her own sorrow. A woman of forty could not show more soul. Her comprehension is astonishing."

"She ought not to have to comprehend all these things, at her age," the old Marchesa said, rather sadly. "But she is reasonably well—eats, sleeps?"

"Fairly well—she is a little listless. But Marchesa, I am rather concerned about her in the future," Fräulein Gelsicher said. "The unfortunate part of this affair is that—" she hesitated "—in effect, she feels that her Mother's action was to some extent the cause of it all, and as she was wholly devoted to Miss Prestwich, she—well, she does not in her mind endorse that action."

"In fact, she blames her Mother?"

"Well, yes. And I feel that—I should not perhaps trouble you with all this," the Swiss said.

"Nothing is more important than Marietta," the old Marchesa said emphatically. "Go on, my good Gelsicher, and don't mince your words too much."

"Well, Marchesa, I do not think it would be a good plan to introduce a new governess into the household at all soon; it would be a constant reminder of her sorrow, and of its cause. And yet I do not see what else is to be done. She cannot be alone."

The old lady considered.

"No—for the present, that would not do. It would be cruel. And Suzy—" she paused, and sighed. "For the moment, no. In any case, she will be delicate, need care, for a long time after this," she said, "even at the best." She thought again. "Could *you* take her?" she asked suddenly.

"I? Here?"

"No no—at Odredo, and in Rome. Elena will need you still, of course, but I imagine mainly for chaperonage now, not lessons. Would you have time? Be willing?"

"Marchesa, there is nothing I should like better," Fräulein Gelsicher said earnestly; "but of course, the decision would not rest with me."

"If you are willing, there should be no difficulty," the old lady said briskly. "Some proper arrangement would of course be made with the Count. Elena is fond of her?"

"Very—and now more than ever. She is beginning to see what she is, for all her youth. Indeed, I should value the companionship for Elena," the governess said, decidedly.

"Very well. Presently it can be seen to," the old lady said. Then, with one of the quick turns so characteristic of old age, she gave her little sardonic smile. "I cannot altogether congratulate you on your present pupil, Signorina."

"Elena? Is something wrong? I wondered that you sent for her," the Swiss said anxiously.

The old lady pulled the Roffredo letter out of her little bag and handed it to the governess without a word. Fräulein Gelsicher read it in silence, and then looked up over the sheet, with eyes in which a distressful conviction lurked, at the old Marchesa.

"This is not—*her*?" she asked lamentably.

"Indeed it is—she sent that, arranged the whole thing, as a stroke of vengeance."

"Oh, Marchesa! But this is terrible. I am unspeakably sorry, ashamed," the poor woman said. "She has caused this illness, then?"

"Not intentionally. She meant merely to leave Suzy alone on the road. But unluckily she had also the idea to put birdlime on the bushes all round the ruin, that day when my son went to paint the flower—yes, yes, that was why she arranged this famous picnic; and so we imagine that Suzy, in the dark and in her confusion, fell into the well."

Fräulein Gelsicher's rejoinder to this startled the old lady. "So *that* was why she took the mackintosh," she said.

"The mackintosh?"

"Yes. She took one with her, and left it there. She will have worn it while she was using the birdlime, and made it too dirty to bring home. But Marchesa, this is terribly wrong of her," the Swiss said. "I cannot tell you how sorry I am."

"Do not distress yourself too much, Signorina. And if I were you, I should not scold her about it. I have spoken to her. But she has made her own judgements on all this affair —on Suzy, and on her Father too. They all have; Roffredo also, and no doubt Marietta as well. One cannot say they are wrong. The thing has gone on too long. To *you*, I speak freely," the old lady said. "I should have seen sooner that it must stop."

"Marchesa, I am glad that you feel this," the Swiss said. "To me, for some time, this has been a matter of great concern. I wished to speak to you about it, but, in effect, it was not an easy subject."

"It was not. But I wish you had done so, all the same," the old Marchesa said. Then she made one of her bird-like hops to a fresh idea. "How is that poor little creature, Prestwich, do you know?"

The Signorina did not know, with any accuracy. It was some days since she had seen the two Countesses.

"H'm. It is almost time some one found out," said the old lady.

## Chapter Twenty-six

IT was in fact some considerable time before La Vecchia Marchesa or anyone else took any definite steps to inform themselves as to how Almina was getting on at Castellone. All that week the Marchesa Suzy's illness overshadowed both houses, Vill' Alta and Odredo, and dominated the thoughts of those who lived in them. In the room with the silver mirror, where once she had sat and looked at her own beauty, and secretly decided to let her late love for Roffredo have its most complete expression, Suzy now lay in the great painted bed, tossing, muttering, moaning sometimes, more often lying in the silence of exhausted weakness. A lot of her beautiful hair had had to be cut off—ill as she was, it had proved impossible to wash the bird-lime out of it, and to the accompaniment of Agnese's bleats and even tears of distress, one of the Padua Sisters had cropped off most of its splendid length—the six inches or so that remained lay in disorderly curls round her head, or damply plastered to her brow, wetted by the compresses of aromatic vinegar which they put on to cool her. The doctor came three times a day, and a specialist was sent for from Milan; but, as is the way of specialists, he had nothing new to suggest, and said, wisely, that the Marchesa undoubtedly had lobar pneumonia, that this was purely a nursing illness, and that they had better get a third nurse. The Marchese Francesco crept in now and then, listened with a face of distress to the short rough breathing, and the little moaning sounds of discomfort which his wife made, and then crept out again and went down, wretchedly, to paint in his study; the old Marchesa walked in with her stick, and asked the Sisters and the doctor sharp questions in a sibilant whisper —while she was in the room she preserved a rather fiercely blank face, but once back in her boudoir she would sit in her chair, staring in front of her with a wistful sadness in her expression, and sigh—and then presently fall asleep. Suzy, with all her faults, those faults which the young people reprobated so energetically, had really afforded the old woman more of that precious warmth of affection than anyone else; this, her one vested interest, was now threatened by the chill shadow of fear which lay over the house—she shivered sometimes as she sat, thinking how cold her last days would be if she had to spend them without Suzy. Iron with herself, she yet found the anxiety extremely tiring; that curious pain which had assailed her on the day when she learnt of Suzy's treatment of Miss Prestwich came more often at present, both in the darkened bedroom, and when she sat afterwards in her own room. She spoke of it to no one—who was there to tell, now? To Suzy she might have mentioned it. As it was, she drank her egg-nog rather eagerly, and dallied with thoughts of having a second glass in the afternoon—but that would be a form of weakness, she told herself irritably, and she refrained from ordering it.

Almina, during that same week, spent most of her time sitting in her room at Castellone, a piece of sewing—which she scarcely touched unless someone came in—in her lap, staring in front of her, and thinking. During the first few days after her arrival she had been, and indeed felt herself to be, a sort of pawn, moved at the will of others—to Castellone, to bed, out of bed, to bed again—without volition or interest of her own. But since the doctor had decided to stop the sedatives, and allowed her to be about, her mind, after that rather dazed lull, had begun to work once more. She had plenty of time for thinking, for she was left to herself a good deal; after the first three or four days, when the excitement of championing her and treating her as an invalid had begun to die down, the two Countesses resumed their usual occupations of running round to their neighbours' houses and receiving visits at home. When visitors were expected, Almina was, quite kindly and thoughtfully, got out of the way—she was told that So-and-so talked loud, and would make her head ache, or it was suggested that an hour in the air would do her good, and she was despatched to the garden. In the evenings, indeed, she sat with the two ladies and heard their collection of gossip for the day; but it was from this background, so to speak, of its not being quite suitable for her to meet people in general that she started when she began to try to straighten the whole thing out in her mind—to assess what had happened to her, what it really meant, and what it was going to mean in the future.

One of the principal things which occupied her was the whole matter of her feeling for Roffredo. She gathered from the Countesses that he was being blamed on all hands for what he had done, and her own heart could not rise in his defence, could not acquit him of the most reckless selfishness and a cruel lack of self-control. This brought her back to the question which she had asked herself that morning at the Villa Gemignana, when his revolver lay on the table before her—of what was wrong with their love, which at the time had seemed to her so dazzling and perfect. Roffredo's love, she saw it now, was clearly selfish; it was not the tender and cherishing emotion which she had read of in the works of Miss Charlotte M. Yonge and other Victorian writers, and it was, alas, fatally evident that it was not 'pure'. But what about hers? What had she loved him *for*? In the cold light of her disillusionment and the clear-sightedness of pain, at last she asked herself that; and the answer was disquieting. It had not been for any of the qualities which she had been taught all her life to value —not for any special goodness, or gifts of mind or character. She had simply been carried away by his good looks, his gallant bearing, his imperiousness and wit, and the flattery of his making love to her. Oh yes, and more than the mere flattery of that—there was more. Almina did not know that convenient and graceful modern expression 'sense-enchantment', so she did not use it; but she did at last realise and admit to herself that those dizzy raptures when she was in his arms were more of the body than of the soul. And it might be—shivering a little, she faced the possibility—it might be that if they had been more of the soul, or if she had not so readily and joyously yielded to them, things might never have come to the pass that they had reached at the villa.

To a person with Almina's strong moral preoccupations this was a painful and shocking admission. No one had ever told her that she might expect to feel these things, that the normal body reacts in a particular way to certain forms of stimulus; she had really been brought up as if she were without a body at all. Neither the novelists, nor her Mother, nor her pastors and masters at Oxford had given her any definite guidance in the difficult and delicate matter of discriminating between sense and spirit in loving, nor in the still more difficult and delicate art—whose mastery is almost a life-long task—of learning how to combine the two. The special kinds of honesty and courage and tenderness needed for this task she might perhaps possess; but as she was not really conscious of the nature or even of the existence of the task, she had not used them. Brought up now by life with a cruel and crippling jerk, she began to feel blindly after some rationalisation of this problem—like Giulio, she was accustomed to live by the mind, but her mind, like his, found this set of facts rather too much for it. She got a little way, far enough to cause her great distress; but anything like clear vision or even light breaking beyond was so far denied to her.

The two Countesses were not the sort of people to be of much help in this situation. Both meant to be kind—in a way both were kind to her; but the difference between the English and Italian mentalities was a great obstacle, besides the girl's youth and shyness. Neither realised the sort of help she needed, nor would either really have been capable of giving it. Roma's inquisitive prying into her feelings was as useless as Aspasia's bland moral unconcern:—young men would be young men, Roffredo was particularly thoughtless, and she, Almina, peculiarly unlucky. This was almost more comfortless than their busy practical curiosity as to whether she was going to have a baby or not. When the Countess came in of a morning after she had breakfasted and enquired briskly if she felt at all sick, Almina could at least say honestly and with relief that she did not. From the two spinsters, indeed, who were fairly well-informed in such matters, she did at last learn the main facts about reproduction; but it was a poor way of doing it—the ladies were not scientific, and the context, usually scandalous, made the whole subject violently distasteful to the English girl. For their practical benevolence, for putting a roof over her head and getting her money for her, for their general supervision of her and her affairs she was deeply and silently grateful, and for Aspasia, with her healthy bluntness, her cheerfulness and her strong character, she was beginning to feel a certain genuine affection. But as far as her own private problems were concerned, during those days of Suzy's illness Almina was very miserably alone.

There was one person in the Province who was even more alone, just then, than Miss Prestwich, and that was Suzy herself. Who can say where the sick go during the long days and hours of acute illness? Watching them, one has the feeling that they are neither here nor there—words do not reach them, their responses—a hand flung out, a slight movement, low confused sounds from the lips—seem to be to some other stimulus than that of our compassionate speech. What does the spirit do, then? Does it move in some world of its own, or does it lie dormant, dulled by the same heavy confusion that clouds the brain? The sick can seldom say, for the brain is the channel through which we communicate the movements of the spirit, either to ourselves or to others—the words, the ideas in which we try to clothe those experiences are furnished by the brain's mechanism. But from all human communication, once illness has blanketed the brain's activity, the sick are cut off. So Suzy lay, alone in her own world, with who knows what bitter companionship of thought drawn from her last conscious experiences.

To those beside her—to the old Marchesa and to Francesco —this withdrawnness was peculiarly troubling. The old Marchesa, like most healthy old people, disliked the very sight of illness; all the complicated apparatus of poultices and gamgee jackets filled her with alarmed distaste. But far more distressing was the strange feeling of impotence; seeing Suzy there before her, and yet not there, not within reach of her love and sorrow, utterly unresponsive to speech or touch. As the days drew on towards the crisis, though the fever persisted and even rose, a great weakness checked the clearer signs of delirium—there was hardly any evidence of mental life at all, no sounds but those moaning unsyllabled breaths. During the final twenty-four hours they would not let the old lady go into the room—the Sister on duty sat, her fingers lightly on the wrist to note the pulse, her head bent low to mark the breathing, watching, waiting, trying to gauge whether the body would have enough resistance left to survive the shock when the temperature came down with a crash. On Sunday night the doctor stayed in the house; he forced Giacinta to give the old Marchesa a sleeping-draught in her evening glass of warmed wine, after which she was put, unresisting, to bed—he was almost as anxious about "La Vecchia" as he was about his patient. As a result the old lady slept deeply and long; when she woke, she at once sent Giacinta to enquire for the night's news. A few moments later there was a tap on her door, and the Marchese Francesco walked in. He was still in his flowered dressing-gown, his beard untrimmed, his thin hair anyhow, but his face was luminous with happiness. "It is past," he said. "It is past, and she lives! She is terribly weak, but she lives. Oh, Mama"— and the poor man knelt down by her bed and put his dishevelled grey head in her lap, as he used to do when the hair was brown and thick, sixty years before, and fairly sobbed in his relief.

Messengers to enquire had been coming all that week from all over the Province, and from Odredo and Castellone at least twice a day; by midday on Monday it was fairly generally known in the neighbourhood that the crisis was past and that the Marchesa Suzy was going to recover. At about five o'clock a little pencilled note was brought up to the old Marchesa, who had had her first good afternoon nap for several days, conveying warm congratulations on the news from the Countess Aspasia, and asking whether the Marchesa felt equal to receiving her in person for a few moments? "I, too, have some good news for you," the note concluded.

The old Marchesa sent a message requesting her to come up —after the solitude and anxiety of the past week she felt quite in the mood to see Aspasia. When the usual flow of greetings and congratulations was over, and a full account of the course of Suzy's illness had been given by the old Marchesa, and almost visibly pocketed by the Countess Aspasia, "And what is your good news, my dear Aspasia? Is it about *her*?" the old lady asked.

"Yes, Marchesa. It is all right, the Virgin be thanked! *That*, at least, that poor child is spared."

"I am glad. I am thankful," the old lady said gravely. "Poor little creature, she is a good girl—I cannot feel that she was really much in fault. Tell me, how is she?"

"She is relieved, of course, but she is still low in herself," the Countess replied. "I think that morally, the thing preys very much on her mind," she added, with unexpected penetration. "She was childishly innocent, ignorant, about all such matters—really, it is ridiculous! She knew nothing! I cannot think what her Mother was about."

"You know what the English are," the old Marchesa countered, with a fine inflection of disdain. "Since the little Victoria came to the throne, they decided that to ignore love would save young girls from the consequences of it! This is, in fact, an error." She considered, and tapped. "For any girl, however, this is a trying experience," she pursued. "So she frets. You can do nothing?"

"I have tried. But the English are so reticent! She is

dumb as an animal about her feelings," the Countess said, with quite unresentful detachment. "She is perfectly gentle, and docile, and good-tempered—but when she is alone, she just sits and looks! It is not good for her. It may be better when she goes home."

"In my opinion, she should not go home just yet," the old lady said. "My dear Aspasia, you have done a good work for that little thing—could you continue it for a week or so more? I should like a little time to consider—I think I might possibly arrange something. But perhaps this is inconvenient?"

The Countess Aspasia assured her that it was not in the least inconvenient.

"Va bene. I am obliged to you. These last few days, with Suzy so ill, I have done nothing. But now—I must see," she repeated.

The old Marchesa's "seeing" involved, in the first place, the writing of two or three letters, and a brief and rather acid interview with Count Carlo. She told him roundly that he must now let Giulio have his wish, and go to Oxford. She did not mince her words. "His being mewed up at home in this old-fashioned way, with a sister and a governess, was always ridiculous; now it is become impossible. You must let him go."

Count Carlo did not like the idea, and was unwise enough to advance one or two arguments against it. They were decisively dealt with. At last—"And if he goes to England, who knows but that he may marry this girl, Postiche. He is mad about her. What then?" he asked, with a comically dismayed face.

"What then.. He marries then the granddaughter of an English peer, whose misfortunes are due solely to the very discreditable behaviour of your nephew and your mistress," the old lady retorted, suddenly angry. "Yes, and I have this further to say to you, Carlo—this affair with Suzy must now stop. It is enough. ✦ Marry again, if you must, or take a mistress in Venice; but this business *en famille* I will *not* stand." Quelled and routed, the unhappy man eventually agreed to both propositions—he was mopping his brow with his fine cambric handkerchief as he walked down the broad staircase after leaving La Vecchia's room.

The old Marchesa's next move was to send, on the following day, for Giulio. In a rather curious way, it was precisely her tender and protective feeling for Suzy, her sense that she had somehow been tripped up by Life and betrayed her better self, which was making the old lady so energetic in her efforts to straighten out the tangle and repair, as far as possible, the damage that had been done. Almost unconsciously, she felt that if most of the damage could be repaired, Suzy's wrongdoing would in some way become less. Certainly she would have less to regret, when she was well enough to think of such things again. (At present she still lay, weak and helpless, supported on champagne and sips of brandy and milk—but, to the old woman's infinite relief, once more conscious, *there*, capable of comprehension and response.) The old Marchesa's efforts were of course partly due to the intelligent person's impatient dislike to seeing other people make fools of themselves, and muddle up their lives. Nearly a century of observation of this process had made the old lady unusually intolerant of it; but till recently, beyond occasional caustic criticisms she had looked on with ironic detachment, only interfering rarely, and in the most immediate and urgent cases —she recognised, as she had said to Elena, that playing Providence was usually a dangerous as well as a thankless game. But now some obscure impulse seemed to be driving her on to this remedial activity in all directions. She told herself, half in excuse, that it would be agreeable if these family matters could be made reasonably tidy before her birthday, now only a few days off. She did not want any distresses and disturbances to spoil that day.

With Giulio and his lovesick condition she felt peculiarly

impatient, and she awaited him in a rather irritable mood. He must go to Oxford, of course; nevertheless it was tiresome of him to have caused these extra complications, to worry Fräulein Gelsicher, and to have blurted out everything about the little Prestwich to her darling Marietta. But when the boy actually walked into her room, impatience and irritation died. She was shocked by his appearance; he had a peculiar stricken look, and when he sat down and began to speak, the curious uncontrolled inflections of his voice and the movements of his hands suddenly made her realise that his nervous condition was really serious. He must be got out of it somehow, and quickly.

It was a rather curious interview. The old lady felt more out of touch with Giulio, with his books and his philosophy, than with any of her other young relations; but in the end she managed to reach him. She began by talking to him about going to Oxford, and was further disturbed by his listlessness and lack of enthusiasm at the prospect. "I thought you wished so much to go, but you do not seem very glad," she said at length. "Is it because you are so unhappy about Miss Prestwich?"

Giulio winced. "Yes, Bonne-Mama," he said.

"H'm," said the old lady. "I thought you were to be a philosopher. Philosophers don't go all to pieces because they are hurt."

"You are thinking about the Stoics," the boy said gloomily, argumentative even in his sadness. "And, in any case, it is more for—more for *her* that I mind, than for myself; that is what I can't get over."

"Bother the Stoics!" said the old Marchesa sharply. "And I fancy, Giulio, that you are deceiving yourself. Miss Prestwich has had a cruel experience, which has caused us all distress; but, as it most fortunately turns out, it will have no serious or *lasting* consequences. Do you understand me?" she asked, looking very directly at him.

"Yes. I am glad. Oh, I am very glad," he said, with

more animation that he had yet shown. "If it had been other-wise—" and he covered his face with his hands.

The old lady watched him in silence for a few moments, and then asked him some exceedingly direct questions about himself and his feelings for Miss Prestwich. At first he hedged, but in the end the whole tangled mass of wretched-ness and misery came pouring out, as pus follows the probe out of a wound. When he had finished, with a brisk "Now listen to me, my dear Giulio," the old Marchesa took up her parable, and gave him some of her views on life and love. They were extremely astringent, and they were not Giulio's views, but there was a quality about them which startled him. He felt that this old woman, who had been looking at life for nearly a hundred years, had acquired empirically something of the detachment, the philosophic outlook which he had been seeking through books and learning. This was a new aspect of her, and he listened with respect. She was very open with him. "Your real trouble is pure masculine possessiveness— another has taken what you love. So now you feel that she is spoiled, second-hand—is it not so?" And when, rather shamefacedly, he admitted it—"But that is fundamentally all nonsense," she exclaimed vigorously; "especially since she will not have a child. Men have always these ideas! We should be in fine case, we women, if we could no longer look at a man because he had taken some other woman! Do not feel this, my child; it is a false feeling. A loose woman is one thing—a girl whom misfortune has overtaken is quite another. This is a *good* girl, whatever happened to her, just once. *Once!* Good Heavens!—and our husbands deceive us once a week, and we smile and bear them children! And at my age, are still glad that we did. No—be at peace; presently you shall see her, before she goes—I will arrange it. And if, after a time, you find that you love her still—well, you will be in England, and no doubt you will be able to meet her. In the meantime, you will have your Oxford." She paused; then—"In any case, for all your life remember this—do not

exaggerate the importance of the body.    Dio mio, have we
souls, or have we not?    And with which does the good God
concern himself?"

These preachments did Giulio a great deal of good.    She
had laid strong and even rather ruthless hands on those feelings which everyone else, in shrinking compassion, had not
dared to touch directly, but it seemed to him, even as he
listened, that this was exactly what he had been needing.
She had seen so much; she was so little and so old—one
*had* to believe her, and belief in what she said was comforting and somehow cleansing.    He thanked her, and was
beginning to wonder if he ought not to be taking his leave,
when suddenly she spoke of Marietta.    She asked how the
child was, and when Giulio said vaguely that she seemed all
right, the old woman snapped out at him with a return of her
normal sharpness.

"She is all right, you think?    My good Giulio, have you at
all realised, in your concern for your own troubles, what *she*
must be feeling?    She too has lost Miss Prestwich, whom,
remember, she also loved; and—" she hesitated for a moment
—"in addition she is necessarily very unhappy about her
mother, precisely on this account.    She has had all this to
bear, and as well, she is grieving and worrying over you and
your unhappiness."    She sat looking rather sternly at him,
and when he did not answer, she went on—"Might you not
try now to do something to comfort her, to help her in *her*
unhappiness?"

Giulio looked at her, slightly startled.

"I don't think I should be much good at that, Bonne-
Mama," he said slowly.    "I—I am very fond of Marietta,
she's a darling; but you see I am not much accustomed to
helping people in such ways."

"No, I see that clearly.    And it is high time that you
began," said the old Marchesa.

## Chapter Twenty-seven

GIULIO walked very slowly homewards from Vill' Alta, thinking as he went. Yes, he felt better; he felt encouraged; that poisoning misery and hatred and despair had as it were been washed out of him by that vigorous directness. But the old Marchesa's matter-of-fact acceptance of his love for Almina, her hint that it might some day come to fruition, and not be frowned upon—this did more to lighten his mood than anything else could have done. The worst part of his misery had actually been the feeling that in Almina's humiliation his love had been humiliated, that this love itself was somehow tainted and soiled by her disgrace. Whether the old lady realised that or not—she had not said so in so many words, but (unlike the moderns) she frequently did not think it necessary to express *all* her thought on a subject—she had in fact administered precisely the right treatment for this state of mind. As he strolled along the ridge path through the sun-warmed resinous fragrance of the stone pines, out of sun into soft shadow, out of shadow into patches of sun, he found himself aware, with a sense of pleasure and wellbeing which he had lost for a long time, of the strength of that aromatic scent, the brilliance of the arbutus-berries among their leaves, and a new hope and happiness sprang up within him. Like the Ancient Mariner, and moved by the same unconscious spring of love for the artless beauty of natural things, he blessed them unaware. There is no surer sign of returning mental health than this unexpected willingness to let beauty come in and help.

Suddenly a new sweetness reached him. He sniffed it appreciatively, and recognised it as the scent of that hedge of 'rampicante' near Odredo. He stopped, sniffing again—yes,

354

it was. How extraordinary!—for the hedge was at least three-quarters of a mile away. Some light drift of air from the eastward must have carried it all that distance. As he stood, enjoying it, he was startled by a rush of painful feelings which, without any obvious cause, overtook him, shattering for the moment his mood of new-born hope and happiness. What was it? What was wrong? Then, slowly, the memory came back to him of the first time that he had smelt the 'rampicante' this year—on his return from that agonised walk to Castellone, after he had been to see Roffredo at the Villa. And as he remembered, the pain, the unreasoning unhappiness sank away again like the outgoing tide. It was not *real* any more, not with that acuteness—the scent had brought it back, in the strange way that smells and music, above everything else, do bring back emotions associated with them. He walked on again, remembering, calmly now, his talk with Marietta that day. Some of her words came back—what she had said about the person who was tipped out of a boat not having committed suicide. But that—he stopped a second time, astonished, as the thought struck him—that was almost exactly what La Vecchia had said! "A person who is overtaken by misfortune." And Marietta too had spoken, as the old lady had done, about the soul—something about the unconsenting spirit holding up its head in Purgatory. He walked forward once more, thinking how extraordinary it was that a young girl like Marietta should have had the same ideas about such a situation as the old old woman. Still under the strong impression which the old Marchesa had produced, his little cousin's words, unheeded at the time, took on a new weight; and he began now to think of what the old lady had said of Marietta and her troubles. Yes—she must indeed be very unhappy; and he had never even thought of that, had done nothing to help her! A rush of real affection and penitence, such as he had hardly ever experienced, warmed his heart still more. Always at odds with his surroundings, the young man's eager search for the good life had been carried on through the medium of books and thought, rather than in his immediate experience; he had admired moral beauty and hated moral ugliness in those about him, but without making any serious attempt to express this sense of the aesthetics of right-eousness in his own person.   Now at last the old Marchesa's words—this one little task which she had set him, to help Marietta—opened his eyes.   He began to hurry—he wanted to see Marietta quickly, and tell her about all this, and do whatever he could to comfort her.

He found her, as he had done on that evening nearly a fort-night before, sitting ready dressed for dinner by the marble table under the stone pine.   Marietta in these days liked her own company better than ever; she loved the late evening light, too, and made a practice of dressing early—then, while the rest of the family were getting ready, she was fairly sure of half an hour to herself on the terrace, when she could sit and watch the level golden rays of the sun catching the near tree-tops in the Park below, and the still, distant shapes of the mountains slowly changing from blue to lilac, from lilac to a silvery rose.   She was so sitting now, her chin propped on her hands, gazing at them; as the young man approached he was struck, this time, by something curiously desolate about that small figure, in the unbecoming stiff white dress, all alone under the great tree.   He went over and put an awkward arm round her small shoulders.   "What are you thinking about, cara?" he asked.

The unwonted caress and endearment startled the child, shook her out of her usual self-control.   Her eyes were swim-ming in sudden tears as she turned them up to her cousin.

"Oh, *her*," she said sadly.   "I am almost always thinking of her."

He sat down beside her, and again put his arm, with clumsy tenderness, round her little thin form.

"Listen, I have some good news for you about her," he said. "She *isn't* going to—to have a baby."

"Who told you?"

"Bonne-Mama.   Marietta, that *is* good news, isn't it?"

"Yes, it is.   Yes, it is very good," she said, warmly and gladly, fumbling for her handkerchief to wipe her eyes.

"Here, have mine," Giulio said, pulling it out with his free hand; releasing his hold of her, he actually wiped her eyes himself, gripping the back of her head to steady it, as a nurse does when she washes a child's face.   The absurd little kindness touched and amused her; it brought her smile running like quicksilver over her face.

"Giulio, you would make quite a good *bonne*!" she said. "Tell me, what else did Bonne-Mama say?"

"Well, you know I am to go to Oxford?   Gela told me yesterday, but she said I was not to speak of it; but now that Bonne-Mama has told me too, I do not see why I should not, especially to you."

"Oh Giulio, I am glad!   I am so very glad!   How was this settled?"

"Oh, it is all Bonne-Mama, of course.   She sent for Papa, and arranged it.   Gela told me that.   Papa did not like it, and to me he has not spoken of it; but he has agreed, and I am to go."

"That is *very* good," the child said thoughtfully.   "It is right.   Bonne-Mama always knows what is right; and she causes things to happen, as others cannot.   She has some special force in her."

"Yes, she is wonderful," the boy said, earnestly.   "But, Marietta, do you know, I think you have something of her way of knowing what is right also."   And as she looked at him in surprise—"Do you remember what you said to me that first day, over there—" he waved behind him towards the ridge "—about—about Almina?   That because—what happened—was not of her intention, it did not affect her soul?   Not touch her, really, at all?"

"Yes," she said.   "I remember.   I am sure it is true."

"Well, Bonne-Mama said almost the same thing to me this afternoon.   She said that she was good, that it was only misfortune. And she spoke of the soul being what mattered. You know," said Giulio simply, "I did not know that Bonne-Mama thought much about such things."

"Oh yes—I am sure she does, in her heart; she knows nearly everything. But she does not speak of it—she laughs and is sarcastic, because that is somehow easier," the child said. "But I am very glad she told you this, because you will believe *her*," she added, quite practically and without the smallest resentment.

"Another time, I think perhaps I shall believe you too," the boy said. "I think you are much wiser than I realised. But, Marietta, has it helped you, also, to believe this—to be less unhappy, I mean to say?" Giulio felt vaguely that he ought to be getting on with the business of comforting his little cousin; this talk was in itself easing and consoling, but so far *he* was not doing much.

"Yes, in a way. But I miss her so dreadfully, all the time; and I hate not knowing how she is, and thinking of how un-happy she must be, all alone over there," the child said sadly, looking across to where Castellone showed white and maroon above the tree-tops. "You see, *she* may not know that we think this. She may feel about herself as—as you felt about her, till now. Oh, I wish I could see her!" she said, on a long breath.

"I wonder if you could not!" Giulio said suddenly. "I believe it might be possible, Marietta. Because, do you know, Bonne-Mama has promised that before she goes back to Eng-land, *I* shall see her! She said that. And she was quite amiable about all that; she said that when I was in England, after a time, if I found that I—that I loved her still," he dropped his voice—"and I am sure that I shall—she spoke of my meeting her there. It was as if she even thought of my perhaps marrying her."

"Shall you want to, since she isn't going to have a baby?" Marietta asked.

"I think—you see, I have never thought of marriage, only

of loving her," Giulio said, with perfect candour. "But indeed I think I should wish to; if I marry anyone, she would be the one." He looked thoughtfully ahead of him, then back at Marietta. "But I think you ought to see her too. I shall tell Bonne-Mama that you wish to."

"She might not like that," Marietta said.

"She wants you to be happy," the boy said. "Anyhow, I shall try."

"I wish Bonne-Mama would see her herself," the child said musingly—"that is what would help her most of all, if Bonne-Mama would say those things to her that she said to you. *I* should try to say them, if I were allowed to see her; but I don't suppose she would pay any more attention to me than *you* did!" she said, a momentary glint of amusement crossing her small face. "I am too young—no one pays any attention to what people say till their hair is up! There's the bell! Giulio, you must fly," she added, as the deep musical notes boomed out across the garden.

In fact, this was another of the cases where Marietta and the old Marchesa thought the same thing right. A couple of days later, unprompted by Giulio, the old lady did something she very rarely did nowadays—after due preparation, and exchanges of notes, she ordered out the closed carriage and, escorted by both Giacinta and Roberto, she drove over to Castellone, in the teeth of the impassioned protests and lamentations of the Marchese Francesco, who was sure that it would be too much for her. The birthday was now only three days off; there was, in spite of Suzy's illness, to be a big reception in the afternoon—she ought to be saving up all her strength for that, her son said; and the Doctor and Giacinta said likewise. The old lady swept their objections aside. She wished to go; she was the best judge of her own powers; she was going. She went.

Her first call was on the Countess Livia. It was very formal—the old Marchesa found Livia, with her lack of vitality, her sour righteousness, and her religiosity singularly unsympathetic. And she was a rare hand at keeping her powder dry; she was not going to waste her strength—which was by no means as great as she had given the Doctor and the Marchese Francesco to understand—on a discussion of recent events with Livia, which would certainly irritate her. No— she had only one serious thing to say to the widow, and after ten minutes exchange of courteous trivialities, as she rose to take her leave she said it. "My dear Livia, I am sure you will understand me when I say that the more your son Roffredo is in Milan, and out of the Province, for the next few months, the better. Goodbye. This has been such a pleasure. Till the twenty-third! A rivederci!"

Then she drove on along the wide terraced drive to the red wing, and called on the Countesses Aspasia and Roma. This interview, though less chilly, was also brief. Sitting very erect in her chair, the old lady formally thanked them both for what they had done for Miss Prestwich. "You have performed a work of charity, and you have conferred a real benefit upon my family. I am grateful to you." The sisters said how utterly nothing their action had been, and what a pleasure it was, but it was evident that they were both gratified and warmed by this deliberate and gracious act of courtesy.

And then the old Marchesa said that she had a request to make. "I should like to speak with Miss Prestwich, alone. Is this possible? I beg that you will not derange yourselves —her room, the garden, wherever is most convenient!" But of course there was really no question of her moving from the chair in which she sat—the sisters left, and after a few moments the door opened slowly, and Miss Prestwich came into the room.

She stood for a moment, hesitating, just inside the door, looking with large and rather timid eyes at the old Marchesa. "You wished to speak to me, Marchesa?" she said at last, in her pretty polite Italian. The hesitation, the absence of the social greeting showed the old lady with painful clearness how uncertain the girl felt about her position, that she was wondering what to expect.    This for some reason touched her rather sharply.

"Yes, my child, I do," she said, very pleasantly.    "Come and sit down here by me, and let us have a little talk."

The ready colour came into the girl's face as she crossed the room.    La Vecchia Marchesa had never called her " My child" before.

"You look pretty well," the old woman said, scrutinising her in the light from the window as she sat down.    "How do you feel?"

"I am quite well, I thank you, Marchesa.    May I ask how the young Marchesa is?" Almina said rather nervously.

"Better—steadily getting better.    Though she is extremely weak still, of course," the old lady replied.    "But I wish to speak about *you*.    Do you sleep?"

"Fairly well," the girl said, colouring again.    It was time I came, the old woman thought to herself, noting that flying colour and the slightly tremulous voice—she is all to pieces still.

"That is right.    Well, my child, I am not over-proud of the way my relations have behaved to you," the old lady said, without further preamble.    "It has distressed me very much that this should have happened to you while you were with us.    I wish to tell you, on behalf of—of us all—that I regret it very deeply."

This, which practically amounted to an apology, surprised and embarrassed Miss Prestwich so much that she was almost incapable of speech.    She blushed more deeply than ever, and said "Thank you, Marchesa."

"Niente.    There is something else that I wish to say to you.    I had occasion recently to have an interview with my great-nephew, Roffredo, who told me, with all possible emphasis, that there was no foundation whatever for an accusation which was, I believe, made a ground for your dismissal— that of impropriety with him while under my son's roof.    I believe him—and I wish you to know that I believe him."

AA

This time Almina made no answer at all—speech was quite beyond her. She sat struggling to maintain her self-control for a moment or two, and then hid her face in her hands. The old lady let her be for some minutes, saying merely—"Cry, my child—it will do you good." Presently the girl raised a flushed and disordered face. "Marchesa, I—I am glad. I beg your pardon," she gulped out.

"My child, that is quite unnecessary—I have just been begging yours! But now—are you sufficiently composed to listen to me? For I have something more to say to you."

The girl nodded.

"Listen, then. First, a piece of advice. When you are acting as a governess, *never* have anything to do with young men. You may be innocent as the dawn, but it does not pày. Dismiss them all; if they do not accept this, tell your employer, or leave. There is no other way."

The girl looked at her. "Marchesa, I did mean—I did at one time refuse to see him. But then—it began again, and I found it almost impossible, in the circumstances——"

"Enough! I know the circumstances. You were most unfortunately situated," the old Marchesa interrupted. "I do not blame you, in this case; I am merely advising you for the future. And *à propos* of the future, have you made any plans?"

At that Almina fairly broke down. "No," she sobbed out. "How can I? I have no reference, from here—and it has been so short. I do not know *what* to do! I suppose I must go home. But—my Mother! She had counted so much on this! And all my clothes! I cannot think what she will feel. And I, myself—*now!*" she shuddered, and covered her face with her hands once more. "I feel so—strange; and wicked—I do not see how I can go home to them," she went on, in a low despairing tone. She took her hands down again and looked at the old Marchesa with desperate eyes. She had always liked and respected the old lady, and now that her defence of silence had so to speak been breached, all the wretchedness which she had been bottling up for the last two weeks came surging to the surface —the despair at her failure, the sense of assoilment. "I cannot really understand it," she pursued. "I must have been—oh, in some way horrible myself, or it could not have happened. And yet, at the time"—again she struggled with sobs—"it seemed so beautiful!"

The old Marchesa sat, during this outpouring, watching and listening to the girl. Some of her words, half-strangled by sobs, she missed, but the sense of what Almina was saying, the whole of her bruised and wounded state was perfectly clear to her. And once more she was unusually moved. From the heights of her immense age, the cool wisdom which those long decades of experience had taught her, she now, at the close of her hundredth year, stretched out a hand to the stricken creature, the pretty conscientious little foreigner whose good-breeding and integrity had been so evident to her from the outset.

"Listen," she said again—"listen to me. In the first place, do not, I beg you, exaggerate what has happened. My nephew is, unfortunately, a reckless and selfish creature—he treated you shamefully when you went to him, as I believe in all innocence, for help. Tell me, were you not drunk that night?"

The girl bent her head in assent.

"So. In the circumstances, one cannot be surprised at that, nor seriously blame you for it, in the state you were in; and without food for many hours. And in that condition, when you were really not responsible for your actions, he took you at a disadvantage. That, really, is his responsibility, not yours. Now, in this matter I wish you to see clearly, to envisage things as they are, and not falsely," the old lady said, with emphasis. "You are not guilty—no sane person could hold you so. To love a selfish man is unwise, but it is not a crime; and you have had little experience. In your country, girls are very oddly brought up, according to our ideas; they

are taught nothing about love—which, after all, is a very
common occurrence. And I think that you perhaps over-
estimate the importance of this embrace. Is it the body which
is immortal? Did your soul, willingly and of set purpose,
yield yourself to him? Of course not—I knew it already,
perfectly. Then let your soul rest in peace, for this. Call it
an accident, if you will."

She paused. Almina was looking at her with wide eyes
and parted lips, but she said nothing.

"After all, it might have been much worse," the old lady
pursued briskly. "You have escaped the embarrassment of a
child. That would have been a real complication! But as it
is, you are what you were—try to remember that! And
now," she went on, fumbling in the little bag at her waist, "I
have a plan for you. I heard not long since from my friend,
the old grand-duchess of Saxe-Greinau, that she was seeking
an English governess for her grand-children; she knew that
you had come to us, and she thought I might help her to find
one. I wrote already yesterday to her, recommending you.
I have told her that we no longer need you now, since with
my daughter's illness, it is proposed to let Marietta be for
several months, at least, with her cousin Elena, in the good
Gelsicher's care."

She stopped, and began to remove from its envelope a letter
which she pulled out of her bag. "Does this plan appeal to
you?" she asked.

"Oh Marchesa, yes," the girl said, the colour flooding into
her face again. "But especially for Marietta! That is just
what she needs, that is just what will help her most, at present
—to be with the Signorina! I am so *very* glad. Nothing
could be better," she said, almost eagerly.

The old lady looked oddly at her. "H'm! Well, no one
could call you selfish," she observed. "I am sorry the child
has to lose you; and I am more than ever certain that I do right
to recommend you to the Grand-Duchess. Now, here is a
recommendation which I have written for you," she said,

handing her a couple of sheets covered with her fine quavering writing; "when the time comes, you can send it to her."

"Oh, Marchesa, I am grateful. You are very good to me," the girl said, with the warm accents of happy sincerity.

"Read it," was the old woman's only response.

Almina did as she was told. Her colour rose once more as she read. With characteristic dry precision, but in no uncertain terms, she saw herself here praised and recommended as the most admirable of governesses. "Her conscientiousness and her devotion to her pupil are beyond praise." "In spite of her youth, she shows a certain discretion." "I have formed a very high opinion of her character"—these were among the phrases which stared out at her from the thin striped paper. When she came to the rather florid signature, "Isabella di Vill' Alta", she looked up at the old Marchesa with an almost bewildered face.

The old lady nodded at her, very pleasantly. "That is precisely what I think about you, my dear Miss Prestwich," she said. "As for the discretion," she added, with something like a chuckle, "we have a proverb that no one is so discreet about fires as a burnt cat!"

The girl tried to speak, and could not. "I—" she began, "I—"

The old Marchesa nodded at her again. "Enough, enough; it is said. You are relieved—I understand," she said. "Now, tell me about your Mother. Has she heard anything of all this?"

Almina's mouth quivered. "No," she said. "I—I have not written. I have tried, but I could not! That is the worst part of all, to tell her this. She—I do not know how she will bear it."

"You must not tell her," said the old lady, very emphatically. "Why should you? It will cause her very great distress, and for what? How will she, or you, be the better for her knowing this?"

Almina muttered that she had never concealed anything from her Mother.

"So be it. Well, for her sake you will now begin! To tell her would be cruel—you must carry this burden alone. I repeat, you are not guilty—then keep your sorrow to yourself. As to the reason for your leaving here, *I* will write to her." She got up as she spoke, and moved over to another of the spindly writing-tables of the Province, and sitting down, wrote in silence for some time, while Almina sat looking on. She, like Giulio, felt extraordinarily encouraged by the old Marchesa's words; the future was not so dark and hopeless any more.

Presently the old lady called to ask for her Mother's address; while she wrote it, she bade Miss Prestwich read what she had written. The letter was not a long one; it referred to the Marchesa Suzy's grave illness, the probable need for a journey of recuperation later, the consequent necessity of making some other arrangement for Marietta, and the obvious desirability of her being with her cousin—it went on to mention the Grand-Duchess's need for an English governess, and what pleasure the Marchesa had in recommending anyone so well-qualified, so conscientious, and so pleasant a member of a household as Mrs. Prestwich's daughter. There followed some very kind expressions about that daughter, and the great regret with which the family at Vill' Alta in general, and Marietta in particular, would part from her. Almina tried to read this document with her Mother's sensible and slightly suspicious eyes—even to them, she felt that it must be completely convincing. There were tears in her own as she handed it back to the old lady.

"You are *very* good to me, Marchesa," she said, rather tremulously; "I cannot thank you as I should wish."

"Don't trouble, my child; your face speaks," the old woman said. "And now," she went on, "before I leave I should like to speak once more with the good Countesses. Farewell, my dear Miss Prestwich,"—and as the girl rose from the little curtsey she had learned to make in the Province, she tapped her on the arm. "Remember, you are what you were," she said. "Don't forget it," she called after her, as the girl left the room.

To the Countess Aspasia, when she returned, she mentioned the proposed arrangements. "And in the meantime, my dear Aspasia, *air* is what she needs—of that I am sure. I should let her be constantly in the garden; let her sit there to read, to work. This has pulled her down." Then she drank the inevitable Marsala which was offered to her, and went back to Castellone in her carriage. She told the Marchese Francesco that she was none the worse for her outing, and insisted on going down to dine with him. But on the drive home Giacinta noticed with concern that once or twice her aged mistress laid her little gloved hand to the left side of her bosom; and in the *salone* after dinner, even before the coffee came, she fell asleep in her chair.

## Chapter Twenty-eight

Two days after La Vecchia Marchesa's visit to Castellone Miss Prestwich was sitting out in the garden, whither she had been duly hunted by the Countess Aspasia. With a book and some needlework, she had wandered along to the wild part, and was now settled on a seat shaded by a group of cypresses at the top of the eastern slope. Below her the ground fell away fairly steeply, the dry whitish grass barred by the pointed solid shadows of the cypresses, or blotched like a snow-leopard's coat with the round mottled patches of shade thrown by the umbrella pines; above their domed dark-green tops the eye travelled off to the distant circle of the mountains. Almina was neither sewing nor reading. From where she sat she could see the Monte Canone, its blunt squarish summit silvery with a powdering of new snow, the first of the year; she was thinking of the day when she had first seen it, from the churchyard wall at Macerbo, and Roffredo had told her its name. She had met him and the mountain, for the first time, together! She recalled that scene now with a curious cold detachment; she felt as if she were cut off from all personal connection with it by the events which had come in between. So a man might look at a hand or foot which, after hurting him intolerably, had been amputated, she thought.

La Vecchia Marchesa's visit had effected an even more profound change in Almina's mood than the old lady's intervention had made in Giulio's. To understand how profound one must remember that for nearly three weeks, after the most severe shock of her life, the girl had been living in almost complete mental isolation, without anyone to whom she could speak freely about her feelings. Only those who have lived through that particular experience, of receiving a crippling blow while among strangers, can have the least idea what this means—how exhausting, how stifling is the effort, renewed day after day, to talk with composure on indifferent subjects while one is ready to scream with mental distress; never to know the relief of easing by speech, even for a moment, the pressure which is so nearly unbearable—and only those also know how overwhelming, when at last it does come, that relief is, and the mind is freed from its spiked prison of solitude and silence.   Almina's conversation with the old Marchesa, short as it was, had afforded her something of that relief, and released the accumulation of anxiety and pain which had been piling up within her.   And the arrangements for her future which the old lady proposed had given her a further sweet relief; not only new hope, but—in the circumstances almost more important—a fresh orientation to her thoughts. How she had slept, that night—what a breakfast she had eaten the next morning!   And with how thankful a heart, on the following day, she had written to her Mother, giving her own account of the Marchesa Suzy's illness, the arrangements for Marietta, and the old Marchesa's plans for herself, for which she asked her Mother's sanction.   She had apologised for her silence, pleading, not quite ingenuously, the general stir and upset; but the mere fact of being in communication with her Mother again, even disingenuously, had afforded her a quite exquisite comfort.

But the writing of that letter had somehow, for her, brought Gardone to an end.   Even as she set down the sentences with her pen she had had a curious feeling of finality; and it persisted.   Her body in its clothes, her trunks and boxes, would only go presently, but she herself had already left the Province, she felt.   With an almost dreamy sense of the strangeness of this feeling, as she sat now gazing at the silvered head of the Canone she found herself looking back at Gardone as one does at a place that one has recently quitted.   The strangeness lay in the fact that for months now life as it was lived there, so differently from in England, had seemed part of the very stuff of her own life, so familiar was it grown—and now she was remote from it. She thought of that life:—the food—its tastes, and still more its smells, which travelled the wide corridors and passed out into the garden; of the clear eastern light in her high-windowed room at Vill' Alta in the early mornings, and the tray coming in with her breakfast—the fruit, the coffee, the starfish rolls; of the hot golden glow in the school-room when they sat working there with the sun-blinds down, and the droning noise of the bees in the terrace flower-beds came up from below, and mingled with the irregular scratching of Marietta's pen; she thought of the afternoon walks through all the delicate detail of that country-side—the roadside vines, the high blocks of maize and gran turco throwing black solid masses of shade, and the slender tufts of acacias on the little green knolls; of the smell of dust, the white horses' hairs on their clothes when they rode in the carriage, and after, the syrupy sickliness of Marsala in cool shaded rooms, and the high, rather nasal, penetrating gabble of Italian voices there. All this had been part of her; Italy was this to her now. And as she reviewed it, still with that wondering sense of being severed from it, those who had peopled this scene came clearly into her mind, in a sort of procession;—the old Marchesa, with her black stick and her white lace, her crisp sentences; the Marchesa Suzy, indolent and graceful in her hammock, with her flowing skirts, her gold mesh bag and her tiny cigarette; the Marchese Francesco peering through his thick glasses, the Marchese Paolo eating incredibly and gobbling out the story about the Bach manuscripts that were tied round fruit trees to keep off the insects; Graziella carrying in hot water, and pausing to gossip; Marietta—oh, Marietta doing everything, everywhere! She turned away from that thought to the other household—Umberto bowing and beaming at the front door, Count Carlo stroking his beard and talking about vines or manures, Giulio's impatient face then, and his quietly eager one when he came

to work with her, his occasional bursts of mischief with
Marietta and Elena; Elena herself, with her shining fashionable
head and her lively malice, affectionately tormenting Fräulein
Gelsicher; and the Swiss with her plain kind face, her shrewd
speech, and her *bonté*, preoccupied always about Anna or
Ospedi or someone, but still lending a kindly ear, and poking
constantly at the pads which always showed through her
thinning grey hair.

Last of all, almost reluctantly, her thoughts moved again to
Roffredo. The strangest thing of all was that he was now
somehow less clear, less solid than the rest of this procession.
Though she did not fully realise it, her own past feelings had
blurred him to her—he had been a mouth and hands and a
voice murmuring endearments, an excitement and a pain for
so long that his face, his bright head and his laughter, his
splendid movements and his imperious manner had become
ghostly. She struggled for a little while to clothe this ghost
with life, so that she might, from this distance, this new remoteness, see him as he was. But it was too difficult, and
hurt too much—she gave it up, for the moment. Of them
all, of those figures which had filled her world, she found that
the most vivid and solid were, not he, but Marietta, the Swiss,
and the old Marchesa.

The thought of the old Marchesa switched her mind off this
reviewing of the past, and brought it back to their interview
of two days before. She was an incredible old woman, to
have thought out this plan, driven all that distance to give
this help to a stranger, three days before she was a century
old! Almina recalled the picture of her, sitting there in
the Countesses' drawing-room, with a sort of awe. For the
twentieth time she went over in her mind the old lady's words
to her. It seemed very strange to the English girl that there
should have been no condemnation, no hint of cheapening
of her in the old Marchesa's attitude. On the contrary,
in an utterly startling way she had minimised the episode at
the villa, brushing it aside as an accident. "Is it the body

which is immortal?"    The very tone in which she had asked
the astonishing question still rang in the English governess's
ears.    But the Marchesa had always seemed to her wise—was
it not possible that she was right?    Right not merely in an
Italian way, but ultimately right?    Were the sins and disasters
of the body perhaps not so all-important, so finally ruinous as
she had been brought up to believe?    "You are the same,
remember"—she could hear the old woman's thin sharp voice,
with its great precision of syllables, saying that too.    Since
this idea had been put into her mind, forty-eight hours before,
the girl's nature, eager to revive, had begun tentatively to embrace it—she began to find that her feelings now followed her
thought.    "I do feel almost the same," she said, half-incredu-
lously, to herself.

But she was beginning to see another side of the whole
affair more clearly too.    If she was not irremediably stained
by Roffredo's embrace, when she was hardly conscious of it,
still there had been conscious wrong-doing.    She could face
that, now.    She had been wrong when she had not, at any
risk of losing her job, told the Marchesa about Roffredo;
wrong when she had persisted, framing excuses, in those secret
meetings.    These things *did* affect her; they were the things
of the will.    And there had been a measure of something like
error when she had surrendered her standards of what was
really lovable and admirable to a purely physical charm.    As
she sat there, on a seat quite close to the one on which Roffredo
had first kissed her, she went on to think—shyly, but with a
quite novel attempt at honesty and clarity—about the nature
of love.    Oh, why had no one told her that the body exists,
that the body has its own life and needs, and may betray the
mind and the will?    Why had no one ever told her what to
expect, and how to deal with those overpowering blisses
which could be, apparently, so unrelated to the soul?    Why
had no one ever spoken of all this to her?    "It is there!" she
said aloud, in a sort of anger: "it must often happen.    They"
(she meant Elena and Marietta) "know it does.    I can't be,

I'm not the only one.   Why should I not have been allowed
to know?   I don't see how I could have known, alone."

She thought again, as she had so often thought in Gardone;
of her Mother's final injunction to her—"Be prudent."   Now
she was critical of it.   She had not been prudent, it was true;
but all the same the advice struck her as inadequate.   "That
really comes to telling you *not* to love," she said to herself.
"What one wants to know is *how* to love.   There must be a
right way of loving; just being careful and holding back can't
really be the *best* thing.

In this critical mood she thought again of her relation
with Roffredo, and now her thought was more gentle to it.
Spoiled as it had been, wretched as it had left her, it had not
been wholly ugly and bad—there had been elements of beauty
and tenderness in it.   Oh yes, there had, she thought, tears
starting to her eyes; and if only she had known more about it,
known how to love, those things might have been preserved.
Elena had whole codes of rules for dealing with men which
she, Almina, had brushed aside as Italian and not very nice-
minded; it occurred to her at last that even these might be a
very useful and practical branch of knowledge.   But now it
was too late, she thought sadly, staring out over the green
domes of the stone pines at the soft outlines of the mountains;
she was leaving Gardone now, she would never profit by what
Elena could have taught.   She would have to go on with only
her own bitter and unillumined experience to guide her.

A cracking of dry twigs on the slope below and to her right
made her glance down in that direction.   Giulio di Castellone,
looking very hot, was scrambling up through the trees towards
her.   When he reached her side he bowed and shook hands,
saying "Buon giorno, Signorina," rather formally; then he
pulled a note out of his pocket, and handed it to her—"Bonne-
Mama asked me to bring you this," he said.

Startled and embarrassed by this unexpected visitor, Almina
took the note; "Read it, read it!" he said, as she hesitated.

The girl did so.   It was one of the old Marchesa's usual

command-requests, to the effect that she desired Miss Prestwich to come over to Vill' Alta on the following morning—"to see my grandchild, who will be spending the day here, since it is, as perhaps you know, my birthday." The note added that the Vill' Alta carriage would be sent to fetch Miss Prestwich and would take her back to Castellone in time for lunch; and desired her further to have the goodness to inform the two Countesses of the arrangement.

Almina looked up from the sheet to Giulio with a stir of colour and shining eyes.

"How good the Marchesa is!" she said. "I am to go over tomorrow to see Marietta!" In her pleasure and surprise the first embarrassment of this visit was quite swept away.

"I know," he said, standing and nodding at her with an air of great self-satisfaction. "I arranged it."

"*You* did?"

"Certainly. I knew Marietta wanted to see you very badly, and I thought you would also wish to see her, so I told La Vecchia; and she settled it, and told me to bring the note."

"That was good of you. I did want to see her, very much. How is she?" Miss Prestwich asked.

"Oh, she is well," the boy said, rather off-handedly. "She misses *you* terribly," he added abruptly.

This brought embarrassment back again, and now in full force. Giulio had by this time seated himself by Miss Prestwich on the rough bench; as he spoke he looked at her. Her colour rose painfully at his remark—she turned her head away. He watched her for a moment, remembering suddenly the first time that he had seen her blush—on the day of her arrival, when she caught sight of the geraniums which he had stuck behind the fingers of the Venus on the terrace at Vill' Alta. That brought such a rush of memories of one sort and another that he too felt his face begin to burn, and in his turn he looked away. They sat so, bound in a curious helplessness, for a moment or two. Then he said, with an effort, "I am going to Oxford."

She turned at once. "Oh, are you? I am *so* glad. How has this been settled?"

"Oh, Bonne-Mama, of course! And Gela. She told her that I wished it, and so it was done. Bonne-Mama just sent for Papa and told him he must do it! And he agreed. She *is* like that."

"She is very good," the girl agreed fervently. "Do you know what she has arranged for—for me?" she asked, rather shyly.

"About Germany? Yes, she told me yesterday. Are you glad?" he asked slowly, his face clouding a little.

"Oh, so glad! It will be wonderful if it can really be arranged," the girl said eagerly. "Then I need not—I need not go home," she ended lamely. Embarrassment supervened once more.

He sat looking rather gloomily at her. "Shall you ever go to England, if you take that post?" he asked at length.

"Oh, I suppose so. Sometimes, in the holidays. It is not so far as here. Why?"

"I had thought, if I was in England, that I might see you occasionally," he said. "I had hoped it."

"If you don't always come back here in the Long" (she used the idiom of her day) "I expect I should be at home then, some of the time. But I imagine you will come home, won't you?" she said.

He hadn't understood her, naturally.

"And I might come and see you?" he pursued.

In her turn she looked a little troubled. She had hoped to cut off all connection with Gardone, with everyone who knew of her disaster. Giulio at Beamington would be rather more than she had bargained for—talked to by her Mother with that disarming confidential affection, cross-examined by May! Something might come out.

He was watching her face, and he saw her hesitation. A quite unwonted instinct, born of his love (Giulio was not at all good at instincts) prompted him to the right move.

"I hope you will let me come," he said. "I shall wish to, I think, very much. I—there is something I have to say to you," he brought out, with a jerk. She turned, surprised, and sat looking at him with perfectly unsuspecting calm, while he remained, stuck fast in embarrassment. "I—I shall not say it well; you must forgive me; I have never said, never thought such a thing before," the boy brought out at last, almost stammering in his nervous haste. And as she looked at him, with her clear grey eyes, in mounting astonishment— "I love you so much!" he burst out.

Almina was, quite simply, astounded. "*Me?*" she said, incredulously.

"Yes, you—who else? Who is like you? With knowledge, and goodness—it seems to me that you have everything! Everything that one needs; everything to satisfy, to rest the heart—and to raise the spirit. I have never known anyone who approached you."

She sat absolutely still, looking at him. It was incredible. He was saying these things to *her*, *now*? After what had happened? Or did he perhaps not know?

"Count Giulio, do you know why I am leaving?" she said, slowly and stiffly, but on an irrepressible impulse.

"Of course! I know everything," he answered, the colour flying into his pale face. "In fact, Roffredo told me himself," he said, with characteristic impulsive tactlessness. "O cara signorina, what is it?" he cried distressfully, as she hid her face in her hands. "Oh, forgive me—I told you I should say it badly!—you see I have never loved anyone before. Do forgive me!"

From behind the girl's hands came a funny little sound, between a laugh and a sob. "And still you say this to me?" she said, taking her hands away, and looking at him.

"Yes, I do," he said. "Why not? Everyone knows it was not your fault." And as she turned her head away again, he took her hand and kissed it. "I love you, cara Almina," he said gravely. "I think I had better stick to that, for if I try to say anything else, I trip on something which hurts you! That is natural—there is so much to hurt you just now; you have been so much hurt! But if you will let me love you, perhaps you will forget that, a little."

The tears gathered in her eyes.

"Count Giulio, you are very good to me. I cannot understand this at all," she said, lamely and vaguely.

"Can you not? But it has been so, almost from the first moment you came," he said earnestly. "I used to think women were—well, were somehow unhelpful, a hindrance to my life, except Gela. But then in you I found everything I valued—like in Gela, only with more learning. And with—" he looked at her very shyly, and raised her hand to his lips again —"with beauty as well," he said.

She found nothing to say but "Oh." But Giulio was now well started, and needed little help from her. Sitting on the seat under the ilexes, in front of that lovely blue circle of mountain crests, he proceeded to give in his own person an admirable illustration of a very true and percipient saying of Vico's, quoted by his own favourite philosopher—"*I ragazzi sono i migliori poeti.*" (Young men are the best poets.) His reverence, his adoration, his pain, the delicate ardours which, now that he saw her again, seemed to spring from it, and the shy hopes which leapt to birth from the very telling of his love to her, so face to face—all this came pouring out, expressed with a directness which had the very quality of poetry. The girl, listening in a sort of stilled wonder, was suddenly reminded of that evening at Pisignacco, when they strolled together through the little streets under the stars, waiting for the carriage. Even then, all drugged as she was with her love for Roffredo, she had recognised something of the vital comprehension that had informed the speech which flowed between them, and even their silences; now, undrugged and disillusioned, fully awake, the reality of Giulio suddenly knocked at her heart and mind. For the first time she really saw him. He was not just a moody difficult bookish boy; he was a person, a lovable and valuable person, single-minded in his passion for truth as in his passion for her, someone who with all his immaturity and his faults *did*, ultimately, conform to those standards which in Roffredo's case she had flung aside, to surrender to physical charm.   And he was offering her his whole soul's worship, in words which rang like the words of songs.   Further than that, at the moment, in her astonishment, she did not go; the numbed dryness of her heart, scorched by the blast of her passion for Roffredo, would not react or respond at once.   But when he had gone, after a farewell from which their shyness could not quite exclude a stirred tenderness, she sat on alone, quietly wondering, and astonishingly raised in spirit.   This declaration had done, would go on doing for her, something that nothing else could have achieved at that moment—nothing less than the rebuilding of her shattered personality, the re-creation of her belief in herself.   The old Marchesa had begun it; but this went far further.   And she was never to know that it was the old Marchesa who had told the boy, when she gave him the note as an excuse for finding Miss Prestwich alone in the garden, to do just that.   "Tell her what is in your heart—and don't forget to kiss her hand!"

Old ladies of a hundred do in fact know a great deal.

## Chapter Twenty-nine

THE one-hundredth birthday of the old Marchesa di Vill' Alta dawned as one of those still, blue-and-golden days which make late September in the Province of Gardone a reminder of Ovid's Golden Age. On such days, there, one expects to see perfect beings, moving with simple gladness among the golden maize, under the yellow poplars, lifting calm brows to the blue circle of mountains beyond the white trunks of the trees, and plucking the red strawberry-like berries which hang glowing among the dark foliage of the arbutus. One does not see them; but one expects them to appear, so complete is the Latin perfection of light and landscape and clear simplified colour. So the day dawned, and so it moved to its still and quiet close.

The Vill' Alta carriage arrived early at Castellone, and carried Miss Prestwich through the yellow fields to the grey house on the hill. Tommaso's straw Homburg swayed slightly against the sky in front of her, the green and beige carriage rug shrouded her knees, the hairs of the fat white horses blew back and settled on her sleeves. It was all as it had been, she thought, on the day of her arrival. And the likeness was completed when, as the carriage approached the little gate in the wall, the iron whined on the stone, and Marietta ran out, her black plaits flying, her face alight, to greet her governess. She carried her off to the *torrino*, avoiding the family gathering of sons and daughters which had assembled during the previous two days at the house, and they sat there, the two of them, the child's arm tucked confidingly through that of Miss Prestwich. "Oh, I have so wanted to see you! I have so missed you! It has *not* been at all nice without you," the little creature said, and flung her arms round Almina's neck, and hugged her almost with passion.

"I wish you were not going away," she said presently, sitting back and looking at her companion—"but I see that it is best; necessary. You would not be happy here, now. Oh, how difficult love is!" the child said, unexpectedly. "There are so many sorts—and they all seem to hurt people! They die, like Zia Nadia—after all, she really died for love; or they are ill, as Giulio was; or terribly hurt, like you. Do you mind my saying that?" she asked.

"Marietta darling, I don't mind *what* you say," Almina said. Somehow with her little pupil there was no embarrassment.

"I am glad. I do think that for today, for this last time"—the delicate Donatello mouth quivered a little—"I think that you and I might speak freely. Oh, I have been so—so suffocated at Odredo, really speaking to no one. I have never needed to speak much before," the child said with great simplicity—"because until all this happened, there was not much to say. But now—how I have needed you to speak with! Gela was so worried about Giulio, and Elena—I love her, but she is not always discreet, and she will take such a *mondaine* view of things, it does not suit me! And Giulio was ill, and Bonne-Mama I have not seen."

"What is it you most wished to speak of?" Almina asked— her sense of loving responsibility for her pupil rose up again then, and overcame any private feelings of shyness.

"Oh, you—what happened; and Mama. About you, I see it clearly, I think; that it did not touch you; that it was an accident, not you. I said that to Giulio, when he was so miserable, but he was no good to talk to, then. Yes, though I have been—oh, so sorry about you, I am not *disturbed*, really; only it would have been nice to speak of it, because it was swelling in me, *here*—" she pressed her hands against her small breast. "No, the worst has been Mama."

"She is better, now, is she not?" Almina asked—even at

that moment her English governessy instinct prompted this slight wilful misunderstanding.

"Yes, oh yes. It is not *that*. It is what she did to you, and the reason. I find that so hard to understand—and to bear. Mama—" she looked away to where the swifts wheeled in the soft blue above the road, as if she were pursuing a thought that flew and wheeled like a bird—"Mama has always been—oh, very important to me, though I really see her very little; she has not the time for much conversation with *me*," the little girl said simply. "And so, that she should do something wrong and cruel, not in a mistake, she who is always kind and generous to others—I have felt that I could not bear it! And to do it on account of someone like Roffredo, who is really *not* very valuable." She paused again, and then looked round quickly at Almina. "That is tactless of me. But perhaps now you yourself see what I mean, cara Postiche?"

Almina, with a rising colour, gave a little nod. The child squeezed her hand affectionately, and administered a quick kiss.

"So," she said, in a tone which made Almina almost laugh, it was so like the abrupt finality with which Marietta's grandmother used that particular monosyllable. "Of course," she went on, "I am accustomed to people paying court to Mama, and even having flirts with her—she is so beautiful and gay, one expects that; I do not mind it. But to let such things make her unjust and cruel—that—oh, it *does* make me so miserable," the poor child said, and put her head down on Miss Prestwich's shoulder.

A month, a week even, before, Almina would have been quite incapable of dealing with this situation in any way that would have been of the smallest real use to her pupil. She would, with the utmost kindness and rectitude, have damped the discussion down, and told Marietta that it was no concern of hers, that all she had to do was to be good herself, and other meritorious but unsatisfying platitudes. Now, stroking the child's head, she thought quickly, and on quite new lines.

And at last, still doubtfully, but on an imperative impulse, she spoke.

"I can understand that," she said slowly; "how you feel, I mean. But, Marietta, because I have—loved—Count Roffredo myself," her voice was a little unsteady—"I think I can understand about her too. He has a sort of spell about him, when he chooses; it is like a kind of magic. It might move one to anything." And as her pupil raised her head, and looked at her with wide and rather astonished eyes, she went on—"And she—perhaps I ought not to say this to you, but I think he was possibly careless with her too; pretending to more love than he felt, and not thinking about *her* feelings. And I was wrong not to tell her about him—I see that. It put her in a false position." She hesitated, and then said— "Since you have heard so much, I feel you ought to know all this too; to realise that it may all have been much harder for her than you can understand. She may—I think she must have felt deceived, both by him and by me; and that would make one very angry."

The child looked at her thoughtfully.

"Yes," she said at last. "I see that—I do see it. I am glad you have told me this." And suddenly she flung her arms round Miss Prestwich again, burying her face. "Postiche, you have no idea how good you are!" she exclaimed. "Oh, how glad I am that I have seen you today!" She raised her head to look into her face. "No one else could have told me this, helped me in this way."

Almina was touched, and thankful too. Even in her own troubles, she had given quite a lot of thought to the repercussions on Marietta of all this affair. She decided to go on.

"I am glad this has helped you," she said steadily. "It is very important, I think, how one feels to one's Mother. I should have been very unhappy if you had been—had been at cross-purposes with the Marchesa because of me."

Marietta looked at her consideringly. "What is your Mother like?" she asked suddenly.

"My Mother?" Almina too considered. It was difficult to think of Mrs. Prestwich in connection with the Marchesa Suzy; the whole structure of English life, so different to that which she had come to know in Italy, stood between the two women. The idea of men paying court to her Mother, of "flirts", even of the most innocent description, going on in the house at Beamington was so wildly improbable as to be almost comic. But Marietta's question made her think, for the first time in her life, of her Father and Mother as two human beings, a man and a woman, who had had a relationship which—once at least—must have borne some resemblance to that between her and Roffredo. It was a startling thought. Absorbed in it, she was silent for a long time. She could not really deal with it, and the sight of her pupil's little brown hand on the rough parapet of the *torrino* brought her back to the present. All this was no good to Marietta. At last—

"Things are quite different in England," she said slowly. "But my Mother and I—that is the same thing; at least it could be, perhaps, with you and your Mother. I feel—oh well, with her one is always perfectly *safe*. She would never stop loving one. But because of that, some things are difficult." She paused, and then said, in a burst of confidence—"I have not told her about this. It would have hurt her too terribly. And the old Marchesa said I should not; that made me glad. But I feel with her—well, that I can pull and pull on her love, and it will never break."

Marietta took this in slowly, looking in front of her.

"That is beautiful—and happy," she said at last. "That is what I should like. With Bonne-Mama, you know, I feel something of that too. Only she is *so* indulgent to me— almost too much. But with Mama—I am not sure. She is somehow further away. She must love me, I suppose—but I am little, and not pretty; I think beautiful Mothers are just a little vexed, generally, to have daughters who are not! Mama would have liked me more if I had been something of a beauty."

This quiet simple statement moved Almina almost unbearably. Her own observation entirely bore out its truth. And once again the new insight and frankness that her own pain had given her spoke from her mouth.

"Marietta, I believe you could do something to alter that," she said. "You know you are very—" she cast about for a word—"You walk very much by yourself," she said, quoting her contemporary Kipling; "you do not open out much to people, not even to your Mother. I think perhaps if you tried, you could get nearer to her; if you"—she pushed up her hair with both hands and wrinkled her soft brows—"if you let her see that you wanted to be. I may be wrong, but I think this." As she spoke she was trying to imagine what her own Mother would have made of a daughter who at intervals appeared, dropped a curtsey, proffered a docile cheek for a kiss, answered any question that was asked her, and then slipped away to stare at a view or to read a book. But then Mrs. Prestwich always had time to talk to even the plainest of her daughters. "She might really like it very much, if you did," she ended rather lamely.

At that very moment, in the Marchesa Suzy's room, up in the house, the same subject was under discussion. Hardly that, perhaps; rather La Vecchia was speaking, and Suzy listening. The old lady had planned her day carefully. The reception was to be at five o'clock, and she must take a good rest after luncheon; the late morning was always her own best time, and in these days of convalescence it was also Suzy's— Suzy, she considered, was now strong enough to be talked to seriously, and the birthday was a good occasion on which to make an impression on a difficult point. So while Miss Prestwich and Marietta were in the *torrino*, the old woman made her stiff slow resolute way to her daughter-in-law's room, and sat down by the bed, where Suzy lay, slightly propped up now on lace-fringed pillows, the gamgee jacket which she still wore concealed by white crêpe-de-chine and swansdown, pearls on her neck, and her short curls arranged with some attempt at art. She was much thinner, and with the loss of flesh lines had become apparent in her face and neck; but her eyes in their shadowed orbits were as beautiful as ever, with that peculiar tender look that comes after illness, and her whole appearance had a fragile delicacy which conveyed something of the old charm; her voice, when she greeted her Mother-in-law, had the caressing quality it had always had. The loving warmth of the greetings which passed between the two women disguised itself presently in little playful sentences.

"You are very elegant today, my daughter," the old Marchesa said, touching the swansdown and the pearls.

"Of course—I have made a *grande toilette* for your birthday, Bonne-Mama. One does not celebrate such an event once a week!" Suzy responded, smiling.

"Ah! I suspect you of having made it for Anastasia's benefit, and to coquet with Edoardo and Filippo!" the old lady said in the same tone.

"No—for *you*! I am not sure that I shall see them today," the young Marchesa said, a little wearily. "But they are all right—they amuse themselves? It seems so odd not to be able to see for myself that all is well, with such a houseful," she said rather sadly.

The old Marchesa assured her that everything was in train, and marching perfectly. "Though without *you*, it will not be the same thing at all, my fête," she said; "indeed, all will miss you!"

The Marchesa Suzy made a graceful deprecating gesture with her head, very slight, and smiled; she was not much good at talking yet, and all she said was "Cara Bonne-Mama!"

"It is true," the old lady pursued. "And my dear Suzy,' she laid her hand on the younger woman's—"on this day, when I have reached the fantastic age of a hundred years, I should like you to know, from my own mouth, how pleasant you have made life for an old woman, ever since you came into the family, fifteen years ago. I can tell you now, frankly, that I was dismayed, a little, at Francesco's marrying a

foreigner—I dreaded it! But you have been one of my
greatest sources of happiness, from the very first. It is right,
and for me a pleasure, to tell you this," she concluded, with
an attempt at her usual firm manner, but with an irrepressible
quaver in her old voice.

The ready tears of weakness had sprung to Suzy's eyes.
"Oh Bonne-Mama, if you only knew what your goodness to
me has meant!" she said—and then, with a little half-sobbing
laugh: "But it is *sixteen* years, cara; Marietta is fifteen."

The old lady bridled for a moment—then her fine thready
laughter pealed out. "So she is—I had forgotten!" But
her face changed then, to a gravity that was still charged with
tenderness.

"My daughter," she said, "I have something to say to you
about Marietta. I think you know, that she is beginning to
need you now."

Suzy looked puzzled.

"To need me? How, Bonne-Mama? Till just now, I
have always had her with me."

"In your house, yes; with you, cara mia, no," the old
woman said, with unusually gentle firmness. "In fact she
has had almost nothing of you. What she needs from you
now is your time, your thought, your attention—all the
practical evidences of an affection which, I feel sure, exists,
but which might as well not exist if it is not fully demon-
strated." She paused, and then went on—"I think perhaps
the same is true of Francesco. He is not a young man any
more; it would help him, comfort him, I fancy, to feel himself
the object of such a loving attention as you have always
shown to me."

In all their sixteen years together, these were almost the
first words of direct criticism that Suzy had ever had from
her Mother-in-law. She looked at the old lady almost in
amazement, and then turned her head away—tears welled up
in her eyes again and began to run down her face. But the
old Marchesa went steadily on.

"To give them both—the child and my son—what they need may well involve the sacrifice of some of your other relationships," she said, leaning a little on the last word; "but I believe you would find this worth while. At my age, it is one's children and one's grandchildren who count —it is unwise to sacrifice them to more ephemeral affections." Again she paused, and still the tears ran slowly down Suzy's face.

"Those pass," the old lady went on. "Who in their old age has been comforted, supported, by a lover? But by their children and their children's children, many—as I by you." Again she took Suzy's hand, grown thin and blue-veined, in her small old one. "Sometimes it is possible to have both things, lovers and an ideal family life," she continued. "But to combine the two perfectly, so that no one suffers, requires a very great output of energy—as I know. It is not easy to concentrate that necessary affectionate attention in two directions at once. And I rather doubt whether after this illness, and at your age, you will have the requisite strength. I would like you to consider seriously whether you should not now try devoting yourself to family life."

She paused again, and sat waiting for a response. Suzy gave her hand a slight squeeze, but still she said nothing. Very gently, but with a certain remorselessness, the old woman pursued her object, and once more began to address words to that silent weeping figure in the bed.

"Marietta is a very remarkable child in some ways. Beauty she has not—importance she has; she is full of intelligence, of soul. She needs comprehension, affection—and an object for her loyalties and her love. You are the natural object for that, at present; and I cannot but feel, cara mia, that this exaggerated feeling of hers for the little Prestwich is in some sense a criticism of her relation to you. If you had chosen to fill her heart, she would hardly have looked at her governess! And if one is to enjoy the love and support of one's children in later years, one cannot indefinitely postpone giving them some tangible proofs of one's own affection. Do you not feel this?"

The direct question drove Suzy di Vill' Alta to speech. It was a curious unexpected little thought which came out. "Marietta is really so—so different to me," she said through her tears; "she is all for books and ideas. That is why she liked Miss Prestwich so much, I think."

"No difference is so great but that affection can overcome it," said the old lady vigorously. "She would have worshipped you, given the chance. She will now, if you will let her have what is, my dear Suzy, her *right*—a full measure of your thought, and time, and above all interest." She waited a moment, and then said, in a different tone, one Suzy had never heard her use, far-away and wistful—

"I love her more than anything in the world; I wish this for her. So much—so much . . ."

Weak as she was, those words, the last ones so faintly spoken, moved Suzy very deeply. "Oh Bonne-Mama, I will give her this—I will try!" she sobbed out. "Children are—are not in my line, very much; if she had been a boy, it might have been easier! But I will do my best. I would like you to have everything you wish, today."

The old woman rose, bent over the bed, and kissed her. "Thank you, figlia mia," she said, gently. "You have made me glad. You will have your reward," she added, with characteristic precision.

The old Marchesa did not get quite everything she wanted on her birthday, though she got a great deal. When she left Suzy she went back to her own sitting-room and sat for a little in her upright chair, among the hydrangeas in pots, the baskets with beribboned handles, the bouquets which crowded the room, brought by the family, sent from all over the Province, and even from Bologna and Rome. Well, that had not gone so badly; Suzy had certainly taken the point, and she was quite sufficiently intelligent, quite generous and skilful enough in her dealings with people to carry her promise into effect, once she gave her mind to it.  One could hope, now, that things would go better, the old woman thought.  And some time today she must find a moment to say a word to tha darling child, that ardent brilliant creature, her precious little Marietta.  A faint mist clouded her eyes at the thought oi Marietta.  What should she say to her?  That life could be hard, but not as hard as it sometimes seemed? and that it was also good?  That the trick of it was—was—what had she been going to say?  She put her hand up to her left side—that tiresome little pain again!  She was so fond of Suzy, it had been hard to say those severe things to her—tiring.  She was really not equal to seeing her darling now—besides, perhaps she was still with her nice little Postiche.  No, just now she must sit quiet—she was really rather tired.  She rang her little silver bell for Giacinta, and told her to take out all the lilies—the scent was almost overpowering, quite stifling! She sat on, in her chair, and presently dropped off to sleep.

But there was no sign of fatigue or weakness about her that afternoon, when she sat in the great cool *salone*, in her richest black brocade, with the marvellous ruffled "front" of Point d'Alençon, and the little cap to match.  She was seated at the further end, in one of her favourite high-backed chairs, with the flowers from her room, lilies and all, banked behind and around her—a figure at once formidable and gracious, for all its tiny stature.  Because of the Marchesa Nadia's recent death it was only a "family reception"; but the stranger would hardly have guessed it from the names and numbers which thronged the room and the terrace; only the fact that the dresses were all black, white, grey or lilac might have given it away.  The ramifications of the Vill' Alta and Castellone families were so widespread that half the Province could claim relationship, and every known cousin of every conceivable degree had contrived to be present, from near and far; Odredo and Castellone were full to overflowing with relations from a distance, Asquinis, di Montes and Barbellinis— all come to celebrate an occasion which made half Italy vicariously proud.    On a small table, under alabaster paper-weights, were set out telegrams of congratulation from the Queen, from members of the houses of Aosta and Piedmont, and other notabilities; out on the terrace was an open-air buffet with madeira, coffee and sweet champagne, of which the centre-piece was a vast cake surrounded by a hundred candles.    At one point the old Marchesa proceeded out onto the terrace, to cut the cake and have her health drunk, and listen to speeches, seated in her usual wicker chair; but for the most part she remained at the end of the *salone* among her embattled masses of flowers, like royalty on a throne, while one and another was brought up to her by Anastasia Colonna, to kiss her hand and utter compliments and felicitations.    They were brought one at a time, and as a rule swept away after a moment or two —Anastasia was anxious that the old lady should not overtax her strength.    But a few La Vecchia kept by her, waving them to a chair placed conveniently at her right hand, for a little talk.

One of these favoured ones was the Countess Aspasia. After suitable compliments had been suitably acknowledged, and enquiries after the Marchesa Suzy satisfactorily answered, the old lady asked the Countess how her little visitor did?

"Marchesa, she is another creature!    Your visit and these arrangements that you have made for her have worked a miracle!    She eats, and sleeps, and talks more cheerfully— she came in from the garden yesterday with quite a colour!"

The old Marchesa smiled finely.    But—"Youth needs hope" was all she said.    "With the young, health and hope are practically the same thing.    But she owes all this, really, to *you*, my dear Aspasia; your resource and promptitude, and your kindness.    I hope to hear any day now from the Grand Duchess—and that will put a term to your charity and your patience.    As you know, I thank you."

"Dear Marchesa, there is no occasion for thanks.    It has been a pleasure to have her—really most interesting," the Countess said, truthfully.    "Roffredo, I hear, is going back to Milan to see about this famous invention," she added—"he expects to be there some time."

"A most suitable arrangement," was La Vecchia's only comment.

A little later it was Giulio's turn. Ushered up to kiss La Vecchia Marchesa's hand, he was detained, and Anastasia imperiously waved out of earshot—"Giulio and I have a thousand secrets!" the old lady said. She was in tremendous spirits by this time. "Well, and how did you get on at Castellone?" she asked him, with an arch shrewd glance.

The boy turned very red, but he spoke up stoutly. "I did as you told me, Bonne-Mama."

"Famous! And what did *she* say?"

"Not much," he said simply. "She hardly spoke at all."

"She did not rebuff you?"

"No no—she was gentle, as she always is," he said, a tone of warmth coming into his voice on the last words.

"So!—well, for the moment, I think that suffices. I am glad, Giulio. Coraggio!—and good fortune to you." And he was dismissed.

Later still Fräulein Gelsicher was made to sit in the small chair beside the old Marchesa—she had modestly waited to come forward almost till the last. The old lady accepted her congratulations with brief sincerity, and then said abruptly—"Well, our little Marietta had her heart's desire this morning! I hope it made her happy."

"It has made her very happy, I think, Marchesa—it has soothed her, and put her mind at rest. She looks more serene this afternoon than she has done for weeks."

"She has too much mind for that little body, and more feeling than her experience can carry," the old woman said—"that is what is the matter with her. But you will help her in this, for the present." She smiled very pleasantly at the Swiss. "It is the greatest comfort to me, that she will be with you. And as for later on—" she paused and looked significantly at the governess—"I think that perhaps from now onwards our dear Suzy will lead a *simpler* life," she said blandly. "If she does so, there will still be time for her and Marietta to become to one another what they ought to be."

Fräulein Gelsicher agreed, perhaps not quite sincerely. She did not herself entertain much belief in a serious change of heart or habits on the Marchesa Suzy's part. But much had been done that would be of permanent benefit—Count Carlo, in the tone of his conversation about the young Marchesa, had not been able to avoid betraying a change of attitude towards her; there was the solid gain of Oxford for Giulio; and there was a future of hope and usefulness for Miss Prestwich, in spite of her disaster. Fräulein Gelsicher had a strong feeling for the old Marchesa, and took this occasion to express, warmly and sensibly, her satisfaction and admiration for the way in which she had arranged everything so well for so many people. "No one else could have done it, she ended.

"My good Gelsicher, there are *some* advantages in being a hundred years old!" the old lady chuckled.

But a few minutes later, when the Swiss had gone out onto the terrace again, something of a stir and commotion became evident in the great drawing-room. The sons hastened in, Roberto and Giacinta were hurriedly summoned, Anastasia asked people to step outside. Anxiety and consternation flew through the assembly. "She is ill." "She has collapsed." "They are taking her upstairs." "The Doctor has been sent for"—the rumours ran from mouth to mouth. In five minutes the gossips of the Province had killed the old Marchesa off outright. Some people left at once; the majority however remained, standing unhappily about on the terrace, in whispering groups, waiting for further news, for confirmation, for certainty. "*Listen* to Aspidistra!" Elena muttered indignantly to Fräulein Gelsicher—"she has practically arranged the funeral already! Such rubbish—as if Bonne-Mama, of all people, would go and do anything so melodramatic as to die today!" And in fact, after less than a quarter of an hour

Anastasia reappeared on the terrace steps, to give to those nearest her a reassuring report.    It was no more than a sudden faintness—after all, the day had been one of great exertion; the old Marchesa was now quite herself again, and was resting quietly in her room.    She regretted extremely not to be able to bid her guests goodbye; but they would realise, Anastasia said, with something of her Mother's firm smoothness, that it would be most unwise for her to come down any more that day.

"There you are!" Elena muttered to Fräulein Gelsicher. "What did I say?"    The company, taking the hint, dispersed gradually.    The Sorellone drove off in their pony-carriage, Aspasia saying to Roma that Anastasia was always one for putting a good outward face on things—for her part, she did not believe the old lady would see the night out!    Count Carlo, taking a last glass of champagne, expressed the belief that the Old One would live for ever, and drank to her two hundredth birthday; Fräulein Gelsicher and Elena, disapproving of this levity, hurried him off—Marietta was to spend the night at home, by the old Marchesa's wish, and to return to Odredo next day.    Countess Livia drove away with two carriage-loads of guests to Castellone; she had just heard from Countess Roma of Miss Prestwich's visit to Marietta that morning, and while her lips moved silently in the words of the Office for the Dying, her mind was actively condemning the immoral levity of the old woman, who could have allowed a pure young girl like Marietta to speak to "that creature". In one of the Odredo carriages Giulio, made grumpy by anxiety, quarrelled with his sister—"She knows all that is necessary, she has done everything she could—why should she desire to live longer?    To wish her to live till today was fundamentally absurd—there is no virtue in number!    Why a hundred, rather than ninety-eight or ninety-nine?"    Elena told him curtly that philosophers were well known to be usually also fools.    In the back premises at Vill' Alta, Umberto, lent for the occasion with a quantity of Odredo china and glass, washed up and packed his effects, exchanging views the while with Valentino. "She always knew what she meant, the Old One, and saw to it that you knew it too. Such are the best employers," Valentino observed sententiously.

"Come, she is not dead yet!" Umberto replied, wrinkling up his square face in a comic grimace. "But, my word, she *does* know what she means! You should have seen my poor Master the day she told him that the young Signor Conte was to go to school in Inghilterra! He was like a hunted calf, when he came home! She is the one!"

Up in the old Marchesa's sitting-room the sal volatile and the brandy stood discarded on a table—they had done their work. The old lady had insisted on leaving the couch where they had placed her at first, and sat now in her high-backed chair—"It is more comfortable so" she protested impatiently to Anastasia. It was only that tiresome little pain over the heart—"which I may tell you I have constantly, lately"—which had suddenly overtaken her downstairs, this time with surprising strength. "It is nothing—probably indigestion. That fine cake of Apollonia's was very rich." And then she demanded to see Marietta.

But one birthday wish La Vecchia Marchesa did not get. As a result of her insistence the little girl was sent for, and presently slipped in, light and slim as an elf, in her white muslin with the black ribands, and kissed her grandmother and asked her how she did? "Well, well—it was nothing," the old lady said. "Sit there, by me, my child—I want to talk to you." Marietta did as she was bidden, taking a low chair beside the old woman, who retained her little hand and fondled it caressingly. She sat for some time in silence, trying, for the second time that day, to recall what it was that she had wished to say to this precious young creature, this treasure of her old heart. But it was no use—she could not remember, she could not do it. She was too tired. There had been so many people, that afternoon.

"It is no good," she said at last, rather wistfully. "I had something to say to you, but I find that I am rather too tired now, my little one. I will tell you tomorrow, when I am fresher. Give me a kiss."

The child put her arms round the old woman's neck and kissed her—to her surprise, Bonne-Mama rubbed her fine old ivory-coloured cheek gently, lingeringly, against the soft apricot-white one. "Thank you for letting me see Postiche, Bonne-Mama," the little girl said; "it has made me so happy, seeing her again. And I am so so glad that you have made this nice plan for her. She is so good!"

"Yes, she is," the old woman said. "Now, run away." She kissed the child again. "God bless you, my darling one, my treasure. I will see you in the morning."

Marietta slipped out, quietly as she had come; she ran downstairs and made her way on to the stone pine ridge. Darling Bonne-Mama, she did not really seem very ill; only rather tired and vague. How funny and tender she had been, too; generally she only just stroked one's hand! And what could she have wanted to say? The child at once wondered if she could have done something wrong—wandering along between the stone pines, chewing a dry grass-stem, she ran her mind over the day, the past week or so, but she could think of nothing serious. But coming to one of the open spaces between the trees, where a great segment of the arc of mountains to the North opened on the eye, she stopped with held breath, and gazed and gazed—in a moment she had forgotten all about her grandmother, or possible naughtiness. Here was beauty; here was that strange source of the uplifting of the heart—sorrow or uncertainty must be stilled before this. Her spirit took wing, planing off into those remote realms of aspiration and bodiless worshipping bliss which are youth's special home and kingdom. She stood there, lost and happy in her private world of wonder.

After Marietta had left the room the old Marchesa sat on, half-dozing, in her chair. Anastasia crept in, but seeing her quiet and comfortable, crept out again. Giacinta was in the bedroom beyond, with the communicating door open—she too came in several times and fussed quietly about, pulling up the light indoor rug over the old woman's lap, tidying the bottles on the side table; the old Marchesa, accustomed to these ministrations, paid no attention to her. In a dreamy vague way, behind her closed eyes, she was meditating—little scraps of thoughts that came and went. It had been a pleasant day, a pretty party. She wished Suzy could have been there —Suzy would have enjoyed it. She had enjoyed it herself. Everyone had seemed happy, had met contentedly—even Marietta and the little Prestwich. She was glad that was all arranged. And Giulio—how red he had turned when she asked him about Castellone! *That* had gone all right, evidently. And he would get his wonderful Oxford now, and a year or two would show how much there really was in it. A year or two—somehow there was a cold feeling about that thought. Would she hear at the end of a year or two what had happened? But her old mind slipped off to something else—Giulio and the little Prestwich led back again to Marietta. It was a pity she had not been able to talk to Marietta—it was the one thing left undone. But she would be with the excellent Gelsicher now, the little thing. And she had really been too tired—*too* tired. She was *very* tired, still; she had never been quite so tired before, she thought. In a strange remote way she felt that perhaps the call was near, now—not today, or tomorrow, but soon. If one was as tired as this, really rest was the only thing left. Still more dreamily, her mind skimmed over the long past—touching the landmarks, some great, some small, that stood up out of the misty distance. Oh well, life had been, on the whole, good—sometimes painful, often pleasant; never so important as one imagined at the time, as these young people imagined still. And she had had a good long spell of it. A childish sense of triumph stirred in her, and she startled Giacinta by murmuring aloud—"And I have lived to be a hundred!"

The maid hurried forward. "Does the Marchesa want anything?"

"No no—what more should I want?" the old Marchesa said.

The woman went over to the window and raised the sun-blind; it was getting rather dark in the room. The striped yellow awning rolled up with a little rattle, and settled into place with a click; the soft sunless light from the upper sky, faintly warmed by the evening gold, filled the room. Still holding the cord, Giacinta turned and looked at her mistress. 'She looks old', she thought; 'at last she looks very old. But she looks quite happy.' She turned away again, and fastened the cord round the double hook, leaning forward over the sill to do so. Outside, the tops of the cypresses below the terrace stood up against that soft evening sky, burnished like green spears in the last sunlight; beyond, from the foot of the hill the autumn countryside stretched away, golden with harvest, the completed fullness of the year's cycle, and lit by the late sunshine, till it faded gently into a far invisible horizon. The maid turned back into the room. "It is a beautiful evening, La Marchesa," she remarked. But the old lady did not answer. The maid went over to her, pulled the rug up to cover the little old hands, put another shawl round her shoulders, and then, taking her work, seated herself under the window, where she could keep watch over her mistress, and sat sewing, as the light faded.